Once Burned

Once Burned

A Northstar Novel

SUZIE O'CONNELL

SUNSET
Rose
BOOKS

ISBN-13: 978-1-950813-04-9

HENRY STARED AT THE PLAIN white envelope and tried to ignore how his hand trembled. In just a few seconds, he'd know for sure. He raised his gaze to study the pudgy, silky-soft face of the one-year-old boy with those wide, innocent brown eyes and crown of downy brown hair. Brown hair and brown eyes, so different from his own blond and blue. When Dylan noticed him watching, he squealed in delight and walked with wobbly but determined steps to him. Henry indulged the little boy for a few minutes, then distracted Dylan with a favorite puzzle ball and returned his attention to the letter.

He positioned the point of the blade of his Leatherman under the flap of the envelope and hesitated again. Clenching his jaw, he sliced open the envelope. Reverently, he slipped the letter out and unfolded it with delicate care, scanning the columns of numbers that meant nothing to him. Finally, his eyes reached his answer. *Based on the DNA analysis, the alleged father Henry Hammond is excluded as the biological father of the child Dylan LaBrie-Hammond because they do not share sufficient genetic markers.*

"Well? What does it say?" Melanie asked. Her voice trembled.

It took Henry a moment to form a coherent answer. He didn't want to say it. Didn't want it to be true.

"He's not mine," he murmured.

Melanie's eyes rounded. "Wh-what?"

"He's not mine," Henry repeated more loudly.

His chest tightened as his heart hammered against his ribs, crushing the breath out of him. No matter how hard he tried, he couldn't seem to draw enough air into his lungs.

I have to get out of here.

Abruptly, he stood and walked out of the room.

"Dada!" Dylan pleaded.

Henry ignored him even though it broke his heart a little more. Everything in him begged him to turn around and scoop the toddler up in his arms, but Dylan wasn't his son, and if he gave in now, he might never be able to summon the courage to leave. And he had to. He couldn't continue this charade, couldn't shackle himself to a relationship built on lies.

He strode into the bedroom he had shared with Melanie for a year and a half—the longest they had managed to stay together—and grabbed his duffle bag. The sight of his college mascot, a snarling red bulldog, solidified his resolve. He was heading home to Northstar in three weeks for a wedding. Maybe he should stay there for a while. He had enough money saved to cover his living expenses for a year, longer if he was back home in his rent-free house on his family's ranch.

The floorboard in the hallway creaked, and he didn't have to look to know Melanie now stood in the doorway; he felt her eyes on his back. He opened his mouth to say something, then closed it again. What else there was there to say? At any rate, the nauseating mixture of pain and fury would probably send accusations flying out of his mouth, and he didn't want to fight with her. He just wanted to leave.

"I'll be back for the rest of my stuff tomorrow or the next day," he managed to say.

"Please stay. I love you."

No, you don't. You love my wallet. He barely refrained from saying it as he whirled on her. "No, Melanie. Dylan is—*was*—the only reason took you back."

He stuffed enough clothes in the duffle bag to last him a week without doing laundry, then brushed past her and returned to the living room to pick up the paternity test results. He wanted to keep that heartbreaking piece of paper just in case he got to thinking he should come back. Dylan wasn't his son, so there was no longer any reason to stay with a woman he didn't love. Thank God he hadn't decided to marry her.

"Please, Henry. You're the only father Dylan knows."

He glared at her and held the paternity test inches from her face. "I am *not* his father, and as much as I love him, I cannot—*will* not—be your meal ticket. I suggest you get in touch with his real father, if you can even remember who he is."

"Henry...."

Tears glittered in her eyes, and he nearly retracted his harsh words. Instead, he only shook his head. "We were ever a long time ago, but I tried to make it work for Dylan. I can't do it anymore. I *won't*. You broke my heart this time, Mel. Thoroughly."

Henry scooted out the door without another word and refused to give in to the temptation to hold and hug Dylan one last time to apologize for leaving. *Dylan is too young to remember any of this*, he told himself again and again as he strode out to his truck. It did nothing to stop the guilt from pounding through him. He chucked his duffel bag into the passenger seat, jumped in behind the wheel, and slammed his door. He hazarded a glance at the front door of the two-bedroom cottage and immediately regretted it. Melanie stood on the quaint, white-trimmed porch with Dylan in her arms, screaming and reaching for him, his face blotchy and red. It took every drop of willpower Henry had to put his truck in gear and drive away.

He drove aimlessly for almost an hour before he decided to check into a hotel. When the clerk at the front desk asked him how long he would be staying, he inquired about weekly rates. The price she quoted was high enough that he balked—he didn't want to blow that much money for three weeks' lodging—but he didn't have much choice. He had no family here and only one friend he might consider calling, but Doug had dated Melanie before Henry had dated her, and he couldn't handle that kind of reminder of Mel and Dylan right now. So he paid for the hotel room and hauled his duffel bag upstairs, then dropped it and his keys and cell phone on the desk in the far corner of his temporary living quarters and sprawled on the bed.

He balled his hands into fists and pressed them to his forehead, his body rigid as the full force of the truth hit him. Damn, it hurt. Grief saturated his heart, cold and poisonous. Had she truly believed he was Dylan's father... or had she only picked him because she knew he'd stand up and support her and her son? Her friend Tam had said Mel had mentioned "a couple" men but no other specifics when she'd confessed what Mel had let slip to her.

Are you sure Dylan is yours? she'd asked.

Mel says he is, he'd replied. *I have no reason to doubt her.*

Except all the comments from friends, family, and complete strangers that Dylan looked nothing like him. A lump lodged in his throat.

Tam had offered him a sympathetic smile. And then poured fertilizer on the seeds of doubt.

With brutal clarity, he recalled the brilliant sunshine streaming through the windows of the salon and the scent of the hair care products and the chatter of the stylists and customers. He'd stopped by at her request, blissfully unaware of what was coming. She and Mel had fought again, and she was looking to strike a blow in retaliation, so she'd told him of the confession Mel had made over drinks a month or so prior before they'd started fighting over the salon and how Mel's irresponsibility was jeopardizing it.

She told me slept with a couple other men right after you two broke up, Tam had told him. *One the night you broke up. The other a couple days later. So I ask again—are you sure you're Dylan's father?*

Henry choked out a sob. Dylan's cherished face filled his mind and the words he'd uttered to Mel less than two hours ago echoed again and again in his mind. *He's not mine.*

Pressing the heels of his hands to his eyes did nothing to stop the tears from flowing, and he gave up trying to fight the grief. As the tide washed over him, he allowed himself to be completely honest.

He'd doubted all along. But he'd *wanted* that little boy. He'd wanted fatherhood in a way he'd never imagined until Mel had uttered those terrifying, wonderful words. *I'm pregnant.*

She'd begged him to take her back, and he had, but not for her. He'd done it because the idea of *his* child had sparked something in him that watching his brothers becoming fathers had not. His family had been stunned at how readily he'd embraced it. He, not Mel, had been Dylan's first word. Dada.

And it was a lie.

He dragged his hands over his face, drained and empty. *What the hell am I going to do now?*

The sounds of the city, barely muffled by the walls of the hotel, grated on his frayed nerves, and right at this moment, it was difficult to remember the reason why he'd come to Denver. He'd craved adventure and the freedom to figure out what he wanted from life, and while he'd certainly found both, what little sense of purpose and direction he'd gained in the last eight years had vanished the moment he'd read the words confirming that Dylan was not his son. That sweet boy had become the focus of his life and his expectations for the future, and he had no idea what would fill that gap.

Throwing himself into his job wouldn't replace what he'd lost. Of that he was certain. He was a good enough welder and machinist that he could probably find a new job just about anywhere, and while he loved his job and the pay that came with it, the lure of home was far stronger than his desire to return to his company. In fact, he felt no desire to return to work at all.

Of course, going home meant he'd have to tell his family why he'd quit his job, and he hadn't even told them he had doubted Dylan's paternity let alone doubted it enough to request the paternity test; he hadn't wanted to upset them in case he was wrong. The thought of telling his parents was especially troubling, and a new wave of despair pulsed through him.

"Mom and Dad are going to be devastated," he murmured. Glancing at his cell phone on the desk, he winced at the jolt of anxiety and immediately decided against calling them. This was the kind of news he needed to deliver in person.

"What am I gonna do?" he asked himself again.

There was no answer in the empty hotel room.

* * *

"Wake up, Linds. We're home."

Lindsay opened her eyes and rubbed the bleariness from them before glancing out the window of Evie Gunderson's SUV. All she saw was a wall of pines, so she leaned a little closer to the window and looked up. A heavily forested ridge rose above the vehicle, a picturesque backdrop to the log cabin at its base. The photos she'd seen of Vince and Evie's new home did *not* do either the cabin or the ridge behind it justice.

She pushed her door open, peeled herself out of the car, and groaned as she stretched. She'd been cooped up in various vehicles—a transit bus, a plane, and most recently

Evie's SUV—for almost eight hours. As she reached sky-ward and turned around, she inhaled sharply, too awed to drop her arms again. Before her, a wall of mountains stood tall against a cobalt sky littered with fluffy, blindingly white clouds, and below them, thick pine forests blanketed rugged foothills that grudgingly gave way to rolling sagebrush hills, lush hayfields and pastures, aspen groves and willow-lined streams. In the clear, early afternoon light, the colors and details of the landscape were so crisp and vibrant.

"Wow," she breathed.

At last, her arms fell to her side as her gaze swept from north to south and back again. Unwillingly, she pulled her eyes from the stunning view that surrounded her and turned to her two best friends, who had also climbed out of the SUV and now stood beside her. "Am I turning green yet? Because I am jealous as hell." She looked out across the narrow valley again. "Skye, I bet your camera hasn't been out of your hand for more than a few minutes since you got here."

"I haven't been *quite* that bad, but yeah, I've taken a lot of pictures," the taller woman replied, beaming.

She glanced between her friends. Evie, the shortest of them, had a cherubic beauty and was sociable and bubbly. In contrast, Skye was tall and slender with rich, dark hair and amber-colored eyes and was as reserved as Evie was outgoing. Lindsay herself fell somewhere between in both physical appearance and disposition, though she leaned with Skye on the extroversion-introversion scale, so it amused her that it was Evie who would be settling in this sparsely populated ranching community.

"Speaking of my camera," Skye remarked. "I need to

8

run down to my cabin to get it. See you both back here in twenty?"

"Sure, but when do I get to see this cabin you rented for the next six weeks?"

"Maybe we could pop down after the rehearsal dinner. It's gorgeous, Linds. You'd love it."

"If it's anything like Evie's place——" She gestured to the two-story cabin behind her.

"——I'm sure I would."

"It's smaller but tucked up against that big aspen grove across the way. Cozy. Private."

With her divorce from her philandering ex nearly finalized, the vacation rental—and Northstar in general—was exactly what Skye needed, and Lindsay was glad her friend would have the peace and quiet she needed to repair her fractured heart. But it was hard to stifle the jealousy.

"I could really use six weeks here, but I know you need it even more than I do," she said, trying and probably failing to keep the bitterness from her voice. "You won't mind if I live this experience vicariously through you, will you?"

"I promise I'll keep you posted on everything I see and do." Skye studied her, frowning. Then she wrapped her arms around her in a sympathetic hug. "I wish you could stay here with me. And I'm sorry Noah decided he didn't want to come. I know that hurt."

Lindsay nodded. "He would've loved it here." Shifting her weight, she hugged herself. How wonderful would it be to spend six blissful, worry-free weeks here, surrounded by all this natural beauty... to have the freedom to up and decide on a whim to do it? Stubbornly, she forced her envy down, pushing it deep into the darkest recesses of her being, where it belonged. "You should probably go get your camera so we can get this show moving."

Skye gave her a reassuring smile. "I'll be back in a few."

Without giving Evie the chance to remark on the turn of the conversation, Lindsay promptly said, "I probably ought to call my folks first and get changed into something that isn't completely wrinkled from travelling, but after that, how about you show me your beautiful wedding gown and my bridesmaid dress?"

Evie eyed her briefly, but for once, didn't press her. It wasn't long before her excitement took over, and she was soon babbling about her impending nuptials. Awash in her friend's vibrant joy, it was easy to let go of her bitterness. As they walked up the flagstone path, Lindsay listened to Evie's descriptions of the wedding planning and wished she could have helped more in the process. But the way Evie told it, there probably wouldn't have been much for Lindsay to do; the groom's family had done much of the heavy lifting with the matriarch of the Carlyle clan—Vince's grandmother, Livia—marshaling everyone like a drill sergeant.

"It all sounds wonderful, Evie," Lindsay remarked. "But did you *have* to pick red for the bridesmaids dresses?"

Evie rolled her eyes. "You'll look absolutely gorgeous, Linds. I promise. I picked a red that won't clash with your red hair."

"I'll withhold judgment until I see it, but I doubt such a shade exists."

With a laugh and a comment about Lindsay's lack of faith, Evie opened the front door of her home. Lindsay inhaled sharply. The place was *beautiful*—log and native stone. There was a loft over the back half of the spacious great room. Below the loft and directly back from the massive front windows were the kitchen and dining room. Down the short hallway to the right were two bedrooms and a bathroom, and to the left through a door beneath the stairs up to the loft was the master suite. A beautiful stone fireplace commanded attention from the corner between the angled walls at the front of the great room, though even its grandeur could not compete with the view the big windows provided of the Northstar Mountains and Valley.

"It isn't huge," Lindsay remarked, "but it *feels* huge. Is it really yours and Vince's now?"

"Not officially until the wedding, but yes, his grandparents are giving it to us as a wedding gift."

Must be nice to have a family that can just give you a house. As soon as the thought wormed its way into her mind, she buried it. Evie deserved every bit of happiness she'd found here, and Lindsay *would not* begrudge her friend any of this. Besides, even if her wants frequently went unmet, her needs didn't, so she had no room to complain.

"I know I said we were putting you in one of the guest bedrooms, but we've had a last minute change of plans. My grandmother decided to get over being mad at me for moving to Montana, and she came out with Mom and Dad. Since she just had knee surgery last week, she can't make it up these stairs. And you know my dad's irrational fear of heights...."

"The loft is fine, Evie. I rather like it, actually."

"There's not much privacy. Just those screens."

"Why would I need more privacy than that?"

11

"Well, you never know. There are some attractive men in these parts."

"Are you suggesting I should find one to hook up with while I'm here?" Lindsay inquired flatly, more intrigued by the idea than she was willing to admit. A fling to satisfy her long-ignored carnal needs with a man she'd never have to see again had a certain no-complications appeal.

"Your words, not mine," Evie teased. With more seriousness, she said, "You're a great mom, Linds, and I know you work your ass off to make sure Noah has everything he needs, but you're only twenty-six and single, and you need to think of yourself sometimes, too." She nudged Lindsay with her elbow. "Besides, with that perfect body of yours, I imagine you'll have just about every single man in Northstar dying to take you out."

Not perfect, Lindsay thought, hugging herself. No matter how hard she tried to erase them, faint reminders of her pregnancy remained, and more than one man had been put off by them. Abruptly, she asked, "Um, where's the phone?"

"There's one beside the bed in the loft."

Nodding in thanks, Lindsay hauled her suitcases upstairs. As her friend had said, the queen-sized bed was shielded from view by a pair of tri-fold screens. The bed itself was adorned with what appeared to be a handmade heirloom quilt of bold blue, green, red, brown, and tan in a pattern that invoked thoughts of a rustic mountain cabin. She settled her suitcases on the cedar chest at the foot of the bed and made her way around to the log nightstand where the phone sat beneath a wrought-iron lamp with a moose-print lampshade. With a flicker of hesitation,

Lindsay picked up the phone and dialed her parents' number.

"Hello?" her mother asked after the second ring.

"Hi, Mama," Lindsay greeted. "I'm in Northstar, safe and sound."

"I'm glad to hear that. Is it as beautiful as the pictures?"

"More so. And you should see Evie's house. It's incredible. She's so lucky."

"I bet she was glad to see you."

Lindsay smiled fondly. "It's so good to be together with her and Skye again—at the same time. It feels like it's been forever. I don't think I realized just how much I missed them."

"Did you get any rest on the way over? You sound tired."

"It's been a long eight hours, but I dozed a bit on the plane and slept the whole way from Butte to Northstar.

"So you really haven't had much time to catch up with them yet."

"No, but at least I might be of some use for the rehearsal this afternoon. Besides, we'll have a week and a half to catch up."

"I still wish you would have given yourself a full two weeks off."

Exasperated, Lindsay sighed and pinched the bridge of her nose. They'd gone around and around about her trip to Montana, and it was only because her mother and father had been so stubbornly insistent that she'd agreed to ten days instead of the bare minimum to see Evie married off. "I can't afford it, Mama. I can't really afford ten days."

"Your father and I could've helped out."

"I don't want you to have to help me out."

"I know that, honey. I just wish…. Well, you know what I wish."

That Max would put as much effort into taking care of his son as he did into making him. Lindsay sneered. She had no need to say it out loud; this was a conversation she and her parents had on a regular basis. They wanted Max to step up and willingly do his part for Noah, but Lindsay had come to believe that she and Noah would be better off—emotionally, at least—if Max would just do what he obviously wanted and step out of their lives. The constant pull on Noah couldn't be healthy, and the never-ending strain on Lindsay was bound to make her old before her years.

"Anyhow… we'd like to take Noah school clothes shopping while you're in Montana," her mother continued.

"I can't afford to buy him clothes right now, Mama." Lindsay was able to restrain her growl of frustration, and it came out as a subdued sigh. She would have been able to take Noah shopping sooner if she hadn't agreed to Evie's request that she stay in Montana until the newlyweds left on their honeymoon. It was difficult to swallow the guilt even though she knew she needed the time off. She hadn't taken more than a sick day or two here and there in over two years, and it was wearing on her.

"I said *we* would take him, Lindsay. And don't you dare offer to pay us back. He's our grandson, and you don't let us spoil him nearly enough."

"Max does a pretty damned fine job of spoiling him," Lindsay muttered.

"Different kind of spoiling, dearest. This is the good

14

kind. Anyhow, your son's just come in from the beach. Noah, your mom's on the phone."

There was some shuffling on the other end of the line, and then Noah picked up. "Hey, Mom," he said sullenly.

"Hi, baby."

"Why do you keep calling me that. I haven't been a baby for a long time."

"I know that, but you'll always be my baby just like I'll always be your grandma's baby."

"Dad says that's stupid girly talk."

Lindsay's face snapped into a scowl. "I really don't care what your father says, Noah, and you'd better put that attitude in check right now, young man."

"Sorry," he retorted.

"What's your issue? Grandma said you just came in from the beach, so you *should* be in a good mood."

Noah didn't immediately answer, and she could see him digging the toe of his tattered Keds into the carpet. "I wanted to go to Montana with you," he said at last, his voice taking on a whiny note.

"Back that up. I had your plane ticket *bought and paid for*, and you decided you didn't want to be stuck having to go to a wedding and doing all the 'stupid girly stuff.' So I cancelled your ticket. Lost fifty dollars on it, too. Remember that?"

"Yeah, but——"

"*You* made the choice to stay with Grandma and Grandpa, so you can't blame anyone but yourself." Lindsay sat on the bed and tipped her head back. "I love you dearly, but every time you come back from your father's, you become this... this obstinate, rude little boy I don't recognize."

"I do not!"

"Yes, you do, but I'm not going to run up Evie's phone bill arguing with you about it. Find a way to get back to being my sweet, polite young man again. Please."

"Fine. Whatever."

Irritation surged, but she swallowed it. The last thing she wanted right now was to fight with her son. This wasn't him talking—it was his father.

"Did you sleep all right last night?" she asked, forcing a tenderness she didn't feel into her voice.

"Yeah, I guess." Noah paused, and when he spoke again, he was more cordial. More her little boy. "It was nice not having to share a room with Spencer."

"I bet it was."

"How come we have to live with him and his mom, anyhow? He's such a butthead."

And... there was Max again. "You know why."

"Yeah. We're too broke to afford our own house. But we're not too broke for you to go to Montana for a week and a half."

"Noah Steven Ulrich!" Lindsay barked. She heard her mother utter the exact same on the other end of the line.

"That was an incredibly rude thing to say to your mother!" Debbie Miller snapped. "Give me that phone and get your backside to your room *right* now!"

Lindsay flinched at the crack of a door slamming.

"I don't know what's gotten into him," her mother said. "That was absolutely uncalled for."

"He's right," Lindsay replied, her voice catching on

16

the lump in her throat. She swore under her breath and wiped furiously at her eyes to stop the tears from spilling down her cheeks.

"No, he's not. Your best friend is getting married tomorrow, and Evie deserves to have you at her wedding."

"It won't take ten days for me to get her married off. That's a lot of money I'm not at work to make."

"Maybe so, but even if you worked every single one of those days, it wouldn't be enough for you to move in to your own place, so he'll just have to get over it."

Lindsay sniffed and tried to subdue the pounding guilt, but it was a difficult meal to swallow. This had been her life the last eight years, so she should be well used to it by now, but it never got any easier. It just ground her down a little more with each passing year, and it would only get worse as Noah got older and the things he needed got more expensive.

"Not to add any more to your plate," her mother said, "but Noah told me today that Peewee football is starting up soon, and he'd like to play again this year."

"Crap, I forgot." This time, Lindsay let the growl out. Speaking of expensive needs…. "None of his gear from last year is going to fit."

"Max is going to help with that, right?"

Lindsay snorted. Max had been less than thrilled that Noah wanted to play football last year and had gone so far as to blame Lindsay's "obsession" with the sport for Noah's desire to play it. She could lie and say she needed the money for school clothes, since her parents weren't going to let her talk them out of paying for those, but she couldn't bring herself to do it. She wasn't *that* person. "I'll call him and ask."

"I'd do it right now. Otherwise you'll find an excuse not to ask. Better yet, don't ask him. Tell him he needs to support his son."

Sighing, Lindsay admitted that her mother was right. "If I get it out of the way now, maybe I'll be able to enjoy my trip."

"Exactly. I need to go deal with my grandson, so I won't keep you any longer. Love you, baby."

Lindsay could hear the wink in her mother's playful tone and smiled despite the torrent of despair. "Love you, too, Mama. When Dad gets off work, tell him I love him, too."

After she hung up the phone, she allowed herself a few moments to regain her composure before she dialed her ex's number. Several deep breaths were evidently not enough to quell the anxiety, but she made the call anyway. *Just get it over with.*

"Hello?"

She flinched at the sound of his voice with the familiar jolt of loathing and longing. "It's Lindsay."

"Where the hell are you calling from? Four-oh-six?"

"Montana. Evie is getting married tomorrow."

"And she's in Montana?"

"Yes," she replied, her jaw clenching.

"I can't say as I'm surprised the little pudgeball had to move all the way to Montana to find herself some blind cow's ass to take pity on her."

Lindsay's hand twitched. If he had been standing in the same room instead of four hundred miles away, she would have slapped him for that. "I see you're still pissed that she called you an insufferable ass, but I guess the truth hurts."

"I presume you didn't call me to exchange pleasantries, so just put Noah on the phone already."

"He's not here."

"What do you mean he's not there?"

"He didn't want to come, so he's staying with my parents."

Silence met her response, and Lindsay had plenty of time to ponder the accusations he'd surely make.

"Why wasn't I consulted about this?"

"I didn't *consult* you because I had to beg you to take him for a week not so long ago, This time, Lindsay let the growl out, and then you couldn't send him back to me fast enough."

"It was a bad time. I had all those city planning meet—"

"Bullshit. It's *always* a bad time, Max. You just don't want to be troubled with the reminder that you, Mr. Perfect, screwed up once upon a time. Say what you want about me, but at least I've shouldered the responsibility of raising *our* son without bitching about every little *inconvenience*." Lindsay drew a deep breath and plunged ahead without giving Max time to form a rebuttal. "And since we're on the topic of responsibility, Noah needs new football equipment because he's outgrowing everything. Do you think you can help out without turning it into a battle like you always do?"

"You know how I feel about him playing football, Lindsay."

She gripped the phone so tightly her fingers ached, willing her voice to remain level. "He wants to play, and he's

19

good at it, too."

"What if I refuse to help pay for his gear?"

"Then I'll find a way to pay for it myself."

"You would, wouldn't you? What if he gets hurt, Lindsay?"

Pulling the phone from her ear, she started at it, certain she hadn't heard him right. But no, she had. His words echoed in her mind again and again with each thud of her heart. Nope. There was no keeping a leash on her anger now.

"Funny how you never give a shit about Noah until you want to malign me," she snarled. "So fuck you, Max. I'll find a way to pay for his gear and I'll make sure he knows you refused."

"I didn't ref—"

She slammed the receiver down on the base and jumped to her feet, then paced the length of the bed for almost a minute, flexing her fingers at her sides to keep them from curling into fists. Rage trembled through her. Damn him. He had a singular talent for infuriating her, but right now, she had to put on her happy face—the one she had perfected waiting tables and could affect without giving anyone around her a clue to the turmoil beneath it. She located a small mirror hanging on the wall beside the window and stared at her reflection, willing her expression to smooth.

I am strong. I am honest. I am enough.

She repeated those thoughts to herself until most of the anger had left her eyes. With fury still seething, it would be impossible to totally erase it, but this would do.

Turning away, she surveyed the loft and set herself

focus on the series of tasks she needed to tackle to prepare for Evie's wedding rehearsal and the dinner to follow. First, figure out to wear. Then freshen up her hair and makeup.

Opening her suitcase, she pulled out a lavender sundress with a hem that was a perfect balance between flirty and innocent. She changed out of her travel-wrinkled jeans and tank top into the soft dress. Her ivory lace ballet flats would go well with it, so she dug them out and slipped her feet into them. Then she took out her makeup case and hairbrush and stepped over to the small mirror again. After applying minimal eye makeup and lip gloss—forgoing the more elaborate makeup she used for work—she ran her brush through her long, deep red hair and decided to pull half of it back with a silver floral-patterned barrette to keep it out of her face for the day's activities. Glancing over herself, she pronounced herself presentable for the informal rehearsal.

"All right, Evie," she called as she descended the stairs. "I'm ready to see this gown of yours."

Evie appeared through the door to the master suite still dressed in her jeans and T-shirt. The rehearsal was supposed to be an informal affair, and Lindsay would probably be a tad overdressed, but hopefully that would help her keep a lid on things and remind her of what was important tonight.

"Come on in." Evie jerked her head toward the master suite. "I've laid it and your dress out on the bed."

It wasn't difficult to make the appropriate compliments about the bride's dress; with its cascade of red silk roses, the gown was stunning and the cut would flatter Evie's curvy build. Lindsay's and Skye's bridesmaids dresses were beautiful, too. The red, mercifully, was on the blue side and would complement rather than clash with Lindsay's deep copper hair, but she couldn't resist teasing Evie regardless.

"I still say I'm going to look like a tomato."

"You will not, and once you try it on you'll see I'm right. But that'll have to wait," Evie retorted. "It's time to head over to the main ranch house for the rehearsal."

As if on cue, Skye strode into the room with her camera bag over her shoulder. "You ladies ready for this?"

"Yep. Let's get this thing done so we don't screw up the real deal tomorrow," Lindsay replied.

If Evie noticed anything strange in her friend's choice of words, she gave no sign. Skye, on the other hand, had always been the more intuitive and regarded Lindsay with a quizzical frown. At Lindsay's subtle headshake, Skye nodded and kept her questions to herself.

They piled into Evie's SUV and headed over to the main house of the C-Diamond Ranch. It was a sprawling, two-story affair laid out much like Evie's place but at least twice the size. As Lindsay listened to the plans for tomorrow—how, where, and when everyone would be getting ready—she watched Skye practice her craft, at once proud and jealous that her best friend had been free to pursue her dreams while she'd had to set hers aside.

"How is this going to work? You being the maid of honor *and* the photographer?" Lindsay asked to distract herself.

"Evie found me an assistant—a college kid. She promises me he's good."

Lindsay tipped her head to her friend's camera bag.

22

"You're going to trust him with your baby?"

Skye shrugged. She leaned in close while Evie was chatting with the minister who would be performing the ceremony. "Are you all right?"

Not trusting her voice, she only nodded.

They walked through the ceremony a few times, and all the while, Lindsay managed to keep her smile in place and make friendly small talk, but irritation continued to gnaw at her. She suspected it would come bursting out of her at some point and prayed she could contain it at least until she was alone tonight with Skye and Evie after the rehearsal dinner. Why did she keep letting Max do this to her? And why, oh why, after he'd spent years making it perfectly clear that he had long ago lost all interest in her, did her heart still jump when she heard his voice or saw him?

Two

HE WAS A COWARD. There was no other explanation for why he was pulling up in front of his house in Northstar when the sun slumped so close to the crests of the western ridges. If he had left when he'd planned to, he would have arrived home four hours ago, but he'd found one excuse after another to delay his departure.

Henry knew his parents and brothers loved him and would offer sympathy, but he'd always felt like he wasn't quite understood, that his disinclination to stay in Northstar to help run the family ranch and his pursuit of a welding career in a big city made him a bit of an outsider. Looking back, his relationship with Melanie had intensified that feeling. His parents had treated Melanie kindly enough, but there was something about her they didn't approve of. Until recently, Henry hadn't a clue what that might be, especially considering how deeply in love they'd fallen with Dylan from the moment of his birth. He had wondered, since they adored the mothers of their other two grandchildren, why they couldn't seem to warm to Melanie.

"They didn't trust her," Henry observed as he stared out his windshield at the Northstar Mountains. "And I understand all too well why now."

He climbed out of his truck and grabbed the first two of his bags off the passenger seat. With tired, defeated steps, he climbed the stairs to the covered front deck of his single-story house and unlocked the door before pushing it open with his foot. He dropped the bags just inside and returned to his truck for more. Without his furniture, which he'd left behind because his house here was fully furnished, all of his belongings fit easily in the bed of his pickup, and it took him less than twenty minutes to unload everything and stash it temporarily in the spare bedroom.

When everything was unloaded, Henry stood in the living room and glanced around his house. It had been his since he'd turned twenty-one—ten years now—but he hadn't spent much time in it. It was the ranch foreman's house in times when that position wasn't filled by a member of the family—currently Henry's older brother, Nick, held that title—and with two bedrooms and a single bathroom, it was on the small side. The living room, dining room, and kitchen formed an open L, and large, south-facing windows flanked the front door and let in plenty of light, which did a lot to make the place feel bigger. Surrounded by wide-open spaces, Henry had no need and no desire for a big house, which made this one a perfect fit. At any rate, it felt more like home than any place he'd lived besides the main ranch house.

"All right," he said, hooking his thumbs in his pockets. "Now what?"

First, he needed to call his parents to let them know he was home. His mother was probably getting worried by now, so he grabbed the cordless off the kitchen counter. After he called his folks, he should call his twin brother. It was his first night back in Northstar, so by tradition, he was supposed to have a drink with Aaron at the Bedspread, but he really wasn't up to seeing his twin… or being social at all, for that matter. Aaron would be disappointed, but he'd just have to get over it.

He briefly debated whom to call first and punched in his parents' number.

"I was beginning to wonder if you were going to make it," his mother said.

"Sorry, Mom. I got a late start."

"That's all right, honey. I'm just glad you're home."

"Me, too."

"When do I get to see you and that darling grandson of mine?"

"Well, I'll see you tomorrow, but Dylan and Melanie didn't come."

"Oh? Are you and Mel on the outs again?"

He winced. He should tell her right now, but he couldn't bring himself to do it. "Yeah, we are," he said instead.

"I'm sorry to hear that."

She offered no other comments and asked no questions, but the tone of her voice said plainly enough that she had noted something amiss in his voice.

"I love you, Mom," Henry said, trying to reassure her that he would be all right.

"I love you, too, Henry. I'll see you tomorrow, and you can tell me about it then… or whenever you're ready."

"Thanks, Mom."

Next, he called Aaron.

"You ready to go get that beer?" his twin asked by way of greeting. "Jessie's down at Mom and Dad's, so I'm ready whenever you are."

"Actually, I think I'm going to have to take a rain check. Sorry, bro," Henry replied. "I'm wiped, so I'm just going to take a shower and hit the sack."

"No problem, Hen. I'll see you tomorrow morning? We're supposed to help set up for Vince's wedding."

"Yeah. I'll be there."

"All right. Get some sleep, and I'll see you in the morning."

Henry ended the call and set the cordless back in its cradle feeling more than a little guilty because a beer sounded very good right then. He was probably a terrible sibling for ditching his twin, but he took a quick shower and headed up to the Bedspread Inn.

* * *

By the time Lindsay sat down at a table beside the big windows in the restaurant of the Bedspread Inn, she wasn't sure she was going to make it back to Evie's house before she either broke something or started crying. Her smile had become too much to maintain, and she stared out the windows at the Northstar Mountains awash in golden evening sunlight, drumming her fingers on the table while she waited for her meal. The food arrived, and it looked and smelled delicious, but she was no longer hungry and pushed the ravioli around on her plate.

"Are you all right?" Skye whispered.

"I'm fine," Lindsay replied—unconvincingly, she knew. She tried again, but only managed to say, "Why do you ask?"

"You've been pretty tense since we left Evie's. So, what's going on?"

Lindsay debated telling Skye and decided it might be a good idea to vent a little. "Noah's mad at me because I didn't force him to come with me and because he has to share a room with Spencer, and then I called Max to ask for help with football gear. You can imagine how *that* went."

She tried to stop the words but couldn't. They tumbled out, and she ended up repeating the entire conversation to Skye. By the end of it, Evie was leaning in, listening intently.

"It's not like I *wanted* to get pregnant in high school or go into labor a couple hours after we graduated, and I sure as hell didn't want to be a single parent who is so broke she can't afford her own place, who had to set aside every dream she ever had to raise her son as best she can—which is apparently *not* good enough."

"And you certainly didn't ask to be stuck with a self-centered asshole of an ex, either," Skye said gently.

Lindsay drew a deep breath and glanced at the rest of their party, but no one else seemed to be aware of the conversation at the bride's end of the table, so she exhaled slowly.

"No, I didn't," she said.

"Look at it this way, Linds," Skye remarked. "At least

you were smarter than me because you didn't marry your asshole ex."

"Given the chance, though, I *would have*. I might have begged him to marry me if I'd thought there was any chance.... But he didn't want us."

Skye shook her head. "No, you *never* would have begged. You have too much pride and self-respect for that."

Evie sat up suddenly and asked, "When was the last time you went on a date?"

"You know when," Lindsay replied.

"You're telling me you haven't been on a date since Logan?"

"That's exactly what I'm saying, Evie." *It turned into such a disaster that I haven't recovered the courage to try again.* Thinking about the only other man she'd been with long enough to earn the designation of "ex" wasn't going to put her in any better mood than would dwelling on her ongoing issues with Max.

"I think we need to send you on a date while you're here," Evie said brightly, oblivious of her friend's inner turmoil. "You don't have Noah here to worry about and all the time in the world to yourself."

Before Lindsay could respond, the bell on the dining room's door jingled and in strolled one of those attractive Northstar men Evie had mentioned not less than a dozen times today. Clad in Wrangler jeans that hugged long legs and narrow hips, a fitted white T-shirt that accentuated strong arms, shoulders, and chest, and a pair of dusty work boots, he looked every bit the quintessential Montana cowboy even without the trademark hat. His mouth was set in a firm line, and his blue eyes were stern. Or were they agonized? When their gazes briefly met, Lindsay decided it was the latter, and her heart stumbled over itself, smitten and concerned all at once.

What's wrong, cutie pie? she wondered as the thought of a one night stand returned with sudden and breathtaking appeal.

As he strode past their table on his way to the bar at the back of the room, she turned in her chair to enjoy the view and thought of the photo of six cowboys sitting on the log rail of a corral Evie had emailed shortly after she met Vince. *Cowboy butts drive me nuts*, she had captioned it.

Just before the stranger settled on a bar stool, he glanced back at Lindsay, and her pulse quickened. *The rest of him might drive me nuts, too,* she mused, absently poking at the ice in her glass of Coke with her straw.

"Well, what do you think?" Evie asked, apparently taking Lindsay's lack of response to mean she was considering the matter of a date.

"Let's get you married off before we start trying to fix me."

Lindsay covertly studied the stranger. He did not again glance her way—at least, not while she was looking. He sat hunched over his beer with his fingers knitted around the bottle and talked quietly to the tall man behind the bar whose expression spoke of a deep conversation rather than a light-hearted chat. A questionable urge to join the blond cowboy for a drink or three—one unhappy soul commiserating with another—fluttered in her chest. Considering Evie's recent comments, she didn't think her friend would mind too much if she missed a bit of their girls' night in, so when everyone in their party stood to leave, she excused herself from the group.

"Where are you going?" Evie asked. "I thought we were—"

"I want a drink," Lindsay replied. "And I promise to be better company when I get home."

"Do you want us to stay with you? I don't drink, but I—"

"No. You don't want to be around me right now, Evie, and I don't want to be the thundercloud to rain on the eve of your wedding, so I'll just have a drink or two and clear my head a bit before I rejoin you, all right? Then I'll be home, and you, Skye, and I can have a laughing good time like we always do."

"If you're sure…."

"Let's leave her be for a bit, Evie," Skye said, gently guiding the bride toward the door. Before she followed their friend outside, she turned to Lindsay and added, "I know Evie's house is just up the road from here and plenty close enough for you to walk, but call if you want a ride."

"Thanks, Skye. Not just for that, but for—"

"I get it, Linds. I've had my share of moments recently when I just wanted to be alone." She glanced toward the bar, then back at Lindsay. "Or not so alone."

Without a word, Skye left, and Lindsay made her way toward the bar. She doubted she'd act on the flash-fire impulses the stranger had unknowingly triggered, but it was refreshing to consider the possibilities. Evie *was* right that she needed to treat herself to a date if only to remind herself that she was more than Noah's mother, more than Max's and Logan's unwanted ex-girlfriend.

She hesitated, catching snippets of the quiet

conversation between the cowboy and the bar tender. What she heard made her heart ache, so she slid onto the barstool beside the man centered so pervasively at the forefront of her attention and smiled warmly when he turned toward her. Maybe she could find a way to cheer them both up.

"Is this seat taken?" she asked. "Because I'd like to join you for a drink, if that's all right."

He hesitated a moment, adding further evidence that he was here for some serious drinking and not a quick beer after work, and she thought he might decline her proposition. Instead, he extended his hand. "I don't mind at all if you join me, but I'm not likely to be the best company tonight."

"So I gathered," she replied, taking his hand and enjoying the firm heat of it. "And that's quite all right because I probably won't be, either. Maybe we can salvage the evening together."

"Interesting proposal... as long as some guy doesn't stroll in here spoiling for a fight because I bought his woman a drink."

"I haven't been anyone's woman for a long time."

He eyed her disbelievingly for a moment. Then one corner of his mouth lifted in a devastatingly sexy, lopsided grin. "Well, all right then. What are you drinking?"

* * *

A large party occupied the front of the restaurant, and a moment after stepping through the glass doors, Henry realized it must be Vince and his fiancée's wedding party sitting down to the rehearsal dinner. He recognized Vince and his wife-to-be, Vince's parents and grandparents, and the two groomsmen—Vince's college buddies—but he didn't recognize the two younger women sitting beside the bride, the middle-aged couple, or the older woman beside them. They must be the bridesmaids and the bride's parents and grandmother.

A cursory glance at the bridesmaids required a second look. Both were attractive, taller and slimmer than their friend, but the one with the mane of shimmering dark copper that ended in soft curls commanded his attention. Her expression was decidedly *not* one of enjoyment but of distress. Blue eyes that took on the lavender tint of her summer dress met his briefly, and his breath caught in his throat. With her graceful neck and shoulders, a face with delicate features, and full, feminine curves, it was all he could do to keep from staring. He managed, but he couldn't help glancing back at her. When he caught her watching him, he turned quickly away so she didn't see his lips quirk upward.

"Welcome home, Henry."

"Thanks, Pat," he replied to the man behind the bar.

"Where's Aaron?" Pat asked. He popped the top on a Harvest Moon Beltian White and set it in front of him.

"I postponed our drink together," Henry replied. He stared at the bottle a moment, turned it around twice with the tips of his fingers, and finally took a sip, then briefly met Pat's concerned gaze. "Found out three weeks ago that Dylan isn't my son."

"Ah damn, Henry," the other man murmured with a genuine regret that soothed Henry's sore heart. "I'm very sorry to hear that."

"I was, too."

"How'd you find out?"

"Paternity test." Henry took a long swallow of his

beer. "About three months ago, Mel's friend Tamlyn asked me if I was sure Dylan was mine."

"Seems an odd thing for her to ask. I thought she and Mel were best friends."

"They are. Were. I don't know anymore. They've been butting heads over the salon for months now. Tam's serious about it, and Mel.... Well, you know how Mel is with money. She spends it faster than she makes it. Anyhow, before all that started, they went out for drinks one night, and apparently Melanie confided to Tam that she slept with a couple other men right after we broke up. When I confronted Mel about it, she admitted that Dylan might not be mine."

"Have you told your folks yet?"

Henry shook his head. "Haven't worked up the courage to break their hearts yet."

"Something tells me they may not be entirely surprised."

"Why do you say that?"

"Your father made a remark to Old Matt a few weeks ago. Seems he thought you should ask for a paternity test."

"What else did he say?"

"That he hoped he was wrong," Pat replied. "I take your surprise to mean he's never mentioned this to you."

"Not exactly, but he and Mom never liked Melanie much. And you know my parents. They love everyone."

"They're good people. So what happens now?"

"I left. For good this time. Quit my job so I could move home for a while and regroup."

"That's drastic."

Henry shrugged. "I couldn't stay in the city anymore.

I may spend most of my time fighting it, but I am a country boy at heart. Besides, the fact that you know more about my father's suspicions than I do.... Well, maybe it'll be good for me to spend a little quality time with my family."

"And just maybe you'll realize you're not as much of a black sheep as you've tried to convince yourself you are."

Henry studied Pat for a moment, wondering what the former detective was getting at. Shrugging again, he decided not to worry about it tonight. He had enough to drown already with Melanie's deceit still fresh in his mind.

When the pretty redhead perched on the stool beside him and asked to join him for a drink, he almost declined her offer, but when she wasn't put off by his bad mood, he smiled and decided the company of a beautiful woman might be just the thing to get his mind off Melanie and Dylan. Unless she had a boyfriend and was looking to cause trouble.... So, he asked and wasn't sure he believed her when she said she hadn't been anyone's woman in a long time until he saw the shimmer of something in her eyes that sliced right to his heart. She was telling the truth, and there was surely a story behind *why* she was single—and had been for some time, apparently.

"Well, all right then," he replied, curious. He offered her a lopsided smile, trying to be as playful as she had been a moment ago. "What are you drinking?"

"Rum and Coke. Thanks. I'm Lindsay Miller, by the way."

"Henry Hammond. It's a delight to meet you, Lindsay Miller."

Pat moved off to make her drink, and Henry turned to face her fully. With time to gather the pieces of a more accurate impression, he was quite intrigued. Despite the fact that she'd asked to join him, there was a subtle shyness and caution about her that provoked the same instinctive need to shelter and protect that Dylan's conception had initiated.

"So, you're a Hammond," his companion inquired. "Any relation to Vince's sister Beth Hammond?"

"Her husband Nick is my older brother."

"I'm guessing then that you'll be at the wedding tomorrow."

"Yep. Of course, just about everyone from the Valley will be there, too. Welcome to Northstar," Henry said with a laugh.

"It's the quintessential small town, then, huh?"

"Oh, yeah. But in the best way."

"From what I've seen so far, I have to agree. I love small towns." She leveled those exquisite blue eyes on him, narrowing them briefly and pursing her lips as she studied him with an intensity and curiosity that kicked his pulse up a notch. "Should we just get our reasons for being bad company out in the open so we can get down to the more pleasant task of salvaging the evening?"

Playful, Henry noted, *but serious, too.*

The thought that she might be maneuvering for more than a drink tiptoed across his mind, and he ignored it. No way. She might be, but he knew himself well enough to know that anything beyond drinks and conversation would be a very bad idea.

"I'm sure you heard most of my reason."

Pat briefly interrupted when he brought Lindsay's drink and another beer for Henry, then ambled off to tend to other patrons, leaving them alone to talk.

36

"I'm sorry for eavesdropping," Lindsay said. "That's a terrible thing to find out, and I'm sorry for that, too."

"Thanks. What about you? Why are you bad company tonight?"

"Right before the wedding rehearsal, I had the displeasure of engaging in yet another fight with my ex regarding our son."

Henry sat up in surprise, unable to recall seeing anyone under the age of twenty at the wedding party's table. "You have a son? Where is he?"

"Back home in Washington because he didn't want to come to Evie's wedding with me."

"How old is he?"

"Eight. And before you ask, yes, I got pregnant in high school—senior year."

"Tough break. But can I ask you a question?"

"Sure."

"Do you always begin conversations with such deeply personal information?"

"I think I might make it a habit." She took a sip of her rum and Coke. "It should save a lot of time and frustration if the guy I'm interested in can't handle the fact that I have a son."

"I take it that has happened more than once?"

She nodded but offered no other information on the topic. He watched her for a moment, distracted by the rather adorable way she chewed on the slender straw in her drink, and waited for her to enjoy her beverage a bit before he asked what had happened between her and her ex.

"At first, he acted like he wanted to stay in our lives and wanted to be a father to Noah, but then he went off to college at Washington State University, found a new woman, and our relationship faded into nothing."

"Wait. When did he meet her?"

"During his junior year when he and I were still technically together. Just before graduation, he called to tell me that he was getting married."

"Christ, that's low. I'm sorry, Lindsay."

She shrugged. "It's water under the bridge, as they say, but if I could find a way to make it happen, I'd burn the bridge."

"I don't blame you," Henry said gently. Then he let out a self-mocking snort. "Makes me feel even worse for walking out on Mel. But I couldn't stay with her anymore. Honestly, she was never a long-term prospect for me, and we only got back together because she told me she was pregnant with my kid."

"Why'd you break up before?"

"Too many incompatibilities. She's a city girl through-and-through, hates to do all the things outdoors that I love, and—forgive me for saying this because it will probably sound cruel—her favorite thing about me was my steady paycheck. I wouldn't call her a gold digger, but she tends to seek stability. Maybe that's because her dad walked out on her and her mom when she was seven, or maybe she just likes spending money. I don't know, and I don't care anymore."

Lindsay tilted her head and studied him again. "Let me guess. You feel guilty because you're doing the same thing to Dylan that her father did to her."

"When you put it that way... yeah, that's exactly how I feel."

"You realize none of that is your fault, right?" she remarked. "I'm also going to guess that she said the kid was yours to keep your steady paycheck."

"That makes her sound exceedingly manipulative."

"Granted, I don't know the exact timeframe of all this, but it sounds like she slept with two other guys very soon after she slept with you the last time, so there's no way she could have known for sure you were her kid's father."

"I'd like to hope she at least believed I was Dylan's father. It's better than the alternative—that she picked me without even considering that I might not be because she knew I'd support her. Yeah, we always used some form of protection, but accidents happen."

"I can attest to that." Suddenly, Lindsay grinned. "Who's divulging deeply personal information now, hmm?"

Despite the ache that had trickled back into his heart, Henry laughed. "You are a very intriguing woman, Lindsay. I'm not in the habit of opening up like this so quickly… or so easily."

"That sounds like a good thing."

"Jury's still out, but since I'm already in a better mood, I'd say it's a *very* good thing."

"See? Aren't you glad I invited myself over?"

"Yes, I am. I wish you could stay longer, but I don't want to take anymore of your time away from your friends."

"I should head back to Evie's," Lindsay agreed. She made no move to leave him, though her drink now sat empty and she shook her head when Pat asked if she'd like another.

Henry chuckled, then swallowed the rest of his second beer and contemplated the wisdom of the question he wanted to ask. It was likely foolish, but he asked anyhow. "You said announcing the fact that you have a kid up front will help you screen men you're interested in. Does that mean you're interested in me?"

"That depends. Do you have a problem with me having a son?"

"Until three weeks ago, I thought *I* had a son, so it's safe to say that I definitely don't."

"Then, yes, I'm interested. I think I'd like to get to know you better while I'm here, if you're agreeable to that."

"I don't know if it's a good idea right now, and I think you know why," Henry said slowly, "but if you're okay with *my* issues, I'd like to get to know you better, too. Just probably not tonight."

"No, not tonight. I'm supposed to be having a girls' night in with the bride, anyhow, and thanks to you, I think I might actually be able to enjoy it now."

"Not sure how I helped, but you're welcome."

"*How* is not important, but you did. I'll see you at the wedding tomorrow?"

"Yep. Looking forward to it."

"Me, too. Thanks for the drink and the commiseration."

"Right back atcha."

He watched her walk away until she disappeared into the deepening twilight, captivated by her natural poise and subtle confidence. He stayed at the bar, had more than a few beers, and chatted with Pat but ignored the other customers who came and went. Melanie and the paternity test hovered at the edges of his thoughts, but for the first time in three weeks, he wasn't consumed by them; he was too captivated by the enchanting Lindsay Miller. As the night wore on and his senses dulled with alcohol, he wondered if he'd imagined their entire conversation. Recalling her almost shy invitation to get to know him, he sincerely hoped not.

At ten, Pat closed the restaurant and the bar and drove Henry home. When Henry climbed out of the passenger seat, Pat leaned across the cab and said, "I'll stop down and pick you up on my way to the C Diamond tomorrow morning so you can get your truck."

"Thanks, Pat. For driving me home, picking me up tomorrow... and for listening."

"Any time, Henry. That's what friends are for. And hey, it's heartbreaking that Dylan isn't your son, but now you're free to find the kind of good woman you'll *want* to spend the rest of your life with."

A good woman, Henry mused as he climbed the steps to his front deck with surprisingly steady legs. Maybe he should ask Pat in the morning what a good woman was like because he couldn't say for sure, but Pat had certainly found one in his wife, Aelissm. The thought stayed with him while he prepared for bed. As he crawled between his sheets, he decided he was glad he hadn't declined Lindsay's offer to join him for a drink because her openness and honesty was, right then, very appealing. *And if those two traits are a good place to start, Lindsay might just be one of those good women Pat mentioned.*

Three

WITHIN FIFTEEN MINUTES of arriving at the Carlyles' ranch house, Lindsay wished she had thought to pack a button-up shirt for the day of Evie's wedding. The yellow, curve-hugging dress she wore was the only thing she'd brought that could be taken off without pulling it over her head when it was time to change into her bridesmaid dress, but it was entirely impractical for setting up for the wedding. At the moment, Livia had her hauling chairs out to the backyard. Everyone else who had already arrived to assist was out front setting up tables and the dance floor for the reception or in the kitchen finishing up the food prep, so she was alone, but Livia had promised to send any new arrivals out to aid her.

At least she'd had the forethought to wear flat sandals. She couldn't imagine how difficult and slow it would be trying to set out two hundred and some folding chairs on this lush, squishy lawn in heels.

Pretty comical, too, she mused as she hauled the last two chairs for the first row into place and unfolded them.

"Livia says you might appreciate some help."

She straightened, and a smile lifted her lips as she turned to the owner of the newly familiar voice. Henry strode toward her with two chairs in each hand and that same charming lopsided grin. Desire uncurled inside her, yawning and stretching after a long dormancy, and her pulse jumped as she took in the sight of him. He was again dressed in a white T-shirt, jeans, and work boots, but today he'd added a straw cowboy hat to the casual ensemble. The dim lighting of the Bedspread Inn's restaurant last night hadn't given her as clear an impression of him as she'd thought, and as she took in every line of him in the brilliant morning sunlight, she nearly let out a whistle. The man was pure sex appeal without a trace of arrogance.

"Well, howdy stranger," she drawled. "Fancy meeting you here."

His smile turned slightly sheepish. "When Livia mentioned you were out here by yourself, I may have volunteered to help you with these before I head out front to help my brothers with the picnic tables." He leaned the chairs against his legs and handed one to her. "Something tells me you'll be much more interesting company. At the very least, you're certainly more *attractive* company."

"And here I was just chastising myself for not packing something more practical for the pre-wedding activities." She glanced down at her sunny yellow dress with its flirty hem and neckline and laughed. "To think there was a time I wouldn't be caught dead in a dress."

"Coulda fooled me."

She snorted and unfolded another chair. "I know, it's hard to believe since that's all you've seen me in, but before I bowed down to the pressures of society, I—"

"Bowed down to the pressures of society? You don't seem the type to bow down to anyone or anything."

"Okay, let's say then that I gave in to pressures of my poverty. I figured out I got better tips when I wore dresses and skirts instead of slacks. I'm still not fond of them, though."

"I take it you were a bit of a tomboy growing up."

"Total tomboy."

Henry glanced over her with a brow lifted. "Not sure I believe that, either."

"I was one of the managers for my high school football team because that was the next best thing to playing. Skye was the other manager, though she spent most of her time taking pictures. That's what got our feet in the door, so to speak—her photography. She asked me if I wanted to manage with her, and how could I say no?" Lindsay grinned. "It was damn fun."

"Mel hates football, so I find this revelation entirely fascinating."

"Max doesn't like it, either. In fact, he hates it. He prefers baseball, which—I'm sorry—bores the hell out of me."

"You and me both," Henry replied. "Are you still a football fan?"

"Diehard. I've never really gotten into the NFL, but I love watching a good high school or college game, and

Skye and I go to a couple Husky games together each year. Our folks have season tickets."

"Okay, I have to ask because you've mentioned her twice. Who is Skye?"

"Skye Hathaway. She's my other best friend. I don't think you've met her yet, but she's renting your folks' vacation cabin for the next six weeks, and you might have spotted her last night at the Bedspread Inn. She's the tall brunette."

"Ah, no, I'm sorry. I don't remember her from last night. I must've been too distracted by you."

Lindsay looked up at him with an amused smile. "Are you always such a flirt?"

"I try. I hope you don't find it offensive."

"Not at all. I'm actually rather enjoying the flattery. It's not often I get to feel like a girl anymore. Most of the time, I'm Mom."

"And I'm sure you're a great one, so enjoy the attention for a bit."

"Thanks… again."

"You're welcome. Speaking of your son and turning back to football, I'm going to go out on a limb here and bet he's a big fan, too."

"I don't know if he's as big a fan as I am yet, but he's always liked watching it and going to games… and he started Peewee football last year, which he *loves*. He wants to play again this year."

"How'd that go over with the ex?"

"Not well, but it was Noah's idea." Lindsay scooted another chair into position, then looked up and grinned smugly. "It's probably terrible of me, but I was pretty proud

45

when he tried tee ball—at Max's insistence—and hated it."

"From what you've told me so far about your ex, I'd probably feel the same in your shoes... or sandals," Henry said, making a show of leaning over to take note of her foot wear. He winked. "They look pretty practical to me."

"You wait tables long enough, and fancy, uncomfortable shoes lose their charm," she explained. "So, what about you? You seem to appreciate my football fandom, which makes me think you're a fan yourself. Did you play?"

"Yep to both. I played Little Guy all the way on up through college. Occasionally, I stepped in at running back, but mostly I played cornerback. What position is Noah playing?"

Lindsay smiled. "Running back, but I think his coach may try him at cornerback this year."

"A kid after my own heart."

They fell into an easy silence as they set out chairs in row after row around the as-of-yet undecorated arbor where Vince and Evie would become husband and wife in a few short hours. Lindsay found that she enjoyed working quietly with Henry every bit as much as she delighted in their playful banter. She felt no pressure to engage in meaningless small talk, and at the same time, she knew that anything they said wouldn't *be* meaningless.

After a while, she asked Henry what he did for work, and he informed her that he had worked as a welder and machinist in Denver but had quit to move back to Northstar following the results of the paternity test. Unwilling to taint the beautiful day, Lindsay redirected the conversation to other interests and discovered that, in addition to football, they shared several other passions including classic rock music, books in the fantasy and science fiction genres, and action adventure and fantasy movies. When he made a comment about her being every man's perfect woman, she snorted.

"So far, I haven't seen proof of that," she murmured.

"Then you must be dating the wrong men."

"Apparently so." She laughed softly. "Thanks."

"Just keeping up the tradition you started last night. Speaking of which, I forgot to ask how long you'd be in Northstar."

"Eight more days. I fly out of Butte next Sunday when Vince and Evie leave for their honeymoon."

"Eight days. That's it?"

"Yep."

"What do you have planned for those eight days?"

"I don't really know, but I think Evie just wants to hang out for most of it. We don't get to see each other much now that she's out here."

"I imagine not. I guess I'll have to ask the bride what her plans for you are."

Lindsay tilted her head. "Why are you so curious?"

"Well, we agreed that we'd like to get to know each other while you're here, right?"

"Yes...."

"I am thoroughly intrigued by you, Lindsay Miller. Your openness is refreshing, so I'm going to have a talk with your friend and do a little scheming. In the meantime, we're done here, so I should probably head out front to help my brothers with those picnic tables."

All at once, Lindsay realized that they had indeed finished setting out the chairs and felt a pang of disappointment that Henry would be leaving her momentarily. Gallantly, he took her hand and kissed her knuckles.

"Until later, my lady."

She watched him until he disappeared around the house, captivated by his relaxed stride. Then she sighed and headed inside to see where she was needed next. Livia was in the living room with Evie and Skye going over the specific shots they wanted. Lindsay waited politely for them to finish before she inquired about her next assignment.

"I think it's probably time for you girls to start getting ready," Livia replied. "So, Skye, you should probably go track down your assistant. I believe he's out front helping with the tables. While you're doing that, Lindsay can help Renée and Evie get everything laid out and ready."

"Remind me again. What is my assistant's name?"

"Luke Conner," Evie answered. "He's the tallest and youngest of the blonds out there and pretty hard to miss."

"All right. I'll be back."

Skye zipped out of the house. Lindsay stared briefly after her with a wistful twist of her lips, wishing she could have gone in her friend's place. It was silly, she knew, because she'd likely have many opportunities to sneak in a word or two with Henry Hammond throughout the day.

"Oh, sugar," Livia said. "I forgot I was going to have her ask if we can send the centerpieces out. Lindsay, dear, would you mind?"

"Of course not," she replied quickly. A little too quickly, perhaps, if Evie's quirked brow was any indication. Before her friend could question her, she trotted out the door after Skye.

They located Skye's assistant photographer with the

Hammond brothers and a dark-haired man Lindsay didn't recognize. Like Evie had said, Luke Conner was easy to spot, standing a good three or four inches taller than Henry and his brothers, who weren't exactly short at six feet or so. He was boyishly handsome with golden hair styled in a center-parted bowl cut and a lean, athletic build that made Lindsay certain he played some sport or other in college.

"Pardon the interruption," she said when she and Skye reached the group.

Henry glanced up from his task and grinned. "What can we do you for?"

"Mrs. Carlyle wants to know when she should start sending out table runners and centerpieces," Lindsay replied lightly so as not to reveal the rush of heat and anticipation triggered by the insinuation beneath his words. Still, she couldn't help but glance appreciatively over him. They hadn't openly discussed the topic that had been flirting with her mind since she'd first seen him last night, but that didn't mean either of them was unaware of it. Last night hadn't been right, but if Lindsay had her way, she'd find out if he was as good in bed as his strong, capable hands and easy, rocking gait led her to hope.

"This is the last load," Henry answered.

From the corner of her vision, she caught the amusement on the face of his brother, who looked to be the same age as Henry, and the warmth of embarrassment climbed her neck. Reminding herself that she was a grown woman and not a young girl who'd been caught at something naughty, she turned her attention more fully to him. Were he and Henry twins? Fraternal, if so. They certainly weren't identical, though they were similar enough in appearance

49

that no one would doubt they were brothers. There was one difference, however, that she noted immediately. Henry exuded energy with a hint of simmering anger and resentment while his twin was reserved with an air of deep-seated sadness. He glanced away, his attention drawn to Skye, who met his gaze with a coy smile and blush pinkening her cheeks.

Interesting, Lindsay mused.

"Tell Livia she can start sending the decorations out," the dark-haired man added, interrupting her observation.

Skye at last shifted her attention from Henry's twin to the tall, young man and said, "Evie described my assistant as the tallest and the youngest of the blonds, so I'm guessing you're Luke Conner."

"You must be Skye," the kid replied. "When do you need me?"

"Right now if you can be spared. The families want some pictures of everyone getting ready, and since I'm in the need-to-get-ready camp...."

Luke glanced at his companions, silently asking if he was free to go.

"We can handle these last eight tables," Henry's older brother, Nick, replied.

Lindsay turned to follow Luke and Skye back to the house, but Henry stopped her.

"We just keep bumping into each other, don't we," he remarked.

"We do, but I don't know that I'd call it 'bumping.' That implies it has happened by accident, but I'm pretty sure it's been intentional every time."

"So it has," he said with a quirk of his lips. "I have a

thought about this getting-to-know-each-other idea. Luke's starting in his first college football game on Saturday."

"He plays football?" She glanced over her shoulder at the young man. "Why am I not surprised? Quarterback?"

"How'd you guess?"

"He's tall and lean, has strong, graceful hands, and I'd bet he's pretty quick both on his feet and with his head. As far as I can tell, he's what my dad would call an ideal quarterback."

"You really do know your football," Henry said, obviously impressed.

"Obsessive might have been a more fitting term back in the day."

"I like dedicated better. Anyhow, a bunch of us from Northstar—including, I believe the bride and groom—are going. Care to join me?"

Before Lindsay could respond, Henry's twin barked, "Henry!"

"I gotta go," Henry said quickly. "Think about it?"

"I will definitely think about it," Lindsay replied. "I'll find you later."

So she didn't get him in any more trouble with his siblings, she hurried after Skye. Just as she passed out of earshot, she heard him utter something under his breath that made her beam.

* * *

"Hot damn," Henry said softly.

Lindsay was as beautiful as she was intriguing in that cheerful yellow dress, which showed off proud, graceful shoulders and long, toned legs and hugged a trim, exquisitely feminine body. He knew it was stupid in the extreme, but he couldn't seem to tell her no. He had a pretty good idea of what she wanted—a brief, casual affair—but instinctively he knew it wouldn't be a purely physical romp. She wasn't the kind of woman who could disassociate her heart from sex. With her, it would be making love, and he wasn't sure he could set his anger aside long enough to let that happen.

"Would you quit thinking with your dick long enough for us to finish this?" Aaron snapped.

Henry jerked back in shock, but surprise quickly gave way to anger as his temper flared. Aaron had no room to talk. If anyone in his family could understand the anguish boiling in Henry's heart, it would be his twin, whose wife had died in his arms nearly half a decade ago after being shot in the chest. But no, Aaron was still too wrapped up in his own grief to give a passing thought to anyone else. He'd been a different man since Erica's death—sullen and withdrawn, going through the motions every day instead of living. Like someone had opened a door in his mind, Henry realized that he'd needed his twin's understanding over the past three weeks, but a rift had opened up between them that had prevented him from seeking it. Anger darkened into bitter and helpless fury.

"Maybe you oughta *start* thinking with yours again so you wouldn't be such an uptight ass all the damned time," he retorted and stalked away a few paces.

"Henry!" Nick growled. "Would you give him a break?"

"Why? It's been almost five years, Nick. I miss Erica, too—we all do—but she's gone, and he needs to get that through his head."

"Jerry Mackey's getting out on Friday," Nick explained, "but you'd know that if you had bothered to talk to him instead of heading straight for the bar at the Bedspread as soon as you rolled into the valley last night."

He ignored the flash of guilt. Learning that the brother of the man who'd accidentally killed Erica would soon be released from prison had undoubtedly brought the agony of her death back to the surface of Aaron's thoughts, but Henry was in no mood to offer sympathy. He spared only a moment to pray the dumb kid had learned his lesson and wouldn't foolishly try to come after Aaron again because the last time hadn't turned out so well for him; he'd ended up with a black eye and a return trip to prison to serve the remaining two years of his original sentence. Curtly, he responded, "We've all got problems, Nick."

"You were at the Bedspread last night?" Aaron asked.

Henry eyed him warily. "Yeah, I was. Pat had to drive me home." He looked up at Pat with a humorless smile. "Thanks, by the way, in case I didn't say it last night."

"You did," was Pat's reply. He offered to help Ben unload to give the brothers a chance to talk.

"It's been a long time since someone's had to drive you home," Aaron remarked, suddenly concerned. "What's going on, Hen?"

"Don't ask like you give a rat's ass any more than anyone else in this family."

"You're my brother, Henry. Of course I care."

"Bullshit. Since Erica died, you've been too lost in your own sorrow to care." He glanced at Ben Conner, then added, "For a little while, when you dated June, I thought you might be starting to come back, but then you gave up and slunk away with your tail between your legs."

"Oh, come on, Henry, I haven't been that bad."

"Maybe I'm exaggerating, but you sure haven't been the same Aaron who used to party with me back in high school and college, the Aaron who was up for anything, any time."

"I have a daughter."

"Yeah, you do."

Aaron studied him for a moment with narrowed eyes, and Henry looked away as his anger fizzled and left a hole that filled too quickly with despair.

"You and Melanie on the outs again?" Aaron asked.

Henry sat heavily on the nearest picnic table. This was *not* how he'd planned to break the news to his family, but it was too late to stop the conversation from happening now, so he said, "That's one way to put it. You remember me telling you that everyone always says Dylan looks nothing like me?"

"I do. I've thought the same myself."

"Well, that's because he's not my son."

"Ah, hell. You're sure?"

"Yep. She isn't sure who his father is, but the paternity test confirmed that it's not me." Henry's voice faltered, and he swore under his breath. He'd had three weeks to come to terms with that piece of information, so he should be able to keep a tight grip on his emotions, but his eyes stung with the threat of tears. The memory of the moment he'd hopped in his truck to drive away, when he'd foolishly looked back to see Dylan reaching and screaming for him, crashed into his mind and made it difficult to speak. "He's a year old, and she's had me thinking all this time that he's my kid."

"I am so sorry, Hen."

"I am, too. I love the little stinker."

"That means you're over for good, right?" Nick asked.

"Yeah." He forced the memory away and sought anything that might help him swallow the pain. Suddenly, an entirely different image popped into his head... and a plan. Recalling that interesting look between Aaron and Lindsay's friend Skye, he wondered if he could turn Luke's football game into a double date. That might keep him from acting on the raging desire to take the pretty redhead to bed and might also be good for Aaron. He hadn't seen that particular expression on his twin's face in a long time, so he plunged ahead with his scheme. "Have either of you met the new tenant in Mom and Dad's rental yet?"

"We met her briefly last night," Nick replied. "And you met her just a few minutes ago—she's the brunette. I get the feeling she's going through a divorce right now, so go easy on her, all right, Henry?"

"Hey, I'm always easy."

Aaron and Nick both laughed.

"I *so* want to make a smart-ass remark right now about you and Melanie, but I won't because I can see it's still a tender subject." Aaron gave him a good-natured pat on the back. "Contrary to your earlier accusations, I *do* care."

"I know you do," Henry replied. Then he chuckled and relaxed some more. This was more like it—the light-hearted teasing between brothers, just like the old days. "Thanks for *sort of* not being a smart ass."

Aaron pushed to his feet and went back to work. As he strode away, Henry said to Nick, "I wasn't asking about the tenant for me. I was asking about her for Aaron because the man seriously needs to get laid. Besides, I'm a little partial to that redhead in the yellow dress."

Nick grinned but said, "Let's leave things alone for now and get back to work."

"Fine." Henry grabbed one side of a table, and Nick grabbed the other. "I haven't told Mom and Dad."

"You should probably do that soon because you know how Northstar is. It won't take long for word to get out, and it'd be best if they heard it from you."

"Last night, Pat said he didn't think they'd be too surprised, that he'd overheard Dad telling Old Matt I should ask for a paternity test. Did he ever say anything like that to you?"

"No, but he and Mom have both commented on Dylan's lack of resemblance to you. Look, Hen, it's a gorgeous day, so don't let this get you down. Go back to daydreaming about that redheaded friend of Evie's if that'll keep you in a good mood."

Henry laughed. "Now, *that* is a wonderful suggestion."

"Just... be careful with her. You're probably not in the best state of mind at the moment to be diving into a relationship with a new woman, and it wouldn't be fair to mislead her."

"Something tells me she's a pretty sharp cookie and she knows exactly what she's getting into with me," Henry said. "But I *will* be gentle with her."

"I take it that wasn't the first time you've met her."

56

"Nope. Last night at the Bedspread… and we set out the chairs for the wedding together. She's a very fascinating woman. Football fan."

"Why don't you ask her to Luke's game?"

"I already have, but Aaron interrupted. I thought maybe he should ask Skye, too, and we could turn it into a double date."

"That's an interesting idea." Nick glanced at their brother. "There was definitely a spark there. Good luck convincing him, though."

Thoughts of Luke's football game and Lindsay carried him all the way through setting up and decorating the reception area. When it was finally time for the wedding, his troubles had been pushed far enough to the back of his mind that he was able to fully appreciate the stunning August day and accept that his decision to come home to Northstar was the right one. The quiet of the valley, which could not be disturbed by even the boisterous wedding preparations, was a soothing balm after the constant noise of Denver, and it was refreshing to again gaze upon clear, sapphire skies undimmed by pollution. Maybe he'd drag his old Harley out of his garage and take it for a ride over the pass to Wise River to blow the spider webs, dust, and carbon off the valves. Maybe he'd ask Lindsay to join him. And maybe he'd take her horseback riding across his family's ranch and give her a proper introduction to Montana's beauty.

The woman who had so firmly captured his attention strode down the aisle with her hand resting lightly on the arm of Vince's friend from college, and Henry noted the smug gleam in the man's eye. He couldn't blame the groomsman—Lindsay was breathtaking in that deep red, floor-length sheath with her hair piled in loose curls at the back of her head. Her hair was a dark enough auburn and the red of the dress was cool enough that the colors didn't clash, and the rhinestones glittering from the pins in her hair threw dazzling sparks of rainbow-hued light and added a glamorous quality to her.

That, or I'm just smitten. The thought didn't concern him as much as it probably should. *No harm in that as long as we keep it casual and remember to resist any expectations of more.*

He figured they'd be safe as long as he kept telling himself that and as long as he adhered to it. Of course, plotting a week of adventures with her definitely wasn't the best way to keep it casual. Still, watching her throughout the ceremony and catching the occasional, coy glance she tossed his way, he went on plotting.

It wasn't until the reception was underway that he finally got a chance to put his plan for Saturday into motion. He joined his twin and a very pregnant June Conner near the refreshments tent.

"Wow, June," Henry announced, striding over. "You are looking absolutely stunning these days."

"You're such a natural liar, Henry, that I actually believe you," she teased.

"I never lie."

Her husband strolled over, and they gathered around a nearby picnic table. Shortly thereafter, Pat and his wife, Aelissm—who was nearly as far along as June—ventured over with their two children in tow. Moments later, Nick and his wife, Beth, and their son, Will, joined their party. They watched the goings-on in companionable silence until

Henry noticed his twin's preoccupation with the dark-haired photographer as she reviewed the shots Luke had taken of the ceremony. *This may not be so difficult after all.*

"Ms. Hathaway sure is easy on the eyes, ain't she, Aaron?" Henry inquired lightly.

"Mmm," Aaron replied distractedly. Without turning to Henry, he added, "Yes, she is. Beautiful."

"Fascinating," Henry remarked.

Aaron finally met his gaze with narrowed eyes. "Mind your own damned business, Henry."

"Can't, bro. Sorry. Because I have an idea. You and I should take her and that sexy redhead out on a double date in Devyn or maybe Butte. Better yet, we can take them to Luke's game on Saturday. A little birdie told me that Lindsay—she's the redhead—and Skye both like football. *Really* like it, as in they were managers for their high school team. C'mon, Aaron, how can we go wrong with that? We'd better make our move fast, though, because the groomsmen are interested, and they already have a foot in the door, being part of the wedding party and all."

Henry waited for Aaron's dismissal of the idea, but it didn't come. Instead, his twin changed the subject to June and Ben's son, Luke, who Henry learned was at last starting to recover from the hell Pete Landers's second personality, JP, had put him through two years ago. Toward the end of the conversation, Jessie asked to go play with her cousin, Will, and the O'Neil kids.

"Sure. Just stay out of the way of the photographer and the wedding party, okay?" Aaron told her.

As talk shifted to more pleasant topics, Henry watched his niece stalk Skye, Lindsay, and Luke until Ben's niece Becky joined them and dragged Luke over to his group's table. Not half a moment later, Jessie did exactly what her father had told her *not* to do, much to Henry's delight.

"Hey, Aaron, you might want to go get your daughter," he said. When Aaron didn't respond, he glanced at his brother, who was too busy staring at the photographer to notice what his daughter was up to. "Yo, Aaron! Are you asleep, or what?"

He blinked at Henry and frowned. "No. Why? Did I miss something?"

"Your daughter seems to have taken a sudden interest in photography," Nick responded, inclining his head.

"Oh, hell. What is she doing?"

"Looks to me like she might be playing matchmaker," Henry remarked. "Atta girl, Jessie."

"Keep it up, smart ass," Aaron grumbled and jogged after his daughter.

When he was gone, Nick leaned over and said just loud enough for Henry to hear, "I'd say it's pretty low to let Jessie do your dirty work for you, but that may just be the key to getting Aaron to go along with your double-date idea."

Henry offered his older brother a sly grin.

Bridesmaid duties kept Lindsay occupied through dinner, but as soon as she could sneak away, she joined Henry's party.

"Doesn't the bride need you?" he inquired.

"If her remarks earlier are any indication, I'd say she's rather pleased Skye and I are opting to spend the rest of the evening with you and your family and friends. You and

Aaron are twins, right?"

"Yep. Used to be inseparable."

"Used to be?"

"When he married Erica, that changed. He mellowed a lot. And then, when she died...."

"Evie mentioned he was a widower. I'm sorry to hear that."

"Me, too. Erica was a wonderful woman."

The DJ briefly interrupted their conversation when he announced it was time for the bride and groom's first dance as husband and wife. Henry leaned back against the table.

"Have you thought about that football game? Because I even tried to convince my brother to take Skye just incase you were feeling pressured."

Her smile was gentle. "That's really kind of you, but since I'm the one who started this whole thing when I asked to join you for a drink last night, it would be a bit hypocritical of me to feel pressured. Besides, I may have tried to do a little convincing of my own. All I got out of Skye was 'I'll think about it.' So, in answer to your invitation, I'd love to go. I wanted to go anyhow, and I will, but this is me clarifying that I want to go with *you*."

Henry grinned. "All right, then. It's a date. And I may have a few other ideas for your vacation, too, but we'll talk about them later. Right now... how about a dance?"

"You dance?"

"Not willingly, but for you, I'd like to make an exception. Are you up for that?"

"I am."

Grinning and entirely pleased with himself, Henry

offered to help her up and pulled her to her feet when she laid her hand in his. *Keep it casual,* he reminded himself as they stepped onto the dance floor and took Lindsay into his arms. She evoked a depth of desire he wasn't sure he'd ever felt for Melanie, and he nearly snorted at his promise. *Why do I get the feeling that's going to be a* lot *easier said than done?*

* * *

Stars glittered across the cloudless night sky, which was a glowing blue instead of the inky black Lindsay was accustomed to back home in Washington where the city lights dulled the brilliance of the heavens. There were so many even with a full moon outshining many of the dimmer stars, and they mesmerized her nearly as delightfully as her partner. She danced and talked and laughed until she was breathless and enjoyed herself with a carefree abandon she hadn't felt in years.

She sat to take a breather with Henry at his group's picnic table, leaning back with his arm propped on the table behind her. She wasn't exactly tucked into his side, but the warmth of him chased away the descending cool of night.

Today had been nothing short of marvelous. For once, she wasn't worried about money or housework or Noah's homework or any of the myriad of other troubles that took the joy out of life, and though Henry hadn't yet broached the subject again, she looked forward to whatever plans he had for her.

Since he seemed unwilling to discuss them with so many people around, she asked him to drive her home to Vince and Evie's house. It wasn't that she wanted the night to end—she certainly didn't. She wanted him all to herself.

"Won't Evie be disappointed you're leaving her

wedding reception so early?"

"Early? It's almost ten. Besides, I'm still pretty tired from traveling yesterday, so I'm sure she'll forgive me."

Lindsay said her goodnights to the newlyweds and Skye, who was preoccupied with Henry's twin. No one questioned her desire to head home, undoubtedly figuring she just wanted to catch up on the sleep she'd lost. Having satisfied her duties as a bridesmaid, she didn't feel too guilty, either, and followed Henry into the main house. She quickly gathered her belongings, and then they headed out to his truck.

They were quiet on the short drive to Vince and Evie's home, and Lindsay wasn't sure how to ask Henry to come in let alone how to invite him to sleep with her.

Is asking for sex always this awkward, or is it just me? she wondered.

Too soon, Henry pulled up in front of the cabin and shut the truck down, then climbed out and walked around to help her out. The confidence that had bolstered her last night and today evaporated, and she was suddenly over-come by shyness. Henry must have sensed it because he turned to face her with concern drawing his brows together. After a moment, he took her hand and led her up the flag-stone path.

They were nearly to the door when he stopped and turned her to face him. "I feel like I'm getting ahead of my-self with my ideas for your vacation," he said. "I don't know what you expect of me other than what you said earlier about enjoying feeling like a girl instead of your son's mother. So, I guess before I ask you out on a date, I—"

"You mean, a date other than Luke's football game?"

"Yes. I need to ask what you want out of this, Lindsay."

She didn't answer for a moment and considered how best to answer his question. She thought back to what had driven her to join him for a drink last night and reviewed their initial conversation. Recalling his remark about not wanting to land himself in trouble for buying some man's woman a drink, she said slowly, "I have spent so much time alone or being Noah's mom that I'm starting to forget that I'm more than that. I guess what I want is to remember what it's like to be someone's woman for a little while... even if it isn't real."

Henry frowned, silent, and Lindsay chewed on her bottom lip. Had she turned him off? To this point, he seemed to have appreciated her frankness, but if she'd gone too far, he certainly wouldn't be the first man to tuck tail and run. Defensively, she said, "I know I have no right to ask that of you, and I completely understand if you want to back out of... whatever you want to call this thing we've started."

"I don't want to back out," he said firmly. "To be honest, spending some time with you might make me remember that not every woman is like Mel. If I haven't said it yet, I truly do appreciate your candidness and your independent spirit."

"You're one of the few who do, then."

"Now I'm certain you've been dating the wrong men." He paused, and in the bright moonlight, his grin was plainly visible. "So, how about that date?"

"What do you have in mind?"

"Showing you a good time in Montana. I know Vince

and Evie have a swim party at the Ramshorn planned for tomorrow, but I thought I'd start you off with a trip to Virginia City on Monday. It's about an hour and a half from here, and I think you'll enjoy the Virginia City players. Live theater with an air of vaudeville. It's always a good time, especially the variety show they put on after the play."

"Sounds like a lot of fun."

"Then dinner with my folks. Sorry, I can't get out of that, but I'd like you to join me."

"Meeting your folks already?"

"Well, you did say you wanted to feel like someone's woman, and I'm pretty sure that involves meeting the parents."

Laughing softly, she nodded, unable to argue with that logic.

"And since you're a self-professed tomboy, I bet you'd enjoy a horseback ride across the ranch, some crystal digging, and an exploration of our local ghost towns."

"Is that all?" she inquired, trying uselessly to keep her face from breaking into a broad grin.

"Nope. If you're up for it, I'd like to take you on a ride on my Harley later in the week because that's the best way to experience the scenic highways in these parts."

"You have a motorcycle?"

He nodded. "Are you up for all that?"

"I am. Sounds like a blast." Not giving herself the chance to chicken out, she asked, "And sex? Is that part of the deal? That's really all I had in mind to begin with."

"I got that impression, but let's save it for your last night in Montana."

"Why wait? We have the house to ourselves.

Everyone else is still partying it up at the reception and likely to continue for a while yet."

"You deserve more than a meaningless fling."

Lindsay's eyes rounded, and she stared at him for several thuds of her heart. Not one of the men she'd been with since Max—*including* Max—had ever left her with that sentiment, and to hear it from a man she'd known barely more than twenty-four hours did something strange to her insides. They quivered with hope even as doubt threatened. She cleared her throat to dislodge the lump that had formed and hoped Henry took it as a sign of playfulness rather than the moment of vulnerability that it was. "Isn't that what we're proposing?"

"No. I mean, yes, we should keep it in the here and now and not expect anything lasting to come of this, but that doesn't mean it has to be cold and impersonal."

"I highly doubt it would be either."

Henry's lips curved. He leaned toward her, and she met him halfway. When their lips met, she purred. After the hours of flirting and dancing, she was glad to finally kiss him. He was willing and eager but also considerate and restrained. She pressed her body against his and curled her arms around his neck as he took her face in his hands and deepened the kiss. Waves of sensation flooded her, and she gleefully gave in to it.

"Well, it definitely won't be cold," he murmured.

"Are you sure you don't want to come in?"

"I am, but if you keep kissing me like that, I might just change my mind."

"Would you regret it if you did?"

He leaned back in her arms. "Not in the way I think

you mean, but I am serious about making it mean something—for both of us. I don't want to hurt you."

"You can't possibly hurt me worse than Max did."

"Maybe not, but that doesn't mean I *couldn't* hurt you." He wrapped his arms around her and sighed. "I'm still in a place that I want to hurt Melanie for breaking my heart, but I can't. How did you feel when Max told you he'd not only found someone new but that he was going to marry her?"

"I wanted to hurt him like he'd hurt me," she admitted. "But I couldn't… because he didn't love me like I loved him."

"So you turned that anger and pain on someone else."

She shook her head. "No, but I wanted to."

"Exactly. You needed an outlet. I don't want to use you and cast you aside, and tonight, I'm afraid I would." Gently, he kissed her again, then lowered his lips to her neck. She shivered and sighed. "Believe me, I would love nothing more than to take you inside or—better yet—back to my house and spend all night exploring every exquisite inch of your body."

"But it's not a good idea tonight," she said, seeking confirmation.

"No, it's not."

"What do you expect will change between now and Saturday?"

"If you keep making me forget her like you have been all day… everything."

He walked her to the door, kissed her once more after she opened it, then vanished into the night. Lindsay closed the door and leaned against it with her head tipped back. Raw desire quivered through her, but even as she wished she had tried harder to convince him to stay, she knew he was right. As she climbed the stairs and slipped out of her bridesmaid dress, she thought about what he'd said. His frame of mind and current inclination to inflict pain on someone in retaliation for the pain he was suffering should concern her, but the fact that he was aware of it and taking steps to avoid it had the opposite effect. It was nice to know, for once, that a man cared enough about her to try to protect her from himself. And in that, her time with Henry was already a success.

Four

LINDSAY STEPPED OUT of Henry's truck as soon as he shut it down in the parking area on the western edge of Virginia City. A small creek bordered by dense foliage blocked most of her view of the well-preserved gold rush town, and she was anxious to get busy exploring. They had only an hour and a half until the show started, which wasn't nearly enough time to see everything, but she wasn't willing to forgo the play to indulge her curiosity about the town. Vince and Henry had both spent a good portion of the ride from Northstar lauding the good time to be had watching the Illustrious Virginia City Players.

Lindsay leaned against the tailgate of the truck and waited as Henry opened the stubborn back doors to let Evie and Vince out of the back seat.

"Are you sure you don't mind us tagging along?"

Evie asked Henry as she climbed out and stretched.

"Positive," he replied. "Lindsay's here first and foremost to spend time with *you*. At any rate, it's a little late to change my mind now that we're already here."

After Henry closed all the doors and locked his truck, he strode around to Lindsay and hooked her index finger with his. She glanced up at him and was greeted by a gentle, reassuring smile, so shyly, she twined the rest of her fingers with his, loosely joining their hands. She expected him to drop her hand when Vince and Evie joined them, but he didn't. Evie glanced at them, and though her lips twitched upward, she withheld comment for the time being. Henry started toward town, and the newlyweds fell into step behind them.

"Since we girls haven't been here before, where do you gentlemen suggest we start?" Lindsay inquired as they cleared the trees and the town sprang into view.

"We'll start on the south side and save Cousin's Candy Shoppe for last because we're sure to make purchases there, and I don't know about you, but I don't feel like packing sacks of candy around for the next hour and a half," Henry replied. "It's sort of a family tradition to get a few sweets for the play, and I thought you might like to bring a few treats home to Noah. They have everything from old-fashioned rock candy to giant jawbreakers to salt-water taffy."

She glanced up at him, surprised he had thought of her son, and started to thank him but refrained as they stepped up onto the boardwalk and her attention was diverted. They passed several old buildings with locked doors, but when she peered in the windows, she saw that they had been maintained with all the supplies and tools and miscellany that had filled them during the height of the placer gold rush that had brought droves of hopeful miners to Alder Gulch in the mid 1860s. Other buildings were still in operation and housed touristy-type shops with everything from era-style clothing to figurines carved from various rocks and crystals to Montana-themed mementos.

As they explored the town together, Henry kept hold of Lindsay's hand. Vince and Evie made several purchases, but Lindsay's wallet remained in her slender purse. While the newlyweds nosed around the Vigilante Mercantile, Henry pulled Lindsay outside.

"Are you having fun?" he asked, snatching her other hand and pulling her against him.

"I am."

Maybe this wasn't real and maybe she shouldn't be so comfortable in the embrace of a man she'd known only a few days, but it felt good to be held with such casual, easy intimacy, and Henry was already an old friend. That felt good, too.

They'd spent most of yesterday together thanks to Evie's insistence that he and his twin brother join their party at the Ramshorn Hot Springs, and they'd talked and laughed and flirted shamelessly. Lindsay's impulsive decision to be completely open from the get-go had set the stage for their friendship, and that in turn was well-needed therapy for her weary heart. She felt alive and sexy and clever, all thanks to Henry's unwavering attentiveness. He made a fantastic pseudo-boyfriend, all the more because he seemed to be enjoying their charade as much as she was.

With a smug smile threatening, she examined an

exquisite lantern with a base carved from a weathered fence post. Her mother would love it, but a glance at the price tag drove the idea of purchasing it from her mind.

"Not much of a shopper?" Henry inquired. "I would have thought you'd want some souvenirs of your trip."

"I can't really afford to splurge right now," she replied. "Noah needs school clothes and supplies. This trip has already stretched my budget pretty thin as it is."

"I may have to remedy that."

"Henry, that's not part of the deal. I'm already imposing on you."

"No, you aren't. Come on. I have an idea."

Henry briefly let go of her to step into the mercantile to let Vince and Evie know he and Lindsay were taking a detour. Lindsay waited outside in the bright sunshine and let her gaze wander. Cars rolled slowly over the pavement while people milled along the boardwalks and ducked in and out of the many shops that lined both sides of the bustling street. She pulled her little point-and-shoot camera out of her purse and took a few pictures for keepsakes, wondering what amazingly beautiful shots Skye would have found had she decided to come along. A light smile played across her lips as she waited, and she was too absorbed watching people to notice the two men approaching her.

"Hello, sweet thing."

The voice jerked her attention back to her immediate surroundings, and she took a step back toward the mercantile. There was nothing overly threatening about either of the men, but she didn't like how close they were—neither stood more than five feet away—nor did she like the way they blatantly looked her over. Irritated and uneasy, she folded her arms across her chest and was suddenly glad she had decided to wear jeans and a modest lace-trimmed tank top instead of her lavender dress.

The taller, dark-haired man extended his hand, and she ignored it as she studied them both. If she had to guess, she'd say they were tourists rather than locals. Both wore cargo shorts, muscle shirts, and the kind of rugged sandals one might find at Cabela's.

"My name's Braden Hennessy," the dark-haired man said. "My friend here is Todd Gilman."

"Lindsay."

"Well, Lindsay, what's a pretty thing like you doing here all alone?" Braden asked.

"I'm not alone," she responded. "My friends are inside shopping."

"Sure they are."

"I'm not kidding. I just stepped outside to take some pictures."

"Easy there, sweetheart. I'm not trying to scare you. I just want to know if you'd care to join us for lunch."

"Thanks for the invitation, but I'm not interested. Like I said—"

"Yeah, we heard you the first time," Todd retorted. "Your friends are inside."

"I'm not interested, gentlemen," she said more slowly to make sure they heard her. "But really, thank you for the offer. I'm flattered."

"Are you sure I can't change your mind?" Braden asked.

"I'm sure."

"What if I say please?"

"My answer is still no. I'm sorry." What did she have to do to get her point across? The men who hit on her at work were rarely so persistent, and her patience evaporated. Did he honestly believe that making her nervous with his relentlessness was going to win her over?

"Come on, pretty girl. It's just lunch."

"No. You can keep asking me until the sun goes down, and my answer won't change, so why don't you save yourself the breath and walk away right now." She started to turn away and head back into the store, but Braden grabbed her hand. She whirled on him and jerked her hand free. "Don't... touch me again."

"Easy there, sweet thing. I just—"

"Hey, babe," Henry interrupted.

Relief surged through Lindsay at the sound of his voice. He stepped out of the mercantile and immediately slipped an arm around her waist before kissing her cheek. Then he straightened and addressed Braden and Todd. "Is there something I can do for you gentlemen?"

"No," Todd replied arrogantly.

"Good. Because if you touch her again, we're going to have a problem." Henry's smile was icy and left no doubt about his intentions.

"You her boyfriend?" Braden inquired, his face darkening.

"I would have thought that was obvious, but regardless, she made it very clear she wanted you to leave her alone. Or are you the kind of asshole who can't take no for an answer?"

For a terrifying moment, Lindsay feared it would come to blows, and she stood rigid, clinging to Henry's arm as if that could stop him from acting on the anger that burned in his rich blue eyes. Braden had him by a good twenty pounds, but she suspected he was all bravado that would fizzle against a smarter, more levelheaded opponent... and that's exactly what Henry's outwardly relaxed posture and furious but calculating gaze told Lindsay he was. The last thing she wanted was for him to get in trouble for protecting her when it wasn't his place.

At last, Braden held his hands up and muttered, "Whatever, man."

After the two men walked away, Henry turned to Lindsay without letting go of her. "Are you all right?"

She nodded.

"Are you sure?" He took her face in his hands, leaning back a little to inspect her, and brushed his thumbs across her cheeks. "Because you're shaking."

"I'm okay. Honestly, I was afraid for a minute there that you'd end up in a fistfight because of me." She inhaled deeply and let it out before adding, "I'm not used to having someone defend me, which is having the odd effect of making me feel a little fragile. And the way you're looking at me right now isn't helping."

"Sorry."

"Don't be. It's... nice."

"I take it that isn't the first time you've had to dissuade jackasses like those two."

"I deal with crap like that at work a lot."

"Where do you work?"

"Donovan's Bar and Grill. It gets a little rowdy on occasion, but the tips are better there than at other restaurants, so I've learned to deal with it."

"So I noticed." He touched his lips lightly to hers before taking one hand and leading her across the street. "Now that we've narrowly avoided making a scene in the middle of the boardwalk, let's see about getting you some souvenirs."

"Henry, I—"

"I know what you told me, but humor me. Let's go take some old-fashioned photographs. They're cheap, and I'll pay."

He pulled her over to a shop decorated with sepia-toned photographs of people dressed in period costumes. It took a moment before she realized what Henry meant, but before she could object, he yanked his wallet out of his back pocket and paid for a session for them, then directed her to the woman who ran the studio.

"I think I have the perfect thing for you two," she said and pointed Lindsay into the women's changing area, then pulled out a beautiful sapphire blue saloon girl's gown with detailed black beading. To that, she added a black feather boa and a gem-encrusted hair comb with a long black feather.

Lindsay quickly changed into the costume and stepped out of the changing area to find Henry dressed like a rugged outlaw. Somehow, it was perfect. The photographer had Henry sit on the stool with Lindsay draped around him, then told him to put his arm around her waist.

"The outlaw and his lady," the photographer said. "Perfect. Now, we'll do a serious shot because that's how they were posed, but for the two of you, I'd like one of you smiling."

By the time their session was over, Evie and Vince

76

had ventured over from the mercantile. After Lindsay and Henry changed, Henry made arrangements to pick up their photos after the play, and they all headed back across the street to Cousin's Candy Shoppe. As soon as she stepped through the door, Lindsay's olfactory senses were drenched in the sugary fragrances of the wide array of old-fashioned candy.

"What's going on with you and Henry?" Evie asked not two seconds after Vince and Henry had stepped out of hearing in search of their favorite candies.

"A mutual ego boost," Lindsay replied. She selected a couple sticks of flavored rock candy and settled them gently in her brown paper sack.

"What, exactly, does that mean?"

"He's helping me remember that not all men are assholes like Max and Logan, and I'm helping him remember that not all women are deceptive, self-serving whores like Melanie. That's all."

"*That* sounds like a lot to me."

"Well, it's not, and it's a temporary arrangement, so don't get your hopes up."

"I can't make any promises, Linds, because I have eyes."

"That's all part of the deal," Lindsay said. That wasn't entirely true because she and Henry hadn't discussed the exact details. "This is what you wanted, isn't it? For me to go on a date with one of your sexy, single Northstar men? To put my wants and needs first for once?"

"Well, yes, but more importantly, I wanted you to enjoy yourself and be happy."

"I am, Evie. Henry is definitely upholding his end of

the bargain."

As soon as she said it, she wished she hadn't because Evie's face split in a wide grin.

"Didn't I *just* tell you not to get your hopes up?"

"Yes, and I won't... yet."

Rolling her eyes, Lindsay returned her attention to selecting some candies for Noah. He was definitely going to be kicking himself for a good long while for not coming with her. As she browsed and made her way over to where Henry was picking through the crates of saltwater taffies, she recalled his suggestion that she bring home some sweets for her son and was again surprised that he had considered Noah. Then again, he'd been a father for a while, so he was undoubtedly familiar with the urge to indulge one's child. She wasn't in the position to be certain, but she doubted the habits and instincts of parenthood ever went away once established.

She slid her hand around his arm and, since he'd apparently given her permission to act like his girlfriend the moment he'd told Braden and Todd she was, she rested her head on his shoulder.

"Thank you," she murmured.

"You're welcome. Are you having a good time?" he asked. "Other than those two dickheads outside the Vigilante Mercantile."

"I'm having a wonderful time, and even they couldn't ruin it."

Having located everything they wanted, they headed up to the counter to pay. Deftly, Henry snatched Lindsay's sack out of her hand.

"Henry!" she piped.

"That's liable to get you in trouble," Vince remarked. "Lindsay's a proud one."

"So am I," Henry remarked.

"Henry, you can't pay for everything."

Too quietly for Vince and Evie to hear, he said, "That's one of my conditions. You said you wanted to feel like someone's woman again, and since—for the time being—you're mine, let me treat you like it."

"I don't need to be taken care of."

"I'm well aware of that, and I'm not offering to take care of you."

Lindsay squared her shoulders and clenched her jaw. "I won't be like Melanie, letting you pay for everything."

"No, you won't because Melanie *expected* me to pay." He straightened. "Now, if that's settled, here you go."

Scowling, Lindsay took her sack back from him. She held on to her irritation all the way to the café where they scarfed a quick lunch of burgers before heading over to the Opera House. Her excitement grew, and she found it difficult to maintain her annoyance, but she tried because she had no intention of allowing Henry to pay for her ticket and couldn't think of any other way to convince him of that. A few paces from the ticket booth, Henry snatched her hand and yanked her toward him.

With his lip sticking out in a mock pout, he said, "Please don't be mad at me, Lindsay."

"I'm not mad at you, but I work damned hard to make sure I can take care of myself and my son because I refuse to have to rely on anyone ever again."

His pout disappeared, and the same anger she's seen in his gaze less than half an hour ago returned. "If I ever meet Max, it will take every shred of willpower I possess to resist knocking him right on his ass." Without giving her a chance to respond, he turned to the booth and greeted the woman behind the glass. "Hey, Joanie."

"Henry Hammond, how the heck are you?" the woman replied.

"Good. Yourself?"

"Can't complain. Here are your tickets." Joanie slid four tickets under the window. "Enjoy the show."

"You know I will."

Lindsay's scowl returned. "So much for paying for my own ticket."

"Sorry. I paid over the phone when I called this morning to reserve our seats."

"Don't even bother apologizing," Lindsay muttered, "because that Cheshire cat grin says pretty clearly that you're not remotely sorry."

Henry laughed, took her hand, and kissed her palm. Tingles shivered across her skin, and she smiled, unable to maintain her irritation.

The play itself—the Sherlock Holmes mystery *The Sign of the Four*—was marvelous fun, but it was the variety show afterwards that was the best. The actors sang and danced and cracked jokes and brought the show out into the audience. During one song about a lonely sailor wishing for a wife for Christmas, the man singing sat on the arm of Lindsay's chair.

"What's your name?" he asked.

"Lindsay."

"Well, Lindsay, I must say... you are very fetching."

"Thank you," she replied, blushing.

"Hey, Ma!" the actor called to the stage. "I know what I want for Christmas."

"I agree she's lovely," Ma replied, joining him. She made a show of inspecting Lindsay and Henry. "But something tells me she's already taken. Best keep lookin', Sonny."

After that, the male actor found another target a few rows back and asked, "How 'bout this one?"

Lindsay turned her gaze on Henry. He was grinning like he'd just pulled some great joke. "You knew they were going to do that. And that's why you let me sit on the aisle."

"I couldn't have guaranteed it, but it has been known to happen during the variety show." His pout returned. "Am I in trouble again?"

Smiling, Lindsay kissed him lightly. "No, that was actually pretty cute."

* * *

After Henry dropped Vince and Evie off at their house with a promise he'd bring Lindsay home after dinner, he drove down to his parents' house. They were early, so his father and brothers were still out working somewhere on the ranch. He suppressed the twinge of guilt for spending the day with Lindsay in Virginia City instead of helping out, but he'd only just come home, and there'd be plenty of time later to start pulling his weight around the ranch. Besides, he didn't know how long he'd be here.

As soon as that thought entered his mind, he dismissed it. He'd be here for a while this time. Certainly long enough to get back into the habits of ranch work.

They headed into the house and found his mother in the kitchen prepping for dinner. She greeted them with a wide smile, then embraced Lindsay.

"I'm so glad you decided to come," she said. "Henry wasn't sure you'd want to."

"I didn't want to impose, Mrs. Hammond, but he assured me I wouldn't, so how could I say no? Especially since he's been bragging about your smoky pulled pork and coleslaw all day. If it's not too much trouble, I'd love to see how you make it."

"It's no trouble at all, and please, call me Tracie. Henry, why don't you take my four-wheeler out to the upper pasture and tell your father and brothers to get down here."

"Sure, Mom. I take it Beth has Will and Jessie."

"She does. They should be down in about half an hour."

"Good. I haven't gotten to spoil either of them enough yet." He glanced between his mother and Lindsay and wondered what his mother had up her sleeve. Unable to come up with another excuse to linger and find out, he quietly asked Lindsay if she would be all right alone with his mother. It was a stupid question because of course she would be, but their encounter with those two assholes in Virginia City hovered at the edges of his mind, and the instinctive need to protect her lingered. He didn't like recalling the fear-fringed annoyance on her face or the way her body had trembled afterward.

"I'm sure I'll be perfectly fine," she said brightly. "Besides, I enjoy cooking, so it'll be fun."

He gave her a quick peck on the cheek, bid the women farewell for a few minutes, and stepped back outside. His mother's four-wheeler was waiting for him, so he swung his leg over the seat, started it, and headed to the upper pasture. He found his siblings and father sitting on the top rail of the jackleg fence, each with a beer in his hand. The corner of Henry's mouth lifted, and he admitted that he'd missed this particular end-of-day tradition.

"Grab a beer out of the cooler on the back of my four-wheeler," his father said, "and come join us for a minute."

Henry popped the cap off with the blade of his Leatherman, then perched on the fence on the other side of Aaron. Together, they sipped their beers and surveyed their sprawling ranch. The pastures nestled up against the thickly forested foothills of the Northstar Mountains were dotted with black and red Angus, and the waist-high hay and native grasses waved mesmerizingly in the soft afternoon breeze.

This is where I belong, Henry thought as he let his eyes roam.

"So, Dad... do you need an extra hand for a while?" he heard himself ask. "Because I could use something to do."

"You know I can always use a good extra hand." His father glanced sideways at him, then turned his gaze out across the upper pasture. "I'm glad to have you home, Henry, even though I'm sorry about the circumstances."

Frowning, Henry studied his father. Somehow, John Hammond knew what had brought his wayward son home. He turned an accusing glare on his brothers. "All right, which one of you jackasses talked?"

"Sorry, Henry," Nick said. "But Mom and Dad deserved to hear it from family."

"And I didn't deserve to tell it when I was ready?" he

snapped.

"Well, you have a habit of waiting too long. Come on, Hen. You didn't even tell anyone you requested a paternity test. Or do you not trust us enough to be there for you?"

"I don't know, Nick. Did you trust us to be there for you and Beth twelve years ago when Trey raped her and you were arrested for—"

"That's not the same thing, and you damned well know it. I did what I thought best to protect her from more pain."

Nick's eyes hardened and the muscle in his jaw twitched. There weren't many things that could set his irritatingly steadfast older brother off, but bringing up Trey Holt and the hell he'd put Nick and Beth through their senior year of college was guaranteed to do it, and Henry was well aware of that. He was pissed at Nick, sure, but he respected his brother and was more than a little disgusted with himself for taking such a low shot in retaliation.

"I kept my mouth shut, didn't I?" he muttered. "I was going to tell Mom and Dad at dinner. As to why I didn't tell anyone about the paternity test.... I hoped I was wrong, and there wasn't much point worrying anyone until I knew."

With anger and despair again swirling through him, he swallowed the rest of his beer, jumped down off the fence, and headed back to the four-wheeler. "Mom wants you all to head down to the house to get cleaned up for dinner."

"Henry!" his father called after him.

He ignored the summons and sped off. *Goddammit.*

No less angry when he arrived back at the house, he

skidded to a stop at the front door and yanked the key out of the ignition before he headed inside. When he slammed the door behind him, his mother and Lindsay jerked their heads up from whatever they were huddled over. Curious, he craned his neck and saw a notebook on the counter in front of Lindsay.

"What?" she asked when she noticed his perusal.

"Notes?"

"Yeah," she said shyly. "Your mom doesn't have a recipe for this."

"I guess you weren't kidding when you said you like to cook."

"No, I wasn't."

"Yet… you're a waitress instead of a chef."

"Tips," she said simply.

There was a sharpness to her voice that made him wonder what she wasn't saying. With his mother watching him with a curious expression, he didn't dare ask for clarification.

"What?" he asked Tracie.

"You came stomping through that door all fired up about something," his mother said. "Yet you seem to have been at least momentarily distracted from whatever it was."

He wished he hadn't asked because he *had* been distracted, and now his anger returned full force. Scowling, he said, "I assume you know, too."

"Know what, dear?" Tracie inquired. Her too-nonchalant tone was evidence enough that she knew exactly what he referenced.

"You know about Dylan."

She sighed and offered him a hug and a sympathetic

smile. "Yes, honey, I know about Dylan. Nick told us this morning, but to be honest, it wasn't much of a surprise. I assume you're angry that he told us."

"Yeah, I am. It wasn't his to tell, goddammit."

"It makes it easier, though, doesn't it?" Lindsay asked gently. "The secret is out, so you don't have to worry yourself sick over how to tell your parents anymore. I imagine your brother was simply trying to make it easier on everyone by being the bearer of bad news."

Stubbornly, Henry tried to hold on to his anger, but it withered, leaving him deflated and hollow. He wandered a few steps to the dining room table and sank onto the nearest chair. In truth, he'd been prepping himself all day to break the devastating news to his parents—since he'd found out, really—and now that he didn't have to, he wasn't sure what to do next. Lindsay was right, however. It *was* a relief to have his secret out in the open. When she pulled out the chair beside him and sat facing him, he met her concerned gaze.

She had such beautiful blue eyes, he thought, so full of compassion and kindness. It was unusual to be so soothed by her presence when Melanie's attempts to defuse his anger only ever added more fuel to the fire. What was it about Lindsay that had the power to make him take a deep breath and refocus?

"I'm probably overstepping my bounds," she murmured, "but I think you need to let your family help you through this. They all love you. Your mom told me you've always liked to work things out yourself, but this may be one of those times that you can't do it on your own."

Henry had the overwhelming urge to wrap his arms

around her and hug her until the rest of his bitterness settled into a manageable ache again, but he resisted.

"You're right," he said. "I don't know if I can do that, but you're right that I need to. How is it that you know me so well?"

"I've been where you are," she replied. "Maybe not *quite* the same situation, but I know what it's like to be used and betrayed and how it makes you feel like you're somehow flawed. And I thought I could handle it myself, but I was wrong. I needed my family and friends to remind me that I wasn't the defective one."

"You're most definitely *not* defective," Henry whispered and leaned forward to kiss her cheek. "*I* may be, but you're not."

"You aren't, either." She stood but didn't immediately return to the kitchen. With a mischievous gleam in her eyes, she said, "Now, if you're about done with your pity party, may I get back to helping with dinner?"

She didn't wait for his response and instead turned away with little more than a sassy wink. Despite himself, he chuckled, once again finding himself glad he'd accepted her proposition at the Bedspread. The composure she helped him find remained firmly in place even when his father and brothers came in and immediately started in on him about Dylan and Melanie. It probably helped that Nick began with an apology.

"I should have let you tell it in your own time."

"I appreciate that, and I'm sorry, too, for the cheap shot. Lindsay's right that you made it easier on me, and I'm glad it's out in the open. And it sounds like I was more surprised by the results of the test than any of you."

"I don't know that you were surprised, either," Aaron said. "But you were hopeful, and believe me, we all understand why."

"I suppose I should have listened to you all. You never cared much for Mel, and I didn't want to open my eyes to see why."

His father studied him with narrowed eyes. "I think that may be the fastest you've ever gotten over being mad at your brothers."

"Curious, isn't it?" Tracie asked from the kitchen.

"Very."

"I would think you'd be pleased by that," Henry muttered.

"We are," John replied.

After that, the conversation turned toward happier things, and Henry detailed his day with Lindsay, Vince, and Evie in Virginia City for them. Beth arrived with Will and Jessie just as Tracie and Lindsay were finishing dinner. During the meal, which was as delicious as usual, they all discussed in detail what other plans Henry and Lindsay had for her stay in Northstar.

Throughout the conversation, Henry noted his family exchanging furtive glances and once or twice caught a sly quirk of lips or the wiggling of eyebrows. *Oh, goody.*

When everyone had finished eating, Henry volunteered to help his mother wash the dishes while Nick, Aaron, and their father and Beth, Will, and Jessie entertained Lindsay with tales about ranch life and all there was to see and do in the outdoorsman's paradise that was Northstar. Both youngsters were instantly charmed by Lindsay and clamored for her attention, which she gave freely while talking with the adults. Henry listened passively, both amused and excited to learn that she quite enjoyed the great outdoors even if she didn't get much opportunity to indulge herself. She mentioned playing on the wide sandy beach near her parents' Indianola, Washington, house with her son.

"Indianola?" Henry asked. "That's where Bill Granger lives—he's Aelissm's uncle. Do you know him?"

"Of course I know the Grangers! My parents' house is right across the street from theirs, and they let us use their stairs down to the beach whenever we want. They're great people."

"Yes, they are."

"She's a very nice girl," Tracie remarked quietly to Henry after the others had returned to their conversation. "I quite like her."

Henry eyed his mother as he handed her a plate to dry. "She's refreshingly different from Mel, that's for sure."

"Indeed she is, and from where I'm standing, that's a very good thing, which means I have to ask if you know what you're doing. You two seem to be getting pretty friendly for knowing each other only a few days."

"Mom, please don't go reading between the lines. That's all just part of the deal."

"I know what you and she *say* it is. She told me about your *arrangement*."

"She did?"

"Mmm-hmm. She was rather candid about it, so I'm going to tell you right now that you'd best keep treating her like the gentleman your father and I raised you to be."

Her tone left no room for misunderstanding; she'd

make him pay if he did anything to hurt Lindsay. He shifted his weight and took a moment to organize his response. He hadn't had a conversation like this with either of his parents since high school, and it was at once unsettling and comforting. That his mother was looking out for Lindsay like she never had for Melanie further intensified the peculiar sensation.

"That's why I'm taking my time to get to know her before we jump into bed together—and, for the record, *she* propositioned *me*." He paused and met Tracie's gaze head on for a moment before looking away. "Mel screwed me up pretty badly this time, and I don't want to take any of that out on Lindsay."

"Then why didn't you just tell her no?" his mother asked.

He couldn't immediately answer that question. Why *hadn't* he just said no to Lindsay? He'd wanted to. "She intrigues me," he said at last.

"Then tread very carefully, Henry. Not just for her sake, but for yours, too, because I think you may have found your match, and I don't want to see either of you get hurt if you can't tell the difference between a harmless, casual affair and a deeper attachment."

With that, Tracie turned away to finish drying the dishes and, in her not-so-subtle way of getting him to think about what she'd said, refused to be drawn back into the same line of conversation. Henry gave up and wiped down the stove and counters before joining everyone back at the table for a dessert of homemade apple pie and vanilla ice cream. Lindsay was naturally the center of attention and didn't seem to mind. In fact, she chatted with his family as if she'd known them for years instead of hours. The way she doted on Will and Jessie confirmed Henry's belief that she was a great mom, and his chest tightened a little at the thought, so he hastily shoved it aside before it could take root.

It was almost midnight when he drove her back to Vince and Evie's. He walked her to the door, but before he let her go inside, he took her hand and kissed her knuckles.

"I hope you enjoyed yourself today," he said.

"I had an amazing time, Henry. Thank you."

"I know this is only a temporary, fill-a-void-for-each-other deal, but I think... when you go back to Washington, I'd like to stay friends and keep in touch."

She tilted her head back to study him in the bright moonlight. "I'd like that, but I'm a little surprised at the offer."

"So am I, but you have this strange effect on me. You can make me stop and think when all I want to do is stay angry, and that is a rare quality and an even rarer bond."

"Your mom *did* warn me that you have a bit of a slow-burning, handle-it-yourself temper that takes a while to burn out."

"Of course she did," he muttered.

"Mmm-hmm, right before she said that she was amazed at how willingly and easily you listened to me and how quickly you let go of your irritation with Nick."

"Why can't my family just mind their own business?"

"Because they love you and they want you to be happy."

"And did she happen to say she thought you would make me happy?"

"No, but I think she likes me. We had a good time cooking together. Did she say something to you about it?"

"Oh, she definitely likes you, and she gave me a crystal clear impression that she would castrate me if I did anything to hurt you."

"I think I really like your mom."

"She's a wonderful woman." He cocked his head. "She thinks I've found my match."

"Henry… neither of us is looking for a relationship, remember?"

The way she said it made him think she wasn't exactly opposed to the idea, either. But he, at least, was not yet in a place to entertain the idea of getting involved in a serious relationship again.

"I'm well aware of that," he said. "But in some ways, she may be right… because I *did* listen to you. That's something of a miracle, as I'm sure you gathered. It's easy to talk to you. I was *never* able to talk to Melanie like we are now."

"If I was ever able to talk like this with Max, it's been so long that I've forgotten," Lindsay said by way of agreement. "So, yes, I'm open to staying in touch after I go back to Washington. I think we could both use another good friend. Perhaps with a few extra benefits by week's end if you're still game for that."

He slipped his fingers along her jaw and angled his body toward hers as he caressed her cheeks with his thumbs. Before he lowered his mouth to hers, he whispered, "I definitely will be."

Five

SHOWING LINDSAY A GOOD TIME in Montana had the unintended side effect of reminding Henry how much about his home he took for granted. Until he'd taken her to Crystal Park on Tuesday, he'd forgotten how much fun it was to play in the dirt and how addicting the hunt for those clear rocks was. Also, prior to their excursion to Bannack State Park on Wednesday, it had been years since he'd last visited Montana's first territorial capital, and he couldn't remember the last time he'd ridden a horse across his family's ranch purely for the pleasure of it. Yesterday's ride with Lindsay, along with the endless laughter that accompanied her total inexperience with horses and her wide-eyed awe, had driven home just how much there was to love about his family's way of life and how lucky he was to live it.

As he headed out to his small garage a quarter after

seven on Friday morning, he tried not to think about today being Lindsay's last full day in Northstar. Tomorrow was Luke's football game, and after, she'd be checking into a hotel in Butte because Vince and Evie would be staying in Butte tomorrow night, having the early flight out the following morning. Despite his vow to avoid it, he wondered how she'd spend the hours until her late afternoon flight and wished he could come up with a decent excuse to spend them with her.

It was a pure and simple truth that this week had been an incredible adventure brightened by her vibrant smile, her frank honesty, and her quick wit, and he was going to miss her more than he was willing to admit out loud.

Again, he had to remind himself that this wasn't real.

That's not true. The relationship isn't real, but everything else is. Thanks to her initial openness, he was able to trust that she and their friendship were absolutely genuine even after Mel's wrenching deception. *That* was something else he needed to thank Lindsay for. The desire to inflict pain on someone else as an outlet for his own had faded into nothing. It'd be a long time yet before he was able to forgive Melanie and longer still before he stopped wishing the paternity test results had been different, but the anger was gone.

Shaking his head, he grabbed his helmet and the spare he'd bought for Melanie just in case she ever wanted to go riding—she never had—and swung the doors of the garage open. He straddled the bike, shifted it into neutral, and walked it backwards outside. Briefly settling it on its kickstand, he trotted into his house to get his mother's old leather jacket. Lindsay was about the same size as his

94

mother, so it should fit her. He folded it tightly and stuffed it in the saddlebag. The spare helmet he strapped down with a black bungee.

He had told Lindsay he would be at Vince and Evie's to pick her up at eight sharp, but he was a bit early. Still, when he rode up to the newlyweds' home, she was sitting out on the front steps with Evie, sipping a cup of something hot and steaming. She was dressed, as he'd suggested, in jeans and long sleeves, and she smiled when their gazes met. His heart tripped a little.

"Are you ready for this?" he asked after he shut his bike down.

"I surely am." Lindsay drained her drink—French vanilla coffee by the smell of it—bid her friend farewell until later, and joined him in the driveway.

Henry pulled the leather jacket out and handed it to her, then the helmet.

"Melanie's?" Lindsay asked.

"The jacket was Mom's, and the helmet is a spare."

"Mel never rode with you?"

"Nope."

"She doesn't like motorcycles?"

"She likes them well enough. We just never took my old bike out. Then again, I think we only came up here four times when we were together, and two of those trips were over Christmas, which is not a good time to ride Harleys around here."

"I imagine not."

Once Lindsay had pulled on the jacket, which fit perfectly, and secured her helmet, she climbed on the motorcycle behind Henry and waved one last time to Evie. Her cherubic friend returned the gesture with a broad grin.

"Any instructions, boss?" Lindsay asked.

"Hold on to me, try to stay relaxed, and lean with me. Other than that, it's pretty easy, so enjoy the ride."

She tucked her legs in behind his with her feet resting on the back pegs and wrapped her arms loosely around his waist. He started the bike and drove slowly down the Carlyles' driveway to the main road through the valley. After waiting for Ben and June Conner to drive by on their way to the Ramshorn for work, he pulled onto the road, following them north on the Northstar Mountains Scenic Byway. The Conners stuck their hands out their windows and waved as Henry and Lindsay continued around the bend past the Ramshorn's driveway. Lindsay said something, but Henry couldn't hear it over the Harley's engine.

"What was that?" he called back to her.

"I like it here!" she yelled. "Everyone's so friendly!"

"Yeah, they are!"

The road snaked up through dense lodgepole pine and Douglas fir forest with occasional glimpses of the towering peaks of the Northstar Mountains until just after it crested the pass between the Northstar and Crystal Valleys. Then, the landscape opened up into lush alpine meadows still dotted with wildflowers even this late in the summer. To the east, the more rugged northern peaks stood proud against a deep blue sky brushed with long streamers of cirrus clouds. On the other side of the Crystal Valley, the road twisted around two sharp switchbacks on its way down into the Wise River Valley, and Lindsay asked if they could take a detour to see the Coolidge ghost town. He pulled off the scenic byway on the road to the ghost town but turned the bike back toward the main road rather than up to Coolidge.

"It's six miles up a gravel road to the trailhead, and another three-quarters of a mile to the ghost town on foot," he told her. "I don't want to take the bike up there, but how about we plan a trip up there the next time you're in Northstar to visit Evie?"

"I don't know when that'll happen, but I'd love that if you wouldn't mind playing tour guide to me again."

"I would love to. You're great company, and besides, playing tour guide to you is helping me reconnect with my home. I'd forgotten just how much I love this place."

She briefly wrapped her arms higher around him, and he captured her hands and held them against his chest in silent gratitude for her presence. Without his deal with her, he wasn't sure if he would have bothered to take the time to visit all the places and do the things that made Northstar home. Most likely, he would have plunged into work on the ranch and gone on as the rope in the game of tug-of-war between his wanderlust and his soul-deep appreciation of this place.

Always at odds, he mused. *But not when I'm with Lindsay.*

If he let himself think about it for more than a moment, the realization that she somehow satisfied his desire for adventure and simultaneously provided contentment might have terrified him. So he didn't let himself think about it and instead concentrated on keeping his Harley rubber-side down on the winding mountain highway. They spotted several whitetail and mule deer, a large coyote, a moose, and three cow elk by the time the valley widened into the sagebrush flats just north of the tiny town of Wise River. Since they were making better time than he'd planned—he was somewhat surprised Lindsay hadn't asked him to stop—Henry pulled off the highway west of Wise River into one of the many recreation areas along the Big Hole River so they could stretch and walk out any numbness brought on by the vibration from the frame-mounted engine of the bike.

"Enjoying the ride so far?" he asked.

"Absolutely! You're really lucky to call this place home, Henry. The country up here is stunning."

"Yes, it is and, yes, I am."

"What river is this?"

"This is the Big Hole, and it's prime trout fishing."

"That's it. I'm going to have to find a way to come back sooner rather than later. There is just too much here to see and do in the limited time I have."

"You like to fish?"

"You bet I do. My dad used to take me out salmon fishing in the Puget Sound and Hood Canal every summer. And we've been lake and stream fishing a few times, too."

"You really *are* an outdoors kind of girl."

"When Evie wanted to play dress up, Skye and I would try to talk her into building forts in the woods behind my parents' house or running through the tide pools on the Indianola Beach. I was a total tomboy, remember?"

"Yes, I do. I'd ask if your parents wanted a boy and tried to make up for not getting one, but I get the feeling tomboy is just in your make-up."

"It really is," Lindsay said and laughed. "They actually wanted a girl, and for a while, my mother tried to turn me into a proper one... until she realized it wasn't going to happen. Then she embraced her little tomboy and encouraged me to be whatever I wanted to be."

"Your parents sound like great people."

"They are. They've been there for me through everything, even when I didn't want anyone's help."

"A little stubborn?" Henry asked. "Or just proud?"

"Both, and more than a little."

"No wonder you and I get along so well."

"You? Stubborn? Say it isn't so."

"Har har. How 'bout we get back on the bike for the second leg of our ride to Anaconda?"

"Did I touch a nerve?" Lindsay asked. The playful note was still thick in her voice.

"Well, I *do* have my pride you know."

When she tipped her head back and laughed, Henry found himself grinning. God, she was fun to be around. He offered his elbow, and she slipped her hand around it, and they walked back to his bike as several rafts of fishermen drifted by on the lazy current of the river.

"So, how long have you and Skye and Evie been friends?" Henry asked.

"Since elementary school. We were all in the same second grade class. I should've gone to a different school because I lived in Indianola, but my mom taught at Poulsbo Elementary, so that's where I went."

"Your mom's a teacher? What grade."

"Was. She retired last year, but she taught sixth grade, mostly."

"Retired already?"

"I wouldn't say *already*. She taught for forty-two years."

Henry stopped and stared at his companion.

Something didn't add up. "How old are your parents?"

"Sixty-six. They were forty when I was born and had given up hope of ever having children. Needless to say, I was quite the surprise."

Henry chuckled. "I bet so. I'd also bet they were thrilled."

"They were. I am so blessed to have the parents I do, and if I do even half as well with Noah as they did with me, I'll have done a good job."

"I'm sure you'll do every bit as well."

They climbed back on his bike, and he thought she held on just a little tighter for a moment. He almost told her that he hadn't said that just to ease her maternal doubts, that he firmly believed every word, but he sensed doing so would cheapen the compliment, so he started the bike and pulled back onto the highway.

The Mount Haggin road was more open than the Northstar Mountains Scenic Byway but no less gorgeous. The towering peaks of the Anaconda Range, still bearing the ragged remnants of the past winter's snows, rose majestically to the west and north while tall ridges blanketed in pines and firs and groves of quaking aspen flanked the valley on the east and south, and meandering streams kept the narrow valley bottom vividly green beneath the burning August sun. The wind was warm on Henry's exposed skin, but periodically they passed through pockets of cooler air, particularly when they neared one of the streams and as they climbed higher toward Mount Haggin. Pastures and meadows were still flooded with wildflowers, and Henry recalled his family remarking that the winter had been cold, wet, and long. Good. The area had been experiencing drought conditions for much of the past decade, and he hoped the dry spell was coming to an end.

Henry chuckled at himself. *Yeah, coming back was the right move if I'm already thinking like a rancher again.*

In Anaconda, they found a small mom-and-pop sandwich shop and ordered their lunch to go, then headed back toward Northstar to eat their meal picnic-style somewhere along the road. Henry pulled off at a point-of-interest turnout overlooking an old homestead, and they ate at the picnic table just beyond the parking area.

"It's neat how you can feel the differences in air temperature on the back of a motorcycle," Lindsay remarked.

"Yep, you definitely don't get that in a car. Or quite the sense of scale, either."

"Indeed not." She set her sandwich down and leaned forward on her elbows. "So, what's the story behind the bike? I know it has a story."

"Not much of one. I bought it when I graduated from high school from an old guy down in Devyn for cheap. It needed a little love, so I used it as a project in college. Had it ever since."

"College," Lindsay murmured wistfully. "I can't tell you how often I've wondered what I missed by not going right after high school."

"You could still go, you know."

"Maybe, but if I *do*, it won't be the same experience I would've had going straight out of high school. I lost that wide-eyed wonder of new independence a long time ago."

"What does that have to do with anything?"

"My parents used to tell me that the experiences of discovering themselves, making friends, and testing their independence were even more valuable than the degrees they earned. I already know how I am, and maybe I struggle a lot, but I've proven that I can be independent. Do you think they're right?"

Henry thought back over his four years at the university in Devyn, and with one appalling exception, which he didn't feel comfortable divulging without Nick and Beth's permission, he very much agreed with Lindsay's parents. "I'd say yes, definitely. I had a great time, and while I don't know if I discovered who I am at college, I certainly made great friends and learned a lot about being independent... even if I did go to school less than an hour's drive from home."

"Skye and Evie agree, too."

There was a touch—just a hint—of bitterness in her voice, and when she grimaced, he suspected she was both envious of her friends and proud of them.

"Were you supposed to go to school with them?"

She nodded. "But I had a brand-new baby to take care of."

"I'm sorry, Lindsay. I really am."

She glanced sharply at him. "I'm not. Maybe things haven't been all sunshine and roses for me, and maybe I often wish things had happened differently, but I love my son, and I will never regret having him. That beautiful little boy is worth every dream and luxury I've given up and then some."

Henry held his hands up. "I was just trying to say I'm sorry for everything you must have been through and that you had to give up so much for your son."

When her scowl deepened, he swore under his

breath. Obviously, he was not communicating his thoughts very well, and undoubtedly, she'd had to defend herself and her son in similar conversations against people far more judgmental than Henry.

"I'm not sorry you had your son," Henry said gently. "I admire your strength. What I'm trying to say is that I wish you hadn't needed to sacrifice what *you* want. I wish you could've had your son and your dreams."

"Life doesn't work that way for young, single mothers."

Lindsay's tone wasn't any less defensive, so Henry replied, "Unfortunately not. Which is probably why I didn't question Melanie too closely when she told me I was going to be a father." He hoped that he could salvage the conversation by redirecting it back to his mistakes because her circumstances were apparently too tender a subject for Lindsay. "I'm not sure she could do what you have. In fact, I know she can't. She can't even make the payments on the loan I gave her and her friend Tamlyn to open up their own salon. Tam had no problem paying me back, but I have yet to see enough from Mel to cover two full payments."

Lindsay stared at him with blatant disbelief. He offered her a self-mocking smile and nodded.

"Yeah, I was that stupid. I sold almost half my cows to do it, too, and it's taken me the two years since to rebuild my herd, but I don't regret it because Tam has busted her ass to make that salon into something lucrative, and she deserves all the success she's seeing." He reached across the table and took Lindsay's hand, skimming his thumb over her knuckles for a moment before he pressed his lips to them and gazed up at her with one corner of his mouth lifted. "I suppose that's why I appreciate that you got mad at me for paying for your candy and tickets when we went to Virginia City on Monday."

"And for the pictures. Which I love, by the way."

"I might have kept pushing because you're pretty cute when you're indignant."

"Uh-huh," Lindsay said with a quirk of her lips. Then her brows dipped in a frown. "Is she pretty? Mel, I mean. Not Tam."

"They're both beautiful," he replied. "But not in the same way you are. Their looks are deliberate and styled like you might expect from professional beauticians—not natural like yours. And since I get the feeling you don't hear it enough from people other than your parents and friends and assholes like those two in Virginia City who are too stupid to really see *you*...." He took her by the chin and lightly kissed her lips. "You are a very beautiful woman, Lindsay. Inside *and* out."

Her shy smile was confirmation of his suspicion as was the way she focused her attention on smoothing out the wrinkled corner of her sandwich wrapper. After a moment, she met his gaze again, but when she spoke, her voice was quiet.

"I'm sorry, Henry. I didn't mean to get so defensive. Habit."

I'm sorry that it *is* a habit, but I understand. People can be pretty judgmental."

"It's getting better as I get older, but at first, yeah, I heard some pretty nasty things from people I knew... and from complete strangers."

"As if you didn't already have enough to deal with."

"It is what it is." She sighed. "I guess I'm a little edgy right now, too, because as much as I miss my son and can't wait to see him again, I'm not ready to go home. Mostly, I'm not ready to get home, find no check in my mailbox, and have to call Max again."

"Why would you have to call him? Isn't child support handled through the state?"

"Yes, but he wasn't making any money then, so it's barely enough to buy a few days' worth of groceries. I have to call him on occasion to ask for more when things like Peewee football come up."

"Can't you petition for more child support?"

"It's not worth getting embroiled in that kind of battle with him. He turns everything into a fight as it is, but me asking him for a little extra help makes him feel powerful, and so he complies."

"I'm not sure I'd call that complying."

She shrugged again. "It's better than what he'd do if I tried to go after him for more child support. Besides, we're doing all right." She glanced at her sandwich but continued to ignore it. "Honestly, I'd rather struggle on my own without any help at all from him because Noah comes back a total brat every time he goes to see his father. He had just returned from Max's when he decided—at the last minute—that he didn't want to come to Montana with me."

"Do you think Max does that on purpose?"

"I'm sure of it."

"What an asshole."

Lindsay snorted. "There is *one* thing I would change, if I could. I would go back and leave him before Noah was born instead of trying to hold on to him."

"Why didn't you? It doesn't sound like there was much love between you."

"Back then I thought there was. And I was young, stupid, and scared, and I thought we needed him. Now I know all to well that we'd be much better off without him."

"Sounds like it." The bitterness was beginning to creep back into her voice, so Henry abruptly changed the subject. "You gonna finish that sandwich or let the flies have it?"

She regarded him with lifted brows. "Getting tired of listening to my sob story?"

"Not at all, but I brought you out today to have a good time, not to reopen old wounds."

"Fair enough," she remarked and picked up her sandwich again.

He watched her while she ate, perhaps more disturbed by her sudden distance than he should be. He had no claim on her beyond this week, and what claim she allowed him didn't mean it was his place to soothe her or to try to make amends for what her ex continued to do, no matter how much he wanted to. Lindsay was a strong and fiercely independent woman—of that he was absolutely certain—and he wondered if maybe he had gone too far with the doting boyfriend role. Just because she'd said she wanted to feel like someone's woman for a while didn't mean she was actually looking for a man. If that was the case, was it because she enjoyed her independence too much or because she was so used to heartbreak that she had given up on relationships?

Shaking his head, he gathered their trash in the brown paper sack their lunch had come in and stuffed it in his saddlebags as there were no garbage cans. When she climbed on the bike behind him, he said, "If you want me to stop at any time, all you have to do is ask."

"I appreciate that," she replied with a little more of her usual spunk. "But I'm kinda enjoying the excuse to hold on to you. If we stop, I'd have to let go."

"In that case… I could take the long way home and ride down through the Big Hole Valley. It's beautiful, too."

"I'm beginning to believe everything here is."

The way she said it and the way she rested her cheek briefly against the back of his neck for a moment before she sat up to put her helmet on made him wonder if she include *him* in her statement. He reached back to playfully squeeze her leg, and she laughed and again tucked her body against his with her arms snuggly around his waist. Unexpectedly, she returned his caress with one of her own, and shivers trailed from his head to his heels as she raked her teeth over his neck.

"There's my Lindsay," he murmured too quietly for her to hear as he started the bike.

* * *

Lindsay tried for hours to reconcile her conflicting thoughts regarding Henry with limited success. What he made her feel scared her because their arrangement wouldn't last, and she wasn't sure she wanted it to even if he was open to it; every time she had felt remotely like this, it hadn't ended so well.

Her reaction to Henry's innocent expression of sympathy on their ride had baffled her all the way through the Big Hole Valley to the turn off that brought them back to Northstar, at which point she had realized she was attempting to keep herself from getting too attached. She had known full well that his apology was a statement of sympathy and not regret that she'd had her son, but she was so used to being rejected that it had become a habit to shield herself in preparation for it when she could. Since what she and Henry had was make believe, she was guaranteed to get her heart broken again if she forgot that.

She was painfully aware of her precarious situation, but she was also mindful that the part of her that hadn't been destroyed first by Max and later by Logan wanted this thing with Henry to be real. Their easy banter, the playful caresses, the easy intimacy—it all felt so wonderful and right. And now that it was Friday and the football game was tomorrow, she found herself wanting to spend every last second she could with him. So, even though she needed to pack, when he'd invited her, Vince, Evie, and Skye to his house for a fire in his backyard, she hadn't been able to say no. Nor had she been able to say no, once he'd gotten the fire going, to curling up on the chaise lounge with him, which was why she was now enjoying the warmth of the fire with her head resting on his chest and his arms tucked comfortably around her.

"Too bad Aaron had to work tonight, eh, Skye?" Evie asked.

"It *is* too bad," Henry remarked. "I haven't seen him smile like he did last weekend, so, I'm quite interested to see what tomorrow will bring."

"Don't get your hopes up, Henry," Skye said. "I don't know that I'll be much company for a while yet."

"Bullshit," Lindsay said. "You're always good company."

"To you, maybe, but we've been best friends most of our lives, and you'd put up with me no matter what."

"Yes, I would, but not just because we're best friends. Because you're worth it. Darren on the other hand.... Well, he and Max really are two peas in the same rotten pod. So, quit feeling sorry for yourself and enjoy the attention of your sweet, sexy Hammond twin."

"Like you are?" Skye asked with laughter thick in her voice.

"Yep. Just like I am."

"You're starting to sound like someone else I know," Skye remarked, turning her gaze pointedly on Evie. "What have you done to her, Evie?"

"I haven't done anything. That's all Henry."

"Hey, I haven't done anything, either. This was her idea."

"Uh-huh," Lindsay said flatly. "You haven't exactly been an unwilling participant in this little charade, either, mister."

"What can I say?" he asked with a chuckle. "I'm a sucker for beautiful, stubborn, strong women, and you can blame that on my amazing mother."

"She *is* amazing," Lindsay agreed. "I never felt as welcome or wanted by Max's mother as I do by her. And she hardly knows me."

"Take that as a compliment because she never warmed up to Mel, even after Dylan was born."

"Believe me, Henry, I do."

She stopped short of saying she'd felt almost immediately a deeper connection with Tracie Hammond than she'd ever had with Max's mother, who hadn't seen or called

Noah once in the five years since she and her husband had moved to Virginia to help Max's sister during her battle with aggressive breast cancer. She couldn't fault the Ulrichs for that move, but Noah was their family, too, and she knew they'd been back to Washington at least twice to check on their house, which they had decided to rent out rather than sell. And it took little effort to pick up a phone or send a birthday card.

Thank God he doesn't remember them.

"Whatever you're thinking about," Henry whispered close to her ear, "stop."

Her eyes widened. How had he known? Because, the way she sat, he couldn't see her face or the scowl plastered to it.

"You tensed," he murmured before she could ask. "So I'm guessing it had something to do with Max."

"His parents," she confirmed, "who seem to have forgotten they have a grandson. Given the choice, I think they would have preferred to ignore Noah from the get-go."

"I guess that explains where Max gets it. What made you think of them?"

"Comparing them to your mom. Both your parents, really. They're such warm-hearted people, and I'm glad I got to meet them while I was here."

"They're certainly fond of *you*."

The others were talking about Vince and Evie's plans for their Hawaiian honeymoon, so Lindsay and Henry let go of their conversation to focus on happier things. She let the solid warmth of the man holding her soothe away her irritation with people who no longer had any right to hurt her, sighing contentedly when she was able to push those feelings aside with ease. She wasn't ready for this thing with Henry to end, and she wasn't ready to leave him or the incredible peace and beauty of Northstar. He'd definitely upheld his end of their deal—perhaps too well. She curled her hand against his chest, then flexed her fingers and smoothed a wrinkle from the soft fabric of his navy-blue T-shirt.

She turned her gaze skyward and took in the stunning peach-colored sunset that had ignited the sky while she was preoccupied. She didn't often see that sharpness of color back home where the marine air usually softened the tones. She was going to miss that, too, and methodically, she committed every detail from the exact shades of orange and lavender in the sky to the dancing flames in the fire pit to the laughter of her friends to the comforting weight of Henry's arms around her to memory.

"Comfortable?"

Lindsay jerked her attention to Evie, frowning in annoyance. "Yeah, I am."

"Obviously. Vince is heading inside to get drinks, and he asked what you wanted." Evie shifted her gaze to Lindsay's six-foot, not-so-squishy pillow. "Maybe we should've let you ask, Henry. She might've heard *you*."

"How 'bout I make it up to you, Evie, by getting the drinks myself. Lindsay, what can I get you?"

"Do you have any of that Belgian White beer you had me try the other day?"

"You mean the Harvest Moon Beltian White? Sure do. I'll bring you one."

"You're a true gentleman, Henry," Evie remarked. "Isn't he, Linds?"

She only nodded and eyed her friend.

"Well, my mama did try to raise me right."

Lindsay stood so Henry could get up, then sat in the chaise lounge and watched him walk up to the back deck of his house. She kept watching until he disappeared inside.

"Babe, would you mind fetching some more firewood?" Evie asked her husband. "We're getting low."

"Sure thing, sweets."

Not a very subtle orchestration, Evie. Glowering at her companion, Lindsay sighed. "Get whatever you feel you need to say out so I can go back to enjoying my evening."

In true Evie fashion, she didn't miss a beat. "Do you honestly think you can just walk away from him without looking back like none of this happened?"

"Yes, I do because that's what has to happen. That was the deal."

"Why, Linds? I've never seen you as comfortable with anyone as you are with him."

"It's all part of—"

"Part of the deal. So you've said. Repeatedly. But I know what I'm seeing."

"You want to know why it's so easy to be with Henry, Evie? It's temporary. No strings attached, no fear of things going wrong, and no expectations beyond distraction. It's freeing, and Henry is a very considerate companion."

"Then why—"

"Give it a rest, Evie!" Lindsay snapped. "I don't have time for a relationship, and I'm not looking for one, anyhow. And Henry's *definitely* not ready for one. Neither of us needs any more complications."

Evie pointed a finger at her. "I call BS. Everyone has baggage, Linds, but there's something happening here, and

I firmly believe that Henry may be the man to help you unpack."

"I thought that about Logan, too, remember? I thought he wanted to be that man, but he had no plans to be and ended up tossing another suitcase on top of my gargantuan pile of baggage."

"Henry is a far better man than Logan ever dreamed of being. Trust me, Lindsay. I may not know him as well as I've come to know the rest of his family, but they're all good people. Every single one of them."

"Maybe so, but he's as screwed up right now as I am. You don't have kids yet, but when you do, you might understand how badly Melanie hurt him by making him believe Dylan was his son."

"What does that have—"

"Leave her alone, Evie," Skye said quietly.

"But she's—"

"Evie. Let it go."

Skye offered Lindsay a sympathetic smile and a roll of her eyes as their friend snapped her mouth shut and folded her arms tightly across her chest.

"Do you think I'm wrong, Skye?" Lindsay asked.

"I don't know, but Evie may be right about you and Henry. There's too much there to be nothing more than an act. It's been so long since I've seen you this happy or this relaxed—maybe not *right* now—and that has to mean something."

Lindsay growled at the smug gleam that ignited Evie's eyes. They waited silently for Skye to continue.

"I'm not saying you should jump into a serious relationship with him… but don't write him off, either."

Lindsay drew her knees up to her chest and draped her arms around with her chin resting on them. "I have to."

"Why?"

She didn't have an answer for that. A thousand reasons pranced tauntingly through her mind—he was too fresh from his break up with Mel, there was too much distance between her home and his, she wasn't girlfriend material.... On and on the excuses paraded, but they were all weak. Some were absurd. The only one that held any weight was Noah. He had gotten so attached to Logan, and it had hurt him deeply when Logan left them. She vowed to never put him through that again, but even protecting her son didn't seem like a strong enough reason to shut the door on Henry. She wanted his friendship, and instinctively, she believed he would never do to Noah what Logan had done or what his father continued to do. A little voice in the back of her mind reminded her that Henry had up and walked out of Dylan's life.

Dylan's not his son, she argued. *And Mel used him. He was right to leave.*

Noah wasn't his son, either.

Abruptly, Lindsay pushed to her feet just as Vince returned with a wheelbarrow full of firewood. Seeking solitude, she headed around to the front steps of Henry's house and sat with her elbows braced on her thighs and her hands folded loosely in front of her. Tipping her head back, she tried desperately to quell the swarm of conflicting emotions. The sunset had faded into a dim reminder of the vibrant colors, and a single star twinkled in a darkening sky.

It was stupid that she wanted to be with Henry right now since he was at the center of her confusion, but when

114

she heard footsteps to her left and looked up to see him striding toward her with two beers in his hand, her heart leapt in relief.

"Hi," he greeted gently.

"Hi."

"Mind if I join you?"

"Please do."

He sat beside her on the steps and took his Leatherman out of its case on his belt, then used the blade to pop the tops on the beers. They sipped in silence for several minutes, and Lindsay was content to enjoy his quiet, unassuming company. Evie was right about one thing. Henry had a way of soothing her that even her best friends couldn't. She took a deep breath and let it out in a sigh.

"Skye said Evie went after you pretty good about us," her companion murmured, "so I figured I'd better come talk to you."

"I love her dearly, but sometimes, she doesn't know when to stop."

"I'm sure she only wants you to be happy."

Lindsay nodded. Inexplicably, tears burned her eyes, and she swore under her breath. Henry must have noticed; he wrapped an arm around her shoulders and pulled her close. Pinching her eyes closed to keep the tears locked behind her lids, she leaned into him, resting her head on his shoulder and cursing her trembling chin. When he set his beer down and tucked his other arm around her, a single tear escaped and slid hotly down her cheek.

She lost track of time, but when she'd regained some control over herself, sunset had vanished into a vivid blue-green twilight. The clouds that had burned so brightly had drifted off to the northeast, leaving the heavens clear and glittering.

"I'm afraid," she said at last. "That's why I have to let this thing we have go even though I don't want to."

"Why are you afraid?"

"My son. I've made mistakes with men in the past that hurt him, and I can't let that happen again."

"I'd never hurt Noah, Lindsay." He let out a long breath. "That may be hard to believe since I just left a little boy only a month ago."

That he'd expressed the exact concern that had bounced into her head before she'd left the fire was oddly reassuring.

"I had to do it, though. I knew I'd never be able to make it work with Mel," he continued, "and it was best to leave when he's too young to remember me when he gets older. It's still killing me to leave him at all, but he's not my son, and his real father deserves to know him."

"Do you think Mel wouldn't bother to find him if you'd stayed?"

"I *know* she wouldn't."

"I'm sorry, Henry."

"Me, too. Feeling better?"

"Yes… and no. I'm calmer, if that's what you mean, but the problem remains."

"What problem is that?"

"I don't want what you make me feel to end. I'm getting attached to you, Henry, and I don't even feel guilty about it. You're a good man."

He didn't respond to the compliment and didn't try to allay her concerns. He only hugged her tighter, and right then, that was exactly what she needed.

"I don't know if I've said it yet, but it means a lot to me that you would take the time to get to know me so you wouldn't use me as an outlet for your pain over what Mel did to you. You don't still feel that need do you?"

"No, I don't. And that is entirely your doing." He shifted momentarily to kiss the top of her head and tuck a wayward strand of her hair behind her ear. "You're a remarkable woman, Lindsay—honest, adventurous, beautiful—and I should have known from the start that I didn't have a chance of walking away from this without becoming attached to you, too. I don't want to, but we can call off the rest of the deal if that's what you need. Take sex tomorrow night off the table and go to Luke's game as friends only."

Without hesitation, she shook her head. "No, I don't want to take sex off the table. I want that memory of you, too."

"All right." He hesitated a moment. "Are you ready to go back to the fire?"

"I think I am. Thank you."

Hand in hand, they returned to their friends and curled up together again on the chaise lounge. To her relief, Evie didn't resume her grilling about Henry, and they were able to spend the rest of their evening together in laughter.

Six

"THAT LAST PLAY of the game, what was your left tackle doing, Luke? He left a gaping hole on your blindside." Lindsay recalled with marvelous clarity how she'd yelled almost that exact question to Henry over the capacity crowd and how her heart had pounded as one of the defensive linemen barreled through the gap left by the Bobcats' distracted left tackle and reached for their unguarded quarterback. Luke had noticed him just in time to bring the ball back close to his body and lunged forward just as the lineman reached to snag him around the waist. With impressive power and agility, Luke had broken the tackle and sprinted down the field to turn what could easily have been the only sack of the game into a touchdown. Though she'd seen ample evidence of his quick thinking and athletic ability throughout the game, Lindsay was still stunned by the play. She'd screamed wildly as the refs threw their hands in the air to confirm the successful extra point, and seconds later, the horn had sounded the end of the game. The Bobcats had won with a score of thirty-five to seventeen and brought Lindsay's fantastic adventures in Montana to a close on a high note.

Sitting a couple chairs down and across the table from her at the front of the Pekin Noodle Parlor in Butte, Luke shrugged. "It was his first game, too."

"Obviously. That was a sloppy mistake, but luckily, the rookie quarterback is amazingly quick on his feet. Quite an impressive debut, Luke," Lindsay remarked.

"You never worried about your blindside when Shane was your left tackle," Luke's cousin and best friend Becky muttered.

"No, I didn't."

Something in Luke's tone—a thread of bitterness or anger or perhaps anguish—made Lindsay sit back in surprise. She glanced questioningly at Henry.

"Long story," was all he said. "And not a happy one."

"So not the stuff for a fun evening like tonight," she surmised.

He nodded. "Are you enjoying yourself?"

"Immensely, but I would have thought that was obvious."

"It is," he replied with a grin. "But I like hearing you say it. You are a fascinating woman. I know I've said it before, but you are. You really do know your football."

Lindsay ducked her head sheepishly. "Sorry if Skye and I have hogged the conversation."

"And Becky." Henry inclined his head to the girl, whom Lindsay guessed was a couple years younger than

Luke. "Like I said, it's fascinating to watch. It's also pretty funny that the three people most involved in the discussion of the game are women."

"I warned you."

In response, Henry dove in for a quick kiss while no one was looking. "Am I complaining?"

His voice was a low rumble, almost a purr, that set her pulse to pounding in anticipation of what they had planned for later in the evening. Then his eyes narrowed and searched her face with a flicker of concern.

"Are you feeling better than you were last night?"

"Yeah. I don't know what my deal was yesterday other than I don't want to leave. And then Evie started in on me, reminding me that I have to. The game today really helped. It was a great game, and with so many people from Northstar there to support Luke…. I needed that. All of it."

"It's nice to know that there are still places in this world where people genuinely care about each other and will do anything for each other, isn't it? Gives us hope that life won't always be so hard or so lonely."

"That's exactly it." She tilted her head, frowning contemplatively. "Life *has* been lonely and it started even before Evie moved here and before Skye's photography business started gaining steam. All I do anymore is take care of Noah and work and worry."

When Henry reached a hand out and slid his fingertips along her jaw with that sympathetic shadow in his blue eyes, she rested her cheek against his palm, closing her eyes briefly to focus on the heat of his skin against hers.

Cheers rose from their table, and Lindsay opened her

eyes to see everyone's gaze turned toward the TV in the corner of the room. It took her a moment to realize it was a brief snippet of Luke's post-game interview that had captured their focus. The commotion drew the attention of several other diners, who peeked out of the enclosed booths that lined the aisle leading to the kitchen at the back of the long, narrow restaurant. One man, noticing that the young man on the screen was seated at the big table in the front of the room, joined them to congratulate Luke on his well-played game. At this point, Aaron and Skye decided to call it a night.

While Aaron and then Henry headed to the back of the restaurant to pay their checks, Lindsay stood to embrace her best friend.

"Travel safe tomorrow," Skye whispered.

"See you when you get back to Washington." Lindsay tilted her head in Aaron's direction and winked. "That is, *if* you make it back."

"Oh, please," Skye said with a roll of her eyes that did little to obscure how her pupils dilated at the reference to her date. "One Evie in our trio is enough."

"Right you are, but have some fun with Aaron while you're here, all right? I can already see the good he's been for you."

Skye glanced toward Aaron, who was making his way back to the table. "Yeah, he has."

"Just two more days until Darren officially becomes your ex-husband." Lindsay hugged her friend again. "It's going to be so lonely in Washington without you, but if you come back more at peace, it'll be well worth it."

"I'll miss you, too. All the more because you won't

be here to keep Evie's romantic imagination in check."

"She'll probably start planning your wedding to Aaron the moment she and Vince get back from their honeymoon," Lindsay said with a laugh. "She can be a pest, but that's why we love her."

"Yes, it is."

Aaron returned, and he and Skye bid their final goodnights to their party, who responded as one with such jubilance that Lindsay marveled at how readily the Conners and O'Neils had folded both friends from Washington into their group despite knowing them such a short time. After six weeks with them and Aaron, Skye was certain to come home a mellower, happier version of herself even if this spark between her and Aaron turned out to be nothing more than a passing attraction. Lindsay immediately quelled the twinge of envy but couldn't stop herself from wondering what good a month and a half in Northstar would do for *her* state of mind.

You can't think like that, she scolded herself. *That isn't your life, and thinking about what can't be will only make you miserable.*

"Shall we head out?" Henry asked beside her, startling her.

Not trusting her voice, she only nodded.

When Henry announced their imminent departure, everyone rose and hugged her in turn, each wishing her safe travels, thanking her for coming to the game and dinner, and expressing hope that she would come back soon. Even though she knew it wasn't likely to happen, she promised she would. Henry offered his arm, and she slipped her hand around his elbow, and together, they followed his twin and

Skye out the door and down the long flight of stairs to the street below.

Lindsay stared out the window of Henry's truck at the brick buildings that rose proudly over the hill that was Uptown Butte, and scattered throughout the historic district, the city's trademark black gallus frames stood as testaments to Butte's hard rock mining history. Henry drove the five miles west toward Rocker, where Lindsay would be spending the night in a hotel just off the Interstate. The music was turned down so low that she couldn't make out what song was playing on the radio, and she was acutely aware of their lack of conversation.

"You're awfully quiet," Henry remarked as he pulled into the parking lot of the hotel and shut his truck off. "You're not having second thoughts about this, are you?"

"Second thoughts about what? Sleeping together or heading home tomorrow and trying to pretend like none of this happened?"

"The first thing," he replied, "because there's not much we can do about the second."

"No, no second thoughts. None at all about sleeping with you. In fact, how I feel about *that* is entirely unclouded." She glanced at him. "What about you? Any reservations?"

"As long as you don't have any... not one."

"Then why are we still sitting in your truck?"

He turned as fully toward her as he could in the confines of his seat and seatbelt, frowning faintly. For what felt like at least a full minute but was probably less than ten seconds, he said nothing. Then, in a voice that was disarmingly tender, he gestured to the hotel and said, "Forgive me for saying this, but after our adventures this week, this feels… cheap. Are you sure you want to spend your last night in Montana in a hotel?"

"I don't exactly have a choice, do I? Vince and Evie are flying out first thing in the morning, and while I'm sure they'd let me stay at their house, I have no one to drive me to the airport tomorrow."

"Sure you do. And you have somewhere else to stay, too—with me. We're planning on spending the night together, anyhow, and your flight doesn't leave until four. That gives us plenty of time to sleep in, enjoy a lazy Sunday breakfast, and maybe even sneak in a quick lunch with my family if you're not opposed before we have to head back to Butte."

"When you put it that way…." Lindsay grinned. "Think the hotel will let me cancel my reservation without charging me an arm and a leg?"

"They probably won't charge you anything. The off season has started."

Sure enough, it was still early enough in the evening—and late enough in the season—that she was able to cancel her room without paying a dime, and within minutes, she and Henry were back in his truck and on their way to Northstar.

Unlike the short ride between the restaurant and the hotel, they talked the length of the two-hour drive back to Henry's house. They talked about his plans for the near future—he was going to help out on the ranch until he decided what to do with himself—and about Noah's favorite activities and what Henry wanted to show Lindsay and her son on her next trip to Northstar, whenever that might be.

Lindsay figured he'd probably find himself a wife or at least a girlfriend who wouldn't appreciate him playing tour guide to a woman he'd slept with long before she made it back here, but she kept the comment to herself. He was trying to steer the conversation away from serious topics, and she appreciated his effort. She wouldn't ruin it with speculations about the lucky woman who would someday get to call this charming, considerate man hers.

While they talked, Lindsay enjoyed the scenery and how the evening sun painted the grassy hills on either side of the Interstate and tipped the pines and firs that blanketed the foothills of the surrounding mountain ranges with sharp golden light. The shadows lengthened as they rolled southward until the sun dropped behind the western mountains, casting the land in darkness while the sky above burned. By the time Henry parked in front of his house, the sky had filled with stars.

He told her to wait in the truck a moment while he hauled her two suitcases up to the deck and opened the front door. When he returned to open her door of the truck, she understood why. *Ever the gentleman, aren't you, Mr. Hammond.*

Her heart hummed with anticipation as she slipped her hand into his and slid out of her seat.

Lindsay had been in his house before but only briefly, and while she had appreciated the simple, open layout, she hadn't paid as much attention to the details as she did now. It was a distinctly masculine space, and she couldn't discern anywhere that Mel might've had an influence. Artifacts of ranch life—an old wagon wheel, horseshoes, weathered barn wood, and various other odds and ends likely dating back to the Lazy H Ranch's beginnings—were scattered through out the house not with a decorator's artful hand but by a collector's loving eye. Hunter green and rich, dark blue accents added splashes of cooler color to the earthy tones of the artifacts and golden tones of the walls paneled with tongue-and-groove slats of knotty pine. The furniture—a plush, stone-colored microfiber couch, log coffee and end tables, and a log dining room set—was all newer. If she had to guess, she'd say the log pieces were all locally handcrafted, and if Henry hadn't built them himself, he knew their crafter personally.

No television, she noted. She liked that. With all there was to see and do here, who needed TV? A tall, narrow bookshelf stood in the back corner and was filled with worn paperbacks and a few hardcover novels, painting an interesting picture of Henry wiling away cold winter nights with a good book. *Nothing sexier than a man who likes to read,* she mused.

The wood stove in the front corner of the living room was cold and dark, and it was too warm to light a fire, but Lindsay smiled as she imagined curling up on the couch with Henry to watch merry flames dance behind the glass. It was a Rocky Mountain fantasy for sure.

Inevitably, she was drawn to the small but well-appointed kitchen. Like the furniture, the appliances were all newer, brushed stainless steel, and the counter tops were solid granite. *Granite!* More golden pine added some warmth to the otherwise utilitarian coldness of the granite and steel. Despite the limited room, it was efficiently laid out with a snack bar separating it from the living room and adding more counter space. Oh, the meals she could cook in here.

It put her tiny kitchen back home to shame.

"Considering your previously mentioned enjoyment of cooking, I suppose I shouldn't be surprised that it's the kitchen that has stolen your attention," Henry remarked. "Now that I think about it, I'm kicking myself for thinking I had to treat you since it was your vacation because I imagine you're one hell of a cook."

"I can make a decent meal without burning anything," she replied coyly.

She spotted a tri-folded letter and envelope resting on the snack bar and nosily stepped over to see what it was. In a tidy house with no other papers visible, it seemed to her that this one must be important enough to warrant being out in plain sight. Upon closer inspection, she decided it was in fact something official.

"The results of the paternity test," Henry said quietly, joining her. He picked up the letter and handed it to her. "Mom was up here the other day and wanted to see it, and I haven't gotten around to putting it away again."

"You kept it?" Lindsay asked after reading the confirmation that Dylan wasn't Henry's son. "Why?"

"I wanted to keep it in case I get to thinking I should go back."

"You think you would?"

"Not to Mel... but I still love Dylan. His paternity doesn't change that. Should it?"

"I don't know, Henry. I can't even imagine what that feels like." Setting the results on the counter, she loosely folded her arms around his neck and combed her fingers through the soft hair at the back of his head. There was a startling unguarded vulnerability in his gaze, and she realized he wasn't questioning her reaction as if she were wrong. He was asking her honest opinion, so she gave it. "No, it shouldn't change how you feel about him. Kids can use all the love they can get because they'll find out soon enough how cruel the world can be."

He pulled her close, touched his forehead to hers with his eyes closed, and let out a sigh. "It's been a lot harder to break those habits than I thought it would be. It's been almost a month, but sometimes I still wake up expecting to hear him crying. And there's only silence."

She said nothing but hugged him tightly for a long while, and he relaxed quickly, almost as if he'd consciously closed the door on his pain. She leaned back in his arms to find him watching her with that sexy lopsided grin.

"It's been a lot easier this last week, though," he said.

"Oh? And why do you supposed that is?"

"Well, you see, I've had this smart, beautiful, and marvelously independent redhead distracting me."

Lindsay smiled playfully. "Tell me more about this woman. She sounds pretty incredible."

"She is. She's a selfless and devoted mother who's given up a lot to make sure her son has everything he needs, she's funny and fun to be around and loves football with a passion that makes her light up like the sun, and she's shown me time and again that good women do still exist and that someday, if I'm lucky, I might find one to call my own... not just for a week-long game of make believe but for the rest of my life."

Her heart fluttered. Was this part of the game or did he really mean that last part? She didn't doubt the rest, but could he be thinking they might have a future beyond this week? She doused the hope that flared. She wasn't going to wonder or worry about any of that tonight because tonight was for enjoying the moment, so she drew herself up to kiss him. Their kisses to this point had been somewhat restrained or playful, but she let loose now, pressing her body to his and demanding more and more as he responded in kind.

"I guess we're done talking," Henry whispered hoarsely. "Hold on for a minute, though. I left the damned condoms out in the truck."

He disappeared out into the night, and Lindsay briefly contemplated stripping out of her yellow and navy MSU Gold Rush T-shirt and jeans and greeting him when he came back wearing only her bra and panties but decided against it. She didn't want to take away the fun and pleasure of him undressing her. She wanted every moment and every pleasure tonight because the memory of it was going to have to last her a long time.

When he walked back through the door, closed it behind himself, and looked up to see her leaning against the snack bar, he laughed.

"Now, that's a look of pure mischief if I've ever seen one."

"Mmm. I imagine so. I was just pondering how quickly I could strip down to my underwear."

Before she realized what he had in mind, he leaned down and swept her off her feet with one arm behind her knees and the other behind her shoulder. "Shall we find out?"

Lindsay could only nod and press her lips together to keep the giggles locked inside. When he carried her back to his bedroom and tossed her lightly onto the springy mattress, those giggles erupted. She'd been waiting all week for this, and now that the moment of her initial proposition had arrived, she couldn't stop laughing. It was absurd, and she had no hope of explaining it other than to admit she was so entirely comfortable with Henry that it made her giddy and lightheaded.

He stepped away for a moment to click on the bedside lamp, and that dizziness faded, and doubt unfurled. She lay on the bed and watched as her soon-to-be lover tossed the condoms onto the nightstand.

"Is that tiny box going to be enough?" she inquired, hoping the desire quivering through her edged the nervousness from her voice.

"If you want me to live long enough to drive you to the airport, it is. I'm not exactly a spring chicken anymore."

"Coulda fooled me."

"All right... you've got a long day tomorrow, so you should probably try to get *some* sleep tonight."

"Right you are."

He sat on the edge of the bed and brushed her hair back from her face with his brows knitted. "You're still sure about this?"

Nodding, she asked, "Why? Do I not look sure?"

"A second ago, you got this look like you might be having a few doubts."

"I still have zero doubts about this, Henry. I'm just feeling a tad self conscious."

"Whatever for?"

"Having a baby... changed my body in ways I'm still not entirely comfortable with. Ways I've been made to feel uncomfortable about."

His frown of concern darkened into a scowl. "By Max?"

"And a couple others."

With a twitch of his fingers, he beckoned her to sit up, and hesitantly, she complied. Gently, he lifted her tank top up her body, over her head, and off. He motioned for her to lie down again, and again, she obeyed but had to fight the urge to cover herself with her arms. Instead, she watched as he traced the fading stretch-mark scars with his fingertips, and the expression on his face was entirely different than the ill-concealed revulsion Max and Logan had both regarded them with. A faint smile, almost of awe, graced his handsome face, and something shifted inside her. She let out a breath and relaxed a bit.

"Are these what all the fuss is about?" he murmured.

"It's silly, isn't it?"

"No, it's not. They should never have made you feel ashamed of your body. This body worked hard to bring your son into this world, and these are a reminder of that, which makes them beautiful. Max, especially, is a damned fool if he thinks differently because you are exquisite, Lindsay."

From anyone else, she might have thought such a comment was a come-on—which, considering where they were and what they were about to do, would be redundant—but she knew Henry believed every word he uttered. She clasped his face and pulled him down to her for a kiss, wishing she could find the words to thank him and tell him how much his sentiment meant to her. Her eyes burned with the force of her gratitude, but she determinedly held the tears back, and when he slid his hands over her bare skin with a potent demand, desire re-ignited and burned away her self-consciousness.

She deepened the kiss and swept her hands under his T-shirt, delighting in the firmness of muscle beneath smooth, warm skin. She let the primal hunger for more guide her and override her mind. After a week of waiting, she was ready for this and boldly yanked Henry's shirt over his head, then pushed him over and onto his back. Straddling his waist, she skimmed her hands over his chest, stomach, shoulders, arms, and neck, and over every inch of bare skin she could reach—lightly at first and then with increasing pressure as her attention was captured by each and every toned line of his body.

He let her play for a while, watching her with his pupils so dilated by pleasure that she thought she might get lost in his eyes. When she leaned over him to trail kisses from his navel to the hollow of his throat and her hair brushed across his skin, he shivered and goose bumps rose. Lindsay sat back, entirely pleased with herself.

"You know, you're pretty cute when you're smug," Henry said with laughter in his voice. He rolled them over with an effortless strength that left her breathless, and the playful glint in his eyes vanished, replaced by an intoxicating intent. "My turn."

With deft fingers, he unbuttoned her jeans and slid them down her legs, then pushed the heels of his hands up her thighs and smoothed them around the curves of her hips. Instinctively, she rocked her pelvis into his touch, and when he trailed his fingertips with startling tenderness across her belly, she whimpered. How could he make her feel so fragile and delicate and so powerful and beautiful all at once?

Wanting to have only skin against skin, she unbuckled his belt, unbuttoned and unzipped his jeans, and shimmied beneath him to drag them down his legs. He paused briefly in his investigation of her body to kick them off. Then his touches turned more feverish, and their limbs tangled as they sought to satiate ravenous need.

"Feel good?" he asked, his voice rough.

"Amazing. I'm pretty sure I've never felt like this before."

"Yet more proof that you've dated the wrong men. Taking a little time to warm you up will make it better for both of us. Didn't they know that?"

"They did, and they tried, but… they didn't care like you do. You've managed to excite my emotions as well as my body, and you make me feel more desirable than anyone else ever has."

He kissed her, tugging on her bottom lip. "You aren't just desirable, Lindsay. You're irresistible. You also have a valid point."

"And what is that?"

"That an emotional connection makes it even better. I never realized that before—not like this—so you could say this is new territory for me, too."

"Does that mean you have an emotional connection to me?"

"You've undeniably captured my heart's attention."

She didn't know how to respond to that, and he didn't give her time to figure it out, kissing her so fiercely that she had no choice but to submit to the passion of it.

He returned his attention to her body, massaging each limb and everything in between, and it didn't take long before she felt as pliable as clay in his hands. Soon, her need for more became insatiable.

"Much more of this and I'm going to start begging for the rest," she murmured. "So let's get to it while my dignity is still intact."

The rest of their garments were shed in a rush, and Henry hastily tore open the box of condoms and sheathed himself before positioning his arousal teasingly between her legs. Fire exploded in her core, and she moaned, angling her hips in readiness, but he didn't act on the invitation. Instead, he braced his hands beside her lower ribs and lowered his head to kiss her neck. Shivers coursed through her body, and she pressed her fingers into his back with a blatant demand.

At last, he pushed inside her.

"Finally," she sighed.

As sensation overwhelmed her, there was no room for conscious thought. Her body tingled pleasurably, and she moved with him, driven by pure, spontaneous instinct, and gasped when he drove deep. She gripped his hips with her thighs and shifted her body to take him deeper, glorying in the groan that escaped him.

He kept their rhythm slow, increasing the speed of his thrusts so gradually that she figured he must be pacing them for a marathon. One fleeting thought danced across her mind.

This is going to turn me into mush for the rest of the night.

Her body trembled as muscles she hadn't used in months were reawakened, but she was able to match him thrust for thrust, and the build toward climax deliciously consumed her. When it came, the orgasm slammed through her with a new and incredible power, and moments later, Henry uttered a strangled cry, then swore under his breath. He hung his head as they panted for air, and the muscles of his shoulders and back quivered with the effort it took to hold himself above her, so she pulled him down, comforted by the weight of him and the fullness of having him still locked inside her. They were one as she had never been one with anyone else.

"Diesel engine," he mumbled.

"Huh?"

"You're like a diesel engine. Get you warmed up and you run a very… long… time."

Inexplicably, she laughed. And then she laughed harder when he pushed himself up to stare at her with one corner of his mouth lifted and his brows drawn together in amused confusion. A comment her mother had once made regarding relationships popped into her head, and she laughed harder still.

"What is so funny?"

"My mama once told me that if you haven't laughed during sex, you're doing it with the wrong person."

"Does that mean I'm the right person?"

"By that logic, I guess you are."

His smile widened, and he was soon laughing with her. "I like that. I suppose it means you're the right person, too, because I can honestly say that I haven't ever laughed during sex, either."

She took his face in her hands and kissed his lips. "I think you've ruined me for the rest of the night. You do know this wasn't a competition to see if you could outlast my exes, right? Even if you *did* win it... by a lot."

With his body slackened by mirth, he flopped onto his back. "Just wanted to give you a night to remember, but I may have ruined myself, too. Like I said, I'm not a horny teenager or even a horny twenty-something anymore."

"Maybe not, but I'd say you definitely know how to compensate for that. How old are you, anyhow? Since I've never bothered to ask."

"Just turned thirty-one in August."

"Oh, you poor baby. Did it make you feel old when you crossed that thirty marker?"

"Not really because I don't feel old."

"You don't act it, either." She walked her fingers across his chest. "You put the teenager and the twenty-something I knew to shame."

"Well, thank ya, ma'am. One benefit to having those idiotic, hormone-fueled days behind me is that I've learned not to rush things. Traded rabbit sex for...."

"Diesel engine sex?" she supplied with a giggle.

"Exactly." He kissed her again. "We should probably try to get some sleep, since it's now after eleven."

"It's that late already?"

"Yep."

"But it wasn't quite nine when we got home."

"Yep."

"Um... wow. No wonder I feel like jelly."

"We did play around for quite a lot of that time, so it's not as impressive as it sounds."

"Hush up. Now is not the time for modesty, stud."

Henry laughed again. Then he climbed out of bed to

clean himself up only to return moments later to turn down the covers. Gently, he lifted Lindsay onto the cool sheets, slid in beside her, and yanked the blankets over them to ward off the chill that descended as the heat of their love-making faded. Lindsay shifted onto her side while Henry reached to click the lamp off. When he fit his knees in behind hers and tucked his arm around her waist, she sighed happily.

Worn out by the day's excitement and—she hoped—contented by holding her close, Henry dozed off. She lay awake with her head pillowed on his arm, which couldn't be comfortable for him, and listened as his breathing slowed and deepened, soothed by that simple sign of life. She felt entirely relaxed and secure in his embrace, and she thought of their deal to remind her of what it was like to be someone's woman if only for a little while. It had become so much more, leading to this perfect moment when she wasn't just *someone's* woman but *Henry's*. They could only go forward from here because there was no going back. She couldn't just forget this bond, whatever it was, and she hoped he was serious about wanting to remain friends. Henry had altered her expectations about relationships, shown her what they *should* be, and anyone who could do that was worth holding on to however she could.

She knew she should *try* to get some sleep, and she was certainly tired enough, but she wanted to linger in this moment and enjoy the warmth of Henry's skin against hers and the cozy heat he'd kindled in her heart. In the long run, it would do her far more good than even the best night's rest.

Tomorrow can take its sweet time getting here.

137

Seven

SOMETIME IN THE MIDDLE of the night, Henry snapped awake to the cries of a young boy in the thrall of a nightmare. It was a dream, he knew, but he couldn't shake the panic of hearing his son screaming for him and not being able to get to him. He tried to sit up, but his right arm was pinned beneath his sleeping partner, so he lifted his head and looked around. All was dark and quiet, and the dim light of the waning moon illuminated objects he recognized as belonging to his house in Northstar, not the one he'd shared in Denver with Mel. The cool blue glow also caressed the woman in his bed—a woman with a taller, fuller body than Mel's and long, naturally red hair instead of Mel's stylishly frosted blonde pixie cut.

Not Mel. Lindsay.

The realization brushed away the lingering fog of the

dream, and he wondered how long it would be until the habits and instincts triggered by Dylan's birth fell dormant. Seeking any form of reassurance, he shifted a little closer to Lindsay. The tension flowed out of him, and he sagged into the mattress, anchored in reality by the feel of her naked body against his and the memories of all that had led them here.

Comforted by Lindsay's presence, sleep soon reclaimed him.

When he woke again to bright morning, his shoulder ached from being twisted into the same position for hours on end and his arm tingled. The softness of the woman curled with her back to him kept him from trying to move it to get blood back to his limb, and for almost half an hour, he endured it to watch her sleep. He was certain he'd never been as mesmerized by Mel as he was by Lindsay. Everything about her—her honesty, her passion, her vulnerability, even her stubbornness and independence, and definitely her lithe body, her keen blue eyes, and her mane of shimmering dark copper—captivated him and had from that first moment when she'd confidently introduced herself at the Bedspread Inn.

If he had ever doubted that she would fit Pat's description of a good woman, he didn't any longer. There was something incredible about her that calmed him even when he didn't want to be calm. He'd noticed that almost immediately when she'd come to dinner at his parents' after their Virginia City date.

How much of an idiot was he being for holding to the deadline of their arrangement?

Probably a giant idiot, he admitted. But Mel's deception

was still too fresh, and his dream proved it. *But we promised to remain friends, and who knows what might happen down the road.*

Lindsay stirred, though whether because she was simply ready to greet the day or because she'd sensed he was no longer asleep, he couldn't say, but when she turned to study him over her shoulder with concern darkening her eyes, he suspected it was the latter.

"Good morning, gorgeous," he murmured reassuringly.

Her lips curved. "Good morning, cutie pie," she quipped.

God, he loved her quick wit and added that to the long list of other things he loved about her. *Yeah, I'm a dumbass.*

"You up for round two?" she inquired. "One more to hold me over until… whenever."

"I think I might be able to muster the energy."

This time, Henry didn't try to draw it out, and their joining was just as hot with that incredible sense of *connectedness*. He wished he could stay with her all day right here in his bed, but that wasn't in the cards, so with the heat of their passion barely cooled, he rolled out of bed to start breakfast. It wasn't quite nine in the morning, so they still had plenty of time before they had to drive to Butte. He figured if they left by half past noon, that'd get Lindsay to the airport well ahead of the minimum requirement of one-hour prior to take off.

After breakfast, he took her—at her request—down to his parents' house so she could say goodbye to them as she hadn't done it properly the other day. They ended up staying for lunch, and Henry sat back to watch and listen as his parents, Nick, and Beth, and his niece and nephew hugged her and expressed a desire to see her again soon. His mother and Beth even exchanged email and mailing addresses with her so they could swap recipes.

Too soon, it was time to head to Butte. On the drive, Henry didn't say much, content to listen to Lindsay talk about all the people and all the things she was going to miss in Northstar. He hadn't planned to see her take off, but when he pulled into the short-term parking lot of the Bert Mooney Airport, he found himself wanting to spend every last possible second with her and followed her into the terminal to wait while she checked in.

They sat side by side in chairs facing the broad windows, and Henry draped an arm around her. They talked little, content to gaze out at the towering wall of pine and aspen that was the East Ridge and enjoy this last hour of closeness. They watched her plane land, saying nothing as the people on it disembarked. Long before Henry was ready, the attendant at the counter beside the gate announced that it was time to board the plane. Reluctantly, they stood, and Lindsay wrapped her arms tightly around his neck.

"Thank you," she whispered. "For everything."

"You're welcome. And thank you, too." He buried his face against her neck for a moment, then leaned back to study her face and commit every feature of it to memory. "Give me some time, and we'll see what happens."

Hope sparked in her eyes, and he knew that she understood what he meant. He needed to put Mel and Dylan firmly behind him but was leaving the door open to Lindsay and discarding their deadline.

142

"Say hi to Noah for me and call me when you get home. You have my number still, right?"

"Yep, but I won't be home until late tonight... even later by Montana time."

"I don't care."

She kissed him then, smiling. "Talk to you soon."

Not soon enough. He didn't say it, afraid to put too much pressure on either of them. "Looking forward to it."

The attendant made the final boarding announcement, and Henry shooed her away so she wouldn't miss her flight because he couldn't seem to let her go. She was nearly to the gate when he thought of one last thing he wanted to know before she flew out of his life.

"Lindsay!"

She turned to face him, waiting for him to continue.

"Did I uphold my end of our bargain?"

"Absolutely. And then some. Did I uphold my end?"

"Beyond my wildest dreams."

She grinned, waved, and disappeared through the gate.

Henry walked over to the window and stood there until her plane took off, then jogged out to his truck, slid in behind the wheel, and watched her plane shrink beyond his sight into the distance.

"I'm really going to miss her," he admitted to the empty cab. "She's some kind of special, that woman."

The drive home was the second loneliest of his life but for an entirely different reason. Instead of an emptiness brought on by the breaking of his heart over the loss of the boy he'd believed was his son, he was filled with yearning, and no amount of trying to convince himself that he'd just gotten caught up in their game could erase it. His family was going to have a field day teasing him about moping around like the proverbial lost puppy, and he didn't care. He almost welcomed this new loneliness and even the teasing because it was far preferable to the hurting, angry state he would have been in still if Lindsay hadn't breezed into his life like a cool zephyr on a scorching summer day. And besides, it was true. He *was* lovesick.

Two hours later when he stepped through his parents' front door for the second time today to discuss over dinner what his father wanted him to do tomorrow when he jumped back into ranch work, Nick didn't disappoint.

"You don't even have to say it," his older brother said without bothering to greet him first, "because how much you already miss her is written all over your face."

"I'm sure it is."

Nick regarded him with brows raised, surprised perhaps by the lack of anger and sarcasm in Henry's response. Half a second later, he lifted his hands in a show of peace and nodded his head toward the kitchen. "Mom and Beth have dinner almost done, and Dad and Aaron are washing up."

Henry followed his brother into the kitchen and greeted both his mother and his sister-in-law with a kiss on the cheek. They returned his gesture with knowing smiles.

"Lindsay's flight get off all right?" Tracie asked.

"Yeah. Sorry I'm later than I said I'd be, but I stayed until she took off."

"You're here just in time, so I'm not sure why you're apologizing."

"Even if you were late," Beth remarked, "seeing

144

Lindsay off properly is about as acceptable an excuse as there is."

"Don't start in on me," Henry said without any heat. "Yes, I miss her already, and I'm not afraid or too proud to admit it. I'd be a fool not to miss her."

"That's for damned sure," Aaron remarked as he and their father joined the rest of the family—except Will and Jessie, who were still playing out in the backyard—in the kitchen.

"I'll take crap from everyone here but you," Henry retorted. "Because you have no room to talk with the way you've been looking at Ms. Hathaway since Vince and Evie's wedding."

"It's nothing, Hen. Just a little bit of curiosity."

"And *that* is why you have no room to talk—because you're a bigger fool than I am. But I don't want to talk about you and Skye. I want to talk about what work Dad and Nick want me to do this week on the ranch because, to be honest, I'm ready to get to it."

"Fine by me." Aaron slid plates out of the cupboard and took them and the requisite silverware into the dining room to set the table.

Henry turned expectantly to his father and older brother, but neither John nor Nick spoke up. Instead, they studied him with the same quizzical expression. He folded his arms across his chest and waited for one of them to say what everyone was obviously thinking. Before he'd met Lindsay, this tribunal would have annoyed the hell out of him, tightening the muscles in his back and shoulders, but he was surprisingly relaxed and without even a drop of impatience willing them to speak up.

145

"Lindsay was good for you," Tracie said gently. "Even if your arrangement *was* only temporary."

"Of course she was. She's an incredible woman unlike any I've dated before."

John snorted. "I can't believe you're going to just let her leave and close the door on—"

"For now, yes, I am. She was a great distraction from Mel and Dylan, but I still have to deal with that. And until I do, I don't want that tainting anything I could have with Lindsay. I think she understands that and that I need to find the part of my identity that used to be wrapped up in Dylan."

"I hope you're not making a mistake," Nick murmured. "But I guess we'll see if distance makes your heart forget or grow fonder."

"I guess we will."

Tracie pulled the last pot off the stove, and Beth finished tossing the salad, so Henry headed out to the backyard to bring his niece and nephew in to get washed up.

"Where's Lindsay?" Will asked.

"She had to go home to Washington, sport. Remember?"

"Will she come back?"

"I hope so," Henry replied before he could stop himself. He ruffled Will's mop of blond hair and smiled fondly. Both Nick and Beth were clearly represented in the six-year-old's features just as Aaron and Erica were both evident in Jessie, and Henry wondered why he hadn't noticed the absence of himself in Dylan.

The answer was simple but agonizing. *I didn't want to.*

"Did you really mean it when you said you're not

going back to Denver again?" Jessie inquired as they walked toward the back door hand in hand.

"I did. I don't have any plans to go anywhere this time."

"That means we'll get to play lots, right, Uncle Henry?"

"You bet it does."

She bounced in front of him with her hands held up, silently commanding him to pick her up. He obeyed, happy to indulge her, and she threw her little arms around his neck. With her hitched on his hip, he took Will's hand and squeezed. He'd thought he had seen them both and gotten to know them well enough, but in this moment, he understood that he hadn't spent as much time with them as he should have. If there was one good thing to come of thinking Dylan was his son it was the way it had settled his mind on children. He'd never been opposed to having kids, but neither had he been sure he wanted them, and now he was.

Once he stepped inside, he set Jessie on her feet and told her and Will to go wash their hands for dinner, then ventured back into the kitchen to help serve the food. After everyone was seated and grace had been said, they ate.

"So, Dad, what do you need me to do this week?" Henry asked.

"If you wouldn't mind, the hoist truck needs a tune up. We'll be haying the lower fields this week and stacking Friday, Saturday, and Sunday. And at some point in the not-too-distant future, you and Nick probably ought to get some firewood cut for you." John paused to level a questioning gaze on his wandering son. "If you're planning to be here through the winter."

Henry winced. "That's the idea."

"I thought maybe we'd ease you back into ranch work, but you said you were ready for it, so I've got plenty of jobs lined up for you."

"I appreciate that, Dad. It'll be great to be out working with my family again."

"We're glad to have you back home, too, Henry," Nick replied. "It'll be good for us all to reconnect as a family."

Henry nodded, glancing between his brothers. Between Beth's rape, Erica's death, and now Henry finding out that Dylan wasn't his son, their family had been shaken up quite a lot since the boys had left the nest and headed off to college, and though time had healed a lot of the grief and pain, the scars were still there, and Henry should have been here for his brothers instead of off obeying his wanderlust in Denver.

"I'm glad I came back," he whispered too quietly for anyone to hear.

After they finished eating, Henry helped his brothers with the dishes, reminded by the joking and teasing of the good old days before any of those tragedies had rocked their family. It was nice to know that, no matter what happened in his life, he could count on the love of his family. When the dishes were done, Nick, Beth, and Will headed home. Aaron left soon after with Jessie, and Henry lingered for a few minutes more, but it was close to nine, and the promise of hearing Lindsay's voice again began to make him anxious.

"I suppose you need to be home so you won't miss Lindsay's call," his mother sighed when he announced his imminent departure.

"How did you...?"

"You may not have been home much these last few years, Henry, but I know my son. You haven't changed so much that I can't still read your face like a book. Give her our love, will you?"

"Of course."

He bid his parents goodnight and drove home. When he arrived, he didn't immediately head inside but stood out on his porch, leaning over the railing to watch the stars come out as the sky darkened into full night. The air still held summer's balmy warmth, but beneath it, there was the promise of impending autumn. It wouldn't be much longer now until the air turned crisp, and thoughts of cutting firewood next Monday with Nick and of lighting a fire in his wood stove made him think of other cozy things like snuggling with a warm and willing woman to watch the flames while the first snows of the coming winter descended on the mountains. He'd bet the ranch that Lindsay would love it out here in the fall. Or the winter. Despite her struggles, she had managed to maintain her delight in the simple pleasures of life—he'd seen plenty of evidence of that on their dates over the last week—and he imagined this kind of life would suit her perfectly.

At last, he headed inside to flop on the couch with a book and the phone in easy reach.

* * *

Lindsay had spent her entire life in Western Washington, but when her plane had touched down at SeaTac Airport, its sprawling cities, towns, and suburban areas interspersed with towering evergreen trees and lush vegetation had looked foreign to her eyes. After a long seven hours of waiting and sitting in the airport shuttle and then her roommate's car, that peculiar sensation hadn't faded. Neither had the wish that she didn't have to sleep alone tonight. It had been a long time since she'd slept as well and as deeply as she had last with Henry curled around her.

"Thanks for picking me up," she said as Chelsea unlocked their front door. "I didn't want Mom and Dad to wake Noah up since school starts on Wednesday."

"It's no problem, Linds. Spencer's at his dad's tonight, anyhow. How was your trip?"

She nearly sighed in longing. "It was wonderful. Evie's wedding was as beautiful as any I've ever been to, and Northstar is an incredible place. I totally see why she's as smitten with it as with her new husband… and Vince is a great guy. They have a long and happy life ahead of them."

"Sounds like it was a great vacation for you. You certainly look a lot happier, and you *definitely* look more rested."

"I am. Hopefully it'll last for a while."

She expected to feel the relief of returning home when she walked through the door, but it didn't come. There was no gladness to be back in her own space and no welcome to be found in the sight of her scattered knick-knacks and cherished photographs, only the sensation of sinking beneath the crushing weight of her responsibilities as a single parent, and those greeted her far too eagerly. For nine wonderful days, she'd been free to enjoy life, but that was over now, and the reality of her life threatened to overwhelm her.

I've been doing this for eight years. I'll go right on making it work for the next ten, and then….

What about a car for Noah? Auto insurance? And,

God, what about college? The thought that she had no way to prevent her son from being sucked into the bleak cycle of poverty terrified her. She was failing him with precious little hope for better.

Stop thinking like this. Right... now.

Lindsay straightened, squared her shoulders, and hauled her suitcases back to her bedroom, then returned to the kitchen to quickly glance through her mail. The pile was relatively small, and as she'd suspected, there was no check from Max. Sighing, she left the mail on the kitchen counter where Chelsea had piled it for her in her absence and wandered into the living room to collapse into their worn, hand-me-down couch. It was after eleven now, which meant it was after midnight in Montana, so she should probably wait to call Henry, but even thinking of doing so made her heart fall in disappointment. She'd spent most of her flight and the ride home thinking of him and of their many adventures, and those thoughts had kept the burden of her usual concerns and doubts from descending on her, and she couldn't bear the thought of waiting until the morning to hear his voice again.

Mercifully, the cordless was on the coffee table, so she didn't even have to get up to retrieve it. She dialed his number from memory—funny how little effort it had taken her to memorize it—and waited as the phone rang. It kept ringing, and she almost ended the call, figuring he'd already gone to bed and reluctant to wake him if she hadn't already, but on the ninth ring, he picked up.

"Hi, gorgeous," he answered groggily.

"Either you have caller ID or I need to be very envious right now," she quipped.

"I have caller ID. How was your flight?"

"Long and bumpy."

"And the ride home?"

"Longer and bumpier. How was dinner with your family?"

"It was nice. Everyone sends their love. They miss you, and so do I."

There was no stopping the smile that spread across her face, so she didn't try. Across the living room from the tattered Lay-Z-Boy, Chelsea regarded her with unveiled curiosity, and Lindsay lowered her gaze. "I miss you, too, and I miss them. Anyhow, I wanted to call to let you know I got home safe and sound, and I've done that, so now I'm going to let you get back to sleep."

"I wasn't asleep."

"Uh-huh. Sure you weren't."

"Okay, maybe I dozed off while I was reading."

"Must not be that exciting a book."

"It's a great book, but I've read it at least a dozen times before. Larry McMurtry's *Lonesome Dove*."

"One of my favorites. But I'm not going to keep you awake talking about literature." She hesitated, debating if what she wanted to ask was wise. "Talk to you soon?"

"Like when?"

"Is tomorrow evening too soon?"

"Not soon enough."

Grinning, Lindsay said, "No, probably not, but you have to work tomorrow, and I'm probably going to end up spending most of the day shopping for Noah's school supplies and football gear and...." She sighed. "I'm going to shut up about it or I won't get any sleep because I'll be too busy worrying about how to afford it all."

"Sounds like you were right that Max wouldn't send the money."

The sleepy, teasing tone vanished from his voice, and the note of anger mixed with concern for her eased the ache of tension growing in her neck and head.

"Unfortunately so. That's something else I'll have to take care of tomorrow, so by tomorrow evening, I'll *really* want to talk to you because my sanity will need a boost."

"Do you want to call me, or shall I call you? I should be done with work and home to cook myself dinner by six or so my time, five yours."

"Why don't I call you, then, since I don't know when I'll be done."

"All right. Talk to you then. Good night, Lindsay, and try not to worry too much, all right? Worrying doesn't do any good, anyhow."

"I know that, and I promise, I'll try. Good night, Henry."

Reluctantly, she ended the call and let her head fall back against the couch. She wanted to hug someone—either Noah or Henry, she didn't care—but she had to settle for wrapping her arms around herself.

"Henry?" Chelsea asked as soon as Lindsay had returned the phone to the coffee table.

"I met him in Northstar—he's one of the brothers of Vince's sister's husband."

"*He's* the reason you're looking so…. I'll say content, but satisfied seems like it might be a more fitting term."

"It was a fling," Lindsay replied evasively. "And from the start, it wasn't meant to last."

She liked Chelsea well enough, but they'd never developed a deep enough friendship that would prod her into divulging the details of her relationship with Henry to the woman; that kind of talk was reserved for her two best friends only, and probably her parents because she'd already told them about Henry, anyhow, and they'd supported her through everything else.

"Well, whatever it was, it did the trick," Chelsea remarked. "Good for you."

Lindsay pushed to her feet and, with Henry's voice still fresh in her mind, bid her roommate goodnight and headed to bed. She was wiped out by her journey and anxious to get up in the morning to see her son and parents, and the sooner she got to sleep, the sooner she'd be able to do that, but loneliness settled over her, and her weary brain decided now was the perfect time to replay her vacation. She tried to convince herself that what she'd shared with Henry was exactly what she'd told Chelsea it was—a fling that had no a chance to be anything more—because she didn't think holding on to the hope that it would be more was healthy. And yet… hadn't he said, just before she'd boarded the plane, that there might be more for them in the future?

Give me some time, and we'll see what happens.

That didn't sound like something a man intent on closing the door would say, did it?

She knew he needed some time and space to deal with his issues, and she respected that. She respected, too, that he didn't want to drag her through it while he worked through it, and that he cared enough about her to want to spare her whatever pain he thought it might cause *her* only endeared him to her that much more. Old habits instilled in her by the other men she'd dated made her question his intent, but what reason would he have to be anything but genuine? Sex had been on the table from the beginning, and *he* had been the one to put the brakes on when she would have been happy to fall into bed with him that first night... or the night of Vince and Evie's wedding, but he'd wanted to make sure he had enough time to set aside his anger so he wouldn't take it out on her. No other man she'd been with had *ever* put her first like that.

I trust him.

The admission washed through her with sweet intensity, and she tried but failed to remember the last new person she'd trusted as much. She didn't even trust Chelsea enough to tell her the extent of her relationship with Henry, and her roommate had no real power to hurt her.

Drawing her knees in close to her body, she tucked an arm around them and tried not to wish he were here with her. As she'd told him, he'd more than adequately fulfilled his end of their bargain—too well because now she wanted more. The familiar voices of despair began to whisper, and stubbornly, she shut them out and did something she rarely allowed herself to do.

She hoped.

155

Eight

IT WAS PROBABLY A DIRTY TACTIC, but Lindsay didn't care. She withheld the gifts she'd brought home for Noah—both the ones she'd picked up and the ones Henry had bought for her son—to bribe her anti-shopping boy into being on his best behavior while they braved the crowds of Labor Day bargain hunters to find the best deals on what supplies and clothes her parents hadn't already bought him. She'd arrived at their Indianola house bright and early this morning to discover that they had already purchased damned near a new wardrobe for Noah as well as his football gear. She had been simultaneously annoyed and grateful, and promised she'd find a way to pay them back. Her father had told her they'd only accept repayment if it came from Max.

"You can't keep trying to do this all on your own,

Lindsay," her mother had added. "Noah has two parents, and it's well past time the other one was reminded of that."

She didn't like shopping much more than her son, but she drew out their excursion to delay the inevitable phone call she'd have to make to Max this afternoon. At least her son was behaving himself. Maybe she hadn't needed to bribe him. Maybe he was as happy to see her as she was to see him. He'd been a chatterbox, quizzing her about her trip to Montana, but his energy was draining, and in the last hour, he'd almost stopped talking, so they hauled their bags out to her car and adjourned to the mall's food court to refuel before heading for their last stop in the mall—shoes.

While they ate their pizza, she drank in the sight of him, reacquainting herself with his cherished features—the blue eyes he'd inherited from her, the dark hair he'd gotten from Max, and the mixture of them both that had combined into a visage that was uniquely Noah and hinted of the handsome young man he'd become far too quickly. When he caught her watching him, he smiled and blessed her with her favorite funny face. Laughing, she copied him and soon had him laughing freely with her. For the time being, Max's corrosive influence was nowhere to be found.

As a testament to another growth spurt in the works, Noah scarfed two pieces of pizza before she'd finished one. And they weren't small slices. As they cleaned up after lunch, she wondered how long his new school clothes were going to fit him. They talked as they walked toward the first shoe store, and she noted an increasing whininess in his voice, and she figured that growth spurt was probably in progress. If so, she couldn't blame him for being cranky.

They'd been on their feet most of the day, and combine that with impending growing pains…. *Poor guy*.

"We're almost done, bud," she said when they paused in front of their destination and he gave her a withering look when a bubbly store employee almost bounced over to them.

"What can I help you find today?" the clerk asked brightly.

"I don't think we need any help just yet," Lindsay replied, "but thank you."

"Just let me know if you do, and I'll be happy to assist you."

After the woman moved off to assist other customers, Lindsay ushered Noah toward the aisle with his shoe size. She skimmed the prices of several and let him choose half a dozen he liked from those that were within her budget, but she noted how his eyes flicked to one pair that was well out of her price range. She wished she could just splurge—just this once—if only to see him smile. He was only eight, for God's sake, but already he was picking up the look of resignation she frequently had when she thought about the very real possibility that life was never going to get any better than this. Sighing, she asked him to try on the shoes. He stuffed his feet into the first pair and grimaced.

"Too small?" she asked.

"No, but really *not* comfortable." He stood up, wiggled his toes, and took a few steps, trying to make the footwear work, but at last, he gave up and jerked the shoes off and tossed them back into their box. "Just once, I wish I didn't have to pick shoes by price."

"I'm sorry, baby," she sighed. "I wish we didn't have

to, too."

"Mom...."

"I know, I know. I'm sorry I called you baby. Habit. I really missed you while I was in Montana."

Abruptly, he hugged her, clinging to her like he hadn't in a long time. "I really missed you, too."

There's my sweet boy. Lindsay pinched her eyes closed and took a deep breath.

He tried on the rest of the shoes, but only one pair was a good fit. He had such narrow feet, just like her, and most of the shoes were so wide, but to his credit, he didn't look at the pair still on the shelf that he so obviously wanted. She'd hoped to get him three new pairs because he'd either outgrown or worn the ones he had to pieces, but so far....

She stood while he went back through the shoes to make sure he couldn't make any of the others work and grabbed the other pair. There were other shoe stores they could try in the mall, but since they'd started with the cheapest first, they weren't likely to find much else in them. She dropped the box on the floor in front of him.

"Here, try these on."

He glanced between her and the shoes, and the guilt in his eyes nearly broke her heart. "But...."

"Just try them on, all right? And wipe that grin off your face," she added with a smile of her own when he beamed, "because you may have to make them and this other pair last."

The expensive pair naturally fit perfectly. With that item off their list and her purse lighter than she liked, they escaped the crowded mall and drove home to her parents' house. After the bustle of Silverdale, the quiet of Indianola was a welcome relief, and Lindsay had to swallow a surge of claustrophobia. Silverdale wasn't exactly a big town, and the busyness of it had never bothered her before, but after nine days in the exquisite tranquility of Northstar, it was a shock to her system.

Her mother was out watering her garden when Lindsay parked her car in the driveway. The greenness of the surrounding forests and the vibrant splashes of color in the garden were a strange sight, and Lindsay marveled at how much the open landscapes of Montana had grown on her. Noah gave his grandmother a quick hug before racing inside, claiming an urgent need for the bathroom. Lindsay stayed outside and helped her mother deadhead the cheerful multi-colored poppies that lined the front walkway.

"Did you have a productive shopping trip?" Debbie asked.

"We did. Got everything else we needed, so Noah should be set for school."

"Are you still planning on giving him your goodies here, or would you rather wait and do it at home?"

"Here of course. Chelsea's ex was dropping Spencer off just as I headed over here, and I know he'll try to sneak some of Noah's stuff if we wait until we get home."

"You both look tired, so I thought maybe you'd just want to head home."

"If anything, I'd rather stay here a bit longer."

"Well, good because I pulled out enough chicken for all of us, so why don't you just stay for dinner."

"Thanks, Mama. Is Dad home yet?"

"No, he's running a little late this afternoon."

"Just one more week until he retires. Are you looking

forward to it?"

"You bet I am. You'd think having so much time by myself in the summers, I'd know what to do with all this alone time, but I still don't. And speaking of retirement, I finalized our lease of that condo in Sedona."

"How long will you be gone?"

"November first through March thirty-first, but we'll of course be back for Thanksgiving and Christmas. Are you sure you won't move in here and look after the place while we're gone?"

"I can't, Mama."

Debbie paused in her deadheading chore and regarded her daughter with one brow lifted. "Can't... or won't?"

"I should probably call Max before Dad gets home. Mind if I use your phone?"

Her mother eyed her but didn't press for clarification. "Go right ahead, honey."

Lindsay sighed in relief and turned away. She couldn't stay here while her parents were in Arizona even if she kept up rent and bills on her house with Chelsea to make sure she didn't lose it. It would be too hard to leave her parents' spacious custom home and return to the cramped quarters of her rental, and she *would not* move back in with her parents. She had worked too hard to win her independence to give it up now.

With that vow, she stepped inside.

The front door opened into the entryway. To her right was the sprawling living room with its two full-sized couches sitting across the wall from the pair of bay windows that offered a view of the water and Bainbridge Island beyond the Grangers' bluff-top home across the street. To her left behind a wall lined with coat pegs was the dining room. Also to her left farther toward the rear of the house was her favorite room—the large, bright kitchen. A long counter separated it from the living room, and with that and the island, she never had to fight for workspace when she cooked here. Behind that, at the back of the house, was her mother's office, which had a sliding glass door that opened into a backyard she'd thought was fairly large until she'd spent over a week in Montana. The dining room, kitchen, and office were all open to each other and to the living room, and Lindsay had always loved that. Only the master suite, bathroom, and two bedrooms, which sat in an L around the living room down a hall that ran behind the wall with the couches, were closed off. This had been her home for the first eighteen years of her life, and downsizing to her first apartment had been a stifling adjustment. She pushed that memory from her mind and reminded herself of the task at hand.

Dread made each step toward the phone in the airy kitchen heavier than the last, and by the time she dialed Max's number, her lip curled with it. She wasn't going to bother with niceties, she promised herself. She wasn't going to back down, either.

His wife picked up the phone. "Hello?"

"Giselle, it's Lindsay. May I please speak with Max?"

"Max, it's Lindsay."

After a brief pause filled with shuffling sounds, Max came on the line. "To what do I owe this pleasure?"

"I was hoping you might decide to be decent for once and that a check for Noah's football gear would be waiting for me when I got home from Montana last night, but I can't say I'm surprised it wasn't."

"I'm not going to send money for something I don't want him involved in. We've had this discussion, Lindsay."

"I don't give a rat's ass what you do or don't want him involved in. Maybe if you'd been more of a parent to this point, I might, but you haven't, so I don't. He wants to play football. The least you can do is provide the means for him to do it."

"No."

"Then do us all a favor and give up your parental rights."

"Excuse me?"

Lindsay didn't immediately answer, too stunned by what she'd said. Where had that come from? Half a second before she'd uttered the words, her father's comment about Noah having two parents had popped into her head followed immediately by the conversation she'd had with Henry on their motorcycle ride. The conviction that she and Noah would be better off if Max had completely walked out of their lives returned stronger than ever.

She set her jaw. "You heard me. All you ever do is fight me over money and turn my son into a smart-mouthed brat, so it's not like you're actually a parent. Besides, we both know you never wanted him in the first place and that you would have been happy to walk away like you had no son. So why don't you just do what you so obviously want to."

"No."

"Then cut me a goddamned check for—" Lindsay glanced up when her mother joined her in the kitchen. "Mom, how much was Noah's football stuff?"

Debbie rattled off a price, and Lindsay repeated it to Max.

"And put the check in the mail first thing in the morning, or we may have to reevaluate our situation. With lawyers."

She ended the call before Max could answer and met her mother's surprised gaze head on with her arms folded across her chest and defiance in every muscle of her body.

"What got into you just now?"

Forcing herself to relax, Lindsay inhaled deeply and opened her mouth to answer, but Debbie cut her off.

"It's this Henry Hammond you met, isn't it? My, he seems to have had quite an impact on my girl... and a good one."

"I guess he has."

"Did I actually hear you tell Max he should give up parental rights to Noah?"

Lindsay nodded.

"Do you really think that's best for Noah? A boy needs his father."

"A boy needs *a* father, and yes, I do believe that having Max out of his life would be best for him. You know as well as I do that Max is a terrible influence on him. That snotty attitude he always comes home with when he visits Max won't get him very far in life, and...." She stopped short of saying *he's already going to have a hard enough time starting out as poor as we are.* When she spotted her son watching them from the hallway with rounded eyes, she tipped her head back and groaned. How much had he heard? She looked at him again, and his expression darkened. *Too much.*

"Noah," she said, "I'm sorry. I shouldn't have said

any of that to your father. He just makes me so angry. It isn't right that he doesn't do more for you when he has the means to do so."

For a long time, Noah didn't answer, only stared off into space and chewed on the inside of his cheek. Lindsay prepared herself to endure shouted accusations and tearful pleas that she try to get along with his father.

"Is it true?"

Lindsay blinked at him. That wasn't at all the response she expected, rendering her preparation useless. She sputtered for a moment, then asked, "Is what true?"

"That he never wanted me."

She'd been avoiding this very question for years now; he hadn't been old enough to understand, and anyhow, she hadn't yet figured out how she was going to tell him. She glanced at her mother for help, but Debbie only shrugged.

"I know you were really young when you had me," he continued. "Did he want you to have an abortion or put me up for adoption?"

Rendered speechless by his startlingly mature questions, Lindsay could only nod.

"Which one was it?"

"Noah, this is not a conversation we need to have right now."

"Which one, Mom?" he asked more firmly.

"Both."

"But you said no. *You* wanted me."

"Yes, I did. I won't lie and say I wasn't terrified, but I loved you from the moment I found out about you, and there was *never* any question in my mind about keeping you."

In her son's face, she watched a war play out between

a young boy's need for his mother's comfort and a man's anger at Max's callousness. Lindsay leaned back against the island, afraid she'd end up on the floor if she didn't. His need won the battle, and he quickly crossed the distance to her and threw his arms around her. She hugged him tightly and wished she had long ago asked Max to give up his rights instead of holding onto her adolescent fantasy that they could all be a family.

"I hate him," she heard Noah mutter against her shoulder. "I always felt like I was a… a…."

"Hush now. Don't hate him, baby," she murmured. "He *is* your father even if he doesn't always remember it, and he wouldn't keep fighting if he didn't love you."

"But why does he have to fight at all?"

"I don't know, Noah. But come on. Let's not talk or think about this anymore today, okay? It doesn't do any good. Besides, you know that *I* love you, right? And that Grandma and Grandpa love you, too."

He nodded.

"Why don't you show Grandma your snazzy new shoes while I bring out the goodies from Montana."

"Oh, right! I forgot about those."

So he *had* been too glad to see her to give her any grief while she dragged him from one store to the next. That made her feel somewhat better, though she regretted that he'd overheard her conversation with his father and hoped he wouldn't dwell on it. One, he just didn't need to think about it or worry over it, and two, God only knew how Max would use that as ammunition against her. Shoving that mess aside for the time being, she retrieved the gifts from their hiding place in her parents' bedroom and brought them into the kitchen.

Noah was most excited about the crystals she and Henry had unearthed at Crystal Park, but their old-timey photographs were nearly as interesting to him. He thought the various candies were cool, too, and Lindsay made sure he understood they were from Henry, since the man had paid for them. He'd also tossed in a few other things for Noah without her awareness—a picture frame with footballs and helmets and a note saying *for a picture of your first championship*, a small box made of weathered barn wood in which Noah could keep his crystals, and an IOU for a horseback ride on the Lazy H Ranch. They were little things and inexpensive but thoughtful.

"The Lazy H Ranch? Is that Vince's ranch?" Noah asked.

"No, it's Henry's family's spread."

"Who is Henry, and why would he send these home for me?"

"He's a friend I made in Northstar—a friend of Vince and Evie's."

"A friend like Logan?"

The question was innocent, but Lindsay flinched. "No, not a friend like Logan. A real friend."

Noah went back to sorting the crystals and admiring his goodies, and Lindsay picked up the photographs, more glad than ever that Henry had talked her into them. She should ask Skye if she'd taken any pictures of him or of them together at the wedding, and she smiled, hopeful.

"Is that him?" Debbie asked her quietly so Noah wouldn't hear as she looked over her daughter's shoulder at the photographs. "Oh, honey, he's so handsome. And those eyes."

Lindsay glanced at her mother, curious. "What about his eyes?"

"They're kind and generous. He has an honest soul, that one."

Tilting her head, she studied the image more closely. She'd thought it was her frankness that had invited Henry to be as candid as he had been with her, but now she decided he was always that sincere. Maybe he didn't make a habit of telling everyone who'd listen his life story, but she believed he'd answer honestly if asked directly. "I think you'd like him, Mama."

"Just from the way you talked about him, I figured I would, but seeing him... now I'm certain I would." Debbie gazed at her daughter probingly. "Maybe I'll get a chance to meet him one of these days?"

"Maybe so."

Of her parents, Lindsay's father was the cook, and since he wasn't home yet, she decided to start dinner—chicken Parmesan, his favorite. Debbie helped as Lindsay needed her to but otherwise leaned against the daughter and talked about Lindsay's trip and, when Noah headed into the living room to watch TV, about Henry and his family. It was wonderful to have something positive to think about after her conversations with Max and Noah, and before long, thoughts of Henry and the therapeutic, habitual motions she used as she cooked soothed away her anger and frustration and left her feeling almost as rested as she had before she'd left Northstar for Butte yesterday.

Her father arrived just as she was plating the meal and gave her a bear hug. She nearly dropped the two plates she was holding.

"Welcome home, sweetheart," Steve said. "Not only do I get to come home to an incredible meal after a long day of cooking for other people, I get to see my beautiful daughter smiling like the sun. Montana was good for you."

"It was *very* good for me," she replied.

Lindsay, her parents, and Noah gathered around the dining room table, something her parents did only when she and Noah were over—normally they ate on their laps in the living room while they watched the evening news. Her father asked her about her trip, but instead of feeling like a broken record having repeated the tales first to Noah while they were out shopping and then to her mother, she relished the opportunity to revisit Northstar and everyone who called the ranching community home. Her mother refused to let her do the dishes, but she stayed and talked with her parents until the kitchen and dining room were reset to pre-meal orderliness.

"All right, honey," Debbie said, hanging the hand towel on the handle of the oven. "Thank you for dinner, but it's probably time you head home. You have work tomorrow, and I'm sure you could use a few extra hours of rest, so we won't keep you any longer. There will be plenty more time to talk tomorrow and the next day… and whenever. And something tells me the happiness you found in Montana isn't going to fade any time soon, so you just wait to tell us the rest."

"Yes, Mama."

"And tell that friend of yours hello for us the next time you talk to him. You *will* talk to him again, won't you?"

"I'm supposed to call him when I get home."

"In that case, we definitely won't keep you any longer."

Lindsay hugged her mother and whispered, "Thank you."

Noah was quiet for most of the ride home. About a mile away, a scowl pinched his face, darkening the closer they came to home.

"What's on your mind, bud?" she asked after she'd parked behind Chelsea's car out by the curb.

"Spencer's gonna steal all my stuff that you brought back from Montana."

"I'm sure he'll try, so how about you keep it in my room when you're not using it?"

"I wish we didn't have to live with him and his mom. I mean, Chelsea's nice, but…."

"I know, bud. I wish we could have our own place, too."

"How come we can't stay with Grandma and Grandpa? They said we could."

"They need their space. We have to keep making the best with what we have, okay? Someday, it'll get better for us."

"And meanwhile, Dad and Giselle get to live in that giant four-bedroom house with nobody else but them to use it."

Lindsay reached over and squeezed his hand. She wished she could take a magic wand and make all his worries go away. Instead, she hugged him tightly for a long time, gratified when he hugged her back.

"I'm glad you're home," he whispered. "I really missed you. And I'm sorry I was a butthead to you on the phone while you were gone."

"I really missed you, too, and thank you for the apology."

They headed inside, and Lindsay took Noah's gifts to her room while he unpacked his bags from his stay at his grandparents. Chelsea's son, Spencer, wasted no time quizzing him about what Lindsay had brought home for him, and while she didn't condone lying, she wasn't about to chastise him when he told Spencer *nothing*. Some days, she was tempted to sleep on the couch just so he could have his own room, but that wouldn't solve the problem, so she swallowed the urge like she always did.

After the boys headed to bed, Lindsay retreated to her room to call Henry.

"I was beginning to wonder if you'd forgotten me already," he teased.

"Like I could," she replied as a spark of her playful side flared to life. "Sorry I'm calling so late again. We had a busy day, and then we ate dinner with my folks, and I had an uncomfortable conversation with Noah about his father."

"Oh? What triggered that?"

She told him everything about her phone call to Max and about telling her ex to give up his parental rights. Henry agreed that it might be best for both her and Noah and commended her on her guts for speaking her mind. He wasn't too thrilled to learn that Max had suggested she have an abortion—she apparently hadn't mentioned *that* in their conversations—and his anger on her behalf and on her son's kindled a warm glow in her heart that burned away ever last lingering trace of angst over Max's continuing animosity.

"I know you think I'm this amazing, selfless woman, but I am selfishly glad right now that I met you, Henry." She flopped on her bed and stared at the midnight blue ceiling with its large flakes of glitter trying poorly to imitate the stars. "Because you're pretty damned incredible yourself, and you have this talent for making me forget my worries."

"I'm nothing special. It's all you, gorgeous. You bring out the best in those around you."

She snorted. "Evidently not."

"Let me rephrase that. You bring out the good in people who have some to be brought out."

Feeling more than a little like a giddy schoolgirl, she thanked him, shyly glad he couldn't see her blush. They moved on to happier topics, and by the time their yawns began to overtake the conversation, they'd been on the phone almost two hours. Lindsay stared at the clock, certain it must be lying to her.

"We should get off this thing," he said but took no other steps to end the call.

"We should."

"Right. Because we both have to work tomorrow."

"Yes, we do."

He chuckled. "When can I call you again?"

"I have the dinner shifts all week, but I'm off on Thursday. Will that work?"

"Not soon enough," he answered, and she could hear the fond smile in his voice, "but I guess it'll have to do. Talk to you on Thursday."

"It's a date. Good night, Henry."

"Good night, gorgeous."

At last, Lindsay hung up the phone and got up to take the cordless back into the living room. She finished preparing for bed and crawled between the sheets, determined to keep Max from reentering her mind. It was surprisingly easy to do that, and she dozed off smiling with a thought that Thursday couldn't come soon enough.

Nine

"AARON AND SKYE to be hitting it off well," Henry remarked as he caught the sixteen-inch-long block of beetle-killed lodgepole pine Nick tossed to him. He dropped it smoothly on top of the row of other logs already stacked neatly in the bed of his pickup. "Is it just me or does he seem a little lost without her here?"

"They do indeed, and it's not just you who's seeing that. She's supposed to be back from Washington the day after tomorrow, and I know he's looking forward to it." Nick tossed another log and another in an effortless rhythm. "I'm inclined to say your hope for them is well placed. If nothing else, she's distracting him from thinking about Jerry Mackey."

"That's a damned good thing. Mackey's still keeping his distance?"

"Sounds like it. Aaron said Pearl bumped into him a few days ago while she was at lunch, but other than that... Jerry's keeping his head down."

"That's good. Good for Aaron *and* for Mackey. I know I shouldn't because his shitty choice to run drugs for his dirt bag cousin ultimately led to Erica's death, but I can't help feeling sorry for the kid. Life's dealt him one crap hand after another."

"I've always felt bad for him, too, and I know Aaron does. That's a big part of why it's been so hard for him to let go of Erica. He has too much guilt dragging him down."

"Rogers hasn't changed a bit since he arrested you for kicking the shit out of Trey Holt, has he?" Henry shook his head, recalling the way the sheriff—then an officer with the Devyn Police Department—had pompously slapped the cuffs on Nick out in the hall in the view of half the crowded cafeteria on their college campus. No tact whatsoever. "God, he was full of himself, and that old son of a bitch had a hard on for Mackey, like he was the ringleader of that drug ring instead of a first-time driver."

"Don't forget how badly he handled the investigation into the murders of Mike Thompson and Carol Landers."

"I'm not likely to ever forget that. Poor Luke. I hope Aaron is serious about running against Rogers one of these days. The county would be a lot better off with our brother as sheriff."

Nick snorted. "That's for damned sure."

After the last of the logs were in the truck, Henry jumped down and stretched while Nick fetched two bottles of water from the cooler in the back of his truck. They sat on the tailgate and gazed up at the steep, forested wall above them, content to enjoy the quiet for a few minutes. The mid-September day was pleasant with a cool breeze wafting down from the peaks and carrying the promise of impending autumn—a perfect day to be out cutting firewood.

"You've been back to work on the ranch for two and a half weeks now," Nick said after a while. "How's it feel?"

"I'm working twice as hard for less money," Henry replied, "and I feel ten times better. I loved my job in Denver, but right now, this is what I need. And speaking of the ranch, is there any word on hiring a couple new hands?"

Nick shook his head. "No one who's responded is willing to do the work. I think Dad's trying to talk Austin McGuire into coming to work for us fulltime. Even if he agrees to it, though, we're still a hand short."

"At this rate, we may *have* to give up some of the old traditions." Henry glanced through the narrow gap in the walls of the ravine to the lower fields of their ranch at the beaverslide they'd used a week and a half ago to make the stacks of hay that now dotted the fields. "I'd hate to see the old dereks sit and rot."

"I would, too." Nick glanced at the wooden structure in the distance, then turned to Henry. "I'm a little surprised at you."

"Why? This is my home as much as it's yours... even if you and Beth will be the ones to take it over when Dad and Mom decide to retire. It's like Uncle James said. You can take a Hammond off the ranch, but you can't take the ranch out of the Hammond."

"That's not what I mean, Hen. Of course the Lazy H will always be your home."

"And I wasn't being a dick. I meant what I said."

"That's what surprises me. I *know* you love this place as much as the rest of us, but you've spent most of the last ten years trying to convince yourself otherwise."

Henry turned his water bottle around in his hand, staring at it without seeing it. "I guess getting a metaphorical kick in the balls forced me to admit that I was deluding myself."

"How are you doing with that? I know how much you love Dylan, but you seem to be handling it remarkably well."

"I have my moments, but I'm okay. Meeting Lindsay helped. A lot." He drained the rest of his water in one long gulp, crumpled the bottle and screwed the cap on, and set it beside him, then returned his gaze to the distant beaverslide.

"Have you talked to her since she left?" his brother inquired.

"A few times. We've sort of set up a twice-weekly schedule—Mondays and Thursdays, though not tonight. She and Skye are going out to dinner. I miss her a lot more than I thought I would, and it sucks, but even missing her is good for me because if I'm thinking about her, I'm not thinking about Dylan."

"That *is* good, Henry," Nick agreed. "And I'm glad to hear you're keeping the lines of communication open because it tells me you're smart enough to realize you need her right now."

Henry snorted. "Need is a strong word, Nick."

"Tell me I'm wrong."

Henry didn't admit that Nick was right, but he didn't lie and say his brother was wrong, either. Instead, he moved forward on the topic. "Her ex has been more of a prick than usual this week. It's almost like he's trying to make her pay for suggesting he give up his son even though it seems like that's exactly what he's wanted from the start. I didn't know he told her to get an abortion and that, when she refused, he wanted her to put Noah up for adoption. She didn't tell me that until after she went home to Washington."

Nick swore under his breath and leapt off the tailgate. He stalked away a few paces, and Henry noted a sudden and alarming stiffness about his brother.

"Nick?"

The older man turned back to face him and stuffed his hands in his pockets. Henry could almost hear the memories churning in his sibling's head. It was a few minutes before Nick regained his composure and again joined Henry on the tailgate.

"Sorry," he said. "That caught me off guard, made me remember those first hours and days after Trey raped Beth. If she'd gotten pregnant from it… she'd've had to face that same decision."

"I can't even fathom that kind of fear—not what Lindsay must've felt as a young mother and certainly not what Beth went through."

"I can. To some extent, anyhow. The worst of it for me was knowing there was nothing I could do to protect her from it, but I imagine that's nothing compared to what she felt."

"Thank God she didn't get pregnant."

Nick nodded. "I'm truly afraid I would've killed Trey if she had."

"I believe you would have, too. I remember how protective you became of her after that. I mean, you always

178

looked out for her, but that night changed everything."

"Yes, it did." Nick frowned. "What Beth went through was horrible, but it doesn't make Lindsay's struggles any less heartbreaking. I may not have spent much time with her, but it was pretty easy to see the damage her ex did and continues to do."

"I wish...." Henry shook his head, unable to put his desires into words.

"You wish what?" Nick prodded when Henry hadn't continued after more than a minute.

"I wish I could fix it for her. I wish I could protect her from him."

"You probably don't want to hear this yet because you want to put Mel behind you before you think about moving on—and believe it or not, I support you in that— but the fact that you want to take her troubles away suggests a much deeper connection than your bargain. I know you never felt that way for Mel, and I can tell you that I never felt the need to protect Michelle like I do Beth... and it has nothing to do with how strong the woman is, Henry, because Beth proved beyond a doubt that she's even stronger than Michelle is first when she reported the rape and then when she took the stand against Trey, and I'm damned sure Lindsay is stronger than Mel. It's instinctive, and you might want to take that into consideration when you're ready. In the meantime, get your ass back to work. This wood isn't going to cut and load itself, and I'd like to get home to my wife sometime before midnight because she's been hinting that it's time to give Will a sibling."

"You guys are *finally* thinking about having another baby?"

179

"I think so. There's a bit more urgency these days because we aren't getting any younger, and it's beginning to feel like now or never."

"I've never understood why you waited so long to have Will… and then to have another kid. Neither of you ever doubted that you wanted children like I did."

"We promised ourselves to savor every moment of our lives together and not rush anything." Nick grinned. "Dylan settled your mind, huh? In that case, we'd better get your firewood cut and loaded so you can get back to thinking about Lindsay and if she might be the one to make that happen for you."

Henry stared at his brother. For once in his life, he *wanted* to talk about his emotional train wrecks, but Nick made it quite clear that further discussion wasn't going to be allowed.

"Subtle, Nick. Real subtle."

Nick didn't take the bait, so Henry jumped to his feet and picked up his chainsaw.

His conversation with his brother occupied his mind while they finished filling both trucks with firewood. Nick was definitely right that he'd never felt a need to protect Mel. Sure, he'd wanted to make sure she was taken care of and had even enjoyed spoiling her until she started taking advantage of his generosity, but that was the extent of it.

It was a want, not a need.

Nick climbed into his truck, and Henry braced his hands on the open window. "Thanks for helping today."

"With what? The firewood or the advice?"

"Both."

Nick nodded in acknowledgement, then chuckled. "I

like this new you. I'm not sure what Lindsay did to bring it out of you, but it's a good change. It's nice to get to know my youngest brother again."

Henry jokingly grumbled about being the youngest by only a few minutes but appreciated the gentle teasing.

"Well, we'd best get this back to your house and unloaded so I can get home to my beautiful wife. We still have to stop down at the main house, too, to figure out who we can get to help bring the herds down next week."

Henry thumped the roof of Nick's cab and jogged over to his own. He slid in behind the wheel and gunned the engine, then followed his brother down the narrow, rocky road out of the ravine. The road hugged the base of the foothills even after it left the gulch until it turned into Billings Creek Road, at which point it smoothed out and widened. The driveway of the main ranch house was another mile down the road, which now followed Billings Creek through stands of cottonwoods and quaking aspen. In another week or two, the dark emerald leaves of those trees would turn to vibrant gold. Henry was looking forward to that as much as he was anticipating moving their herds down from the summer allotments with something akin to glee.

Lindsay would probably get a kick out of that, he mused as he turned into his parents' driveway.

When he parked beside Nick, he noted a beat-up old pickup parked next to Aaron's newer one. He didn't recognize it.

"Any idea whose truck that is?" Henry asked Nick as they climbed out of their pickups.

"Nope. Maybe Dad found a new hand while we were

out cutting firewood."

"Wouldn't that be nice?"

They headed inside and found everyone gathered in the kitchen. Henry stopped dead in his tracks when he spotted the guest leaning against the counter beside Aaron with his arms folded tightly across his chest and eyes wide with apprehension.

"What the hell is Jerry Mackey doing here?" Henry blurted.

He glanced over the kid, who met his gaze briefly and winced. His medium brown hair was longish and resembled a mop, but his green-tinged hazel eyes were clear and alert if wary. Twenty-two or so now, he'd filled out a bit since Henry had last seen him, but he was still skinny. At five-eight, he was only an inch taller than Tracie, which made him seem even smaller compared to her husband and sons than he was; John, Nick, Aaron, and Henry all stood four inches taller with thicker, more heavily muscled frames. *It's no wonder*, Henry mused, *that Aaron so easily overpowered the kid two years ago.*

He looked to his twin and noted a blossoming bruise on Aaron's jaw. "And what the hell happened to your face?"

"What do you think happened to my face?" Aaron replied. "Jerry and I settled our differences… and then I offered him a job on the ranch."

Henry lifted his brows in surprise. He had no hard feelings toward Jerry, but that didn't mean he'd ever imagined this outcome. At best, he'd hoped the kid would eventually get over his grudge against Aaron and leave him alone. Maybe he hadn't heard right. "You *what?*"

"We need an extra hand, and he needs work."

182

"What's his probation officer think of that?"

"He thought we were both nuts but decided it might be a good idea."

"I called Austin right after they arrived," John said. "He's willing to move into one of the bunkhouses and room with Jerry and teach him the ropes."

"You got Austin to agree to fulltime?" Henry asked.

"Yep. He's struggling a bit with his empty nest with Shane away at college, and it didn't take too much to convince him once I mentioned he'd have a new kid to train. Jerry doesn't know much about ranching, but he does know a bit about construction and maintenance, and he's willing to learn the rest. To start, he'll probably be working mostly with you, Henry, fixing things. We'll ease him into working with the livestock."

"Hope you can keep up, kid," Henry remarked lightly.

"I like to work," Jerry retorted with a spark of challenge.

"In that case, welcome to the Lazy H. I'm Henry, by the way—Aaron's twin."

Henry extended his hand, and for a moment, the kid eyed it disbelievingly. At last, he cautiously shook it.

"You're nervous, Jerry," Nick observed. "Why?"

"I...." Again Jerry shook his head and tried again. "I can't believe how nice you all are. I thought you'd all hate me for what happened to Aaron's wife."

"It was an accident," Nick said gently. "You won't find any animosity here, Jerry, but you *will* find a lot of sympathy. We haven't forgotten that you lost someone you loved that day, too, just like we did. Nor have we forgotten how Sheriff Rogers and his buddy the county attorney rail-roaded you."

"Believe me, kid," Henry said. "We've all had our issues with Rogers and *not* because Aaron works with him. You'll find he's not very popular here in Northstar."

"Thank you." The young man flashed a smile. "Would it be all right if everyone called me Jeremiah? The only two people who called me Jerry are my cousin and my brother, and I've never liked it."

"Of course it's all right," Tracie said. "We've just always heard you called Jerry. Truth be told, I like Jeremiah better, too."

"Thanks, Mrs. Hammond."

"None of that formality. You call us all by our first names."

"Anyhow," Henry interrupted. "I need to head home and get that firewood unloaded. Aaron, do you have a sec?"

Nodding, Aaron followed him into the living room. Henry turned to his twin, eyeing him for a moment before he spoke.

"This is quite the shocker."

Aaron shrugged. "It's time I move past what happened, don't you think?"

"Absolutely. I just didn't expect this to be the way you did it. Skye's had quite a remarkable influence on you."

"This has nothing to do with Skye. I'm finally in a place that I can forgive the past... and forgive myself for my part in what happened. Jerry isn't the only one who made mistakes. I did, too. I should've just let him go or fought harder to see that he got a fair deal because I knew in my gut that he was just a dumb kid in a bad situation with little choice but to do what his cousin told him to do. It was stupid to agree to running drugs for his cousin, but it was also hope in a life that was pretty much devoid of hope."

Henry chuckled. "Listen to you, waxing philosophical. Tell me something, Aaron. Why are you finally at the point that you can forgive the past? I'll tell you why. Skye. She's come into your life now that you've had sufficient time to grieve and opened your eyes again to the good in the world. That's the truth whether you want to admit it or not."

"Now who's waxing philosophical?"

Henry embraced his brother. "It's good to see my twin coming back again. I'd love to stay and chat, but—"

"Yeah, I know. Lindsay's supposed to be calling."

"Actually, no. She's out to dinner with Skye, so we agreed she wouldn't call tonight."

"Bummed?"

"Very, but I'm also hungry, and *that* is why I'm going to call it a day. We'll talk more about our lovely ladies later, though, all right? I still owe you a beer at the Bedspread since I ditched you on my first night back."

"I'll hold you to that, Hen."

Henry ducked into the kitchen just long enough to bid farewell to everyone and grabbed Nick so they could get the firewood unloaded. They drove to his house, and while they tossed the blocks into a pile Henry would stack in his woodshed later, they spoke little. The only mention they made of Jerry—Jeremiah—Mackey was to comment on the "interesting" development. Henry was running low on energy and didn't have any to spare on things other than thoughts of Lindsay. There would be plenty of time later to see how or if hiring Jeremiah would work out.

After Nick left for home, Henry trudged into his house.

His first inclination was to sprawl on the couch and wonder how many sore muscles he was going to have tomorrow—muscles that would've gotten him through a day of cutting firewood like it was nothing before he'd left the ranch in search of adventure in the big city. Admitting that he was either getting soft or old… or both, he ignored the call of the couch and headed to the kitchen to pull something out to cook for dinner. He glanced toward the answering machine and saw it flashing with a new message. While he defrosted a small package of elk steak, he hit play, thinking perhaps Lindsay had decided to call after all before she and Noah headed to dinner with Skye.

The message wasn't from Lindsay.

"Henry, it's Mel."

Immediately, he reached toward the delete button.

"Please don't delete this," she continued.

He hesitated with his finger hovering and his teeth clenched as a stabbing pain lanced through his chest at the sound of her voice and the memories attached to it. There was a long pause, and he had plenty of time to wonder if she had needed to search for something she could say that would prevent him from erasing her message. He knew he should just delete it, but a masochistic curiosity seized him, and he couldn't seem to make his finger do the job.

"I really need to talk to you. About the salon and the money I owe you and… other things. Please call me back. I… Just call. Okay?"

Henry frowned at his answering machine long after

Melanie's message ended. There were no others. His gut warned him to leave well enough alone and ignore her plea, but she *did* still owe him money, and if he ever hoped to get it back, he'd have to call her someday.

Do I even want it back?

Lindsay's face suddenly appeared in his head, and for the first time since he'd loaned Mel the ten grand for the salon, he considered writing off the debt... and *not* because it would be less painful than dealing with her. Lindsay's plight had given him a new perspective, and it made him feel guilty as hell to think that paying back the debt might put Melanie and Dylan in a financial bind. He might not want anything to do with her, but he wasn't callous, and at any rate, he didn't need the money.

It was probably stupid, but he called her back.

"Henry," she breathed when he announced himself. "I wasn't sure you'd return my call."

"I nearly didn't. What do you want, Mel? And don't try to draw me into conversation. Just say what you need to say."

"Tamlyn found a new partner for the salon who wants to buy me out."

"What does this have to do with me?"

"I'll be able to pay you back... except I don't want to be bought out. I love running the salon."

"Again, what does this have to do with me?"

"I need your advice, even though I'm sure you'll tell me to sell my part of the salon so you can get your money back."

"I *am* inclined to think both you and the salon would be better off if you sell, yes, but not because I want my money back. The fact of the matter is that you're not a businesswoman. I'm not trying to be mean, Mel, but you've never been great with money, and you can barely balance a checkbook, so why did you figure you could keep records for a business?"

Silence met his observations.

"On the other hand, you're a great stylist, and as I recall, you only wanted to partner up with Tam so you didn't have to pay such ridiculous station rent. Do you actually love running the salon… or do you love that doing so makes being a stylist a little cheaper?"

Mel didn't respond immediately, and hearing her sigh, he braced himself for what he had no doubt was coming.

"I miss you," she murmured. "I miss being able to ask you about things like this. And Dylan misses you, too."

"I'm sorry, Mel. I am, but that isn't my problem anymore. I wish you the best, but I can't be your safety net. Have you located Dylan's father yet?"

"Yes, I have. And he wants nothing to do with us."

Henry wasn't sure he wanted to know, but he asked anyhow. "Who is it?"

Again, she hesitated, and he suspected it was someone he knew.

"Doug is Dylan's father."

Briefly, a pang of betrayal stabbed him, but it was gone in a moment. He gave himself a minute to absorb the information, and in that time, the flash of bitterness disappeared. Of all the people she could have gotten pregnant by, at least it was someone she cared for and who cared for her and Dylan. Relief surged. Doug was a good man.

"You have proof?"

"A paternity test confirmed it." Mel let out a sob and quickly choked it back. "He wants nothing to do with us."

That didn't sound at all like the friend Henry knew, but he wouldn't have thought Doug would jump into bed with Mel so soon after she and Henry had broken up. Of course, the news that he was a daddy was still probably sinking in, and Henry imagined his friend was angry that Mel hadn't bothered to consider he might be Dylan's father, instead choosing to assume Henry was. Unintentional perhaps, but that was a stinging insult to Doug.

"I strongly suggest you find a way to convince him otherwise," Henry said, "and soon because being a single parent is only going to get more difficult as Dylan grows."

"I'm finding that out."

The thought of her adorable son needing something and not getting it gnawed at him, and before he could begin to consider the consequences, he said, "Listen, Mel. If you find yourself in a bind—and I mean a *real bind*—I'll help. But don't call me unless you have no other choice. I don't want Dylan to go without something he needs, but neither do I want you to lean on me. It's time you learn to stand on your own feet. And the first step you need to take is talking to Doug. No excuses like I know you're tempted to make. Just do it."

"Thank you, Henry. I promise I will pay you back... even if I decide not to sell my half of the salon to this woman Tam wants to bring in."

"I'm glad to hear it." He glanced at his watch. "I need to go fix myself dinner. Take care, Mel."

"You, too."

After ending the call, Henry hunched over the counter with his forehead pillowed on his folded arms. What in the hell had he just done? He *knew* better than to leave the door open to Mel even that fraction of an inch.

Jerking upright, he took the cordless into his bedroom and sprawled on his bed, staring up at the ceiling for what felt like an eternity as his generosity warred with his self-preservation. Why did his every dealing with Mel leave him torn like this? The only time he was torn about Lindsay came when he tried to keep their temporary bargain temporary while everything in him wanted to further explore the intoxicating chemistry—physical *and* emotional—between them.

He glanced at the picture sitting beneath the lamp on his nightstand. Skye had printed it out for him, a shot she'd taken of him and Lindsay dancing at Vince and Evie's wedding reception. Even then, barely twenty-four-hours after they'd met, the connection between them was obvious. The smiles on both their faces and the way they had eyes only for each other, oblivious to everything and everyone around them….

At least Mel hadn't asked him to come back. He wasn't in the least tempted, but that didn't mean he had the energy to explain to her why he couldn't even though his reasons were very simple. He didn't and hadn't ever loved Mel, and even if he had, his hope for a relationship with Lindsay—just the *hope* of something with her—eclipsed it.

He pinched his eyes closed and massaged the bridge of his nose as a million thoughts and emotions danced through is head in a dizzying tango. What a day. Suddenly bone-tired in a way that had nothing to do with the day's physical labor, he dozed off with his dinner still sitting un-cooked in the microwave. Soon after, the ringing of his phone snapped him out of a pleasant dream about Lindsay, and he glanced at the cordless handset's small screen to see her number displayed. Smiling, he answered.

Ten

"I STILL CAN'T BELIEVE you said that to Skye," Lindsay said to her son as they climbed the crumbling steps to the house they shared with Chelsea and Spencer. "At least she waited until she *was* divorced before she moved on to a new man, which is a lot more than Darren did. That was so incredibly rude, what you said, that I can't believe it came out of my son's mouth."

"How many times do I have to say I'm sorry? I didn't mean to be rude. It just sorta popped out."

"Funny how things like that *just sorta pop out* of your mouth after you talk to your father. I guess that means you're over hating him."

"Well, he *is* my dad," Noah snapped. "And you can't take that away from him."

"Yep. There he is," Lindsay muttered. With fury

snapping through her, she whirled on Noah and pointed a shaking finger at him. "Let me tell you something, Noah. I don't want to take that away from him. I never did. I have *always* wanted him to be a parent and to do what every parent should—to take care of his child instead of fighting over every dime and every visit. But enough of this. I'm not going to fight with you about it."

The front door was unlocked, so Lindsay pushed it open and gestured for Noah to enter ahead of her. Chelsea and her boyfriend were making out on the couch but jerked apart as soon as Lindsay stepped inside and shut the door. Chelsea smiled sheepishly. After pausing to regard the couple with brows lifted and a faint sneer of disgust, Noah strode toward the room he shared with Spencer.

"Sorry," Chelsea's boyfriend mumbled.

Lindsay shrugged. "For what? God knows he sees enough of that on TV and… everywhere."

"Um, Lindsay?" Chelsea said. "We have some big—"

A commotion in the boys' bedroom drew Lindsay's attention, and she jogged down the short hall. She popped her head in the doorway to see her son and Spencer wrestling on the floor, and it was immediately clear that they weren't playing. Red-faced and crying, Noah struggled to overpower his enemy while Spencer thrashed violently to free himself. Lindsay barreled into the room with Chelsea right behind her, wrapped her arm around her son's waist, and hoisted him off the ground, nearly losing her grip on him when he pushed off the side of his bed with his foot. When had her little boy grown so strong?

"Noah Ulrich! Enough!"

"He stole my crystals, Mom! The ones you and your

friend Henry found and brought home for me."

"I didn't steal anything, you stupid brat!" Spencer spat.

He'd been face down, and when he rolled onto his back with his mother's assistance, Lindsay saw his bloodied nose and swore under her breath. Chelsea called for her boyfriend and asked him to bring her a paper towel.

"Yes, you did!" Noah yelled. "They were in my mom's room when we left for dinner. I made sure to put them back there because I didn't want you to take them. Because you always take my things and wreck them!"

"Spencer?" Chelsea asked. "Is that true?"

Silence. The older boy glared at Noah, and his lack of response was all the confirmation Lindsay needed. The crystals in question were scattered across the carpet, glinting evidence of Spencer's deed. Noah finally stopped fighting Lindsay, and she let him go so he could pick up his treasures. After a moment, she stooped to assist him, using the task to help her rein in her immediate instinct to defend her son. Chelsea's boyfriend brought the paper towels, and Chelsea took her son into the bathroom to get him cleaned up.

After they'd gathered all the crystals they could find—some were certainly lost elsewhere in the room and wouldn't be found unless everything was moved out—Lindsay sat down on Noah's bed and asked him to sit with her.

"I know you and Spencer don't get along and that he's always taking your things and breaking them, but do you really think hitting him was the right way to deal with it?"

"Well, nothing else works."

"Noah."

He gave her a hooded look, and the wounded pride in his eyes threatened to demolish her shaky composure. She held her ground, and after almost two full minutes of the silent staring contest, he gave in. His boyishly narrow shoulders slumped and his head drooped in defeat.

"I'm sorry, Mom."

"I'm sorry, too, bud." She wrapped both arms around him and hugged him, relieved when he leaned into her. "I know it's hard. You want to sleep in my room tonight?"

"Please."

"And I'll make sure I hide your crystals in the top of my closet, okay? I have to say, though, that I'm a bit surprised they're so special to you that you'd get into a fight over them. I mean, they're just rocks."

He shrugged. "Every time I see them, I remember how happy you were when you told me about finding them with your friend Henry. I liked how you smiled like you couldn't help it."

That was *not* the response she'd expected, and the sentiment behind it made her heart ache with longing and pride. "How'd I get so lucky to have such a wonderful son?"

"I dunno." He sighed heavily. "I really am sorry for fighting with Spencer. He just makes me so mad."

"I know, baby."

"Will I ever get to meet Henry?"

Lindsay rested her cheek on top of his head and hugged him tighter for a moment. "I don't know, but I hope so." She leaned away from him and brushed his hair back

195

from his forehead before inspecting his face. He was going to need a haircut soon. "Back to you and fighting. Are you all right? You don't look hurt."

"I'm fine. I didn't give him a chance to hit me."

"I'm glad you're okay, but please don't ever do that again. Fighting never solves anything and in fact just makes things even worse. Get your PJs out and head up to my room while I go talk to Chelsea, all right?"

Noah nodded, and Lindsay stepped out of the room. Chelsea and Spencer had already left the bathroom, and she found them sitting with Chelsea's boyfriend on the couch. Wearily, Lindsay sat in the desk chair and faced them. Now that he was cleaned up, Spencer didn't look so bad. His pride was bruised, she noted, but as he'd just been outmatched by a boy a year younger and ten pounds lighter than him, it wasn't too hard to figure out why. She heard Noah leave his room and close the door of hers behind him and sighed with relief. A moment later, Chelsea quietly told Spencer to return to his room.

"Anyhow…" the other woman began. "Before the boys got into a fight, I was about to tell you that Dave and I have some big news."

Of course we're not going to talk about the fact that our sons just got into a brawl, Lindsay thought with an inward sneer. *Which is exactly why Spencer keeps stealing and ruining Noah's belongings. What's to convince him to stop?*

"What kind of news?" she heard herself ask. She sounded just as tired as she felt.

Chelsea lifted her left hand and beamed. It took Lindsay a moment to notice the almost obnoxiously large diamond solitaire glittering on her roommate's finger and even longer to recognize what it meant.

"You're engaged?"

With a squeal, Chelsea replied, "Yes! Dave proposed at dinner tonight, and I said yes. Obviously."

"Congratulations," Lindsay said flatly. She probably sounded like she didn't care—not too far from the truth right at that moment—so she sat up a little straighter and attempted a convincingly enthusiastic smile. "I mean that. I'm happy for you both, but I'm tired, so forgive me if I don't sound like it."

"There's something else," Dave said, clearing his throat nervously. "I've asked Chelsea and Spencer to move in with me."

Panic seized Lindsay. Move in…? That meant she and Noah would have to find a new place to rent or a roommate because there was no way she'd be able to afford this place on her own. "When?"

"This week."

"This… week?"

"That's right," Chelsea answered gleefully. "Isn't it wonderful?"

"Yeah… wonderful." Lindsay rose slowly to her feet. "Congrats again. Excuse me."

Without pausing to wonder why, she grabbed the cordless phone and headed to her bedroom. She sought sanctuary—a place where she could cry without an audience—but with Noah sitting cross-legged on her bed counting his crystals to see how many were missing, she wasn't going to find it. He glanced up at her, and she pasted her well-practiced fake smile on her face and asked him if he'd be all right by himself while she stepped out onto the back deck. He nodded and returned to his task without noticing anything unusual about her demeanor.

Still clutching the phone, Lindsay slipped out the back door. The weather gods were smiling on her tonight; the skies were clear, something that didn't happen often in the middle of October. She sank onto one of the cheap folding chairs she'd splurged on at the start of summer and rested her head against the back of it. What were she and Noah going to do? A few days didn't give her enough time to find a new roommate and it sure as hell didn't give her enough time to find a new house. She might be able to pay Chelsea's portion of the rent for next month, but she certainly wouldn't be able to scrape together the money to pay all the utilities, too. She hadn't yet paid back the money to her savings account that she'd spent on her trip to Montana.

Montana.…

It was with a groan half of guilt and half of longing that the name entered her mind, and she lifted her gaze to the darkening sky. In the twilight, a couple stars twinkled, but she knew there wouldn't be nearly as many when the dim glow of dying day faded into black night as there would be in the sky over Northstar, and right now, she dearly missed those stars. She missed a lot more about Montana, and though she and Henry agreed she wouldn't call him tonight, she found herself dialing his number, needing the peace the mere sound of his voice never failed to bring her.

"Thought you weren't going to call tonight," he mumbled sleepily.

"I woke you up again," she said, immediately regretting her selfish need. "But it's not *that* late."

"It's been a long day, and I dozed off. Apparently,

198

I'm getting old and soft, too."

"Say it isn't so."

"It is. Spent the day cutting firewood with Nick, and I am beat. Kinda sad that my older brother can outwork me these days."

"If he weren't just a couple years older, I might agree with you. I should let you go so you can rest up."

"No, you shouldn't. I'm glad you called. I'm glad because I love talking to you, but I'm also glad because I talked to Mel a little bit ago, and I wanted to hear your voice."

At once, her worries slipped away as curiosity needled her. "You talked to Mel? Who called whom, and what about?"

"She called me. What, you don't actually think I'd be crazy enough to call her?"

"No, I'm just checking. What did she want?"

"For one, her friend Tam has someone she wants to bring into the salon... someone who can and wants to buy Mel out of it."

"Which means you'd get the money you loaned her back, right?"

"If she decides to sell, yes. But it doesn't sound like she wants to. I of course told her she should. That's not the most interesting piece of news she had, though. It turns out that my old friend and coworker Doug is Dylan's father."

"Wait. Didn't she go out with him before she and you got together? They were together for a pretty long time, weren't they?"

"Yeah, almost four years. I thought they'd get married, but then they ended up breaking up."

"Why?"

"I don't really know."

"That's good news, though, isn't it, that Doug is Dylan's father? I assume, since he's a friend of yours, that you approve of him, which means you won't have to feel so guilty for leaving Dylan now."

"Yes and no. It seems Doug doesn't want anything to do with either Mel or Dylan, and I'm pretty sure I know why."

"He's pissed at her for assuming you were Dylan's father."

"That's my guess."

He sighed, and even seven hundred miles away, she could picture him frowning and wondered what else he'd said to Mel. Acquainted with his generous nature, she had a pretty good idea. "You didn't offer to help Mel, did you?"

He laughed. "Am I that transparent?"

"Only to me because we constructed our friendship on a foundation of almost embarrassingly intimate honesty. You have a heart of gold, Henry, and that isn't to be faulted, but you *do* remember why you decided to leave her in the first place, don't you?"

"Yeah, I do."

"And you do realize that offering to help her isn't going to achieve that, right?"

"I know that, but I got to thinking about you and how hard it is for you to support your son… and then I thought about Dylan needing something and not getting it, and the offer just slipped out. I told her not to call me unless she had no other choice."

Lindsay wanted to tell him he was a fool and that Mel would likely be calling up for every little "need," but she didn't because she loved his devotion even to a son who wasn't his. He wanted to do the right thing by a boy he still obviously loved even though Mel wouldn't do the right thing by him.

"You know what you have to do, right?"

"Tell her to piss off?"

"No. You need to help her convince Doug to step up and help with Dylan because that's the only way she'll stop leaning on you. Think you can do that?"

"I have my doubts. I know what he's feeling right now if from the opposite side."

"Does it bother you that she slept with him?"

"Not really. Why should it? Her body, her choice what she does with it."

"I admire your stance on that. And I also have faith that you'll find a way to convince Doug to take responsibility for Dylan."

Henry sighed. "I wish you were here right now or I was there. It'd be a really good night to hold you... or make love to you."

"Yes, it would. I should give you a heads up, I suppose, because I let it slip to Skye that you and I slept together on my last night in Montana."

"Why should I need a heads up?"

"Well, she might tell your brother...."

"Who cares? I'm sure he's already figured that out. We didn't exactly keep it a secret from my family what we intended to do."

"No, we didn't."

There was a pause on the other end of the line, and she wondered what subtle cue he'd picked up on.

"Everything all right?"

"Not really."

He waited patiently for her to elaborate, and after a moment, she did. She told him about Noah's snotty attitude after his phone call to his father before they'd gone out to dinner with Skye, and she told him about Noah getting into a fight with Spencer over the crystals, detailing how she'd underestimated how strong her son was and how touched she'd been by his reason for cherishing his crystals. Then she told Henry about Chelsea's engagement to Dave and her roommate's plans to move out within the next week. Henry responded with the exact note of concern she needed to hear, and as he rattled off ideas about what she could do—all things she'd already considered—some of the strain slipped away.

"What about moving into your parents' place? Didn't you say they were planning to snowbird it in Arizona now that your dad is fully retired? As I recall, they asked you to look after their house while they're gone."

"Yes, they did, but housesitting and moving into their house aren't the same thing."

"How do you figure?"

"I can't move into their house, Henry."

"Why not?"

"Because they've only rented that condo through March."

"Lame excuse. What's the real reason?"

Lindsay pulled her feet into the chair and curled her free arm around her knees. "It's admitting defeat... admitting that I can't make it on my own."

"Bullshit. That's your stubborn pride talking, and

you're smarter than that."

"Henry...."

"I *know* your parents have on numerous occasions asked you to stay with them while they were still home, and maybe you can argue that moving back in with them is the same as giving up your independence, but this.... You'll be housesitting for them. It's not a defeat, Lindsay. It's a smart financial move that might just get you ahead. You don't have time to find a new roommate or a new, cheaper place to live, so this is a perfect solution. If *nothing* else, it'll give you six months to look for the *right* living situation for you and Noah instead of the fastest one."

Lindsay tried to find an argument to counter his logic but couldn't. She glanced over her shoulder in the sliding glass door at the dimly lit kitchen, and that sensation of not belonging here again descended on her. She hadn't called her parents' house home in years, but it was certainly more home than this place had ever been or would ever be.

"Besides," Henry continued, "I'm sure Noah will be relieved not to have to share a room with that brat Spencer... or anyone else."

"There's that, too," she agreed. On a whim, she asked, "Would you like to say hi to him? I know he's been wanting to thank you personally for the gifts."

"Sure, if you're all right with that."

"Yeah. Hold on a minute."

Lindsay slipped quietly into the house noticing that Chelsea had turned off most of the lights and figured Dave had left and Chelsea had gone to bed early. When she passed her roommate's room, however, the door was open and there was no one inside. Then she glanced out the window and saw that Chelsea's car was gone along with Dave's. Shrugging, she joined Noah in her own room and, holding the mouthpiece of the phone against her chest, she asked if Chelsea had said anything to him before she'd left.

"Just to tell you she and Spencer were gonna spend the night at Dave's. She saw you were on the phone and didn't wanna interrupt. Is that Henry?"

"Yes, it is. Do you want to talk to him?"

"Yeah."

To Henry, she said, "Here's my son."

She handed the phone to Noah and leaned against the headboard to listen, wondering if this was a good idea. It hadn't been so long since Logan had broken up with her that she'd forgotten how hurt Noah had been by his rejection. She instinctively believed that even if things went south with Henry that he'd never do that to her son, but she didn't ever want her son to feel that disappointment again. Still... watching his face as he thanked Henry for the gifts and—to her surprise—for making his mom happy, she couldn't suppress the hope and excitement that blossomed. It was only a phone call, but they hit it off quite well, talking mostly about football but also about the ranch, which Noah expressed an interest in seeing. While they talked, he was her beautiful boy again, and the sarcastic, rude attitude he'd donned after talking with his father this afternoon disappeared. Finally, he thanked Henry for the chat and said he'd like to talk again and would also like to meet him in person. At last, he handed the phone back to Lindsay.

"Wonderful young man you have there, Lindsay," Henry said.

"Most of the time, yes, he is. Thank you."

"I wanted to say goodnight to you before I hung up. It's getting late here, and I should probably go cook that elk steak that I started defrosting so it doesn't go to waste even though I think I'm too tired to be hungry any more."

"Do you have to? I don't want to say goodbye yet."

"Neither do I, but I keep trying to tell you that I'm not a spring chicken anymore. I can't run all day and all night."

"One of these days, we may have to disprove that." Remembering that her son was sitting just a few feet away and listening intently to their conversation, she added, "But not tonight. I'll talk to you Monday."

"Not soon enough," he murmured. "Good night, gorgeous."

After they hung up, she set the cordless on her nightstand and smiled. The way he said that at the end of every call made her forget her troubles and reminded her of what he'd set out to show her when he'd agreed to their bargain—that she was more than a broke single mother and that she was a woman both strong and beautiful. *Yes, Henry, you definitely upheld your end of the bargain*, she thought, recalling what he'd asked her just before she'd boarded the plane for home.

"He's really nice, isn't he, Mom?" Noah asked.

"Yes, he is."

"I know because you always smile when you talk to him or about him."

"Do I?"

"Yep. You know, it'd be all right with me if you wanted to go out with him. Like boyfriend and girlfriend."

Laughing softly, she hugged him. In this moment,

with Henry's faith in her and her son's love, she didn't have room left in her mind to worry about her housing situation.

"I love you, Noah."

"I love you, too, Mom."

Eleven

HENRY SWORE WHEN HE stepped out of the relative warmth of the barn into the frigid early-November evening. The brief warm spell that had melted most of the six inches of new snow had vanished, pushed out of the region by a powerful cold front. What was left of the white stuff had frozen into crunchy, ragged patches. He guessed the temperature must be in the mid teens above zero but falling quickly. The forecast called for sub-zero lows tonight. There was a time when he'd bemoaned the bitter cold, but he was still too glad to be home to experience them to complain today… and too busy wishing Lindsay was here with him to enjoy a cozy fire in his wood stove. As summer had faltered and bowed to golden autumn and his job on the ranch had shifted from repairs to helping his brothers, father, Austin, Jeremiah, and the Lazy H's two part-time hands drive the herds down from the summer allotments, there had been so much he wished Lindsay were here to experience. When he was willing to acknowledge it—like now, with the moody gray snow clouds hanging over the valley and obscuring the mountains behind curtains of cold white—missing her had become an ever-present ache in his chest. Their now thrice-weekly phone calls weren't enough.

"Witch-tit cold," he heard Jeremiah mutter behind him.

"Not yet, but getting there fast." Henry glanced over his shoulder and smiled. The kid's expression wasn't of resentment but of amusement. "And I bet you'd rather be freezing your balls off out here than sitting in that cell."

Jeremiah flashed a grin. "Damned right."

"Glad to hear you confirm it because you and I get to feed the cows tomorrow morning."

"I guess it's a good thing we got the blower motor for the heater in the feed truck fixed today."

"Yep. Thanks for the help, by the way. I can't remember the last new hire who worked as hard as you do."

"I have a lot to earn back." Jeremiah shrugged. "Besides, it feels good. I'm tired when I go to bed at night, but I know it's because I've accomplished something."

"Amen, brother."

It had taken Jeremiah a while to get to a point that he could keep up with Henry, but it had taken Henry at least that long to rebuild the strength and endurance ranch work required, so he could sympathize. Jeremiah had put on some muscle in that time and no longer looked like a strong wind could blow him away, and the changes had caught the eye of a couple of the local girls. He was still almost annoyingly humble most of the time, but he was also starting to open up a lot, and Henry genuinely liked the kid. When he chose to let his guard down, he fit right in with the Hammond clan, and if he chose to stick around for a while, Henry saw him being folded into the family. It was already happening. Tracie had developed a soft spot for him almost immediately, and Henry suspected Jeremiah reminded her a lot of her sons at that age. Confirmation of that suspicion came when they strolled into the kitchen of the main house and Tracie embraced them both without even a hitch of hesitation and told Jeremiah to go get cleaned up for dinner with exactly the same maternal fondness that warmed her voice when she told Henry the same.

"Dinner's ready. We're just waiting for Aaron and Skye to get here."

Anticipation heated Henry's blood, and he shoved Jeremiah toward the bathroom at the bottom of the stairs to wash the smudges of grease and oil from his hands and forearms. Henry waited his turn, glancing frequently and anxiously out the kitchen window at the driveway. Skye's stay in the family's vacation rental had ended the first week of October, and she'd gone home to Washington to tackle the mountain of work piling up at her photography studio. In the month she'd been gone, it had felt like a part of the family was missing, a sensation deepened by the changes in Aaron. Henry had his twin back. The perpetual melancholy that had radiated from him had been replaced by a pleasing determination and a predisposition for laughter.

After Henry's hands were scrubbed as clean as they were going to get tonight, he ventured back into the kitchen to help his mother and Beth set the table. When Jeremiah also stepped in to help, the women stood back to watch with matching smiles of gratitude.

The Hammond household definitely had an air of festivity, like today was some major holiday like Thanksgiving or Christmas, and Henry thought it was appropriate since they were—he hoped—welcoming Skye *home*. He hadn't talked to Aaron about when, exactly, his twin might take that first step toward officially bringing her into the family, but it was written in every grinning line of his face any time Skye was mentioned.

Hearing a vehicle, Henry glanced out the window again and spied his brother's truck slowing to a stop beside his own. When Aaron stepped out, walked around to open Skye's door, and kissed her as soon as she was outside, Henry grinned and turned away as envy spiked. His brother deserved every second of the happiness Skye brought him, but Henry couldn't deny that seeing them together made him ache for Lindsay. Time and distance had definitely *not* made his heart or his body forget her, and the uncertainty over when he might see her again incited a distracting restlessness.

"They're here," he announced, striding into the living room where everyone else had gathered to wait. "So we probably ought to mosey in the direction of the table."

Everyone was seated and ready to eat by the time Aaron and Skye decided to join them. A swirl of frigid air wafted into the cheerful warmth of the house, announcing their arrival as clearly as Henry's words. Rosy-cheeked with eyes glittering with the glow of new love, they ambled into the kitchen hand in hand. Everyone greeted Skye with a hug and welcomed her home in turn, and Aaron's five-year-old daughter enthusiastically launched herself from her chair into Skye's waiting arms. It pleased Henry to see that Skye was as glad to be reunited with the girl as she was to see Aaron again.

Their love might be too new for her to trust it yet, Henry mused, recalling Aaron's words on the matter shortly after she'd left for Washington in October, *but she wants to.*

She brought out the proof copy of the photography book she was working on about the traditions of the Lazy H, and Henry made the appropriate compliments—easy to do because the book was gorgeous and somehow managed to capture everything he and his family loved about their ranch and their way of life—but he was far more interested in Skye herself, most particularly her noticeably bare left hand. When he had a moment, he pulled Aaron aside.

"Well? Did you ask her?"

Aaron lifted a brow. "Ask her what?"

"You haven't, you dumbass."

Aaron sighed but said nothing.

"But you *are* going to ask her."

"That's the plan. Probably Christmas."

"If not before." Henry winked and gripped his twin's shoulder, so glad to hear those words that he couldn't put together an adequate response to express it. At last, he settled for an early congratulation. "Guess I was right about thinking with your dick."

"Maybe so, but I'll go you one better." Aaron met his gaze head on with a fierceness that made Henry lean back in surprise. "You've got something special going on with Lindsay Miller—and don't try to tell me again she was just a fling. I know you've talked with her on the phone at least a couple times a week since she left Northstar. Thinking with your dick got you into that mess with Melanie, so try thinking with your heart this time. It's a damned sight smarter."

To punctuate his statement, Aaron poked Henry in the chest.

Ordinarily, Henry would've chuckled at his brother's closing quip, but it was too accurate to be funny. Instead, he frowned thoughtfully as his twin returned to his seat beside Skye. A plot hatched, and he asked his father and Nick to speak with him in the kitchen for a few minutes.

"What's up?" Nick asked, leaning against the counter beside the sink.

"Do you think work around here has slowed down enough for me to take a leave of absence from the ranch?" Henry inquired. "We've got Jeremiah now, who is perfectly capable of handling any repairs while I'm away, and Hoyt said he'd like a few more hours."

"Depends on why you're leaving and how long you're planning to be gone," John replied.

"The answer to the first is Lindsay."

Nick's brows lifted in surprise. "I thought you said that mess with Melanie and Doug is still up in the air. And didn't you just send a bunch of winter clothes for Dylan just yesterday?"

"That's something I'm going to take care of in a minute. As to how long I'll be gone... I'm thinking until Christmas."

"Why Christmas?"

"For one, the plan is for Skye to join us, and I'd like Lindsay and Noah to be here, too. I think they'd all like that—being able to spend the holidays together with Evie.

And I'd like to invite her parents as well. As long as it's all right with you both and the rest of the family, of course. The rental cabin is open for all of December isn't it?"

"Yes, it is. Can't imagine why anyone would have a problem with that," John remarked. "Maybe I'm getting ahead of myself, but I think Nick will agree that Lindsay is the kind of woman we all hope you'll settle down with."

"The wild card of the family wants to bring a woman home to our family Christmas," Nick said, "and I'd say that's a damned fine thing to celebrate."

"I hope so."

"Go make whatever phone calls you need to make," John added. "We'll keep the ranch running while you're gone, but you'd better put your time off to good use."

"Thanks, Dad."

John returned to the table to tell Tracie to expect more company for Christmas. If the broad smile she tossed her son's way was anything to go by, she heartily approved. Nick didn't say anything else to him, only clapped him on the shoulder and rejoined their family at the table. Henry snatched the cordless off the kitchen counter, slipped into his coat, and stepped outside. Exhaling in a silvery cloud, he punched in Doug's number. His friend answered on the second ring.

"Y'ello," he greeted.

"It's Henry."

"What do you want now? I told you I—"

"I'm done playing games, Doug. I am still supporting Mel and Dylan, and that's not right when Dylan has a father who has the means to do it."

"Whose fault is that? You don't have to support

them."

"Someone does."

"Not my problem."

"Uh, yeah, actually it is. I know for a fact that she didn't make that kid on her own, and so do you. I need to be done with this so I can move on with my life. Here's my ultimatum. Either you grow up and admit that you have a son—a beautiful, amazing son who deserves your love and support—or I'm going to pay for a lawyer for Mel so she can get what she needs for Dylan from you."

"You wouldn't."

"You bet your ass I would. I'm not saying you have to marry Mel or otherwise involve yourself with her. I'm saying you need to be a father because, like it or not, you *are* one."

Silence.

"I know exactly what you're feeling right now—well, the flipside of it. You're angry and insulted that she didn't even consider that you might be Dylan's father."

"How the hell do you know how that feels?"

"I love that little boy, Doug, and all that time, I believed he was my son. I wrapped that love around me so tightly that when it turned out to be a lie it damn near choked the life out of me."

"She never even *mentioned* I might be his father, and she made it sound after like she was already pregnant when I slept with her. Do you have any idea how insulting that is? How much *that* hurts? She chose you over me without a second thought."

Henry winced at the pain in the other man's voice, all too familiar with it.

214

"So that's it, then. You're pissed that she picked me over you." Henry inhaled as deeply as the cold air allowed. A light blinked on in his brain, and the whole sloppy situation came instantly into focus. "You might want to ask yourself why that matters so much."

Again, no response. Henry paced while he waited in an attempt to warm his limbs. Finally, when it became apparent that Doug either couldn't or wouldn't reply, he spoke again.

"Why did you and Mel break up in the first place? You were together for almost four years, for God's sake."

"We were young," Doug replied so quietly that Henry almost didn't catch what he said. "Neither of us wanted to settle down."

"That's it? No irreconcilable differences? No earth-shattering betrayals? Just the impatient curiosity of youth." Henry shook his head. "I've always wondered."

"Mel never said?"

"No, and I got the feeling you were a taboo subject, so we never talked about it." Henry wandered around to the side of the house and sat on the picnic table. It was bare of the snow that had coated it just last night, but even through his insulated Carhartt work pants, the cold wood chilled his legs. "You know I'm not a religious man, but maybe this is God's way of bringing the two of you back together. You'd best figure out whatever the hell it is you need to figure out because I'm going to wipe this fiasco from my life by any means necessary."

For the third time, Henry received no answer, so he offered a friendly goodbye and immediately dialed the next number he needed to call because he wasn't so sure of himself that he'd start the process of finding a place to stay in Washington until he was certain Lindsay was amenable to the idea.

"Well, hi there, cutie pie," she purred. "I wasn't expecting to hear from you for a couple hours yet. You can't tell me dinner with your family is over already."

"No, it isn't," he replied. For a moment, all his plans fluttered out of his head, replaced by the now-familiar joy of hearing her voice again, and he found himself asking how she was adjusting to living in her parents' house now that she'd been in it a month.

"My pride hates to admit this, but it's been great. Much less stressful, for sure, and Noah loves having his room and me to himself."

"See? It was a good idea."

"Yeah, it was, and honestly, I don't feel like I'm living off my parents because I'm still paying the utilities and setting aside money for the property taxes just like I would if this was *my* paid-off house instead of theirs. That helps."

"Whatever eases that guilty conscience of yours," he joked. "Can I say hello to Noah real quick before I get to my reason for calling earlier than planned?"

"He's actually down on the beach with the neighbors and their son."

"Good for him. How's everything else going?"

"Good other than a customer who seems to think he needs to be my knight in shining armor."

"The one you mentioned when we talked the other day?"

"The very same. He brought me a rose today."

Disappointment filtered through Henry along with a

healthy spark of territorial interest. "We never agreed that we had to be exclusive while I got my shit together," he murmured. "If you want to take him up on his offer, I'll understand."

"I know that, but I'm not interested in him." She paused, and he could almost see the thoughtful frown and tilt of her head. "Before I met you, I might've entertained thoughts about dating him. He's nice—a rare gentleman like you."

"But...?"

"He's not you."

Just the answer I wanted to hear. "I know we agreed that our affair was a one-week deal, but I've put things in motion to clean up the mess with Mel. I've had the time I needed to get my head on straight again, and if you want to explore a deeper relationship with me... just say the word, and I'll drive to Washington. I'm ready to see what happens if you are."

For a moment, she didn't respond, but when she did, hope and excitement warmed her voice. "You're serious?"

"Absolutely."

"What's the word?"

"Huh?"

"What word do I need to say to get you to come see me?"

"I suppose a simple yes would suffice."

"Then yes. I would love that. But just so I'm clear, this means we're officially pursuing a relationship."

"Yep. Officially committed, so if you want to tell your would-be knight he'll have to look elsewhere because you're taken, I'd be all right with that, but try to let him down gently because he obviously knows what a prize you are."

The sound of her laughter brought a smile to his chilled face.

"I mean that, Lindsay. He'd be a fool not to want you."

"As it appears I'm already your girlfriend, flattery is not needed to convince me to date you."

"But I so enjoy it," he said with a chuckle. "I wish I could be there tomorrow, but it'll probably take me a couple weeks to find a place to rent."

"You could just stay with us."

"No, I don't want to make things awkward for Noah. Just in case."

With a touching gentleness that said far more than her words, she whispered, "Thank you."

"I can't wait. Tell Noah hi for me, and I'll see you in a two weeks."

"Not soon enough."

With a smile at their ritualistic parting phrase, Henry grudgingly ended the call and hoped it wouldn't take him longer than a couple weeks to locate a rental near Lindsay. Fortunately, he knew a couple guys who still had connections in that area, and with only a moment's hesitation to draw the number forth from his memory banks, he dialed first Pat O'Neil, who suggested he call either his wife's uncle or Ben as they both maintained contact with people in Kitsap County who owned rentals. Henry called Ben first, who happily gave him the number for his former landlady, Jeanie Miller—incidentally Lindsay's aunt.

Thank God for small-world connections, he mused as the

phone rang.

"Hello?"

"Mrs. Miller?"

"Yes?"

"My name is Henry Hammond, and I'm hoping you have a house available to rent for a few weeks."

"Henry Hammond, you say? Why, I know that name. You're my niece Lindsay's friend from Montana and a friend of Ben Conner's."

"Yes, ma'am." Maybe he shouldn't be surprised Lindsay's aunt had heard of him, but he was. "I'm hoping to come for a visit with the plan to return home to Montana just before Christmas."

"I believe I have just the place for you—a lovely cottage on the bluff overlooking the Indianola Beach with its own access stairs."

"Sounds delightful. When will it be available?"

"Don't you want to know how much?"

"Not important."

As they made arrangements for him to rent the cottage, Henry's excitement increased to crescendo, and as soon as he hung up, he pumped his fist in the air. The time between now and the moment he could take Lindsay into his arms couldn't pass fast enough, and he barely managed to subdue the pulsing joy long enough to explain the situation to his family, whose unanimous support he immediately received. He ignored the knowing grins his brothers exchanged, too busy planning his departure for Washington.

I'll be there before I know it. His grin widened. *Not soon enough.*

* * *

"Order up, Lindsay," the cook called.

Lindsay finished taking her newest order and tucked her notepad and pen in her apron, then smiled at the guests and sauntered over to the order window. She reached for the plate, but the cook pulled it back out of her reach.

"I know this order," he remarked, grinning. "There's only one person I know of who likes mayo and barbecue sauce on his bacon cheese burger—your would-be knight, Sir Dan of Liberty Bay."

"He's not my knight, and may I please have his order so I can get to fending off his admittedly charming and courtly advances? Because the faster I get to it, the faster I can get it over with."

"Girl, you don't have to be so cold. You *could* give the man something to hope for. That poor boy's smitten with you, and sometimes the only thing guys like him and me have to go on is hope. Okay, *most* of the time, that's all we have to go on."

"Don't be so hard on yourself, buddy. You've got a lot to offer a woman."

"You got the 'a lot' part right, but unfortunately, there's just a lot of *me* to offer. At least Sir Dan's got *some* physical appeal, even if he is a skinny nerd."

"He's only skinny compared to you, Mitch. To the rest of us, he's the picture of physical fitness, but I will agree that he's a nerd."

"You say that like it's a good thing."

"Nerds are awesome."

"So, what's the problem with Dan?"

"I'm just not interested in him, Mitch, and it's not fair

to lead him on."

"Ah, that's right. You already have a knight, and he wears a cowboy hat and Wranglers and rides a real horse rather than a two-wheeled, man-powered critter like Sir Dan rides."

"He prefers Carhartt, but close enough. Sir Dan's order please? I'm pretty sure it's getting cold." Lindsay held her hand out expectantly.

Mitch pushed the plate toward her again, pouting. "Spoilsport. How am I supposed to live vicariously through you if you won't consider even one date with the guy?"

"You need to get out more, Mitch, if you're living vicariously through *me*."

"You're a beautiful woman, Lindsay, and unlike me and Sir Dan out there, you actually do have a lot to offer."

"If I didn't know any better, I might think you were trying to flatter me into going out with *you*."

"Hell no, girl. You couldn't handle all this." Mitch shimmied and shook his backside.

Lindsay shook her head, laughing as she headed toward Dan's table with his still-hot burger. Despite their teasing, there had never been anything more than friendship between her and Mitch, and there never would be. Mitch had drawn that line when he'd first hired on at Donovan's a couple weeks after she'd started work here; his heart had already been claimed by a young novelist who was currently halfway across the country at a writers' convention. The term pixie often accompanied Lindsay's impression of Mitch's fiancée, as she was the living embodiment of the fantastical stories she wrote with delicate features, petite frame, and large, ever-inquisitive olivine eyes. When she allowed herself a rare moment of feminine vanity, Lindsay knew on some level that she was attractive, but next to Natasha Harding, she felt entirely unremarkable.

Until Henry made me see differently. Until he made me feel truly beautiful.

That was why she'd first turned Dan down and why she would continue to turn him down. No one had ever made her feel as comfortable with herself as Henry did. Not Dan with his gallant hopefulness. Not Logan with his smooth talking. And certainly not Max with his sexy smile and enticing confidence.

"One more week," she sighed, nearing Dan's table beside the big windows with a view of the Olympic Mountains that she had once thought spectacular. Her trip to Northstar had ruined that view for her just as surely as it had ruined any chance Dan might have had to win her over. She managed to set his meal in front of him with grace, but it almost abandoned her when he snatched her hand and brushed his thumb across her knuckles. Patiently, she smiled at him. He was an attractive man, less rugged than Henry with gentler features, but he had an undeniable appeal.

"Anything else I can get you?" she asked politely, tugging on her hand to cue him to drop it.

"Other than a date… I'm fine, thank you."

"Dan, I am genuinely flattered by your continued persistence, and from what I can tell, you're a great guy, but I'm sorry. It's not going to happen."

"Why not? We seem to be quite compatible."

"At one time not so long ago, I might have agreed with you, but—"

"Hey, Lindsay?" the hostess interrupted. The young woman glanced at Dan and offered a hasty apology. "I need to steal you away for a minute, if I may."

"Excuse me, Dan. I'll be back to check on you in a bit."

Lindsay followed the hostess to the front desk and regarded her with brows lifted and arms folded across her chest. The woman only grinned at her.

"While I am grateful for the excuse to escape, what did you need? I have other tables to check on."

"A man came in a minute ago asking for you. He said he'd wait out in the parking lot."

"A man? Who?"

"He didn't say." The girl grinned and fanned herself. "He's *hot*."

Curious, Lindsay headed out into a rare cloudless dusk. Directly across from the door and leaning against a familiar pickup with Montana plates and looking entirely smug with himself for pulling of a grand surprise was the man who had commanded so much of her attention since she'd met him back in August. At first, she froze midstride as her gaze took in every relaxed line of his body. Even her fantasies about him fell short of the reality.

"Hi, gorgeous," Henry murmured.

That simple greeting broke the thrall, and she ran to him with arms outstretched. He pushed off his truck and lifted her off the ground when she reached him, tucking his arms tightly around her.

"My God, I've missed you," he whispered against her neck.

"I can't believe you're here! Is this real?"

"I certainly hope so."

He set her on her feet, and she slid her fingers over his jaw and down the sides of his neck before knitting them behind his head. She tilted her head up to kiss him, and he met her halfway, splaying his hands across her back to draw her closer. It was incredible to be back in his arms, and in that moment, every worry melted away, leaving her refreshed and alive like she hadn't been since she'd left him standing alone in the Butte airport.

"I thought you said your rental wouldn't be available for another week."

"It came open sooner than expected, and I couldn't wait to see you."

"And you couldn't tell me this yesterday when we talked?"

"I wanted to surprise you. I wanted to see the exact look I saw on your face just a moment ago."

"And what look was that?"

"Pure, honest joy."

His response was an accurate assumption of the emotion glowing so warmly in her heart. "So, where did you end up finding a place?"

"Indianola. One of your Aunt Jeanie's places—the cottage on the bluff overlooking the beach. She said it's just a couple blocks from your parents' place, and it sounded great from her descriptions."

"You haven't seen it yet?"

He shook his head. "I had to see you first. How much longer until your shift is over?"

"About an hour. Why don't you go home and get settled, and I'll bring Noah over to meet you when I get off work?"

"Sounds great. You know which house it is?"

"Yep. You're going to love it. It's sort of tucked back into the trees a bit, but it still has a great view... and it's own access to the beach. I can't believe Aunt Jeanie didn't tell me!"

"I might have asked her not to."

"Brat."

"Sometimes." He leaned down to kiss her cheek. "I'll see you in a little while."

"That's all I get to hold me over? A kiss on the cheek?"

"Mmm-hmm. There'll be plenty of time for more later. Just how much time... well, I guess we'll find out."

She didn't watch him climb into his truck and was already back inside by the time he drove away with the thought that if she plunged into work quitting time would arrive faster. The promise of an adventure even grander than their whirlwind week together in Northstar carried her through the rest of her shift. When Dan again tried to draw her into conversation, she told him as politely as she could her reason for declining his offers. She was as honest as she had been with Henry that first meeting at the bar of the Bedspread Inn, and though he was disappointed, her would-be suitor appreciated her candor.

"I wondered if there was someone else who'd already caught your eye," Dan said as he handed her the check and money to pay for it. "He's a lucky guy."

"Thank you, Dan. I really didn't mean to lead you on."

"You didn't. I get that you were being polite. I was

just hoping that if I kept after you long enough you'd give in."

Finally, her last table left, and she zipped into the kitchen to hang up her apron and punch her timecard. She drove to her cousin Jasmine's house to pick up Noah, who was in no hurry to leave. He and Jasmine's daughter, Jamie, were engaged in an intense Mario Kart race, but Lindsay was in no mood to wait. She had already told him Henry was coming for a visit, and he'd been ecstatic at the prospect of meeting the man he'd talked to a dozen times on the phone and had pestered her endlessly all week about when Henry would arrive and where he would be staying.

"Noah, let's go."

"Just one more race, Mom, please?"

"Not tonight, bud. We've gotta go."

"Why?"

"Henry's here."

Instantly, Noah's attention was yanked from the game. "What? Where is he?"

"He's not *here* here. He's in Indianola getting settled in Aunt Jeanie's cottage."

"The one with the stairs down to the beach?"

"That's the one. Come on. I told him I'd bring you over to meet him as soon as I got off work, and we still have to stop by the house to drop off your school stuff. Speaking of which, you *did* get your homework done before you started playing video games, right?"

"Uh… not all of it."

"Noah!" Jasmine chided. "You said you finished it all."

"What do you have left?" Lindsay asked.

"Just some of my math. I got most of it done, and it won't take me long to finish, I promise."

"Next time, I'm going to check *all* your homework, young man," Jasmine said. "Sorry, Lindsay. He said he was done."

Lindsay shrugged. She was in too good a mood to chastise her son for either the fib or for not finishing his work.

"Sorry, Jamie," Noah said to his cousin. "I gotta go."

"See ya, Noah."

"Bye, Jasmine."

"See you tomorrow, kiddo," Jasmine replied.

It was fully dark by the time they cruised into Indianola. Instead of turning right at the intersection by the Country Store toward her parents' house, she turned left. What did it matter if Noah's backpack sat in the car while they visited Henry? The cottage was two long blocks up the road from the store and the Indianola Dock, a retired ferry pier that stretched out into the waters of Puget Sound toward Bainbridge Island. She pulled her sedan in beside Henry's truck in the house's short driveway. He must've heard her pull up because he opened the door and stepped out onto the narrow porch just as she climbed out of her car. Shyly, she took Noah's hand and walked carefully along the mossy concrete path to the porch.

"Henry, this is my son, Noah," Lindsay said when they reached him. "Noah, this is Henry."

"Glad to finally meet you, Noah," Henry greeted, extending his hand.

Noah shook it. "Yeah. Good to meet you, too."

"Come on inside. Noah, I have something for you."

"Henry…" Lindsay groaned.

"Don't worry. It didn't cost me anything but time and a few dimes for gas money."

They followed him inside into the open, well-lit living area. Two off-white couches sat in an L to the right of the space, and a golden oak dining set occupied the left side of the room. Big windows and a set of French doors leading out to a wide deck looked out across the water toward Bainbridge Island. Seattle's glittering lights were also visible in the distance. Nautical was the theme her aunt had chosen for this place, and the gold and navy blue accents complemented the white walls and dark-stained hardwood floors of the main living area with an elegance that was also quaintly inviting. Around the corner to left was the small but efficiently organized kitchen—nearly identical to the one in Henry's house back in Northstar, she realized. Beyond that was the bathroom and a small bedroom. To the left side of the kitchen, a staircase led upstairs to the finished attic that had been converted into the master suite complete with a half bath and another set of French doors leading out onto a private deck on the beach end of the room. Much like Henry's house, the cottage was small but cozy and very welcoming. If she had the means to do so, she would be very tempted to buy it from her aunt.

Despite the fact that he looked like he'd stepped out of an issue of Cowboys and Indians, Henry looked like he belonged in this house. After a moment, she realized it was how he moved with the confidence of someone who had inhabited the space for months or years rather than a couple of hours. It was the same self-assurance that had caught her eye when he'd strolled into the Bedspread. The bitterness was gone, however, making him at once ten times more devastatingly irresistible.

He grabbed a small Tupperware container off the kitchen counter and handed it to Noah. Whatever was inside was wrapped in a paper towel, so Lindsay couldn't guess what it might be.

"Your mom said Spencer got into your crystals and either lost or stole some," Henry said. "So I brought you a few more."

The thought behind the gift hit Noah as hard as it hit Lindsay, and the boy impulsively hugged Henry. She hadn't mentioned it to him again after the incident, so it was impressive he'd remembered. Even if he'd gone out the very next day to find more crystals or taken them from any he might have already had at his house, a month and a half was a long time to hold on to the thought of bringing them to Noah… especially since he hadn't known he would be making the trip until just a week ago. Unless….

Lindsay shook her head. She wasn't going to overthink this. She was going to enjoy his thoughtfulness and the genuine smile of pleasure at Noah's gratitude.

"I know you can't stay long because I'm sure you have schoolwork left to finish," he was saying, "but I wanted to give you those tonight."

"He does in fact have some homework to finish," Lindsay said.

She wasn't ready to leave yet, but it was getting late, and Henry had had a long drive, so she headed toward the door. He walked outside with them, and when Noah continued out to the car, she hung back.

Sensing her hesitation, he leaned close and

murmured, "This isn't like your trip to Montana. There's no deadline. We don't have to cram everything we want to do into a week. We have time."

She nodded, not trusting her voice.

"See you tomorrow?"

"Not soon enough."

With a chuckle, he brushed his lips across her cheek. "Good night, gorgeous."

"I'm glad you're here."

"Me, too."

For good measure, she took his hand and squeezed it, then turned unwillingly away and strode out to her car where Noah was too engrossed by his new crystals to have noticed his mother's fleetingly intimate moment with her handsome friend from Montana. While she drove home, she wondered if it should be weird or awkward seeing Henry again, but it wasn't. On the contrary, it was as if a piece of her that had been missing had been returned.

Twelve

THE WEATHER HAD BEEN dismal the entire week and a half Henry had been in Washington with flat gray skies and unending rain, and while it certainly explained why the western part of the state was so gloriously green, he was glad to have woken up to clear blue skies this morning. He still couldn't believe the vegetation here, so tall and lush, nor could he quite grasp the fact that he was wearing shorts and flip-flops and heading down a steep set of stairs to a broad, sandy beach on the twenty-third of November. It wasn't warm by any means, and the perpetually damp air left a chill in his bones that even ten below back home didn't, but with the sun out and a high of fifty-two, it felt more like May than almost Thanksgiving. When he'd talked to his mother yesterday, she had informed him that the week's highs weren't supposed to break zero, and the overnight lows were hitting as cold as thirty below.

"Still feeling a bit like a fish out of water here?" Lindsay inquired when they reached the bottom of the stairs. She stepped carefully a cross the rocky, seaweed-strewn shore at the base of the bluff and slipped out of her dainty sandals when she reached the sand lower on the beach.

Today—Saturday—wasn't her normal day off, but she'd switched shifts with another waitress when the forecast had called for a sunny day. Henry was glad to spend more time with her and Noah. They'd spent every available moment together, but it wasn't enough.

"Not so much a fish out of water as a little kid seeing something new. Denver was definitely different from Northstar because it's urban, but the climate and vegetation are very similar. This is totally different. It's incredible."

"You sound like I did when I was in Northstar."

"I'm sure I do." He chuckled and kicked off his flip-flops. Noah followed suit, and they set their shoes atop the barnacle- and mussel-encrusted boulder that sat at the edge between the rockier shore and the sand spit. The sand, still packed and damp from the recently receded tide, was cold beneath his bare feet—an entirely alien sensation to a born and bred Montana boy. A long absent, innocent joy saturated Henry, and right then, his spirit was younger and more inexperienced than Noah's as he jogged a dozen yards to the nearest tide pool. Tiny fish darted through the shallow pool as he ran past, ducking under floating, vivid green seaweed that reminded him of a leaf of lettuce. It was incredible to run for the sheer joy of it. It had been a long time since he'd done that, too, so he lengthened his stride and sprinted around the long, narrow tide pool and back toward his girlfriend and her son. When a long stream of water unexpectedly jetted from the sand inches from his foot and struck him square in the chest, he hit the brakes and turned back to inspect the sand. There was a hole about twice the size of his thumb half-filled with water.

"Hey, Henry!" Lindsay called. "Catch!"

He glanced up just in time to see her launch a football at him with a perfect spiral and impressive aim. He caught it effortlessly and lobbed it to Noah.

"What just squirted me?" he asked, pointing to the hole in the sand.

"Probably a geoduck," Noah replied.

"A gooey what?"

"Geoduck. It's a really big clam. Haven't you ever seen one?"

Henry shook his head.

"Come on. I'll show ya."

Lindsay hung back, content to watch her son and lover scavenge the nearby beach for shells and stomp beside more of the telltale holes to get the giant clams to squirt as they retreated deeper into the sand. Occasionally while they hunted, Henry glanced up to see a contented smile gracing her face and couldn't help but smile in response. He was a bit surprised she wasn't joining in their play, but he suspected she was gauging their interaction, judging him with a mother's protective instinct. And since she was smiling, he surmised she liked what she saw.

"Here's a shell," Noah announced, distracting him.

It was in tact and the largest they'd yet found; the halves of the shell were each as big as one of his hands. "Wow."

"How fast can you dig by hand?"

"Uh… I don't know. Why?"

"Wanna try to catch one?"

"Sure."

"All right. Ya gotta be fast, though, because they're fast. I mean scary fast."

"You'll probably have more luck closer to the water's edge," Lindsay remarked, joining them. "The sand'll be softer and easier to dig."

"Can you help, Mom?" Noah turned to Henry. "She's amazing at catching geoducks. She has a trick. You see, she digs to the side of them and then under them, but you gotta be careful not to move the sand too much because if they sense it…. Poof. Gone."

"What d'you say, Lindsay? Care to show a novice how it's done?"

Grinning, she slung her canvas bag over her shoulder and sprinted across the wide beach nearly to the water. Noah raced after her, and Henry kept pace with him until the boy cheered and told him to catch Lindsay. Damn, the woman could run. With legs pumping as hard and fast as they could, Henry barely managed to pass her just a few strides before she slowed down on the last sand bar before the gently churning waves. A broad, smug grin ignited her stunning blue eyes. With her dark auburn hair pulled back in a single braid, no makeup to hide the soft, ivory skin of her face, and casual tan Capris paired with an ice-blue tank top that peeked from the half-unzipped emerald fleece pull-over, she was exquisitely and spontaneously beautiful. She met his gaze and laughed breathlessly. Henry, raised at a much higher elevation and still not fully acclimated to the air as sea level, had to concentrate on how much air he sucked in so he didn't choke on it. Who would have thought it would be harder to breathe at sea level? Wasn't it supposed to be the other way around?

"How far did we just run?" he asked when he'd caught his breath.

"This part of the beach is the widest at almost two-tenths of a mile from the bluff to the water when the tide is as low as it is right now."

"Incredible."

"Feels good to run just to run, doesn't it?" she asked. "Like being a kid again."

"It really does. But I'm guessing you and Noah do this a lot."

"Yeah, we do," Noah answered.

"You're a lucky kid to have a mom who loves to play."

Lindsay ducked her head shyly at his praise, but Noah offered him a lopsided grin and said, "I know. She's pretty awesome. My friend Tanner's mom *never* runs with us. Never digs for geoducks with us, either. She's always worried about her hair or her nails or her makeup or getting her clothes dirty."

"Speaking of geoducks," Henry said, "I'm kinda excited to actually see one, so shall we?"

Lindsay pushed her sleeves up and located a whole shell to use as a shovel.

"Isn't that cheating?" Henry inquired.

"Not if you want to see a live one."

Henry and Noah stood back to watch the expert digger. With her feet braced wide over a hole where she announced a geoduck was near the surface, she used the shells—one in each hand—to excavate about eight inches from the creature's hole. She was quick, moving the sloppy wet sand much like a dog would but with far more skill and precision and soon had a hole deep enough to sink half of Henry's leg. Then she started digging toward the geoduck's hole, faster and faster. When water shot out like a tiny geyser, she squealed and shoved her hand into the sand. The way she was positioned with her ear nearly touching the ground and her shapely rear end sticking up into the air was decidedly distracting, but Henry was too engrossed by her activity to pay too much attention.

Triumphantly, she rose from her awkward crouch with a pile of sand in her hands. Gingerly, she brushed the sand away, revealing the bright white shell, long leathery neck-like appendage, and a rubbery thing that looked like a pale tongue. After she washed the creature in the tide pool on the bluff side of the sandbar, she held it up for inspection. It was, as Noah had said, a giant clam. "Gentlemen, I present to you the elusive geoduck."

Henry took the shellfish from Lindsay and marveled at it. It had to weigh close to two pounds, maybe more, and the shell—larger than any they'd yet found—had to be nearly eight inches long. The neck, or whatever it was called, was shockingly phallic, and when he poked the tongue-thing, the animal sucked most of it back inside its shell, but it was so large that not all of it fit. "Fascinating."

"That thing that looks like a tongue is called the foot," Noah explained. "That's what they dig with. And that gross-looking neck is called a siphon, right, Mom?"

"That's right."

236

"They use that to breathe and eat and stuff."

"Truly amazing."

Lindsay took the geoduck and settled it in the hole she'd created, making sure to place its siphon skyward, and gently covered it with sand and water. It slowly retreated into the safety of the earth.

"I thought you said they were fast," Henry remarked.

Brows lifted in challenge, she gestured to another geoduck hole a few feet away. "Go ahead and give it a try, Mr. Hammond. Noah, you probably ought to help our poor cowboy because I'm pretty sure he has no idea what he's doing."

Playfully determined, Henry borrowed her digging shells, and he and Noah got to work. They hadn't tunneled half a foot before the telltale geyser erupted, and *whoosh*, the mollusk was gone. They found another hole and again attempted to catch the geoduck inside. Again and again, they failed. Try as they might, they just didn't have Lindsay's finesse, and even digging as fast as they could, they couldn't manage to catch one of the quick creatures.

Lindsay shook her head, smiling. "Amateurs."

They gave up geoduck digging and turned to football for a while. Noah's intensity during their light-hearted game was proof that he loved the sport as much as his mother, and moments after Henry found himself sprawled and laughing in the sand, artfully tackled by the eight-year-old, he decided Max was an idiot if he believed he could ever chase that passion out of his son. For Noah's sake and Lindsay's, Henry desperately hoped Max would stop trying. It did no one any good to try to break such a deep and intrinsic love.

"All right, boys," Lindsay said, trotting over. She offered first Noah a hand up and then Henry. "If we want to eat before midnight, it's time to put an end to our frolicking."

Henry eyed her hand, wondering if she realized he was easily sixty pounds heavier than her. Then he shrugged and took her hand. When it required far less effort on his part than he'd assumed it would for her to pull him up off the sand, he shook his head and chuckled.

"What?" she asked.

"I think I've spent too much time dealing with Mel these last few weeks," he replied, "because I'd forgotten how strong you are… in every way."

She only grinned at him and turned to follow her son across the sand toward the bluff. With Noah's back to them, Henry snagged her hand again and yanked her to him. She smacked into his chest, and he folded his arms around her so she couldn't escape, but she made no effort to and only beamed that adoring smile at him. He lowered his mouth slowly to hers. She met him halfway, and his pulse jumped enticingly.

This trip was, thus far, very different from her vacation in Northstar with an unhurried pace that added to the consuming excitement a euphoric relaxation that burrowed even deeper into his heart and gave them time to explore other aspects of each other that they hadn't had the time to investigate before. And what a ride. Seeing Lindsay with her son was an entirely different animal than imagining it. She was, as he'd suspected, a devoted mother, and her love for Noah hit him in the same place Mel's love for Dylan had… but *way* harder.

"So, what's for dinner?" he asked to divert his train of thought before he proposed to her right there on the beach well before either of them was ready to seriously consider that level of commitment.

"Well... I thought steamer clams, but I suppose I should probably make sure you aren't allergic to shellfish first."

"Nope, and that sounds wonderful. It isn't often we get good seafood in Northstar."

"I hate to ask, but would you mind helping Noah with the homework he didn't finish last night?"

"Is this a test to see if I'm daddy material?"

"Maybe a tiny one. I hope you're not offended."

"I don't mind at all, and in fact, I'd expect nothing less. You have to protect your son, and I admire that. I'd be happy to help him, especially since you're cooking something special for us."

"You two coming or what?" Noah called back to them. He was already at the boulder and stuffing his feet back into his sandals.

"I'm going to go with 'or what'," Henry replied. "Give an old guy a break."

"Oh, don't even try to play the old card again," Lindsay laughed, sliding her hand around his forearm before twining her fingers with his.

Even though her son was watching, he impulsively lifted her hand to his lips and kissed her knuckles, watching Noah's face for his reaction. A delighted grin curved the boy's lips. That was good.

Because it was only two and a half blocks from Henry's cottage to the Millers' house, they walked. Lindsay immediately ensconced herself in the kitchen while Noah and Henry sat at the table to work on the boy's homework. Noah was a willing pupil, but he was distracted, Henry noted, watching as the kid glanced yet again between his mother and Henry with an odd little smile. For the time being, Henry ignored it and conspicuously cleared his throat to return Noah's attention to his schoolwork. While the boy worked, occasionally asking for Henry's assistance, Henry studied him. There was a lot of Lindsay in him—her blue eyes, her nose, chin, and cheeks—but his jaw, hair, and brow line likely came from his father, and the combination of them made him a devilishly adorable boy. He wondered what *his* child with Lindsay might look like and jerked back as soon as the thought entered his mind. Way too soon to be thinking like that... but the idea was in his head and refused to be banished. So he focused on Noah's homework with a renewed fervor and ignored the ache in his chest and the blatant need elsewhere.

They finished quickly, and Noah received permission to play a video game while Lindsay finished dinner.

"Wanna play, Henry?"

"I'd love to, but if it's all right, I'd like to watch your mom cook for a bit."

"You want to watch her cook?" Noah asked skeptically.

"Yeah. It's amazing what she's doing with food."

"Uh-huh."

"I'll be in to play in a few, all right?"

Nodding, Noah disappeared into the living room. Henry glanced around the kitchen and the rest of the house that he could see. Despite the shadows of the towering cedars, hemlocks, and Douglas firs outside, the house inside was remarkably bright with a lot of white and pastel earth tones. "What's with all the white?" he inquired. "I thought it was just my cottage, but this place is overwhelmingly white, too."

"Keeps away the gloom," Lindsay replied. "With all the cloudy and rainy days and the dark forest, white adds a little light. Here, try this."

She held a spoonful of the sauce for the steamer clams to his lips, and he slurped it, groaning in pleasure.

"That is amazing! You can cook, woman."

With Noah distracted in the living room, Henry angled his body toward hers and drew her against him, then claimed her mouth with a hunger of an entirely different kind than what rumbled in his stomach. They'd been able to steal only a handful of kisses since he'd arrived, and the frustration of that fast was evident in the way she kissed him back with uninhibited and potent demand. When they broke apart, he tucked a wayward strand of her silky red hair behind her ear, and she leaned into his hand and closed her eyes, turning her head to kiss his palm. Her lids fluttered open again, and in her eyes, he saw his desire plainly reflected and reciprocated.

"If you had the means to do whatever you wanted with your talent," he murmured, "what would you do? Open your own restaurant?"

She shook her head. "No. I've never wanted to be chained to one place."

"What would you want instead?"

"My own catering business."

"Catering. Really."

"Back in high school when Skye decided she wanted to run her own photography studio, we used to dream we could work together at the same events."

"Sounds like a beautiful dream to me."

"It was."

The sadness that crept into her voice said a lot more than her words. He doubted she'd ever say it, but she was at least a little envious that Skye had been able to make her side of their dream come true. Not envious, he corrected, because he was damned sure she was happy for her friend. Hopeless because she hadn't had the same opportunities to make it happen for herself. With the same powerful need he'd revealed to Nick weeks ago, he wished he could find a way to help her achieve her dreams even though he doubted she'd let him.

A thought sprang into his mind, and while it wouldn't put her on the path to opening her own catering business, it might brighten her day and give her a well-deserved break. "When was the last time you had a couple hours to yourself?"

"Uh… I'm not sure. Probably when I was in Northstar."

"You have the breakfast shift on Wednesday, don't you?"

"Yeah…."

"And Noah gets out of school early for Thanksgiving, right?"

"What are you up to, Henry?"

"I'd like to take him to the mall for a couple hours after school or to a movie and give you a couple hours to read a book or do whatever you'd like to do. Call it another test—a test to prove you can trust me with your son."

Without hesitation, she replied, "I *do* trust you."

"But?"

"For one, he isn't a fan of the mall. It's always a battle to get him to go shopping."

"Ah, that's where I have one up on you. Boys shopping together is a totally different game than a boy shopping with his mom. What other reservation do you have?"

"Logan."

"You've mentioned him before. Who was he?"

"My last boyfriend... only the second serious relationship I've had, not counting the current one."

That she considered their relationship serious intrigued him, but he let the off-handed remark go without comment. "What happened? And how long ago did that end?"

"It's been almost eight months now, I guess. It ended four months before I met you. I thought he might be the one to love and accept Noah and me as a complete package, and he did a good job of making me believe that. He seemed so good with Noah... but it was just an act to get me into bed, and it hurt Noah terribly when I found out I was nothing more than a hot piece of ass to Logan."

"What did he say to Noah? I'm guessing he said something because you would've been able to make up some story to soften the blow otherwise."

"He was honest. He told Noah that he'd only pretended to put up with him and that it was a pain in the ass to constantly be entertaining him just so he could get into my pants and that the annoyance wasn't worth the reward anymore. He said it just like that."

Henry swore and balled his hands into fists. "Yeah, you really have been dating the wrong men, Lindsay. I hope you know I'd never do that to Noah because, to be as succinctly honest as I can be without it sounding scripted, I quite enjoy your son. He's a great kid. But you have to do what you feel is best for him, and if you don't want me to spend time with him alone, I won't."

"No, I do, Henry, and I think he'd appreciate it. Just... don't get his hopes up. He's already attached to you, and I don't want him to get hurt again if this doesn't work out."

"Even if it doesn't, I promise I won't hurt your son. Of course... I'm rather hoping there's a future for us. A long future."

He didn't give her a chance to respond to that, vanishing into the living room with nothing more than a quick peck on the lips.

* * *

Lindsay came with Henry to pick Noah up from school at one on Wednesday, and he dropped her off at home before heading to the mall with her son. She was understandably nervous about letting them go without her but not, she assured Henry, because she didn't trust him. It was an eight-year-old habit borne of being the sole caregiver for her son and a silly worry that Noah and Henry had known each other for only a couple weeks and would therefore find each other's company awkward without Lindsay there to provide a common element. Henry, in turn, promised her he took no offense and fully understood her concerns. He also promised here that they were unfounded.

Henry let Noah pick the radio station while he drove

into Silverdale, unsurprised that the boy shared his mother's fondness for classic rock. The kid was skeptical of their destination, but he was polite about it, and Henry almost felt guilty for using Noah's desire to please him to get him to go along with his plan. Almost.

"I want to get something for your mom," Henry explained.

"Why? Christmas is still almost a month away."

"Because she deserves it, and because sometimes it's nice to surprise people when it isn't Christmas or their birthday to let them know you're thinking about them. That's why I need your help. I was thinking she'd like something for her kitchen, since she loves to cook, but I don't have a clue what she might need or want. Once we get that taken care of, we'll have some fun."

"A new mixer," Noah replied immediately. "Her old one broke months ago, and she hasn't been able to buy a new one."

"That is a great idea. There's a kitchen store in this mall, right?"

"Yeah," Noah sighed.

Henry chuckled, guessing Lindsay's son spent far more time in that particular store than he liked. Noah gave him directions to the mall entrance closest to their destination, and Henry found a parking spot relatively close to the door. They made a mad dash through the cold downpour, splashing in the puddles that littered the asphalt and laughing at their own antics once they reached the shelter of the mall.

"You're a lot more fun than Logan was," Noah remarked.

"Your mom told me a bit about him, but she made it sound like you and he got along pretty well at the beginning."

"I guess so. I thought he liked to play catch and do things together, but he didn't goof around much. Not like you do."

"Lemme guess. He was 'too cool' for that."

"Yeah." Noah looked at him with wide, fretful eyes. "You're not... spending time with me just so my mom will like you more, are you?"

"No, Noah, I'm not." Henry met the boy's apprehensive gaze head on. "I want to be as honest with you as your mom and I have been with each other since we met back in August. I really like your mom. She's an amazing woman, and I can see why some men might not want to share her even with her son. But I'm not one of those men. I fully accept that you will always come first, as you should. It's one of the best things about your mom."

"You really mean that?"

"Yes, I do."

"So you like kids?"

"Yep. Two of my favorite people on this earth are my nephew and niece, who are six and five. Kids have a simplistic way of seeing the world that adults forget as life gets ever more complicated, and I for one appreciate the reminder that it's the little things in life that make it worth living."

"Things like digging for geoducks?"

"Or throwing a football on a long, sandy beach."

"Or running as fast as you can just because."

"All of that."

Conversation about other simple joys in life held their attention all the way to the kitchen store, where they were promptly distracted by their hunt for a mixer for Lindsay. With the assistance of the store's manager, they picked the best one in stock, and Henry carried it to the counter to pay only to be distracted by a set of nice holiday cookie cutters.

"Your mom have any of these?" Henry asked Noah.

"No. It's been a while since she baked cookies, and she just used a cup or something to cut them out."

"And these, too, please," Henry said to the manager, tossing the cookie cutters onto the counter. He pulled out his wallet. "We can all bake and decorate cookies tomorrow after dinner with your mom and grandparents."

"That's kinda dumb."

"Why?"

"Well... baking cookies is for girls."

"Where on earth did you hear *that*?"

"My dad."

"Uh-huh. I used to love baking cookies with my mom. Still do, but I don't get to do it much anymore. I'm also glad she and my dad browbeat me into learning how to dance properly. Wanna know why?"

"Sure. Why?"

"Because it's something we did together as a family. Something I've come to realize pretty clearly lately is just how important family is. You don't want to lose it over something as silly and useless as pride."

"Wait. You *dance*? That's like... major girly stuff."

"Remind me tomorrow after dinner, and I'll show you exactly why it's not girly at all."

"Uh-huh," Noah remarked, unconvinced.

"Just go with me on this, all right? And I promise we'll all have fun with the cookies tomorrow. It's one of those simple pleasures we talked about earlier. You'll see."

Noah picked up the cookie cutters, eyeing them thoughtfully. "I guess it might be fun. Do we get to use the fancy sprinkles and colored icing?"

Henry tucked his wallet into his back pocket and carried their purchase out of the store, smiling to himself as cracks formed and widened in Noah's cool-guy façade, letting his innocent excitement shine through. "Absolutely."

They took their purchases out to the truck so they wouldn't have to carry them all through the mall, then headed back in to explore all the stores Noah didn't usually get to—sportswear shops, the toy store, even the arcade. They had a grand time indulging in some good old fashioned male bonding with no shortage of things to talk about. Noah grilled Henry about his family and the ranch and the work he'd done in Denver, and Henry discovered the boy's aspirations—like many boys his age, he wanted to be a professional athlete, and if that failed, he wanted to work with animals. By the time they had to leave, Noah admitted that he'd never thought the mall could be so much fun.

Lindsay's car wasn't parked in the driveway of the Millers' house when he and Noah arrived, so Henry figured she was still out shopping for last minute necessities for tomorrow's turkey dinner. Of all the things she could have done with a few hours to herself, she was being practical, Henry mused. He was beginning to miss her adventurous side and wished she could be as free to indulge in it here as she had been in Northstar. His heart hurt for her.

Henry located the hidden key, but when he inserted it into the lock and turned, he found the door already unlocked. Motioning for Noah to follow behind him, he called, "Hello? Lindsay?"

A woman in her mid-sixties with medium brown hair that was now mostly silver popped her head around the wall hiding the kitchen from the front door. Noah raced into the house and gave the woman a big hug, and Henry realized who she was. A moment later, a man of the same age with graying red hair joined his wife in embracing the boy. The relation to Lindsay was obvious.

"Mr. and Mrs. Miller, a pleasure to meet you," he greeted.

"You must be Henry," Lindsay's mother said. She stepped around the counter and embraced him. "And please, call me Debbie or Deb. No need for formality."

She reminded him immediately of his own mother, and he smiled. "Yes, ma'am." He shook Steve Miller's extended hand. "We weren't expecting you home so early, or Noah and I would've cut our excursion short."

"We ended up driving through last night," Steve explained. "We wanted to get home to see our daughter and grandson… and to meet you. Lindsay has told us a lot about you, and I must say that so far her glowing praise is well deserved."

"Thank you, sir."

"No sirs, either," the older man said.

Turning to Noah, Debbie asked, "Did you boys have fun at the mall?"

"Yeah, we did! Henry, can we show her what we

bought for Mom?"

"Sure, bud."

They fetched the mixer and cookie cutters out of the truck and brought them into the kitchen. With an enthusiasm that completely belied his earlier skepticism, Noah told his grandmother their plans for the cookie cutters and the decorations they'd purchased on the way home. Debbie was impressed by the idea, and when they revealed the other gift, she sighed with pleasure.

"Oh my. Lindsay's going to love that. It's much better than that old piece of junk she had before."

"That was all Noah's idea," Henry remarked.

"Very thoughtful of you both," Debbie said. "But I believe I just heard Lindsay pull up, so you might want to hide that in our room. That is, if I guess right and you want to surprise her with them at dinner tomorrow."

"That's the idea."

Henry excused himself to hide the gifts in the Millers' bedroom where Lindsay wasn't likely to stumble upon them. As he was leaving the room, he heard the Millers talking with Noah, whose glowing praise of him was a relief. Another test passed, he thought. Lindsay came in and greeted her parents, and just before Henry stepped back into view, he heard her father utter something that made him grin.

"You found a keeper this time, my darling daughter."

* * *

"You just sit down and relax while we do the dishes," Debbie told her daughter. "You and your father have already done more than your fair share in cooking that magnificent meal. Haven't they, Henry?"

"Yes, they have," he replied as he stacked plates on his hand. "For once in your life, let someone take care of *you*."

"Thank you, Henry," Debbie said in agreement.

"Mmm-hmm."

Lindsay sat back in her chair, folded her arms across her chest, and pretended to be mad. When her father got up and headed toward his bedroom with a not-so-subtle nod from Henry, she sat up a little straighter, curious. What were they playing at? She glanced at her son, who suspiciously averted his gaze.

"What is going on?" she demanded.

"We have a surprise for you," Henry replied. "And please don't be mad at me because we—Noah and I— bought you something."

"Henry...."

"I know, I know. Humor me, all right? I think you'll like them."

"Them?"

"Them," Steve confirmed, striding through the kitchen into the dining room.

He settled two white paper sacks on the dining room table as soon as his wife wiped it down. Lindsay instantly recognized the logo on the front of the bags as that of the kitchen store in the mall. Exasperated, curious, and touched all at once, she craned her neck to see what was in the bags, but her father yanked them out of her reach and told her she had to wait.

It wasn't difficult to find a distraction. Henry provided an excellent one. He was dressed casually, as they all were, and his dark blue jeans fit him perfectly, emphasizing his long, muscular legs with slightly bowed knees. And, damn, that ass of his was fine. The plain black, long-sleeved T-shirt tucked into his jeans fit him just as well, showcasing his powerful shoulders and strong arms. No man had any right to be that sexy, she mused. As usual, he wore a plain brown belt and his newer work boots, and though he lacked the classical cowboy touches like the hat and big, shiny belt buckle, he still managed to exude that Western charm.

More powerful than his physical appeal was the emotional one. It amazed her how quickly her parents had taken to him and how he seemed to appreciate them in return. He was ever the gentleman, lavishing her mother with compliments and endearing genuineness. For being an introverted country boy, he sure had a natural way with people.

Since Lindsay had already done most of the dishes while she and her father cooked, it didn't take her mother, Henry, and Noah long to finish up what was left, and they were soon seated once again at the table.

"*Now* can I look?" she asked.

"Have at 'em," Henry replied.

She started with the larger sack first, and pressed her hand over her mouth in shock when she saw a beautiful new heavy-duty mixer inside. "Henry, no. This is too expensive. You have to take it back."

"Not a chance."

"Let the man spoil you," her mother remarked. "And if you think that's thoughtful, wait 'til you see what's in the other bag."

She reached into the second sack and pulled out a set of six cookie cutters—a tree, candy cane, snowflake, snowman, Christmas stocking, and a star—along with an assortment of sprinkles and tubes of colored icing.

"I figured we could make our own dessert," Henry explained. "Together. You, Noah, your parents, and me."

The sentiment warmed her heart, but she couldn't find the words to express it, so she simply stood and unpackaged her gorgeous new mixer, washed what needed to be washed, and started pulling ingredients out of the cupboards for sugar cookies, keeping her back to them so they couldn't see her trying not to cry. To her further surprise and delight, everyone stepped in to help, and before long, they were all laughing and the kitchen was a mess of ingredients. It wasn't that she and her family hadn't done anything together... it was that they hadn't done anything like *this* together in a long time. While the first batch of cookies cooled on the counter and the second baked in the oven, they gathered around the kitchen, and Lindsay glanced from one beloved face to the next. Not one of them had escaped without at least a light dusting of flour, and not one face was unsmiling.

Henry nudged Noah with a grin. "See? Isn't this fun?"

"Yeah, it is," her son was quick to admit.

Lindsay regarded him with a brow lifted.

"While we wait to decorate, I want to show you that other thing," Henry continued. "If your mom will indulge me."

He held out his hand, and she tilted her head in curiosity. His patience fueled her interest, and she found herself slipping her hand into his and following him into the living room. Her family followed, taking seats on the plush couch and recliners to watch... whatever it was he had in mind.

"A dance, milady?"

"Okay… but why?"

"One, I want to and, two, your son seems to be laboring under the incorrect assumption that dancing is for girls. I'd like to show him otherwise."

"In that case, I'd love a dance."

"Deb, would you mind putting some music on?"

"What's your poison?"

"Doesn't matter. Anything with a decent beat, fast or slow, will do."

Her mother turned on the radio to a fast-paced Christmas song—let the holiday craze begin, Lindsay thought with a twist of her lips even as she admitted to herself that she was looking forward to it this year.

"Ready?" Henry asked.

Lindsay nodded. Half a second later, she found herself twirling and swinging in a heart-pounding, energetic dance. Henry handled her with exquisite power and grace. The word *handled* seemed harsh, but there was no other way to describe it because she had no idea what she was doing, and by his skill alone, she moved through the dips and spins with agility. She'd been amazed by his ability back in August, but by comparison, the dances they'd shared then were lazy and playful. This was something entirely different—an exciting seriousness wrapped in a familiarity that shocked her. Back in August, there had been flirtation and curiosity, but now they knew each other's bodies, and Lindsay understood with a start that Henry wasn't playing the doting boyfriend anymore. He was committed to that role.

"You were holding out on me at Vince and Evie's wedding," she remarked. Her voice trembled with more

254

than exertion.

"Maybe a little."

The song ended just as the timer for the cookies buzzed, so Henry let her go with a noticeable reluctance. She glanced over her shoulder and watched as he explained to Noah all that went into a dance like that. It shocked her that Noah listened with the same intensity he reserved only for football.

"To dance like that, you have to be strong," Henry said.

He demonstrated the posture required for other traditional ballroom dances and asked Noah to mirror it and hold the position for a full minute. As soon as the time was up, Noah slouched in relief.

"Not so easy, is it?"

"No."

"Imagine trying to maintain that pose when you're holding your partner, spinning her, dipping her so low her head nearly touches the floor. It's your job to lead her... and you have to show her she can trust you to do it. That requires strength of a different kind."

Noah nodded solemnly and asked Henry to show him some of the steps. Lindsay's mouth fell open.

"Never thought I'd see anything like that," Debbie remarked.

"Like what?"

"Noah interested in dancing, of all things." Debbie grinned at her daughter. "That man of yours can move."

"Yes, he can," Lindsay agreed, squirming with a combination of shyness and possessiveness to hear Henry referred to as *her* man. Her cheeks heated more as memories of other ways his body moved popped gleefully into her mind, and her face heated.

"Oh, my girl. I know that look."

Lindsay groaned. Her mother already knew she'd slept with Henry in Montana, but that didn't mean Lindsay wasn't embarrassed that Debbie could see through her so easily.

"I agree with what your father said yesterday. Henry's a keeper."

"But you've only just met him. How can you know that?"

"In that short time, I've seen more than enough to know it. Take his gifts as one example."

"I love them," Lindsay admitted. "But I'm not happy he bought them. He *knows* I don't—"

"Would you put that stubborn pride of yours away for a moment and listen?"

She snapped her mouth closed and stared at her mother. Debbie hadn't ever been one to hide her feelings, but she wasn't usually so blunt.

"He's not trying to buy your love, Lindsay. If he were, he would've bought something like jewelry or flowers, which require little imagination. Instead, he bought you something you'll use, and maybe the mixer was Noah's idea, but I guarantee you, Henry already had something for your kitchen in mind because he pays attention and knows what you enjoy. More than that, he bought something that brought us all together as a family, which tells me he is not only a generous soul but also one who understands what's important in life."

"But—"

"Stop it, Lindsay. Stop looking for this to fall apart like it fell apart with Max and then with Logan because that is a guaranteed route to failure. I know you haven't had much reason to hope in the last few years, but don't give up just yet."

"I'm not giving up," Lindsay promised softly. "He's here with us because I *do* have hope."

"I'm glad to hear that. Boys!" Debbie called into the living room. "Get your backsides in here. Time to start decorating cookies."

The menfolk returned to the kitchen, and Henry, Noah, and Lindsay got started decorating the first batch of cookies while Steve and Debbie cut out the next and got them in the oven.

Later in the evening, when the cookies were all beautifully decorated, safely wrapped and stored, and the kitchen was once again flawlessly clean, they all headed into the living room to watch Christmas movies—a family tradition Lindsay's parents had started when she was younger than Noah. Lindsay turned off the lights in the kitchen and started toward the living room, but Henry, who'd been rinsing out the washrag, tugged on her hand and pulled her back into the shadows.

"Did I do all right?" he asked.

"You did wonderfully, Henry. We haven't had so much fun as a family in a long time. Thank you."

"You're not mad at me for buying you something?"

"How can I be after that?" She flashed him a smile. "I was inclined to be upset with you, but my mother talked me out of it."

"Mmm. Remind me to thank her." He skimmed his

thumb across her cheek and lowered his head.

She thought he was going to kiss her lips, but instead, he kissed the tip of her nose, flicking his tongue across it.

"What was that for?"

"You had frosting on your nose."

Laughing softly, she curled her arms around his neck and pressed her body firmly against his before claiming his mouth.

"You two coming, or what?" Steve asked.

"Yeah, yeah," Lindsay replied. She sighed at the interruption. "To be continued?"

"You bet. The next time we have a moment alone."

Hand in hand, they ventured into the living room, and without letting her go, Henry sank onto the couch and pulled her down with him so quickly that she lost her balance and ended up in his lap. To this point, they'd refrained from overt displays of affection for Noah's sake, so she was surprised at him. He made a half-assed apology and helped her scoot onto the cushion beside him... but he didn't let her put even an inch of distance between them. She glanced at her son to see what his reaction was. He spared them a fleeting glance, too absorbed by the movie to notice much else.

"Now that we're all settled in," Debbie said, muting the TV, "I have an announcement."

All eyes turned expectantly to her.

"Bill and Mary stopped by yesterday afternoon with two extra tickets to Shannon O'Neil's debut next Friday."

"Shannon O'Neil?" Henry asked. "Pat's little sister?"

"That's the one. She's starring in her first musical at the Paramount Theatre in Seattle... and you and Lindsay are going."

"Mom, I have to work next Friday."

"No arguments," Debbie said firmly. "Switch shifts again or call in sick if you have to. Noah will stay with us so you and Henry can go on a proper date—your first since he's been here, I'd wager. I won't take no for an answer from any of you, so just swallow whatever arguments you're thinking of making and forgive me for being pushy and presumptuous. Also, I don't expect Lindsay home until Saturday... preferably not until she has to get ready for work. Have breakfast together, take a stroll on the beach, whatever you want to do, but enjoy each other for a few hours."

"Yes, ma'am," Henry replied.

Lindsay smacked his arm at the betrayal, but she was smiling. With a laugh, she tucked her feet under her, wrapped her hands around his arm, and rested her head on his shoulder. He kissed the top of her head, and what she'd said to her mother in the kitchen before they'd decorated cookies settled over her again with the warmth of the brightest fire on a cold winter night.

I do have hope. And that in itself is a wonderful thing.

Thirteen

"HELLO, HANDSOME," Debbie greeted when she opened the door at Henry's knock. "I knew you'd look dashing in a tux, but I didn't expect you to look quite *so* gorgeous."

"Thank you." Henry bowed politely at her praise, grinning. "I'm a bit surprised myself."

"That dark blue neck tie paired with the dark gray of the vest and tux really bring out the beauty of your eyes. And I know it's a rental, but it fits you like it was tailored for you."

"Again, thank you. You're sure we won't be over-dressed?"

"It's a semi-formal affair, so you might be a *tad* over dressed, but even so, that's half the fun, isn't it?"

"I suppose so."

"I know you won't be the only ones, though. Bill and Mary are going all out as well, and I believe Pat will be in a tux, too. Seems Aelissm requested it, and with that stunning gown she found, I can't blame her."

Chuckling, Henry remarked, "I'm amazed because Aeli has an even greater loathing of dresses than Lindsay. Speaking of my date...."

"She's almost ready."

As soon as he was far enough into the house to see into the dining room, he spotted Noah and Steve sitting at the table putting a jigsaw puzzle together. They were so intent that Henry was standing behind them, peering down at the colorful tropical island scene—a Christian Riese Lassen painting, if he guessed right—before they realized he was there. Lindsay's father eyed him and nodded in approval. Noah was a bit more vocal about his thoughts.

"You look like a movie star on the red carpet," the boy remarked.

"Thanks, bud. Kinda feel like one, too. Who'd've thought this country boy could pull off Hollywood, eh?"

"You definitely pull it off," Debbie observed.

Henry tapped a puzzle piece and then pointed to where it went. Noah fit it in place. He found another, but this time, he placed it and was sucked into the activity.

A catcall whistle drew his attention away from the puzzle. "Look who's rockin' the penguin suit."

"You're a riot, Lindsay," he remarked. "Very fun...."

When his eyes found her, his voice trailed off. She stood in the kitchen sheathed in a one-shouldered, floor-length gown of shimmery dark blue that hugged her curves before flowing out in a slight flare just below her hips. An off-center, knee-high slit revealed a tantalizing peek of leg and made Henry's jaw drop. Crystal beads or rhinestones—he wasn't close enough to tell which—glittered all over, more numerous toward the top and thinning toward the bottom as if someone had poured a bucket of stars over her and they'd trickled down toward the floor, caught up on the fabric. The cut of the gown was both demure and sexy as hell, drawing attention to her graceful neck and shoulders without revealing too much. When she moved, light danced along the lines of the satiny material and twinkled in the beadwork, mesmerizing him. It was pure elegance.

"Holy cow, Mom," Noah said. "You look amazing. Doesn't she, Henry?"

He swallowed and, still unable to speak, only nodded as his gaze raked over her again. Half her hair was pinned back in a braided bun studded with sparkling rhinestones, and the rest cascaded down her back in soft, silky curls. The only jewelry she wore was a pair of simple dangling diamond earrings. She'd applied very little makeup, even less than she usually wore to work, and the effect was alluringly under-stated and natural. She'd been breathtaking in her brides-maid gown, but in this dress, she was unequivocally exquis-ite.

Finally, he found his voice, but what came out of his mouth didn't feel adequate. "Wow."

He tried again.

Nope. Nothing.

"What? No quick-witted, flirty compliments to make me blush?" Though her words were teasing, her voice was shyly soft.

"Nothing adequate comes to mind."

262

She sidled up to him, needlessly straightened his tie, and gazed up at him with wide, innocent eyes, begging him to reassure her that she was beautiful.

"You are the night sky over Northstar," he murmured, skimming his fingertips under the line of her jaw to her chin, "and I am utterly dazzled by your radiance."

The only thing that kept him from kissing her right then was a vague awareness that they had an audience that included Lindsay's eight-year-old son. Even with their agreement to keep things mostly casual around Noah in the back of his mind, he barely resisted.

"I do hate to interrupt," Steve remarked, "but Pat and Aelissm just pulled up over at Bill and Mary's, so you should probably head over."

Henry helped Lindsay into the knee-length coat Debbie loaned her, and they bid her parents and Noah farewell with a promise to enjoy themselves and their night on the town. As Lindsay lifted the skirt of her dress and sauntered through the front door Henry held open for her, taking the open umbrella as she went, Henry gave Noah's shoulder a squeeze with a twinge of guilt for leaving him behind. He did his best to ignore it, and as he huddled under the umbrella with Lindsay with her hand around his arm, it wasn't *too* difficult. Once they were safely under the overhang of the eaves, Henry collapsed the umbrella and carefully shook the water from it away from Lindsay so he wouldn't splatter the unprotected skirt of her dress.

"I can't remember the last time I used one of these before I arrived here," he remarked. "And I'm pretty sure I've needed one more in the last couple weeks than in my entire life."

"You never use them in Montana?" Lindsay asked after she knocked.

"Not really. They're damned inconvenient when you're out working the ranch, so we just tough it out and get wet. Of course, the rain doesn't keep coming down there like it does here. Rarely does it last more than a day or two."

"Do you not like the rain?" she asked with a note of disappointment in her voice.

"I wouldn't say that. It's just a different world than I'm used to. Kind of fascinating really."

Mary Granger opened the door wearing a beautiful mauve dress. "My, my, my, aren't you both stunning? Come in, come in."

Henry embraced Mary as he walked by her into her lovely house. Furnished entirely in Western style, he felt like he'd stepped out of Washington and back into Northstar and was at home in the space she had so artistically and lovingly decorated.

"It's so good to see you again, Henry," Mary said. "It's been a long time."

"Too long," he agreed. "I'm sorry I missed the last couple trips you and Bill took out to Northstar."

"But you've moved back home. That's wonderful to hear, even if your reason for leaving Denver isn't."

"Thank you, Mary. I've very much enjoyed reconnecting with my family and the ranch, but right now, I'm enjoying your hometown and the company of a certain beautiful, redheaded neighbor of yours."

"So I see. And I hear her best friend is enjoying the company of your twin brother."

"That's the rumor."

They found Pat and Aelissm standing in the living room with Bill. Aelissm's uncle was clad in a tailored three-piece suit, but like Henry, Pat wore a tux—black with a deep emerald green vest and tie that matched his wife's glamorous strapless gown. She was every bit as ravishing as she'd been back in the day when Henry had once taken her dancing and idly entertained thoughts of dating her, perhaps even more so.

"Aelissm, you are absolutely bewitching," he said, taking her hand to kiss her knuckles. "Are you certain you had a baby barely a month and a half ago?"

"I was up three times in the middle of the night with the proof of it, so yes, I'm certain." She glanced up at her husband and tucked her arm around his waist, and a smile of adoration and deeply felt love softened her expression. "But thank you, Henry."

"What a delight to see you here in Indianola, Henry," Bill greeted. "And with our beautiful Lindsay on your arm. I hear there's a story behind this."

"You just keep your matchmaking tentacles to yourself, Unk," Aelissm chided without heat. "By the looks of things, they don't need your assistance."

"Matchmaking tentacles?" Lindsay asked. "*That* sounds like a story to me."

"Bill was rather instrumental in pushing Pat and Aelissm together," Mary explained.

"Pushing?" Bill retorted. "It was barely a nudge."

"Uh-huh." Aeli rolled her eyes. "If that's what you call sending Pat to Montana 'on vacation' to keep me safe from Adam, then you need to reevaluate your definition of the word nudge."

They exchanged a few more pleasantries, but they had a ferry to catch, so they headed back out into the rain and piled into Pat and Aeli's Suburban. The O'Neil children, Henry learned, were with Aelissm's parents, giving them their first no-kids date night in months. On the ride to the ferry, Pat, Bill, and Mary talked about Shannon's new career path, and Lindsay and Aelissm chatted about the challenges and joys of a new baby and the bittersweet inevitably of babies growing up too fast. Henry was content to listen, amused that Lindsay and Aeli chatted like old friends though they hadn't had much interaction during Lindsay's stay in Northstar. When Aeli asked her if she wanted more kids given the right situation, Henry leaned in a little closer so he didn't miss her response.

"I was so young when I had Noah that I hadn't even started to figure out how many kids I wanted someday or *if* I wanted any, and I've spent so long trying *not* to have any more that it's strange to even think about it. But with the right man, yes, I think I would. I know Noah would love to have a brother or a sister."

"With a brother being more likely if Mr. Right is a Mr. Hammond."

Having known Aelissm as long as he had, he should have expected her comment and the blatant sideways glance in his direction, but it floored him, and he turned his head away as his neck and face heated uncomfortably. He swore under his breath.

Lindsay, however, didn't miss a beat, and her response surprised him even more than Aelissm's shameless remark.

"But Aaron has Jessie."

No hesitation whatsoever and no balking at the idea of having children with him. Had she already considered that possibility? He snorted. The thought had already crossed his mind, so he supposed it was a good sign that it had apparently crossed hers, too.

"Yes, and she's the first girl to be born to the Hammonds in... four generations, isn't it, Henry?"

"Yep."

"Beth calls it the Hammond Curse."

"Considering that this tomboy barely knows how to be a girl herself, that might actually be a good thing."

The comment elicited two very different aches, and again, Henry swore, but this time, Aelissm heard it.

"What's wrong, Henry? Is our conversation making that tux a little—"

"Don't you *dare* say it, Aeli," Henry interrupted with a chuckle. "No, it's not exactly the most comfortable conversation for me, but the reason why has little to do with what that dirty mind of yours is thinking right now."

"That's not to say we don't have plans for after Shannon's play," Lindsay added. She walked her fingers up his chest, then smoothed her hand over his collarbone and up his neck before leaning over to kiss him soundly. "Because we do."

"Yes, we do, but unless you want to miss the play, knock that off."

"Tempting, but I wouldn't want those two tickets to go unused."

Aelissm laughed. "Henry, my friend, you're in trouble."

Grinning, he replied, "Maybe so, but I love it."

* * *

Several hours later, Henry and Lindsay stood on the front walk of Bill and Mary's house to say their goodbyes to the Grangers, Pat and his wife, sister, and parents, who'd joined them for late-night snacks out on the Grangers' deck to celebrate Shannon's incredible debut. Henry had met Pat's little sister a few times when she'd come out to Northstar to visit, and he'd heard that she was musically inclined, but she'd blown him and the capacity audience away with her powerhouse voice and emotional performance. He never would have imagined the bold confidence she'd displayed on stage to come out of the outwardly shy young woman with ivory skin, blue-flecked hazel eyes, and hair almost the exact shade of dark copper as Lindsay's. Shannon currently stood with her arms around her brother's and mother's waists to thank Henry and Lindsay yet again for coming to her play.

Without dropping his hand from Lindsay's waist, Henry leaned in to kiss Shannon's cheek. "Congratulations, Shannon. You were amazing tonight, and I can't wait to see what's in your future."

"Thank you, Henry."

"Thank you, Bill, Mary, for an incredible night," Lindsay said, briefly stepping away from Henry to embrace them. "And Pat and Aelissm, I can't even begin to describe how wonderful it was to see you both again. But it's time Henry and I head home to tackle the rest of our plans for the night."

With a wink, Aelissm said, "We certainly don't want to keep you. Hopefully we'll see you back in Northstar soon?"

She slid her gaze to Henry with that last part. He nodded, and she grinned in reply.

"I hope so," Lindsay replied, oblivious of the silent conversation between her date and his friend. "Noah's been pestering me about it."

"In that case… see you soon."

They crossed the street to Henry's truck, which he'd parked in front of the Millers' house, and he opened the passenger door for her and helped her into the cab. She leaned out and rewarded him with a delightfully flirtatious kiss.

It was late enough that Noah would be in bed and hopefully asleep, but the lights were still on in the living room of Steve and Debbie's house, and Henry almost popped in to thank them for providing the means for him to treat Lindsay to a night out. Remembering Debbie's express demand that he and her daughter treat the evening like they were young lovers without a care in the world, he slid in behind the wheel of his truck and started the engine. Some of that adventurous spark Lindsay had treated him to in Northstar had returned tonight, and he'd done his best to stoke it; it was good to see her set her stifling worries aside for a few hours.

At his rented cottage overlooking the beach, he continued his stately gentleman routine and offered his hand to help her out of the truck, and they strolled up the walkway arm-in-arm. Just before they reached the step up to the covered front porch, Lindsay stopped and turned her eyes skyward. Following her gaze, he saw that the last of the clouds had dissipated, and in the narrow clearing between the monstrous cedars that towered above the cottage, the black night sky was studded with a scattering of stars.

"What do you think of Washington?" she asked softly.

"It's beautiful. So green. I love the trees and the beach, and the smell of the salt air is sort of magical. Why do you ask?"

"I was just wondering if you miss Northstar as much as I do."

"Of course I miss it. Just like I missed it when I lived in Denver, but I know it'll always be there, waiting for me whenever I want to come home."

"I miss the stars," she murmured. "Of all the things…. It's the stars that have reminded me the most that I'm here and not in Montana with you."

He reached out and tilted her face toward him. "But I'm right here with you."

"For now, but you have a home and a life you'll have to go back to. And what happens to us then?"

Because he didn't have an answer for that—at least, not one he figured she was ready to hear just yet—he drew her body against his and kissed her deeply, willing her worries away. Then he took her hand and pulled her toward the front door, unlocked it, and closed it behind them. Flipping on the lights, he helped her out of her coat and hung it on one of the hooks beside the door. Then he took a step back, drawing her with him, leading her in the first steps of a waltz.

"What are you…?"

"Shh. Just trust me."

At his entreaty, doubt left her, and without that tension stiffening her movements, her body became fluid grace and elegance. The beads on her dress flashed and winked as they moved across his living room to the stereo so he could turn on some music. Though she had no trouble dancing in her strappy high heels, they paused to kick off their shoes, and before long, they were gliding around the open living area. The concern that had shadowed Lindsay's features vanished, and in its place, an open smile lit up her entire countenance. Laughter danced in her eyes, and in the absence of strain, she was breathtaking. In their time together in Northstar, she had eased his anger and pain without effort, refocusing his attention to her, and now he was glad to do the same for her.

"We move well together, don't we?" he inquired gently.

"We do. Even though I know next to nothing about this kind of dancing."

"I'm not talking about dancing, but yes, we move flawlessly together in that way, too. I'm talking about the way we pick each other up when we're down when no one else can do that for us." He leaned down to press a kiss to the curve of her neck, and she shivered. "I don't know what the future holds for us, but I want to find out because I know what I *want* it to hold."

"And what do you want it to hold, Henry?"

"The same thing that, when Aeli asked you if you wanted more kids and suggested you'd end up with boys if you married a Hammond, spurred you to question the Hammonds' propensity for sons instead of dismissing the idea."

Shyly, she averted her gaze. "You don't want to marry me. I'm—"

"Faulty? Broken? Nothing more than a hot piece of ass?"

She met his gaze again, and pain flashed in her eyes.

"That's what Max and Logan and the other men you've dated have tried to make you believe, but they're too goddamned stupid to see how amazing you are. The fault is theirs, Lindsay, not yours, and I cannot fathom that they could all be so blind. Especially Max. He doesn't have a clue what he lost when he turned his back on you and Noah." He twirled her, brought her against him, and said, punctuating each statement with a kiss on her lips, her neck, her shoulder, "You make that gown look incredible, not the other way around. You are a wonderful mother, a beautiful dancer, and an electrifying lover. You are up for every adventure I can throw at you, my family adores you, and you have become my best friend. You are the first person I want to talk to whenever I have to deal with Mel and Doug and the last thing I think about every night."

"You believe all that? You're not just saying it to make me blush?"

"I've been completely honest with you about everything else to this point, haven't I?"

She nodded.

"Why should or would I be anything else right now? You started something amazing when you laid everything out on the table that first night at the Bedspread." He whirled her away from him, then brought her back, splaying his hand across the small of her back and pressing their bodies tightly together. "Would you believe me if I told you that I never had much patience or passion for dancing before I met you?"

"If you hadn't said something similar at Vince and Evie's wedding, I might not because you seem to be thoroughly enjoying yourself right now."

"I am, but it's all because of you, gorgeous. I just can't get enough of your body."

"Is that so?"

"Mmm-hmm."

"We need to do something about that. But not quite yet."

"No, not yet," he agreed. "When do you have to have that dress back? Didn't you say it's on loan from a friend with a shop in exchange for doing a photoshoot for advertising?"

"Yes, I did. She asked me to come by for that sometime this week, and I'll take the dress back then. Skye's assistant, Joel, will be taking the pictures."

"He any good?"

"Taught by Skye and almost as naturally talented."

"In that case, does your friend have any specific shots in mind? Do you think she'd be willing to incorporate a guy with a tux?"

Lindsay eyed him. "What do you have in mind?"

"I know Pat took a few pictures of us, but it might be fun to get some professional shots, too, to help us remember tonight. Think she'd be up for it if we let her use whatever shots Joel takes of us together?"

"I'm sure she'd love that, especially if you're thinking of shots of us dancing. That'd probably be a lot more visually interesting for marketing than me by myself just standing there smiling. And with how damned fine you look in that tux… she'll be flooded with new business." She smiled up at him. "It says a lot to me that you want keepsakes of us together."

"What can I say? I'm sentimental and I like to have reminders of what I love."

Her mouth fell open at his statement, but she snapped it shut and didn't ask for clarification. He didn't offer further explanation. Instead, he spun her around and pulled her against him with her back pressed to his chest, stepping backwards in perfect timing to the beat of the song. She tipped her head back, laying it on his shoulder and baring her throat. He accepted the invitation and trailed kisses across every inch of skin he could reach, eliciting a shudder of pleasure from her that jammed his sex drive into gear. A fast-paced song came on the radio, and he coached her through ever more complicated steps in a pulse-pounding tango, amazed at how quickly she caught on, and let the physicality of the dance fan the flames of desire.

The steps were forgotten as seeking hands and mouths demanded more. Lindsay grabbed his tie and tugged him toward the stairs and his bedroom at the top. Impulsively, he swept her off her feet and carried her up the stairs. There was no squeal of surprise, no coy laughter, only blatant hunger in the way she kissed him as he ascended to his bedroom. Miraculously, they made it to his room without a single misstep and all their clothing still on. That didn't last long once he set Lindsay on her feet. She had his tie loosened and off faster than he'd ever managed to do it himself, and he quickly reached around her to unzip her gown. With only a fleeting regret that the cultured segment of their date was over, he slipped the dress down her body, pausing to let her step out of it, and tossed it with as much care as his need-driven haste allowed over the footboard of the bed.

"Jeans and T-shirts are *so* much easier to get out of," Lindsay remarked huskily as she unbuttoned his jacket, then his vest, and then his dress shirt. "You are sexy as hell in this tux, but right now, it's damned inconvenient."

He chuckled and assisted her, peeling out of each garment as she finished unbuttoning it. The rest of his fine trappings were shed more quickly, and their undergarments came off even faster. While Lindsay turned back the covers and slid in between the sheets, he yanked a condom out of the nightstand drawer.

"I'm on birth control," she murmured, "so if you want to go without that...."

"I guess we'll be doubly covered. I'd prefer you to be married the next time you get pregnant—" He kissed her neck, intoxicated by the warm, natural scent of her. "—because you deserve nothing less than that guarantee of commitment from your child's father."

He didn't say it, but the desire to be that man was powerful. With that thought in mind, he lavished her body with kisses and caresses, determined to make her feel worshipped and cherished. Because she was.

"Good God, you're beautiful," he sighed. "You make me feel so alive, Lindsay, like my life up to this point was just waiting... waiting for you. You know what I want to say, don't you."

"I do, and I want to hear you say it," she whispered, "but only if you truly mean it. I don't want to hear empty words."

He positioned himself above her, braced on his

forearms, and lowered his head to nuzzle her neck. Then he kissed her with all the tenderness he could muster in the storm of raging need, and against her lips, he whispered, "I love you."

She curled her arms around him and held him tightly, and a tiny whimper escaped her. He didn't expect her to say it back, and he and claimed her mouth in a passionate kiss so she couldn't. He had only his own heart to risk, and so it was easier for him, but she had her son to consider as well, and she needed to know beyond every doubt her heart—abused and burned by callous men—could come up with that he wouldn't repeat what had happened in her past.

He stroked her to aching need, determined to drive any thoughts of anything but the moment from her mind, and entered her slowly, pushing deep until she gasped. His body remembered hers, and the feel of her tight around him drove him wild, but he maintained a firm grip on his control, taking her to the edge and bringing her back down time and again until she begged him to take her over. And then his hold slipped, and he raced mindlessly toward that ultimate satisfaction, driven by need and sensation.

They cried out together, clinging to each other and quivering as the climax broke over them. Henry panted for breath and, derived of the strength to hold his head up, rested his forehead on her chest as his body continued to tremble.

After a while, his heart rate slowed, and he rolled to the side and gathered Lindsay in his arms. He touched his lips to the nape of her neck and exhaled slowly, letting his fingertips dance lovingly over her arm. With her tucked safely in his embrace, he found a peace more complete than he'd ever imagined existed.

"I used to think I understood what changed my brothers when they fell in love."

"How did they change?" Lindsay asked.

"The restlessness of youth stilled. Nick was always laidback, but when he and Beth got together, he found his focus. Same for Aaron. He didn't need the wild thrills of our younger days anymore."

"Why do you suppose that happened?"

"They found what they didn't know their hearts were searching for."

She rolled over to face him, searching his eyes as if she could peer right into his heart. "And you, Henry? What have you found?"

"My center of gravity." He brushed her hair back from her face. Recalling what she'd told him all those weeks ago about what she wanted from their temporary arrangement, his lips lifted. "Tell me, Lindsay. How does it feel to be someone's woman again... for real this time?"

"So wonderful that I realize I've never *been* anyone's woman before."

* * *

Thanks to her mother's scheming, Lindsay had planned ahead for her overnight stay with Henry and brought a set of clothing over before she'd dressed for the play yesterday. She was in no hurry to put them on, however, content to sit up in bed for a while and watch her lover sleep. The sky outside was gray, but the cloud cover was thin, allowing plenty of light to brighten the room and illuminate Henry's sleep-gentled face. In slumber, he was devastatingly handsome, but his physical attractiveness—

undeniable, sure—played only a small part in her perception of him. It was the slow and steady rhythm of his breathing, the new familiarity with the lines of his body, and the memory of last night that captivated her and stirred a possessiveness she'd never felt before. If it was true that she'd never belonged to any man before Henry, it was also true that no man had ever belonged to her. But Henry did, and he'd made that quite clear.

Sighing, she combed her fingers lightly back through his hair, and her heart tripped over itself when his eyes fluttered open and a sleepy smile curved his lips.

"G'morning, gorgeous," he mumbled. "Sleep all right?"

"As deeply as I only seem to when I'm with you." She leaned down to kissed him. "When you call me gorgeous… it's like you're saying *everything* about me is beautiful, inside and out, and I love how that makes me feel. I need to think of a good pet name for you because sexy or handsome just don't cut it. They're both about the physical, and that leaves out too much."

"You can call me whatever you want," he replied. "Just so long as you call me."

"And so long as I don't call you late for dinner, right?"

"Right. Personally, I'm pretty fond of cutie pie. You use it quite a bit."

"Do I?"

"Mmm-hmm."

"Hungry? I thought I'd make us breakfast, and then we can take a walk on the beach. And after that…." She wiggled her brows suggestively.

"Sounds like heaven, but how about we take care of the 'after that' first."

He didn't have to do much to convince her—not the first time in bed nor the second in the shower—and by the time she dressed and headed downstairs, her body was deliciously tingly and feeling a lot like Jell-O again. They flirted shamelessly while she cooked, and it almost turned into round three for the morning. Only the grumbling of their stomachs prevented them from ascending the stairs again. After breakfast, Henry washed the dishes, and after that, they headed down to the beach for a lazy barefoot stroll. They walked arm-in-arm like they had last night, and their shoes dangled from their free hands. Lindsay was blissfully relaxed with no room in her mind for worries. The only time since she'd gotten pregnant with Noah that she had been so carefree had been her trip to Montana, but there, her problems had been far away and easier to ignore. Here, they were just around the corner... and yet, she had no trouble holding them off. The effect Henry had on her was extraordinary.

As they meandered down the beach toward the dock, Lindsay recalled Henry's first day on the beach. They'd all had such fun, the three of them, and the way Noah had taken to him—not just that day but every day since—amazed her. She hadn't allowed herself to wonder what she'd do if they didn't get along, and now that fear seemed silly. Noah adored Henry and had been on his best behavior, wanting to impress him, and while he'd tried to impress Logan, how and why had been different. He'd wanted to get Logan's attention, but with Henry.... She recalled how he'd let go of his too-cool-for-this attitude about baking cookies and how he'd listened so intently to Henry's lesson about dancing, and she realized that her son wasn't trying to garner Henry's attention; he didn't need to because he always had it. No, he admired Henry and wanted to emulate him.

The thought nearly stopped her in her tracks. The one that followed did. *I'm okay with that. More than okay, because I'd be pretty damned proud if he turned into a man like Henry. That'd be a helluva lot better than becoming one like Max or Logan.*

Henry frowned at her, and to cover her distraction, she brushed the bottom of one foot against her leg like she'd stepped on something. She flashed him a smile and started walking again. Satisfied, he matched her strides.

"This is wonderful, us on the beach together," he said after a while, "but something is missing without Noah here with us. The beach just isn't the same without him."

She stopped again and stared at him. "Did I say what I was thinking out loud?"

"No. Why?"

"Because I was just thinking about how well you and Noah get along."

"He's a great kid, Lindsay. You've done a wonderful job with him despite your ex trying to undermine your efforts."

"Thank you."

"Shall we head to your parents' house and go get him? Unless you'd rather have me all to yourself for a bit longer."

"I would, but...."

She chewed on her lip, indecisive, and he chuckled.

"Let's go, then. Besides, I have something I want to talk to your folks about before they start packing to head back to Arizona."

"Oh? And what's that?"

"You're just going to have to wait to find out."

"Race ya to the dock?"

She didn't give him the chance to decline her challenge. Slipping her arm free from his, she shot forward and sprinted across the cold sand. His reaction was faster today than it had been on their first day at the beach, and he caught her halfway to the dock, but instead of passing her to secure the win, he matched her pace and ran beside her. Still, he had to work to run with her, and she took pride in that. When they reached the tall pilings that supported the long dock, they slowed to a walk, stepping carefully to avoid the sharp, broken shells of the mussels and clams that gathered around the dock in greater numbers than elsewhere on the expansive beach.

They passed under the dock and turned toward the long stairs to the top of it. As they climbed, Henry took her hand and kissed the back of it. The gesture wasn't deliberate but habitual, an outward sign that she occupied his thoughts even as his attention was on the tall bluff crowned with evergreens and houses.

At the top of the stairs, they slipped their shoes on and headed up the short street and then left toward her parents' house half a block down the road that ran parallel to the beach. Lindsay entered without knocking, and Henry followed half a step behind. Her parents and Noah sat at the dining room table working on the puzzle they'd started yesterday before Henry had arrived to pick her up for their date.

"You're back early," her father remarked. "We

weren't expecting you until this afternoon."

"That was the plan," Henry replied, "but we missed Noah."

Lindsay watched her son's face light up. The sentiment obviously meant a lot more to him coming from Henry than it would have had she said it, further proof of how attached the boy already was to him. Maybe that should worry her, but with the sensations and emotions Henry had wrought from her still firmly in control of her, she wasn't afraid.

"Well? How was your date?" Debbie asked.

"Incredible," Lindsay replied honestly.

"Hey, Noah, are you up for a game of catch in the backyard while your mom and grandma talk?" Henry interrupted before Lindsay could go into more detail. Both he and her son looked to her for permission, and the matching, hopeful smiles on their faces melted her heart.

"Have fun, boys. But don't be too long because Henry has something he wanted to talk to Grandma and Grandpa about."

Henry didn't take the bait, only winked as he snatched the football off the counter and followed Noah out the sliding glass door to the backyard. After a moment of indecision, Steve rose from the table and headed outside to join them.

"Details?" Debbie asked as soon as the door closed behind the menfolk. "Because I get the feeling something happened. Something good."

Lindsay nodded. "The play was excellent. Shannon was amazing, and it was great to catch up with Pat and Aelissm and Bill and Mary. Henry and I danced in his living room for a bit when we got home, and finished off our evening with a, uh, spectacular finale."

"And?"

"And he said he loves me. First time he's said it."

Debbie digested the information, searching Lindsay's face as she asked, "And did you say it back?"

She shook her head. "He didn't give me the chance to, and I get the feeling he doesn't want me to yet, which I don't entirely understand."

"I do. He wants to make sure you trust it so that when you do—when, I say, my daughter, not if—you'll know for sure that it's real. And judging by the look in your eyes right now, I'd say he's right to be patient with you. What's wrong?"

"It just seems like it's too soon. We've only been dating for a couple weeks, and yes, Montana was amazing, and yes, we've talked on the phone a *lot* since then, but...."

"You two have been together the whole time," her mother commented softly. "Even if you didn't realize it. So really, it's not so soon at all. Let me ask you this. Did you believe him when he said it?"

"Yes."

"Well, there you go."

Her mother started to turn away, making it clear that the conversation was over, but Lindsay wasn't done. She told Debbie what she'd thought on the beach about Noah wanting to emulate Henry and listed out the examples that had led her to that conclusion.

"What do you think about that?" she asked her mother.

"I think Henry is a fine example for your son to

follow."

"Thank you, Mama. I needed to hear that."

"You need to stop worrying and overthinking things, Lindsay. Remember what I told you about expecting this to fail?"

"I'm trying to, but old habits are hard to break."

"I know they are, my sweet girl." Debbie hugged her. "And I wish to God you'd never had reason to form those habits. But I see Henry starting to break them."

Nodding, Lindsay walked over to the back door to call Henry, Noah, and her father inside.

"Is it time?" Henry asked.

"Yes, it is. Spill your guts, Mr. Hammond."

He set the football on the counter and leaned against the island, waiting until everyone had gathered around him before he spoke. "Christmas. I want you all to come to Northstar for the two weeks Noah has off from school. I've already reserved my parents' vacation rental for you, free of charge."

Lindsay's first thought was to reject the idea, but with her mother's words fresh in her mind, she swallowed that urge, which allowed her to see clearly. "How long have you been planning this?"

"Since the day I called you to ask if I could come see you."

Her mother looked pointedly at her, and Lindsay ignored her.

"Can we, Mom?" Noah asked. "Please?"

"You're supposed to spend Christmas with your father, Noah."

Disappointment splashed across her son's face, and

his shoulders fell. "I don't want to go. I'd rather go to Montana and see Henry's ranch and meet his family. Dad doesn't want me to come for Christmas, anyhow. You know he doesn't."

"Considering how much coercing it took to get him to agree to Christmas," she said, "I'm sure it wouldn't be too hard to make different arrangements for you to go see him some other time."

Instant mood reversal.

"Really?"

"Does that mean you'll all come?" Henry asked with an adorable hopefulness that matched her son's.

"I know I'd love to see this place that has stolen my daughter's heart," Steve said. "And with our stay already paid for, how can I say no? What do you say, Deb?"

"I'm there."

"Lindsay?" Henry asked.

"You know I miss your family and Northstar," she replied. "And since I've been living here, I can actually afford to take the time off."

"So you'll come?"

"Yes, Henry, we'll come." She kissed him firmly, and when she stepped back, he was grinning like a fool. "I can't wait."

Fourteen

WHEN LINDSAY WALKED out of Donovan's three days later on Tuesday, Henry and Noah were waiting for her in his truck. Instead of getting off the bus at her cousin's like he usually did when Lindsay worked the dinner shift, Noah had gotten off at home and spent the afternoons with Henry. Her parents had left for Arizona early yesterday morning with the plan to meet up in Northstar on the twenty-first, and when they had suggested Sunday night before their departure that Noah might enjoy being at home in the afternoons instead of at his cousin's and that he might also be more likely to get his homework done immediately instead of drawing it out, Lindsay had surprised herself by agreeing. Henry had liked the idea, and Noah had jumped at the opportunity to spend more time with him. That she was entirely comfortable leaving her son alone with Henry was a monumental step forward. She'd never trusted Logan enough to let him watch Noah, and she hated leaving her son with his own father.

"You boys have fun together this evening?" she inquired when they climbed out of the truck to greet her.

"Once I got my homework done, yeah," Noah replied. "We threw the football on the beach. Actually, even homework was kinda fun. We did our own liquid density experiment like the one I did in class today... only Henry's actually worked how it's s'posed to. I'll probably be the only kid in class with the right answers on the homework."

"I'm impressed by you both. Did you thank him?"

"Yes, he did," Henry replied, leaning down to kiss her cheek. "How was work?"

"Long and exhausting as usual."

"Hopefully we can help with that a bit. We made spaghetti, and while it isn't nearly as good as what you make and will have to be reheated since we ate a couple hours ago, we thought you might appreciate not having to cook dinner for yourself after work."

Lindsay nearly sighed with relief. "I do indeed. You're spoiling me."

"And enjoying it, so get used to it."

"You deserve to be spoiled, Mom," Noah remarked.

She hugged him. "Aw, thank you, bud."

"You were able to get the two weeks off, right?" Henry asked.

"Yep, thanks in large part to Mitch. The manager didn't want to give it to me since we're always busier over the holidays, but Mitch suggested I might quit if I didn't get it—fat chance of that happening, and Mitch knows it—but it worked, and I have the twenty-first through the third off and back to work on the fourth."

"Hey, Mitch!" Henry called, spotting the cook as he stepped out of the restaurant on his way home.

The heavyset man glanced up and waved when he spotted them.

"Thank you!" Henry called.

"You're welcome," Mitch replied. "Take care of my girl over there in Montana."

"You bet I will. Have a good night."

"You as well."

Turning back to Lindsay, Henry grinned. "I like him."

"He's a good man," she agreed. "Like you. Other than Skye and Evie, he's probably one of my best friends even if we only ever talk at work. And I owe him big time." Sighing happily, she gestured for Noah to hop in the truck and climbed in after him. "I can't remember the last time I had two full weeks off. The ten days I took off for Evie's wedding was amazing, but a whole two weeks? I may never want to come back."

She entertained herself as Henry drove out of the parking lot of Donovan's Bar and Grill by imagining all the ways an extra four days off would feel, especially an extra four days off in Northstar with Henry, both their families, her son, her friends…. The end-of-day fatigue melted away just thinking about it.

"Guess that answers the question of whether or not you're having second thoughts with a definitive no."

"I've had second thoughts about a lot of things in my life, but spending Christmas in Montana with you isn't on that list."

"And what about you, Noah?" Henry asked. "Any second thoughts about it?"

"Are you kidding me? I've wanted to go to Montana since Mom came back! Do you think we'll have a white Christmas?"

"Most likely. I can't remember one in my lifetime when there wasn't snow on the ground."

"I've never had a white Christmas before."

"Not even when you were at your dad's? Doesn't he live in Spokane?"

"Yeah, but both years I've been at his house for Christmas, there wasn't any snow."

"I'd say you're in for a first, then. What about you, Lindsay?"

"Two that I can remember. We don't get a ton of snow out here."

Henry drove home, and Lindsay listened as he and Noah talked about all the fun things they could do in the snow on their trip. Now that she knew for sure she'd have the entire two weeks off, she'd have to call Max to tell him Noah wouldn't be coming for Christmas. She didn't think he'd mind too much since it had been such a battle to get him to agree to have Noah over for just three nights, but regardless, she wasn't looking forward to talking to him. Noah had only called him once since Henry had been in Washington, and she hadn't spoken to him at all, and the lack of that chaos in her life had been nothing short of wonderful. Too bad it couldn't always be like that.

Too soon, Henry parked in front of her parents' house. Weariness descended on her at the thought of her call to Max about Christmas. *Just get it over with.*

Henry unlocked the door and held it open for her and Noah. He offered to reheat some spaghetti for her while she called her ex. She took the cordless into the living room, dialing his number as she walked, and sank onto the couch to kick off her shoes while she waited for him to answer. Her heart skittered nauseatingly when he answered, but unlike days gone by, it was only anxiety she felt. There was not even a flicker of her former infatuation with him left to stir longing.

"Noah?"

"No, it's Lindsay."

"Well, isn't this a surprise. It's been a while."

"Not long enough," she said tiredly. "I have something I need to talk to you about or—believe me—I wouldn't be calling. It's about Christmas."

"I thought we had everything planned out for Noah's visit already."

"We did, but there's been a change in plans. We—Noah, my parents, and I—have been invited to spend Christmas in Montana."

"Invited by whom? Evie?"

"No."

"Don't tell me that Henry guy Noah's been talking nonstop about invited you."

"Yes, he did."

"You're not seriously thinking of going."

She ground her teeth. He had a way of making her feel like a chastised child, and he had no right to dictate what was good or right for her. If he'd ever had that right, he'd long since lost it. "Not just thinking about it. We *are* going."

"No, you aren't. It's my turn to have Noah for Christmas. I won't let you take that away from me like you're trying to take everything else away."

"Trying to take...? You've got to be joking."

"I don't want my son around that man, Lindsay."

"Now he's *your* son? You know what, Max? Spending time with Henry has been good for Noah. *Very* good for him. He's getting his homework done early every night, he's actually *enjoying* school for the first time this year, and he's started to *willingly* help out around here. I'm sorry you don't like it, but Henry's a great role model for him."

"Like Logan was? He was a real great role model for our son, chasing after you like a dog after a bitch in heat."

"Don't even go there with me, Max, because right now, I'm inclined to lump you into the exact same category as Logan."

"My dad is *nothing* like Logan was," Noah spat.

Lindsay glanced up, suddenly realizing that he'd been standing close enough to hear Max's end of the conversation along with hers. Anger and pain burned in his eyes. Despair crashed down on her. "We'll talk about this in a—"

"No. I don't want to talk about it because Dad is right. All Logan wanted was you, and you were too stupid to know that he was only pretending to like me."

"I have to go," Lindsay said to Max and abruptly ended the call. By now, Henry had joined them in the living room, but she ignored him and addressed her son with fury and agony fighting for control of her. "Noah Ulrich, how dare you speak to—"

Henry stepped between them, leaning down with his

back to her and his face just inches from Noah's. The boy's eyes rounded, and in the reflection on the glass doors of the entertainment unit, Lindsay caught a glimpse of the reason why. Henry's expression was stony. Shock tinged with a hint of curiosity obliterated any consternation she might have felt over such a blatant and uninvited intrusion into her duties as Noah's parent.

"You owe your mother an apology," he said in a low voice.

"You can't tell me what to do," Noah retorted. "You're not my dad!"

"Obviously not. No son of mine would *ever* treat his mother with such disrespect."

Noah opened his mouth to counter, then snapped it shut.

"I will not tolerate the kind of attitude you are displaying right now, Noah, so until you learn to address your mother with the respect she deserves, our time together is done. No more help with your homework after school, no more football on the beach, no more guy time. You can go back to getting off the bus at your cousin's after school. Oh, and no trips to Montana with your mom, either."

"The trip's off anyhow, so who cares?" His voice wavered, and Lindsay could see the implications of Henry's promises sinking in.

"There will be other trips, Noah, so you might want to head to your room and think about that for a while."

With lip quivering and tears threatening to spill over, Noah dashed to his room and slammed the door. Lindsay winced. Henry straightened but remained where he was, looking over his shoulder toward Noah's bedroom on the other side of the wall at the far end of the living room. The muscle in his jaw pulsed, and his brows were drawn low in regret, and to see that scolding Noah hurt him endeared him even more to Lindsay.

It was almost a minute before he turned to her.

"I'm sorry for overstepping my bounds, Lindsay," he murmured, sitting beside her on the couch with that same pained expression.

"Don't be sorry," she replied. "It's what he needed— to hear that from someone he respects. He gets caught in the middle between Max and me, and he has to defend whichever of us he feels is under attack. I can't fault him for loving his father even if Max doesn't much deserve it."

"I can't fault him for that, either, but you bust your ass to make sure he has everything he needs, and you do not deserve to be talked to like that, regardless of the reason."

He folded her into his arms, and she leaned into him.

"I am so sick of this. So sick of fighting Max and watching him turn my son into that nasty, mouthy brat you just saw... because that is *not* my son. My son is a kind, warm-hearted boy."

"I know who your son is, Lindsay," Henry whispered. "And that's why I had to step in. I had to remind *him* of that."

That undid her, and without warning, she broke down. Tears poured from her eyes as frustration, guilt, and rage melded together with gratitude and hope, and Henry held her with unwavering patience as she cried. He didn't have to say it for her to know she had permission to fall apart, and the freedom to do so began to stitch her ragged thoughts and emotions together again. *Every time*, she thought. *Every time this happens, my heart breaks a little more. But I finally have someone to help me put it back together.*

"I'm not going to let you cancel your trip to Montana," he whispered. "So we'll have to find a way to accommodate Max."

"No." She straightened but didn't move to pull away from him. She wasn't strong enough to leave his embrace just yet. "I don't want to accommodate him, and I most certainly don't want to cancel our trip to Northstar. I need it too much."

"So, what do you want to do about Max?"

Bit by bit, she gathered her courage, bolstered by Henry's gentle support. "As far as I'm concerned, he can go to hell, but unfortunately, that's not an option."

"No, it isn't."

"I don't even want to consider this because I don't want to cut our time in Northstar short, but would it be too big a pain to leave a few days early and spend New Years in Spokane so Noah can spend a night or two with his dad?"

Henry briefly got up to fetch the magnetic calendar from the fridge and rejoined her on the couch. "The beauty of this whole trip is that everything is flexible and negotiable, so that wouldn't be a pain at all. It's only about a six-hour drive from Northstar to Spokane, so we could leave early on the thirtieth or the thirty-first."

"Better make it the thirty-first. I don't want to have to cut our trip any shorter than I have to, and if we leave early enough, Noah will still have plenty of time on New Year's Eve with Max."

"Do you think Max will go for that?"

"Guess I'll find out," Lindsay replied, picking up the

phone again. She pulled Henry's arm tighter around her waist.

"What the hell was that all about?" Max demanded without bothering with a greeting.

"Never mind what it was about," she replied. "Here's what's going to happen, and you can either take it or leave it. I really don't care. We're driving to Montana on the twenty-first, and we'll leave early on the thirty-first so you and Noah can spend New Year's together. We'll leave Spokane on the second, which will give us a couple days to rest before he has to go back to school the following Monday."

"No. I want Noah for Christmas, Lindsay. Giselle and I have already made plans, and besides, I thought I was very clear about not wanting Noah around Henry."

"Maybe if you'd chosen to be more of a father to Noah to this point, I'd give a damn about what you think. As it is… I don't. I've made accommodations to make sure you still get to see your son over winter break, but Noah and I *will* be in Montana for Christmas. What'll it be, Max? Because if you don't want to take the offer, we'll happily spend those extra days in Montana."

Her ex was silent for a long time, and Lindsay might've wondered if he'd hung up on her, but she could hear the television on in the background.

"Well?" she prodded.

"I guess New Year's it is. I'm not happy about this, Lindsay."

"As I said, I don't give a damn if you are or aren't. Your happiness is so far down my list of priorities that I'm not sure if it's even still *on* the list."

"You got what you wanted, so there's no need to be

a bitch."

"That's rich, coming from you." Lindsay grinned triumphantly at Henry, and he beamed back at her. "But I'm done letting you ruin *my* happiness. We'll see you on the thirty-first, Max. I'll call you before we leave that morning with an ETA."

"Fine. Put Noah on the phone, please."

"No. He's in his room thinking over his attitude right now, but if he wants to talk to you afterwards, he's more than welcome to call you. Goodbye, Max."

Deciding to quit while she was ahead, she ended the call without even waiting for Max to respond to her farewell and let out a long breath. She shifted her position to face Henry and found him watching her with profound pride etched into his face. He slipped his hand around to the back of her head and leaned forward to kiss her tenderly.

"I'm going to head home and let you eat in peace," he murmured. "I'll see you in the morning after Noah goes to school."

"What if I want you to stay?"

"It's best that I go. I meant what I said to Noah." He touched his lips to hers again, and when he pulled away and stood, he smiled. "But don't worry. Something tells me he won't hold out for long."

She followed him to the door, leaning out into the chilly, damp night. He hugged her, holding her tightly for a few minutes—just long enough to restore peace to her heart but not so long that she would be tempted to beg him to stay.

"Love you, gorgeous."

Again, he didn't let her say it back, striding out to his

truck before she could. She watched him drive off.

"I love you, too," she whispered, and she knew it was true.

Returning to the dining room, she sat down to eat her dinner even though she was too agitated to be hungry. The house was remarkably quiet with no sound whatsoever coming from Noah's room. It was a little after nine, so it was possible he'd fallen asleep, though that was doubtful. Was he actually thinking about what Henry had said? Lindsay promised herself she'd finish her meal before she went to see.

As it turned out, she didn't have to wait that long.

In the silence, the sound of his door opening was loud, and a floorboard in the hallway creaked as he stepped on it on his way into the kitchen. A moment later, he appeared in the kitchen, but instead of joining her, he headed straight for the door and grabbed his coat off the peg behind the door.

"Just where do you think you're going, young man?" she demanded.

"I'm gonna go talk to Henry."

Then he was gone, and she stared at the closed front door in shock for half a second before it sank in that her son had just vanished outside. She skidded around the counter separating the kitchen from the living room and ran to the door, jerking it open. He was gone, swallowed by the black night.

"Noah!" she yelled.

Instinct compelled her to run after him, but she didn't. It was only two and a half blocks to the cottage Henry was renting, and Indianola was a peaceful town.

There was also the gut belief that he needed a man's advice right now more than his mother's terrified chastisement. She waited long enough for him to reach the cottage, listening intently with her heart pounding for any sound of trouble, then went back in and called Henry.

"Is Noah there?"

"He just showed up. Do you want me to send him home?"

"No. Not until he's ready."

"I'll walk him home when he is."

She thanked him and hung up, then collapsed on the couch and prayed Henry would be able to succeed where she'd failed.

* * *

It tortured Henry to leave Lindsay so soon after she'd broken down, but he knew her well enough to understand that she needed some time alone to talk with her son. As it was, he'd already stuck his foot in it when he'd told Noah to apologize to her. It wasn't his place to discipline her son no matter how much he wanted it to be, so he ignored every instinct to stay to make sure she was all right. Of course she was... or would be. She'd been dealing with this for eight years, and she'd been strong enough to do it all on her own all that time, so he reminded himself that she was more than capable of handling it tonight.

I don't want her to have *to deal with it on her own,* he grumbled as he let himself into his cottage.

As soon as he closed the door behind him, he sank onto the couch facing the windows and stared into the black night with its pinpricks of orange lights. Tonight, the reflections of those lights were distorted; the evening's rain and wind had pushed the salty waters between Indianola and Bainbridge Island into choppy waves that clawed at the shore below his cottage. Normally, that sound intrigued his Montana-bred senses, but tonight, it only made him more acutely lonely. What if Noah took his words to mean he didn't want the boy around? That he would do the same thing Logan had? That couldn't be farther from the truth, but did Noah know that? Henry understood that he needed to give Noah time to think over what he'd done and what Henry had said about it, but that didn't mean it was easy to sit here alone in the cottage and wait.

Sighing, he glanced at the clock. It was after ten back home, and he'd probably wake his early-to-rise parents, but he should call them to let them know of the change in his and Lindsay's plans for Christmas. He needed the distraction, and they'd understand.

"I'm surprised to hear from you so late, Henry," his mother replied, fully lucid. "You usually have more consideration."

"Oh, lord. What did I interrupt?"

"I'm sure you can figure it out," John said, apparently only a few feet away as he was close enough to hear Henry's side of the conversation. "So this had better be good."

"Probably not good enough," Henry replied. "Lindsay and I are going to have to cut our stay short by a few days so we can drop Noah off at his dad's for New Years. I just wanted to let you know."

"I thought the idea was for Noah to visit his dad on that three-day weekend later in January," Tracie remarked.

"It was. Max threw a temper tantrum, partially about not seeing his son for Christmas… but mostly about Noah spending time with me. He said some not-so-nice things to Lindsay, knowing exactly where to hit her to cause the most damage. And then Noah lashed out at her instead of at Max."

"Uh-oh."

"Yeah. It wasn't fun. But we dealt with it, and she called Max back to tell him that Christmas in Montana was non-negotiable, so she and Noah and her parents are still coming."

"I'm glad to hear that. We're quite looking forward to it. With them and Skye and her family joining us, it'll be the kind of raucous Christmas we used to have when your father's brothers and their families all came home."

"You going to tell him about the phone messages from Mel?" Henry heard his father ask.

"I think maybe I should wait," Tracie replied away from the phone.

Not far enough away, Henry thought. "Too late for that now. What messages from Mel?"

"I stopped up to check on your house this afternoon, and I saw the light on your answering machine flashing, which I thought was odd because everyone who would call you knows you're in Washington and has the number there or your cell. I didn't think you'd mind, so I listened to the messages. They were all from Mel—sixteen of them—and all she said was that she needs to talk to you."

"She left *sixteen* messages? Holy Christ. And she didn't say in even one of them what was so urgent that she would call me *sixteen* times?"

"No, she didn't."

What the hell could be so important? He'd made sure

she and Doug both understood that he would be away from home for an extended period of time and that they had until Christmas to figure out what to do about Dylan and each other before he started searching for a lawyer for Mel, and he had purposefully not given either of them the phone number of the cottage because he'd wanted to focus solely on Lindsay.

"Well, thanks for letting me know."

Henry ended the call and wandered into the living room, slumping into the canvas-colored couch again with his legs stretched out in front of him. For a while, he stared out the broad windows at the lights scattered along the shore of Bainbridge Island and debated calling Mel. After the kerfuffle with Max and Noah, he wasn't in the mood to deal with anything that was sure to add more stress, but she wouldn't have called him sixteen times if it wasn't important... would she? She'd been struggling since he'd left, but he had hoped Doug would either let go of his anger and willingly step up to the plate or do it because he didn't want to incur the expenses and frustration of a court battle. What if Doug was still fighting it? The memory of Lindsay crying spurred him to action. He dialed Mel's number.

"Hello?" she answered.

"It's Henry."

"Oh, hi! I didn't recognize the area code."

"I'm still in Washington. My mom said you've left a bunch of messages on my answering machine. What do you need?"

"I don't need anything."

"Then why did you leave sixteen messages?"

"Well, for one, I have good news. Doug and I are

back together."

Henry jerked his head back. That *was* good news—better than he'd expected when he'd last talked to Doug. "That's great, Mel."

"Yeah. It hasn't been easy, but we're working through our issues, and I think we're going to make it. I'm hopeful, anyhow. He and Dylan are bonding pretty quickly."

Relief surged through Henry, and he tipped his head back to rest it on the back of the couch. *Thank God.* "That is a huge weight off me, Mel. You have no idea."

"Actually, I do, which brings me to my other reason for trying to get in touch with you. Doug and I want to come to Northstar for a few days over Christmas. We have a couple things to talk to you about that should be done in person. I know you'll like one of them, and I'm hoping you'll like the second."

"I don't think that's a good idea."

"Why not?"

"For one, my girlfriend and her family are coming out to the ranch for Christmas."

"You have a new girlfriend? Is it serious?"

"Very, but she's not a new girlfriend."

For a while, Mel said nothing, and he wondered what was going through her mind. Then he decided he didn't care. She wasn't his concern anymore, and he certainly didn't need her approval.

"Do you love her?" Mel finally asked.

"Yes, I do."

"Not even the slightest hesitation. It *is* serious."

A knock on the front door yanked his attention from

the call. Who would be visiting so late? Standing, he strode across the living room to the front door and peered out the window beside it. When he saw Noah, he immediately opened the door and stepped back to let the boy in, glancing outside into the darkness but seeing neither Lindsay nor her car. Noah must have come by himself, which was worrisome.

"Mel, I have to go. Noah just showed up without Lindsay."

"Who's Noah? And who's Lindsay?"

"Lindsay is my girlfriend, and Noah is her son. I gotta go."

"Henry, wait. What about Christmas?"

"Why can't you just tell me over the phone?"

"I already told you. It's something we need to do face to face. So… what do you say?"

"I need to think about it."

He hung up right then and regarded Noah with arms crossed and brows lifted expectantly. The phone still in his hand rang, and he glanced at the small screen. Seeing Lindsay's number, he answered it.

"Is Noah there?"

"He just showed up." Henry eyed her son, who refused to meet his gaze. "Do you want me to send him home?"

"No. Not until he's ready."

"I'll walk him home when he is."

"Thank you, Henry."

For the second time in as many minutes, Henry hung up the phone. This time, he walked into the kitchen and set it on the counter, then gestured for Noah to have a seat on the couch. Henry sat on the couch perpendicular to him, angling his body so he faced the kid, and leaned forward to wait for Noah to speak. Surprisingly, it didn't take the boy long.

"I'm sorry," he said.

"Thank you, but I'm not the one you need to apologize to. That was an incredibly hurtful thing you said to your mother, Noah."

"I know it was. I didn't mean to say it, and I didn't mean it. I never do." At last, he lifted his gaze to meet Henry's. "Honest."

"I believe you, but I'm curious to hear why you think you do it."

"Because I can't help it."

"Why not?"

"Because... because I get so mad and I have to get it out. I hate that my dad says things like that to hurt her, but every time I try to tell him so, he just does it more, and I get angrier until I say the same kinds of things to Mom that he says. I don't like it."

"I'm not hearing what I need to hear from you, Noah. Why do you say those things to your mother, who loves you unconditionally, who gives up so much to make sure you have what you need?"

"I don't know!"

"Try harder."

"I do it... because I can, I guess. Because I know she loves me even when I'm a jerk to her."

"In other words, she's the only one who makes you feel safe enough to vent."

"Yeah."

"I'm glad we cleared that up. I'm also glad to know that you *do* understand and appreciate everything she does for you."

"Why do *you* think I do it?"

"You're frustrated without a way to make the person who frustrates you understand that."

Noah braced his elbows on his knees and dropped his head into his hands. "I don't want to spend Christmas with my dad. I'd rather spend it in Montana with Mom and you and Grandma and Grandpa."

"That's still the plan, Noah."

"But, Dad said—"

"Your mother called him back and stood her ground about Christmas."

"But what about Dad?"

"We'll leave Northstar a few days early and spend a couple nights in Spokane so you can see him. That all right with you?"

"I don't want to see him at all."

"Maybe not right now, but you need to. He *is* your father."

Noah snorted. "Barely. How come he can't be more like you? I bet you'd be a great dad."

"Well, thank you," Henry replied. He didn't dare say anything else because the innocent comment felt like a punch to the gut, and he wasn't sure he could hide that it simultaneously made him miss Dylan and hope Noah would accept him as his stepfather should it come to that.

"Do you love my mom?" the boy asked abruptly.

"Yes, I do. Very much."

"Like… enough to marry her?"

"I'm beginning to believe so, yes, but let's give time a chance to do its thing, all right? Your mom and I have both been hurt, and she especially needs to know that this isn't another mistake."

"How were you hurt?"

That particular topic was surrounded by landmines, but Henry had promised he'd be honest with Noah. "It's complicated and maybe a bit much for you to understand just yet, but I thought I was the father of a beautiful little boy—his mother made me believe I was—but it turned out I wasn't."

"Did you love her?"

"On some level I did, but it was nothing like how I love your mom." Henry paused, took a deep breath, and admitted the lie. Compared to how I love your mom, no, I didn't love that boy's mother."

"Kinda like my dad didn't love *my* mom."

"I guess so, yes."

"Except that you loved the boy you thought was your son."

"I still do even though he isn't." Henry watched as Noah's face fell, and his heart went out to the kid. "Your dad loves you, too, Noah. Maybe he doesn't show it. Maybe he doesn't know how."

"Or maybe he's just a selfish asshole." As soon as the words were out, Noah clamped his hand over his mouth and stared at Henry with rounded eyes. "Please don't tell my mom I said that word!"

"I should," Henry replied, pausing just long enough to make the kid nervous. "But I won't."

"I don't mind if you kiss her, you know."

Chuckling, Henry said, "Thanks, bud."

"If you marry my mom, please don't send me to live with my dad."

"Never. You remember what I said to you that day at the mall about you and your mom being a packaged deal? I mean that, Noah. Every word of it. In fact, even if you *wanted* to go live with your dad, I'd probably beg you to stay with us."

"You mean it?"

"Yes, I do. You're a great kid, and I love you as much as I love your mother."

Without warning, Noah launched himself at Henry, wrapping his arm's tightly around Henry's neck. Henry hugged him back and murmured, "You know that it won't be all fun and games, though, right? You live in my house, you'll have to follow my rules, and rule number one is you treat your mother with absolute respect... starting with finding a new way to vent your anger because she doesn't deserve to be the target of it. Let it out on me if you have to, but not on her. All right, bud?"

Noah only nodded. It was a long time before he loosened his hold on Henry, and when he did, he drew himself up with a deliberate composure. "I'm ready."

"All right."

They didn't speak on the walk home, but Noah gripped Henry's hand. It wasn't raining, but a thick layer of clouds blocked out the stars, plunging the areas not illuminated by the orange glow of the streetlamps into pitch-blackness. It was a quiet town, and in Henry's time here, he'd seen and heard nothing to make him believe otherwise, but it terrified him a little to picture Noah making the walk from his grandparents' house to the cottage alone, and he knew there was no way Lindsay would have let him go by himself if she'd had a say in the matter. Unsurprisingly, when they reached the Millers' house, she was furious with her son, but she waited until they were inside before she said anything.

"Go easy on him," Henry said gently.

"Go easy? He walked out with little more than 'I'm gonna go talk to Henry' and—"

"Lindsay. He has something he needs to say to you. Please give him a chance to say it."

She snapped her mouth shut, folded her arms, and turned to her son. "Well, out with it."

"I'm sorry," Noah said. "I'm sorry for leaving like I did, and I'm sorry for what I said earlier. I'm sorry, too, for being such a butthead all the time. I don't ever mean what I say."

By now, tears slipped down Noah's cheeks, and he threw his arms around his mother's waist. When Lindsay's fear-driven anger fizzled and she returned the embrace, Henry stepped outside to give them some privacy.

Because the step was damp from the rain earlier in the day, he leaned against the post supporting the small roof over the front door and exhaled slowly. The door opened behind him, and he glanced over his shoulder to watch Lindsay step outside. Without a word, she tucked her arms around him and leaned into him, sighing.

"Whatever you said to him, thank you," she murmured.

"You're welcome, but I'm not sure it was so much what I said as what he did. Your son has a good heart,

Lindsay. He's just frustrated with Max, like you are."

"Did you tell him about New Year's?"

He nodded. "I hope you don't mind."

"Why would I mind? I think this trip will be as good for him as it will be for me. He could really use the Hammond brand of love to show him what a family should be." She looked up at him and smiled sheepishly. "Not to pile the pressure on you or anything."

Chuckling, he kissed the top of her head. "I'll do my best to prove that your faith in me isn't misplaced. Speaking of Christmas... Mel and Doug want to come up for a couple days."

"To Northstar?"

Lindsay leaned away, frowning.

"Supposedly they have something—something I'll supposedly like—that they need to talk to me about in person."

"Mel *and* Doug?"

"Yep. They're back together."

"That's good news, right?"

"I would think so. I need your opinion, Lindsay. I'm not inclined to agree to them coming."

"But you're curious to know what they want."

He nodded.

"It's not my place to tell you what to do."

"Yes, it is." He touched his lips lightly to hers. "It's your place because I say it is. I love you, and I care what you think."

"You said a while back that a friend of her partner's wanted to buy her out. Could this be about that? Maybe she's agreed to it and has the funds to pay you back. That'd be something you like, wouldn't it?"

"Could be, but why would she need to tell me that in person?"

"Maybe she needs you to sign paperwork."

"So you're saying I should tell her to come? Are you okay with that?"

"I guess I'll find out."

Henry searched her face intently for any sign that she was only saying he should tell Mel and Doug it was okay to come to Northstar for Christmas to humor him. She wasn't entirely comfortable, that was for sure, but neither did she seem overly worried about it, and it was possible the unenthusiastic response had more to do with her recovering from the emotional strain of the evening. He decided to ask. "Talk to me, love."

She smiled at that, but it didn't last long enough. "I'm just wondering how long she plans to keep jerking you around like this."

"What do you mean?"

"She knows just what buttons to push to get what she wants out of you. Just like Max and me. It's a bad cycle, Henry, and we both need to get out of it. I think I took a pretty big step tonight when I refused to let him ruin Christmas for us… and maybe sitting down with Mel and Doug will be that first big step for you. So, no, I'm not entirely comfortable with them coming to Northstar over Christmas, but it needs to happen."

"You're sure?"

She nodded.

"You're an amazing woman, Lindsay Miller," Henry said, pulling her close. "And while it pisses me off to no end

310

how Max treats you, I'm glad he was too stupid to see how wonderful you are because I might never have met you if he'd realized it."

She rested her head on his chest, and he felt the tension leave her body. "I believe it now."

"Believe what?"

"That I love you, too."

He gave her one last squeeze to acknowledge her admission, then took her hand and led her inside. Noah was sitting on the couch with a thoughtful expression, but when he spotted them, he grinned broadly. Lindsay sat on one side of him and Henry on the other, squishing him between them in a big hug. In this moment, they were a family... a family like Henry hadn't known he'd wanted until Mel had told him she was pregnant. Only this time, he was in love.

Fifteen

AFTER TWO NERVE-WRACKING DAYS on the road driving through a monster winter storm that had turned all seven hundred or so miles into a sloppy nightmare of sleet, ice, and snow and a night spent in an uncomfortable hotel bed, they were finally approaching Henry's home. Lindsay shouldn't have the energy left to be awed by the sight of the Northstar Valley and its guarding mountains under a thick blanket of snow and a thicker ceiling of dark clouds, but as Henry drove north on the scenic byway and that view unfolded before her, all traces of weariness fled, and she leaned forward in her seat to better see out the windshield. Plumes of snow wafted over the mountains and foothills, and all the color had been leeched from the world but the hint of gray-blue that was the pine and fir forests and the deep red bark of the leafless willows along the streams. The shades of gray and white lent a stark but staggering beauty and otherworldliness that transformed Northstar.

"Noah, wake up," she breathed, reaching into the narrow back seat of Henry's truck to nudge her snoozing son. "We're almost home."

"Yes, we are," Henry murmured, glancing at her with a tender smile as he navigated the snow-covered road with the ease of a lifetime of practice.

At his words, she realized with a start what she'd said and opened her mouth take the words back… and didn't because that's exactly how she felt in her heart—like she was coming home. Relief and joy mingled with the promise of adventure and excitement at reuniting with the friends she'd made here back in August. She covered Henry's hand, which rested on the gearshift, curling her fingers around his with a squeeze. He briefly met her gaze again, and she smiled in thanks for this gift.

"Wha' did ya say, Mom?" Noah mumbled behind her.

"I said we're almost home to Northstar," she replied. "We're in the valley, so open your eyes and take a look."

A moment later, she heard him whisper, "Oh, wow."

She glanced back at him to see his face nearly pressed to the tinted window with the most open awe she had seen in his expression in a very long time. It was impossible to resist, and even if she tried, she wouldn't be able to stop the grin from claiming her entire face.

"This is amazing," Noah sighed as they passed the road to the post office and the Lazy H Ranch's main house. The main road climbed higher with an ever more commanding view of the eastern peaks.

She'd forgotten how tall and dominating those mountains were, and even Skye's gorgeous pictures of Northstar couldn't capture the scale. She felt so small in the face of their enduring power and more connected with the natural world than she'd ever been before. Gazing up at those wintry peaks, it was easy to understand why Henry and his family, their friends, and now Evie and Skye so loved this place.

"Obviously Noah and I are glad to be here, but what about you, Henry?" Lindsay asked. "Are you glad to be home?"

"You mean this smile that's been on my face so long that my cheeks ache doesn't give it away?" He laughed. "You've given me an entirely new appreciation of my home, Lindsay, and yes, I'm glad to be back. Even more so to have you and Noah with me."

He turned onto Aspen Creek Road toward his house, and Lindsay's heart leapt. Unlike the sense of despair and resignation that had claimed her when she'd returned to the house she and Noah had shared with Chelsea and Spencer, seeing Henry's house with the wall of snowy mountains behind it inspired in her all the joy and relief of homecoming despite the fact she'd spent only one night there. Maybe it was just her excitement to be visiting again and the parade of memories imbibed with freedom, but she doubted it.

Henry turned left onto his short driveway and parked in front of his house beside a snowmobile. "This is it. Welcome home."

Lindsay noted the light glowing in the living room window and the smoke drifting out of the chimney and wondered who was inside. Probably a member of Henry's family. Henry told her and Noah to head in while he grabbed their bags. Lindsay opened the door and poked her head inside to see Nick tossing a couple logs into the wood stove. He glanced up when he heard the door open and smiled.

"Here's a sight for sore eyes," he greeted, straightening. He strode to her and gave her a big hug before turning to Noah. "Welcome back to Northstar, Lindsay. This must be your son, Noah."

"Noah, this is Henry's older brother, Nick."

"It's good to have you here," Nick said, extending his hand.

Noah shook it. "Thank you."

"What do you think of Northstar so far?"

"It's beautiful. I saw the pictures Mom and Skye took when they were here this summer, but it's so much prettier now that I'm here."

Henry entered then loaded down with luggage. He dropped the bags in one hand onto the floor to embrace his brother. "Thanks for getting it warm in here for us."

"Any time, Hen. How were the roads?"

"Terrible," Henry replied. "Snow and ice the whole way. We saw about a dozen semis off the road, and I lost count of how many cars after thirty."

"Aren't you glad you decided to leave yesterday after school instead of waiting until this morning?"

"Yes, I am. We wouldn't have made it today if we hadn't. Eighteen hours of driving between yesterday and today instead of the eleven or twelve it's supposed to take. Although… that hotel bed was so terrible, I almost wish we'd tried to drive straight through."

Henry picked the bags up again and headed down the hall to deposit them in their room and Noah's.

"Don't remind me," Lindsay groaned. "Even Noah didn't sleep worth a darn."

"Yeah, and I can sleep anywhere," her son piped.

"In that case, I hope you took a nap in the truck because Will and Jessie are very excited to meet you."

"Will is your son, right?" Noah asked. "And Jessie is Aaron's daughter?"

Lindsay regarded her son with brows lifted, surprised he remembered that.

"Right." Nick glanced at his watch. "You've got a couple hours until we're all supposed to meet for dinner at the Bedspread Inn, so you might want to use that time to get a little more rest. I'll see you all at five."

Nick gave Henry a hand with the rest of their bags, then left, and while Lindsay ducked into the bathroom, Henry gave Noah a quick tour of the house. After, the three of them retreated to the couch to watch the fire dance behind the glass of the wood stove while the snow flew outside. Just like she'd imagined so many times since she'd left Northstar. Henry lay angled against the arm of the couch with his feet propped on the coffee table, and Lindsay rested her head on his chest with her arm around her son. This was perfect.

"Well, Noah, what do you think?" Henry asked.

"I love it. Thanks for inviting mom and me here. This is gonna be our best Christmas ever."

"I have a feeling it'll be mine, too, but I won't say *ever*. I'll say *yet*."

There was so much promise in that statement that

Lindsay's heart threatened to climb out of her chest, too exhilarated to be contained by her ribs. She didn't want to ruin the moment by questioning it, but she couldn't help it. "Yet? As in you're looking ahead to more Christmases with us and that they might be even better?"

"Yes, yet."

Beneath her ear, his voice was a rumble that sent a breeze of warmth and love straight to the deepest reaches of her heart, and she closed her eyes as hope threatened to swamp her. Not so long ago, she'd almost lost hope for anything better than the lonely fight for survival her life had been since Noah's birth, but now, here she was snuggled up with a man who loved not only her but her son and showed her with his patience and admiration that she was stronger than she'd ever realized.

She didn't want this moment to end, but as soon as she thought of seeing the rest of his family again, a new and different kind of joy blossomed, and she unpeeled herself from Henry's embrace, and stood, offering a hand each to him and Noah.

"Where are we going?" Henry inquired sleepily.

"I don't want to wait until dinner to see your parents."

"All right."

"That's it? No excuses to stay here and relax?"

"Nope. To be honest, I want to see them, too, and I want to introduce them to Noah. They're going to love him."

"You think so?" Noah asked.

"I know so. So let's go."

After the cozy heat of the fire, the air outside sucked

317

the air from her lungs, but she was too excited to complain. It was just one more experience for her, one more thing to love about Henry's home. Noah rode in the middle between them on the way down to the Hammonds', staring out the windshield with the same awe inscribed on his face as what she'd seen the moment he'd gotten his first glimpse of the Northstar Valley.

John was outside splitting firewood when they arrived, and he sunk the ax into the chopping block to greet them. Much like Nick had done, John embraced first Henry and then Lindsay, and offered Noah his hand in greeting. He then sent them inside to see Tracie, but Henry stayed outside to help him bring in the firewood. To her astonishment, Noah volunteered to carry some wood in, too. *Yeah, Henry is* definitely *a better role model for him than Max has ever* tried *to be.*

Tracie was in the living room poring over what looked like financial reports for the ranch, so Lindsay knocked on the wall beside the door to announce her presence. Immediately upon seeing who'd come in, Tracie set her work aside and strode over with arms wide. Lindsay stepped into them, hugging Henry's mother tightly.

"We weren't expecting to see you until dinner."

"I couldn't wait."

"Welcome back, sweetheart. Where's your boy?"

"He's out helping John and Henry with the firewood."

"What a good boy. Come on in and have a seat while we wait for them."

"I feel terrible for not finding out as soon as we arrived," Lindsay said, sinking into the plush couch beside

Tracie, "but have my parents checked in to the cabin yet?"

"They have indeed, about an hour ago, so not much before you arrived, and they promised to join us all for dinner."

Lindsay exhaled, glad to hear that her parents had arrived safely.

"So, you have to tell me all about Shannon's play. Henry sent me the pictures from the photoshoot you and he did for your friend's shop—they're gorgeous, by the way, what a spectacular dress you wore—but he was rather vague on the details other than to say the play was great, Shannon was amazing, and your evening out was incredible."

"That covers it pretty well," Lindsay replied, laughing softly. How marvelous it was to launch into conversation with Tracie like they were already family and had been for years. "We had a wonderful time with the Grangers and Pat and Aeli O'Neil and his parents. It was so nice to catch up with them again. We talked with them and Shannon for a while after the play—I wish you'd been there because she has a phenomenal voice—and then we went home to the cottage Henry rented from my Aunt Jeanie and danced in the living room for a while. Then I spent the night because my parents wouldn't let me come home until the next day."

"I think I like your parents already, but back up a bit. You got Henry to dance? When he was younger and his father and I tried to teach him, he hated it. He humored us, but it was never really his thing."

"So he told me."

"Now, *that* is fascinating."

The front door opened again, cutting off whatever else Tracie might have said, and almost as if she was looking for an excuse not to elaborate on her observation, she jumped to her feet to help John, Henry, and Noah unload their armfuls of logs. Lindsay watched as her son introduced himself to Henry's mother.

"Henry has told us so much about you that I feel like you're already part of the family," Tracie remarked, hugging the boy.

"He told you about me?"

"Of course he has. All good things, I promise. Thank you for helping with the wood." Turning to Lindsay, Tracie added, "Quite a considerate young man you have here, Lindsay."

"Thank you," she replied, suddenly shy.

"Well, it's almost time to head up to the Bedspread for dinner, so let me just get the fire good and stoked, and then we'll be ready to go. Henry, you don't mind if Jeremiah joins us, do you?"

"Why on earth would I mind? He's sort of part of the family now, isn't he?"

"Seems so. He's been a great help around here, and I for one am glad Aaron took it upon himself to offer him a job. But we can talk more about that later."

"Shall we meet you up there?" Henry asked his parents.

They nodded, so Lindsay followed Henry out to his truck with her son's hand gripping hers tightly. She glanced down at him, and he met her gaze with a brilliant smile. No need to ask him if he liked the Hammonds so far; the resounding yes was splashed across his face, bright as day. At least a couple members of their party had already arrived.

She hadn't thought it was so late, but the sky had

darkened considerably in the short time she'd been in the Hammonds' house, and when Henry parked in front of the Bedspread Inn's wide deck, Lindsay spotted a vaguely familiar pickup.

"Isn't that Aaron's truck?" she asked.

"Yep," Henry replied.

Lindsay hadn't seen Skye since late October—before Henry had arrived in Washington—so she was excited to see her friend and hear about everything that had been happening in the interval. Lindsay knew Skye and Aaron were serious, but she was curious to see just *how* serious. And she wanted to talk to her friend about everything she had discovered about her own relationship especially in the last few weeks when they'd only talked over the phone a couple times. Skye had been too busy taking care of business for her photography studio.

Oh, and Evie! She had talked to her other best friend only once since she'd left Northstar, and guilt stung her for not keeping in closer contact with Evie since her friend had moved to Montana. Life and distance always seemed to get in the way, and Lindsay wished they still lived closer together. That thought prompted another. If she and Henry were to get married, would they live here or in Washington? As she crested the steps, she turned to take in the incredible view from the deck and knew instantly which she would prefer, but it wasn't only what she wanted. Noah was awestruck by Northstar, but that didn't mean he'd want to live here in this remote, sparsely populated ranching valley.

"You coming or what, love?" Henry asked.

"Yeah...."

Yanking her gaze from the mountains, she took his

offered hand and Noah's and headed into the warmth of the restaurant. For the first time, she noticed the decorations. Unlike when she'd been here in August, garlands of fresh pine boughs decorated with bright red ribbons and white twinkle lights hung along the two side walls, a sprig of mistletoe hung from the first beam inside the door— Henry promptly kissed her when they passed under it—and each table had a mason jar with a candle floating above cranberries and holly leaves. A towering Christmas tree dominated the front corner of the room to the right of anyone walking in through the double doors, and stockings with the names of the employees of the Bedspread hung from the mantle beneath which a roaring fire cast a lively golden glow.

"This is like something out of a country Christmas fantasy," she murmured.

Skye, Aaron, and Jessie stepped around the massive fireplace, and Lindsay let go of Henry's hand to embrace her friend. Then she introduced Noah to Aaron and Jessie before inspecting her friend while the two kids immediately struck up a friendship investigating the gifts under the Christmas tree. The first thing Lindsay noticed was the brilliant happiness on Skye's face. It had been so long since she'd smiled like that, and it was infectious. The second thing Lindsay noticed was the flash of something glittery on Skye's left hand, but before she could further investigate what she'd seen, Skye hid her hand behind her back. The conspiratorial glance she and Aaron shared gave Lindsay a pretty good idea that it was a ring she'd seen.

"Spill it," she demanded.

Shyly, Skye held her hand out, and Lindsay snatched

it to inspect the diamond solitaire now adorning her ring finger. Without a word, she hugged Skye again. Then she hugged Aaron.

"I'm so happy for you both," she whispered.

"That makes two of us," Henry agreed, wrapping his twin in a bear hug. "About damned time, Aaron."

Lindsay couldn't be sure, but she thought she heard Aaron whisper to his brother, "You're next."

"I certainly hope so."

"What about your studio?" Lindsay asked Skye to prevent herself from pondering the twins' side conversation and getting herself worked into a fluster over the possible meanings of it. "Because I know you're going to stay here. Aaron has his job with the sheriff's department, and I've heard rumors that he's planning to run for sheriff someday in the not too distant future."

"Yes, we'll be staying in Northstar," Skye replied. "He belongs here... but so do I now. Joel will take over the studio, and I'll start a new one here. I've shot a couple weddings for the Ramshorn, and it's sounding like June's party planning endeavor is catching on in a big way, so she'll have a few more events for me this winter and even more in the spring. And speaking of her endeavor, she might have mentioned that she's always looking for someone to cater. The one catering company in Devyn is always booked, so she and the Ramshorn staff end up doing most of that themselves, and it's inefficient."

"Uh-huh," Lindsay said flatly despite the flare of hope. "She just *happened* to mention that."

"Okay, she asked me if you'd be interested. I may have let it slip that you've been wanting to open your own catering business for as long as I wanted to own my own photography studio."

"But I don't have a culinary degree, nor do I know the first thing about running a business."

"Maybe not, but as to the first, you're a natural talent, and I'm sure Henry can attest to that by now."

"I certainly can," he asserted.

"And the rest can be learned."

"What about the money to start it up?"

"That can be figured out. But the question is... are you even interested?"

Lindsay's chest tightened. This was exactly her dream—the dream she had given up to take care of her son while Max went off to college to pursue and attain *his* dream. Given up, she wondered, or only set aside? The way her heart beat faster with anticipation suggested it was the latter. "You know I am. I just don't know how it's possible."

"We'll figure it out," Skye said. "You and me together, just like we used to dream we would."

"You know, you're sounding an awful lot like Evie right now," Lindsay mused. "Pushy, ready with an answer to shoot down all my doubts, looking out for my happiness with an optimism that borders on obnoxious...."

Skye laughed heartily. "Must be something in the air around here. But imagine it, Linds. You, me, and Evie back together like old times... but in Montana and even better."

The arrival of more of their party—Lindsay's parents, Henry and Aaron's parents with a young man they introduced as Jeremiah Mackey, and Vince and Evie—put an end to their conversation.

True to form, Evie immediately launched a lengthy

inquiry into Lindsay's relationship with Henry, and the more she learned, the more excited she became until Lindsay had to tell her to calm down.

"Sorry, Linds, I can't. I'm just too happy for you."

"Well, don't get your hopes up *too* high yet."

"Too late." She grinned, then hugged Lindsay again. "I just *knew* he'd be the one to help you unpack all that baggage you've been carrying around for the last eight years. You just wait and see, Linds. I bet you'll have a ring on your finger before too much longer. And that sparkle in your eyes right now says a whole lot. You're hoping I'm right, aren't you?"

"I've tried to enjoy the moment and not overthink this like I tend to overthink everything, but yeah, I'm hopeful. He's great with Noah, and he makes me feel...." Lindsay glanced at Henry, who was currently talking with his twin and Skye about who knew what, though she suspected by their animated expressions that the topic was likely Skye's new photography endeavor and the possible business venture for Lindsay. Damn, he was sexy. All the Hammond boys were, but Henry had a roguish flair that set him apart from his brothers, a wild and adventurous spirit that burned brighter in him than in either Nick or Aaron and drew her like a moth.

"He makes you feel... what?" Evie prodded.

"Everything," Lindsay said simply, returning her attention to her friend. "Loved, adored, strong, capable, hopeful... everything."

Evie squealed quietly, and promised she'd leave Lindsay and Henry alone for now.

Nick and Beth showed up then with their son in tow,

and Lindsay watched Noah and his new friends while her discussion with Skye about the Ramshorn's need of a caterer flirted with her mind. She wanted it, there was no doubt about that, but no matter how she tried to figure her way through making it work, all she found were the same walls and doubts blocking her. So, for the time being, she pushed it from her mind and focused instead on the love and laughter that filled the air around her.

She loved her family's holidays, but they'd always been somewhat small and quiet—just her parents, her Aunt Jeanie and her daughter Jasmine, her grandparents, Noah, and her. This noisy gathering was something new and wonderful, and she would love to get used to it. Her parents and Henry's seemed to be kindred spirits, and Noah, Will, and Jessie were getting along fabulously as well. When Aaron and Skye announced their engagement, the congratulations and love offered to them washed over Lindsay as well. She could easily picture spending every Christmas like this, with these people.

Henry found her hand and gave it a squeeze, then kissed her cheek. "Having a good time?"

"I'm having the best time of my life," she replied honestly. "I love this, and I love *you*."

"That's good… because I love you, too. And so do they." He leaned back in his chair and folded his hand behind his head as the gleam of adoration danced in his eyes. "Think about that for a second. Every single person at this table loves you, Lindsay."

"It's incredible." She leaned into his side, and he tucked his arms around her. "Noah's right. This is already the best Christmas ever… or the best one *yet*."

He kissed her soundly with everyone at the table watching. "I like hearing you say that."

* * *

It was one of those sharply clear blue and white days, and despite the bitter temperatures, Henry wasn't ready to head back to the house yet, and the reason why was now rolling down Aspen Creek Road. His horse shifted beneath him while he sat motionless and watched the familiar SUV pull up in front of his house. Even at this distance, he knew it belonged to Doug; the customized paint job—matte black with flake metal red scallops on the hood outlined in silver—was instantly recognizable.

"This was a bad idea," he said, suddenly queasy.

"Too late now to change your mind," Lindsay replied. "I'm guessing that's them."

"Yeah."

"Who?" Noah asked.

"My ex, her boyfriend, and their son."

"The son you thought was yours but wasn't?"

"Yep."

Lindsay glanced sharply at Henry. "You told him about that?"

He winced. "Just the bare minimum that night you called Max to tell him about Christmas. I should've asked your permission before I did, and I'm sorry, but it proved a point."

"Don't worry, Mom," Noah said. "He only told me that he'd been hurt by someone just like Dad and Logan hurt you and that she made him believe he had a son when he didn't. That's all."

"What was the point it proved?"

"That I needed to wait and give you two time to make sure you dating each other isn't a mistake like those other times."

"I suppose I'm going to have to get used to you two having these kinds of boy talks, huh?"

"Yep," Noah replied cheerfully. "Isn't that a good thing?"

Smiling, Lindsay nodded. "Yes, it is, and you're going to need it more and more as you get older because I can't teach you everything you'll need to know about being a good man."

"I bet you could," Henry said. "My mother taught me just as much or more than my father did."

"I bet she could, too," Noah agreed. "But I bet having you both will be even better."

"Thanks, bud." Henry glanced back at his house and sighed. "I suppose we should get this over with."

He touched his heels to his horse's sides, and the gelding lurched forward at a lope. Lindsay and Noah nudged their mounts forward, following close behind him. The powdery snow that had piled up almost two feet in the two days since their arrival churned beneath the horses' hooves in glittering clouds. Lindsay was much more comfortable on the back of her mount than she'd been on her first horseback ride in August, and she hadn't been exactly uneasy then, either.

He liked they way she had settled right back into life here in Northstar and the way the strain that was her constant companion in Washington had fallen away again. Was that because she'd known only happiness and relaxation here, making it easier to forget the worries in her life? Or was it more than that?

Those questions and the myriad of others he had about their future—the logistics of it, anyhow, because he was certain now that she and her son were his future no matter where they landed—would have to wait until he finally and firmly closed the door on his past. And that's just what he intended to do today when he sat down with Mel and Doug. It didn't matter what they had to say to him. He was done with that part of his life and moving forward into the next chapter.

Of course, the real test would come when he saw Dylan again. No matter how hard he'd tried to push that little boy out of his heart, it couldn't be done.

"You all right?" Lindsay asked as they rode toward his house. "Because your face is about three shades paler than it was a minute ago."

"I'm not looking forward to this," he admitted.

"If it makes you feel any better, I'm not, either."

"No, it doesn't. It makes me feel worse. I shouldn't be dragging you through a mess that should've been cleaned up before I even met you."

"You're not dragging me through anything, Henry. I'm here for you just like you've been there for me since we first met."

They rode the rest of the way home in silence. Too soon, they had the horses unsaddled and turned loose in the corral behind the house and were climbing the stairs to the back deck, stomping the snow from their boots. Mel and Doug were out front, sitting in the warmth of the SUV, and Henry was both grateful and mildly surprised Mel hadn't let herself in. He'd left the front door unlocked like he always did when he was home in the valley, and she was familiar with that habit of his.

As Henry, Lindsay, and Noah shed their coats and the rest of their winter clothing, Henry addressed Lindsay. "If you'd rather Noah not be here for this, we can call Beth to come get him. I'm pretty sure she was planning to be home all afternoon today."

"If that wouldn't be too much trouble," Lindsay answered, "I think he might like to hang out with Will for a bit. Wouldn't you, Noah?"

"Yeah, that'd be fun."

"We'll tell you what happens later, all right, bud?" Henry said.

The boy nodded, and Henry called Beth while Noah donned the coat he'd taken off only moments ago. Beth said she'd be there in two minutes. Henry waited until his sister-in-law pulled up beside Doug's SUV before he walked to the front door to beckon his guests in. Doug climbed out of his vehicle and followed Beth up the front steps. She offered little more than a nod in greeting.

"If it's all right with you, I'd like to wait until Beth and Noah leave," Henry said the moment Doug stepped inside right behind Beth.

"I don't think anything we have to say would be too much for him, but I understand."

"Thanks." Henry shook Doug's hand. "Good to see you again, man."

"Yeah. It is."

"Beth, thank you. We'll be down to get him as soon as we're done here."

"I'm happy to do it, Henry. Having Noah over for a

while will give me a few moments of peace from Will. Poor kid's going stir crazy today, and I just don't have the patience for it right now."

Beth not have patience? Henry frowned. Something tickled his mind, but he didn't have time to explore it right now. "Everything all right?"

"Everything's just fine, Hen. You worry about yourself, and I'll see you in a bit."

After Beth and Noah left, Lindsay leaned close to Henry. "She's not pregnant, is she?"

"Not that I've heard," he replied, glancing out the window to watch his petite sister-in-law climb into her truck. Lindsay's question put a name to the *something* that had distracted him a moment ago. "It's possible. Nick let it slip a while back that they were thinking about trying for another baby."

"How fun."

"You wanna move out of the way of the door, Doug, so I can get Dylan in out of the cold?" came Mel's voice, jerking Henry's attention back to the matter at hand.

"Oh, sorry, babe."

Doug jumped out of the way, yanking the door farther open and then closing it behind Mel. She looked exactly how she had when Henry had left except that she watched him with uncertainty instead of grief and glanced at Doug instead of Henry for reassurance. Henry felt nothing but the mild recognition of an old friend, but he'd expected that. He'd expected what happened as soon as he shifted his gaze to the dark-haired toddler clinging to his ex, too, but there was a world of difference between the expectation and the reality. His heart thudded as he took in the familiar but

331

changed features of Dylan's face. His gaze sidetracked briefly to Doug, and at once, he wondered why he'd never seen the resemblance between them because it was unmistakable.

I didn't see it because I didn't look.

"Christ, he's grown so much," he murmured, reaching for Lindsay's hand for support.

Recognizing his voice instantly, Dylan turned his brown eyes on Henry and reached for him, and when Mel didn't move any closer, he whined. "Dada!"

"No, honey. That's not daddy, remember?" Mel corrected. "That's Henry."

"No! Dada."

Doug's face fell and he started toward the door, but Mel grabbed his arm with her free hand and stopped him. "We knew this was going to be difficult."

"And why is that, Mel?" Doug snapped over Dylan's increasingly louder shouts. At once, he held up his hands. "I'm sorry. I promised I'd work on forgiving that, and I'm out of line."

"Mama! Down," Dylan demanded, reaching again for Henry with enough strength that Mel had a hard time holding on to him. "Dada!"

"Ah, Jesus." Henry pulled a chair out from the dining room table and sank onto it. He couldn't do this. Dylan's cries cut straight to his soul, and every nerve through his neck and shoulders spasmed with each shriek until he hunched over his knees and curled his hands around his head in a useless attempt to block it out. Lindsay perched on his knees, forcing him to sit straighter as she folded her arms around him. At once, with the soft heat of her body to remind him that he didn't have to do this alone, peace flowed through him, and he marveled at her influence over him.

"I know how much you love him, Henry," she whispered, resting a reassuring hand over his heart. "I can't watch it tear you up, so stop fighting it and just take him. Please."

Lindsay stood but left her hand on his shoulder, and he held his hands out to Dylan. The second Mel set the toddler on the floor, he made a beeline for Henry. Swearing again, Henry murmured, "He was barely walking last time I saw him, and now look at him."

Dylan launched himself at Henry, trusting Henry to catch him. He did, hugging the little boy close, eyeing Doug, Mel, and Lindsay. Doug averted his gaze, and the muscle in his jaw worked. Mel didn't look any less pained, but Lindsay's expression was difficult to read. She was obviously uncomfortable, but there was a light in her eyes that he thought might be pride or even maternal gratification that the man she'd chosen as a mate would also be a devoted parent.

With Dylan once again the happy, smiling boy Henry remembered, the tension and awkwardness left them all, and they gathered in the living room to discuss what had brought Mel and Doug to Montana. Henry held Dylan, who jabbered away about his favorite toy, and Lindsay sat close beside them on the couch with her feet tucked under her and an arm draped over Henry's shoulder. Her posture was outwardly relaxed, but the way she watched Mel was anything but.

"The first thing is this," Mel said, slipping a manila

envelope out of her diaper bag. She leaned across the coffee table to set it in front of Henry. "I decided to let Tam's friend buy me out of the salon. You were right. I'm not cut out to be a business owner, and now that I'm back to being just a stylist, I'm so much happier."

Henry opened the envelope and pulled out a certified check. Instead of the nine thousand six hundred she still owed, it was for exactly ten thousand dollars. Frowning, he read the sticky note on it. *What I still owe plus some interest.* It was paper-clipped to a sheet of paper that was a fairly simple, straightforward letter stating that Mel had repaid in full the ten thousand dollars he'd loaned her. There was a space for him to sign and also a place for the document to be notarized. Dylan made a grab for the paper, and Henry held it out of the toddler's reach.

"That wasn't my idea. Stephanie—she's Tam's new partner—wanted everything in writing."

"Smart woman," Henry remarked. "We might be able to get this notarized in Devyn tomorrow if we leave early enough."

"You don't have a problem signing it?" Doug asked.

"No. Why would I? It's a smart move on the new partner's behalf. I might've gotten my money back sooner if I'd been as smart and set specific repayment terms and had it recorded somewhere other than my safe deposit box." He dropped the paper on the table and paid Dylan a moment of attention before turning back to Mel and Doug. "All right. What's the other thing?"

"Well..." Doug began. "Like Mel told you, we're back together, and we're trying very hard to make our relationship work this time. Things are going pretty well, too.

We still have some things to work out, but the important thing is that we're trying. You were right about that. It wasn't a lack of compatibility or issues we couldn't overcome."

"That's great, Doug. I'm happy for you. But what does that have to do with me?"

"We have a proposal for you," Mel said. She gripped Doug's hand and glanced at him for reassurance. When he nodded, she met Henry's gaze. "We'd like you to be Dylan's godfather."

Henry wasn't sure which emotion hit him first—the relief that he wouldn't have to say goodbye to Dylan forever or the dread that he would always have that tie to Mel and the pain of learning that Dylan wasn't his son. He stared blankly at her for almost a minute before stammering, "Wh-what?"

"I—we—know you'd take good care of him if anything were to happen to us," Mel explained. "And… we want to have a reason for you to stay in Dylan's life because you were one of the biggest parts of it. We don't want either of you to lose that bond."

"And this has nothing to do with money?" The words popped out of his mouth, bypassing his censor, and he immediately felt like an ass for asking but didn't apologize or attempt to take them back. He had to know.

"I can take care of my own family," Doug replied a little too coldly.

"I never doubted that," Henry bit back. "What I doubted was when or if you'd man up and decide you should."

"Henry," Lindsay said gently.

That one utterance averted what would have quickly spiraled into a firestorm of accusations, and Henry inhaled deeply, then let it out. "Sorry."

Mel stared at him with unveiled surprise, but she said nothing. Instead, she steered them back to her proposal. "What do you think? Will you do it?"

Henry didn't respond. On the one hand, saying yes meant he wouldn't have to fight to keep his love for Dylan buried, but on the other, he was moving on with Lindsay and making plans to secure their future, and he didn't want any tie with his past to damage that.

"Henry?" Doug asked.

"I can't make a decision right now," he answered. He scrubbed his hand over his face and took a deep breath, but it did little to relieve the heavy weight of weariness. He should just say no because, if the tension that sapped his energy was what it would bring him, he didn't want it. "I need a couple days to think it over and talk it over with Lindsay. In the meantime, why don't we plan to get this notarized tomorrow morning?" He lifted the letter briefly off the table.

"I guess that'll have to do for now," Mel said. She stood and tried to take Dylan from Henry, but the little boy wouldn't have it.

"Dylan," Henry said quietly. "You have to be a good boy and go with your mommy. I'll see you again tomorrow, okay?"

Only after Henry gave him a big hug and again promised to see him tomorrow did Dylan go willingly with his mother. Henry walked them to the door, closed it behind them, and stood at the window to watch them drive away.

Lindsay joined him, wrapping her arm around his waist and leaning into his side. He draped his arm around her shoulders and kissed the top of her head. He owed her. There was no way he would have made it through seeing Dylan again without breaking completely down if she hadn't been with him.

"What should I do, gorgeous?"

"Exactly what you said you needed to. Think about it for a couple days."

He turned to her and folded his hands loosely together behind her back. "Are you all right?"

"I won't lie and say that was a pleasant experience, but I like that you care so much about me that you're thinking about my state of mind even when yours is probably pretty rocky right now."

"I *do* care about you," he said, lowering his mouth to hers. When she kissed him back, reassurance and relief wove together around him. "And I don't think you realize just how lucky I am to call you mine."

"Sure I do because I'm just as lucky to have you." She touched her lips briefly to his again. "Let's not talk about whether or not you should say yes to being Dylan's godfather for a while and focus on having a good time with your family and mine and the rest of the good people of Northstar. In two days, *then* we'll sit down and talk about it. That should give us both plenty of time to step back and prevent us from making a decision from a place of anger or pain or any other dark emotion."

"I like that plan. I like even more that you said us. How 'bout we start focusing on the fun with a soak at the Elkhorn? Noah hasn't been yet, and after our ride today, he'd probably appreciate it even more."

"Mmm. That sounds delightful. And after... maybe my parents will be up for watching Noah so we can explore other ways we're lucky."

"Someone's awfully playful today."

"Must be the mountain air."

"Must be. Maybe it's just me, but you've been a lot happier since we've been home."

"It's not just you." Lindsay shook her head and laughed. "There's that word again. It keeps popping up in my thoughts and conversations, so I have to wonder if it's true."

"What word?"

"Home."

Sixteen

LINDSAY'S SUGGESTION TO WAIT two days before she and Henry talked about him agreeing or not to be Dylan's godfather had very little to do with a desire to ensure he didn't make the decision purely on his emotional reaction. Mostly, she'd wanted time to see how he interacted with Dylan and if the boy he'd believed was his son would pull his attention away from Noah.

She leaned over to see around the wall that separated the kitchen in John and Tracie's house from the living room, spying on her boys. Henry sat with Dylan in his lap, but his focus was entirely on Noah and their intense game of checkers. In the last two days, Henry had drawn a line between Mel, Doug, and Dylan and Lindsay and Noah, and he'd made it very clear to everyone which side he stood on. Regardless, watching Henry with Dylan made Lindsay uncomfortable, but she had no hope of explaining why.

"I hear a rumor that the Ramshorn is highly interested in your rather formidable culinary skills," Tracie commented from the stove where she was basting the Christmas Eve turkey.

"As a caterer, yes," Lindsay replied, forcing her attention back to helping Henry's mother with dinner. "I assume Henry told you June asked me to put together a small spread for Marvin and Mary Struthers yesterday."

"Actually, your parents beat him to it. They were quite proud about it, and rightly so. How did it go?"

"They asked me when I would be available to cater for them."

"And what did you say?"

"I said I didn't know. I haven't even begun to wrap my head around the possibility let alone started working on the details, but I'm grateful they're willing to give me a shot. June said they were thinking of converting the small cabin right next to the lodge into a kitchen specifically for event catering and that I'd be able to use it until I get my own."

"Well, there you go. Sounds like you could make a go of it."

Lindsay beamed despite her troubling thoughts about Henry and Dylan. She'd made herself proud yesterday with an Asian-inspired menu and sampler for the Strutherses and June and Ben Conner. She was no closer to figuring out how to make a catering business work out here in this sparsely populated corner of Montana than she was to understanding why she was still waiting for her relationship with Henry to fail, but the reactions of the Ramshorn's current and future owners to her dishes still made her giddy. She wanted nothing more than to dive right into daydreaming about it, but with Henry's decision about Dylan hanging over her, she couldn't afford the distraction. One issue at a time, she told herself.

"Henry told you what Mel and Doug want, didn't he?"

Tracie nodded.

"What do you think about it?"

The older woman frowned and, like Lindsay had done just moments ago, leaned around the wall to peek into the living room. She returned to basting the turkey before she answered. "I'm torn. I love that little boy to death, and I selfishly would like to keep him in the family in some way, but Mel.... I've never been fond of her, and her decision to assume Henry was her son's father lost her most of the few points she had with me."

Lindsay wasn't surprised to hear that; Henry's mother hadn't made it a secret that she tolerated Mel, and barely at that.

"This idea stinks of being yet another ploy to keep him around, just like asking him for money to start the salon and just like telling him she was pregnant with his kid when she obviously wasn't sure."

"Why would she need him around now? She has Doug to take care of her, and he made it pretty clear the other day that he could."

Tracie didn't answer. Instead, she shoved the turkey back into the oven and, with her previously graceful movements made rough by anger, nearly sloshed hot grease and drippings out of the roasting pan.

"You don't like that she expects to be taken care of,

and you think she wants to keep Henry on a chain as insurance."

"That's a polite way to put it."

"I'm guessing that's also exactly why you've never cared for her."

"Not quite. I never trusted her to love Henry for who he is. It's one thing if my boys want to take care of or even spoil their women, but I didn't raise my sons to be walking wallets. They have so much more to give than that, and I hated seeing Henry's finer qualities ignored in favor of how much money he earned."

"His finer qualities being his sense of humor, his honesty, his generosity, and the fact that he'd break his own heart before he hurt someone he loves?" Lindsay inquired lightly. She picked up the bowl of potatoes and grabbed the peeler out of the drawer beside Tracie. She started peeling and cubing the potatoes and dropping them in the pot to be boiled and later mashed. "Or perhaps it's his devotion to his family, his thoughtfulness as a lover, and that he'll be a wonderful father that you wish she'd wanted instead of his paycheck."

"All of the above." Tracie grinned, and Lindsay realized that Henry had inherited her favorite devilish smile from his mother. "But you see it, Lindsay. You understand his *real* value and have from the very beginning. It was obvious from the moment you talked him out of being pissed at Nick for telling us about Dylan."

Henry's mother wasn't asking; she was stating fact.

"Yes, I do. Just as he understands mine and reminds me that I have it." Lindsay eyed her companion with one corner of her mouth lifted. "Is that your way of telling me you'd approve of your son marrying me if he were so inclined?"

"I more than approve. I'd be delighted to call you my daughter-in-law, Lindsay, and if it were up to me, you'd already have a ring on your finger like Skye does."

"But you wouldn't have approved of him marrying Melanie."

"If he'd wanted to, there isn't much I could have done to stop him, but no, I wouldn't have approved. It takes a lot of work to run a ranch, and everyone has to pitch in."

"And Mel didn't do that?"

"You look in the living room again and tell me what she's doing right now."

Lindsay craned her head around the wall and peeked into the living room. "She's sitting on the couch with Doug."

"Exactly. She could be in here helping with dinner like you are, but she isn't."

"Maybe she doesn't feel welcome in here."

"I might agree with you, but even in the beginning when she was still trying to impress me, she never volunteered to help out around the place. That says a lot about her to me. Just like the fact that you're right here peeling potatoes says a lot about you. You are a rare gem, and Henry should consider himself blessed to have found you... and I know he does, or he wouldn't have invited not only you and your son but also your parents for Christmas."

Lindsay smiled shyly, unused to such blatant praise from anyone but her parents and Henry. "Thank you."

Tracie abruptly switched topics. "So, what about Mel asking him to be Dylan's godfather bothers *you*? Because it obviously does."

Lindsay started to respond, but Tracie held up her finger for silence.

"No, no, sweetheart. Don't tell me. That's something you need to talk with him about first, and I think it's probably time to do so. Mel and Doug are leaving first thing tomorrow morning so they can make it back to Denver in time to spend *some* of Christmas with their families, and without them here, you both might be tempted to put it off. You don't want that hanging over you when you should be enjoying yourselves and each other."

"Yes, ma'am," Lindsay replied. She finished peeling and cubing the last potato and reached for the ingredients for caramelized carrots.

Tracie blocked her. "I'll get these started. You can do whatever it is you do with them after you've talked with Henry."

Lindsay wasn't ready to talk about Henry and Dylan yet, but Tracie was right that she needed to get it out of the way. The doubts swirling around the topic dimmed her enjoyment of what was otherwise a marvelously fun day with the Hammonds, the Hathaways, and her parents. Since she knew Tracie wouldn't back down, Lindsay wandered out of the kitchen. Instead of going straight to Henry and asking him to step outside with her so they could speak in private—something that wasn't likely to happen indoors with so many people in the house—she leaned against the wall and observed the occupants of the living room.

Henry and Noah were still playing checkers, though by the number of pieces on the board, she guessed they'd started a new game. Will sat on the sidelines with Jessie snuggled up next to him, and the cousins watched the game intently. Henry answered their incessant questions about how the game was played with complete patience and an indulgent smile that told her he enjoyed it. Even when Dylan swatted half his pieces off the board, Henry chuckled and put them back. Ignoring the confusing emotions the sight of him with Dylan incited, she couldn't deny that the two of them together were adorable. Any doubts she might've had that he'd make a great father had vanished entirely over the last two days of watching him play with his niece and nephew, Noah, and Dylan. A pang of maternal longing brought to mind her conversation with Aelissm on the ride to Seattle for Shannon O'Neil's stage debut. Did she want another baby?

With Henry, absolutely I do, she admitted with a certainty that having and raising a child with him would be a partnership and a joy instead of the lonely, often frustrating experience she'd had with Max and Noah.

Before the pang turned into an ache, she shifted her attention to the others in the room. Her mother and Skye's sat on the L-shaped couch with Skye and Aaron at their feet paging through a wedding magazine. Steve, Skye's father, and John sat at a card table playing a noisy game of rummy with Jeremiah Mackey, occasionally asking questions or giving input on the wedding planning. Nick added his opinion once or twice from his seat on the shorter section of the couch, but his attention was mostly on his wife, who lay beside him with her head pillowed on his thigh. Beth's eyes were closed, but Lindsay wasn't sure if she was asleep or merely resting. Tracie had chased her out of the kitchen some while ago when she couldn't stop yawning, and instead of arguing the point, she'd obeyed. Lindsay tilted her head. The ribbed ice-blue sweater revealed something her bulky winter coat had hidden, and Lindsay decided the slender woman's belly was thicker than it had been back in August. Pregnancy would certainly explain Beth's exhaustion and the irritability she'd mentioned the other day. The proud, wonderstruck light in Nick's eyes was further confirmation.

I wonder if Henry's expression was the same when Mel told him she was pregnant with Dylan, Lindsay mused. *Or if it will be whenever he has children.*

Shaking her head to clear those thoughts from it, she glanced at last to the primary reason for her unsettled emotions. Melanie and Doug sat together on the loveseat apart from everyone else, plainly the odd ones out, and impatience was beginning to pinch both their expressions. Cut those two out of the picture, and the scene before her was the image of Christmas joy.

With *that* thought, she asked Henry to join her outside when he and Noah were finished with this game.

"Sure. What's up, love?"

"It's time to talk about Dylan," she said too quietly for Mel and Doug to hear.

"Will, do you think you know enough to take over for me?" Henry asked.

"I said after your game," Lindsay said.

"I know you did, but this is important. What d'ya say, Will?"

"I think I can."

Henry scooted Dylan off his lap and, taking the boy's hand, led him over to his parents. When the toddler realized what Henry was doing, he was not happy. Firmly, Henry told him to stay, then turned hard eyes on Doug and Mel.

"You need to take your son for a bit." His tone was both an order and a reprimand.

Henry started to walk away, and Dylan let out an ear-piercing scream. Henry turned around and gave him a firm *no* followed by a command to stay with his mother.

"Dada!" Dylan screamed.

"I'm not daddy," Henry corrected quickly.

"Henny. Stay."

"No. But I'll be right back." He turned to Mel and Doug. "If you think me agreeing to be his godfather means I'm going to raise your son for you, I'll give you my answer right now with no discussion. No."

"That's not what we want, Henry," Doug said quickly.

"Then prove it by being parents."

Even Lindsay jerked back in surprise, and everyone in the room stared at Henry with a mixture of shock and pride or—from Melanie and Doug—embarrassment. Henry took Lindsay's hand and led her the short distance to the entryway, then helped her into her coat and shrugged into his.

Outside, it was another gray-skied, flurry-filled day but mercifully, it was also relatively warmer than it had been with the thermometer reading twenty degrees. Instead of launching into the matter at hand, Henry pulled Lindsay against him and kissed her soundly.

"Looks like Noah is not only going to get his white Christmas but one with new snow falling." He tipped his head back and closed his eyes with a faint smile flirting

347

about his lips. "I'm so used to this that I'd forgotten how incredible it is, but you and that wonderful son of yours have done a thorough job of reminding me. You both make life so much richer."

"Believe me, Henry, the feeling is mutual."

Alone with him in the hush of the falling snow, her worries slipped away again as they only did when she was here in Northstar with him to show her that there was more to life than survival. And that made her all the more anxious to get the subject of Dylan out of the way so she could get back to wallowing in her happiness.

"I thought you were struggling with the decision about Dylan," she murmured, "but what you said in there makes me wonder if you haven't already made up your mind."

"I *am* struggling with it, but that doesn't mean I don't know how to stand up for myself when I need to. So let's talk."

She expected him to let her go, but he didn't. Instead, he led her around the house to the snow-covered picnic table, brushed off a portion of the table and sat, pulling her onto his lap and folding his arms around her.

"What are you feeling?" she asked.

"Too much that's distracting me from what I *want* to be feeling right now."

"Such as?"

"An overwhelming and amazing love for you and your son." He nuzzled her neck and sighed. "And a gladness that our families get along so well because that'll make other gatherings and holidays just as magnificent as this one."

"Henry... about Dylan."

"I know what you meant." He sighed, searching her face as he tucked her hair behind her ear and brushed snow-flakes from her shoulder. "My heart wants to do it, but my brain isn't convinced this isn't another trick of Mel's."

"Your mom said something like that, and I admit that I've thought it myself. I guess in the end you have to decide if that possibility is acceptable to you."

"How about you? How do *you* feel about this?"

"This isn't a decision I can make for you, Henry, and you should trust your heart rather than your brain. What I feel doesn't matter."

"You are my partner, Lindsay, and how this affects and will affect you down the road matters far more to me than what Doug or Melanie want for their son. I'm not asking you to make the decision for me. I'm asking you to tell me why it bothers you so I can make the right decision for *us*. And don't try to say it doesn't bug you because some of that carefree joy you seem to reserve for Northstar has dimmed since our talk with Doug and Mel. So…"

She chewed on her lip for a moment, wishing she didn't have the fears she did. Resting her head on Henry's shoulder and letting him comfort her, she took a deep breath and plunged ahead. Better to just get it out. "It's stupid to even think this, but when I see you playing with Dylan, a part of me wonders if Noah and I are just a re-bound family for you."

"What do you mean?"

She didn't answer immediately, taking a moment to gauge his response. He didn't sound offended but rather curious and concerned.

"You thought you were a father, and you didn't just

349

accept that, you embraced it, and I understand how painful it was when that was taken away from you. I'm not saying I'd blame you if you're confusing love for us with the filling of that hole because how could I when I know how much that hurt you?"

"I hope I haven't give you any reason to doubt how I feel about you and Noah."

"No, you haven't. You've been nothing but committed to us, which is why I feel so thickheaded for letting this fear get a foothold, but I can't help it. I'm sorry."

"There's nothing to be sorry for, Lindsay. How you feel isn't a reflection of either of us or our relationship. It's a reflection of assholes like Max and Logan, who taught you to look for every relationship including ours to fail like all the rest have."

The words, so similar to what her mother had warned her against more than once in the last few weeks, made her sit back and stare at him.

"Your parents and I had a good long talk yesterday while you and Mom were baking pies and cookies with the kids," Henry explained, "and they advised me I might have to work hard to break those habits. I want to be Dylan's godfather, Lindsay, because he was a big part of my life and had a major impact on me, but I won't do it if it makes you too uncomfortable."

Again, she let him hold her close as a sea of doubt swirled through her. She loved him so much, and she wanted what they had to be the real deal, but he and her parents were right. Max and Logan had taught her too well to expect love to fail.

"What can I do to prove to you that I'll never do what

they did to you?"

"I don't know," she whispered, cursing the tremble in her voice and the tears that burned her eyes. "What you've already done should have proven it to me."

"But you still doubt."

She nodded. "And I don't want to. I want to just *believe* and let go of everything else."

"There's something more I think I can do to prove it. Stay here, and I'll be *right* back."

Lindsay climbed off his lap and stood beside the picnic table to wait, shivering in the absence of the heat of his body. She hugged herself to ward off the chill and let her gaze wander. As her eyes took in the winter wonderland that was Northstar, she asked herself if she could live and work here even if she and Henry didn't work out. It looked like she already had a job if she wanted it—giddily, she admitted that she did—and it was true that this place held a freedom and peace for her that existed nowhere else. Noah loved it here, too, and though he hadn't asked her if they could stay, she imagined he would the second he realized it was a possibility. She didn't know how she felt about him going to such a small school, but Henry and his brothers and Beth and Vince and many others she'd met in Northstar had, and they all seemed to have benefitted greatly from their experience.

Her doubts fell silent, drowned out by hope. Her dream of opening her own catering company was, for the first time in almost a decade, right in font of her just waiting for her to reach for it. She still had no idea how to reach for it, but she definitely wanted to. She'd done everything else by herself, and if need be, she could do that, too. Of course, she didn't want to do it by herself. She wanted Henry to be right there, standing beside her and reminding her that she could because he had that power—the power to make her believe she was strong enough to conquer the world if she so wanted.

That's your proof right there, a voice in the back of her mind whispered. *If you were just a rebound to him, he wouldn't bother to lift you up.*

Henry strode around the corner of the house with Noah almost bouncing through the deepening snow. A matching wonder claimed both their faces, and right then, the sight of them together melted her heart. *My boys.*

"I know what you and I feel is the real thing, Henry. I believe," she said when they were close enough to hear. And when she let go of the doubt, she knew it was the truth. "I don't need any more proof."

"Well, tough because you're going to get it."

He handed her two thick pamphlets, and when he gestured for her to look at them, she saw that one was for the culinary arts program at Olympic College back home in Washington and the other was for a business management degree at the university in Devyn.

"Devyn doesn't have a culinary degree," Henry explained, "but they do offer a restaurant emphasis as one of the options for business management. Since you're already so skilled in the culinary side of a catering business, I thought a business degree might be more useful to you. And before you even *think* of asking how you're going to pay for it, let me show you my proof."

"These weren't it?"

"Nope. Noah, come here for a second."

When her son leaned in close to him, Henry pulled a small box wrapped in heavy metallic blue paper the color of a clear night sky and tied with a ribbon of silver gossamer. He handed the box to Noah to open. With a delicacy Lindsay had never seen, Noah carefully unwrapped the box and lifted the lid off. Inside, there was another box, one with a hinge that looked suspiciously like a ring box. She stared at Henry, but his attention was on Noah, whose face shifted into a mask of shock when he opened the smaller box.

"What do you say, bud?" Henry lifted his eyes and met Lindsay's gaze.

"You really mean it?" Noah asked, eyes wide with hope and excitement.

"That's what this is for—to prove that I mean it. So… may I?"

"Oh my God! Yes, of course you can marry my mom!"

With his arm around Noah's shoulders, Henry took the smaller ring box out of the larger white box and turned it so Lindsay could see. Cushioned on black velvet was a rose gold ring with a round blue diamond flanked on either side by two midsized white diamonds and channels of smaller white diamonds.

"I saw it that day Noah and I went to the mall to get your mixer, and it made me think of your beautiful red hair and your stunning blue eyes. When I was sure, I went back and bought it." His voice was soft, disarming. "What do you think, Lindsay? Will you be my wife?"

Her heart stopped in her chest, and for a moment, she forgot how to breathe. *Yes,* she thought. *Just say yes already.* "I… I can't."

"But, Mom," Noah said, "he loves you. He even loves me. And you love him, too, right?"

"Yes, I do. So much."

"So why can't you marry him?"

"Max."

"What does Max have to do with us?" Henry asked.

"I can't say yes until you've met him and know what you're getting into."

"Do you want to say yes?"

"Yes, I do."

"Then say it because I'm not going to change my mind about you no matter what happens when I meet him."

"But you don't know him."

"Do me a favor, will you, and try the ring on."

She was afraid to. Afraid she would lose the strength to say no if she did. But she held out her shaking hand and let Henry slide the gorgeous ring on her finger. It was a perfect fit, which in itself shocked her because the standard size seven most engagement rings were didn't fit her. Upon close inspection of the band, she noticed the tiny mark left when it had been resized.

"How did you know?" she asked.

"I asked your parents... right after I asked them for their blessing, which, by the way, they gave with an almost overwhelming enthusiasm."

"Of course they were enthusiastic," she murmured. "They adore you. All right! Yes, I'll marry you!"

Henry picked her up, and she beamed, hugging him tightly.

"But you can change your mind if you decide you can't deal with Max."

"You've made that clear, but I won't. Max doesn't matter. Sorry, Noah, but he doesn't. Not to this." Setting Lindsay on her feet but keeping one arm around her, he pulled Noah into the embrace. "All that matters is us. You and Noah and me."

"What about Dylan?"

"What do you think I should do?" He lifted her left hand and kissed her knuckles. "Now that you *officially* have a say."

She inhaled deeply and let it out in a sigh. "Your heart is telling you to say yes, so that's what your answer should be. I think it will bring you far more peace than trying to cut him out of your life would."

"I think you're right. Now, regarding college and paying for it, since I know you won't let me do it, I found a bunch of information on scholarships and grants you can apply for."

She tightened her arms around him and buried her face against his neck, fighting hard not to cry. "I'm not sure I deserve you."

"That's all right because I'm certain you do," he replied. "Let's go break the news, shall we?"

The three of them headed back inside and immediately addressed Mel and Doug. Dylan reached for Henry, who shook his head.

"We've made a decision about your proposal."

"And?" Mel asked.

"My answer is yes, but…." He paused long enough to make sure it sank in that he had conditions. "It will be on our terms. We'll maintain a friendship with you and Dylan and even get together now and again for holidays and birthdays and the like, but I *will not* be another parent for him, and I *will not* be in any way responsible for taking care of him. I have my own family, and I will not put *your* family before them. Ever. I have one more condition. If I am to be Dylan's godfather, Lindsay will be his godmother because we're in this together."

Lindsay glanced sharply at him, at once miffed that he hadn't asked if she wanted to be Dylan's godmother and stunned and gratified that he was so sure of them that he would make that demand. He glanced at her with his expression waxing briefly apologetic and pleading. She nodded. Yes, she was willing.

"Are you both amenable to those terms?" Henry asked.

"*Your* terms? We?" Mel asked.

"Yes, *we* and *our terms* as in Lindsay's and mine." Henry lifted her hand to display her engagement ring.

"Congratulations, man," Doug said, looking interestingly relieved. "Isn't that great for Henry, Mel?"

"Yes. Congratulations."

"And yes, those terms are acceptable," Doug added. "Right, Mel?"

"Yes, those terms are fine."

Melanie's tone confirmed Lindsay's and Tracie's concerns that she was thinking primarily of Henry as an insurance policy, but Lindsay no longer had *any* reason to believe Henry would allow that idea to survive. She wasn't proud of the smugness that pulled her head and spine straighter, but she was proud of Henry for reaffirming the line he'd drawn when he'd walked out of Mel's life.

"Dammit, Henry," Nick muttered across the room.

"You said you didn't have any big announcements to make this evening."

Henry shrugged at his grinning older brother. "Sorry, bro. Circumstances moved it up the schedule."

"Well, we're not going to wait any longer just so you can have the spotlight tonight because I'm sure there are a few here who've probably figured it out anyhow."

"Far as I'm concerned, the more good news, the merrier."

"Good news?" Tracie asked.

Nick held his hand out to his wife and hauled her to her feet. The way the light played over her body, their news was obvious, and Lindsay suspected Beth had worn that particular sweater for that exact reason.

"Oh my goodness. Beth! How did I not notice?"

"You've had two beautiful new soon-to-be daughters to think about," Nick's wife replied. "And I've tried to hide it until we were sure it was going to take. But the real news isn't that I'm pregnant."

Matching frowns from everyone in the room, and for what seemed like at least five minutes, no one spoke. Beth nodded at Nick, and he stooped to pull a present out from under the tree. He handed it to Tracie, who unwrapped it without taking her eyes off her eldest son and his wife. At last, she looked down at the gift and breathed, "Are you kidding me?"

Nick and Beth grinned, shaking their heads.

"What is it?" John asked. Joining his wife, he peered over her shoulder. "Twins?"

"Yep."

"When are they due?"

"Mid July."

"Looks like the Hammond clan is growing by leaps and bounds this Christmas," Tracie said, turning her head over her shoulder to kiss her husband.

Henry turned to Lindsay as congratulations were offered to Nick and Beth, Henry and Lindsay, and Aaron and Skye. Clasping her face, he kissed her to the cheers of their families.

* * *

Following Lindsay's directions, Henry navigated the winding streets of Max and Giselle Ulrich's upscale suburban neighborhood, glancing occasionally at the ring glittering on Lindsay's hand to keep his heart rate at a steady if slightly elevated level. It wasn't nervousness that coursed through him. It was the urge to punch Max the second he met the man. Noah hadn't wanted to leave Northstar to spend New Years with his father and had, last night, lowered himself to begging. He'd even called his father to ask if he could come some other time, but Max had staunchly refused.

So, here they were, pulling into a slushy gray driveway in front of a two-story mini-mansion. Henry sneered as he climbed out of his truck and took in the sight of the house's sharply peaked roofs and professionally landscaped yard. Max and his wife could afford this but they couldn't be troubled to help Lindsay buy things Noah *needed*? They climbed the steep, terraced walk to the front door and knocked. Moments later, a stunning woman who could have graced magazine covers opened the door. Standing beside her, Lindsay was comparatively plain… and ten times more exquisite because hers was a natural attractiveness bolstered by the beauty of her fighting spirit. On the other woman's heels was a man Henry guessed was Noah's father. Max was a couple inches shorter than Henry and dressed smartly in slacks and a crisp button-up shirt and looked Henry over with all the haughtiness his rich suburbanite abode and attire encapsulated.

"What is *he* doing here, Lindsay?" Max demanded, turning sharply to her. "I distinctly remember tell you I didn't want him around our son."

Henry replied before either Lindsay or Giselle could recover from their shock at Max's less than civil greeting. "You gave up any right to tell Lindsay who should or should not be allowed around her son when you left her to raise Noah alone. Let's get something out in the open right now. I don't like you any more than you like me, and we can either make asses out of ourselves by getting into a knock-down-drag-out fight right here on your front steps with all your neighbors watching, or we can act like grown men and set aside our dislike and prevent every dealing we have with each other from today forward from turning into a brawl." He extended his hand in a peace offering, and Max stared at it for a moment. "It's your call, and I strongly suggest you take my offer for Noah's sake because Lindsay and I are engaged, so we *will* have to deal with each other a lot."

Max continued to ignore his hand, so he dropped it.

"I'll excuse your behavior because you don't know me. Allow me to introduce myself. I'm Henry Hammond, youngest of three sons. My family owns a large cattle ranch in Northstar, Montana, that I helped them run until after I graduated from college with a degree in industrial arts. After that, I worked as a welder and machinist in Denver—

making six figures a year, if you care to know—until I moved back home to the ranch in August, which is when I met Lindsay. I love Noah as much as I would love my own son, and I will do everything in my power to make sure he knows that and what it is to be a good man."

He refrained—barely—from adding, *That's a lesson he sure as hell isn't likely to learn from you.*

"Get off my front steps," Max snarled. "And stay away from my son."

"I don't want him to stay away from me," Noah snapped. "He loves me a lot more than you do, and he *wants* me around!"

The unexpected outburst cooled Henry's anger, and equally unexpectedly, one corner of his mouth lifted in amusement and fondness. They were going to have a wonderful life together, the three of them, and as he'd told Lindsay, Max couldn't take that love away from them, and if he tried, well, he'd only end up making it even stronger.

"Noah," he said quietly, giving the boy's shoulder a squeeze. "It's all right. You don't need to defend me because your dad's just looking out for you, doing the same thing I would in his place. Aren't you, Max?"

Noah's father didn't respond, staring at his son in utter disbelief. Noah glared back, unflinching.

"Not fun to be on the receiving end of his frustration, is it, Max," Lindsay remarked without heat. "I've been putting up with it for years, and it isn't fair when I'm not the parent who keeps routinely breaking his heart. And since it's patently obvious Noah spending New Years with you is more about avenging whatever wrong you think I did to you, I'm going to change my mind. No, Noah, you don't have to stay. You can come with Henry and me, so why don't you go wait in the car?"

Noah didn't have to be told twice. He bounded down the steps and had ensconced himself in Henry's truck before Max could pull the words of his objection together.

"No," he said. "I have rights to see my son."

"Yes, you do, but the beauty of our open agreement is that we never specified when or for how long. You're the one who wanted it that way, remember?" Lindsay glanced up at Henry and flashed him a smile before turning again to her ex. "It's past time I let go of whatever ridiculous guilt I feel over your unwillingness to be a father and decide what is best for *my* son."

"And you think this man is best for him?"

"I would have thought the ring on my finger made that obvious."

Giselle, who had been standing rigidly beside her husband throughout the entire exchange, said quietly, "I warned you this would happen, Max. Didn't I tell you to either cut ties or put forth a real effort? You can't be a father when it's convenient for you. You have, by your own indecision, given all your rights to Lindsay when it comes to making decisions for Noah."

"You're against me now, too?"

"No one was ever against you, Max," Lindsay replied. "That's what you've never understood. You think this whole thing is some ploy to ruin your life, but it's not. It's nothing more than a simple error in judgment that just so happened to land us with a son. If you want to stay in Noah's life, that's fine, but I'm not going to force you to be a part of it. From now on, you can tell me when you want to see him or talk to him because I'm done fighting with you. It takes too much energy, and I have too many good things going on in my life now that I plan to hang on to with both hands. Call me later if you want to reschedule this visit."

Henry couldn't remember when he'd ever been as proud of someone as he was of Lindsay right now as she threaded her fingers with his, wished the Ulrichs a happy New Year, and headed down the walk to the truck. Neither she nor Henry turned to watch Max and Giselle disappear inside, and when they reached the driveway, Henry yanked her into his arms, grinning.

"I think that went well," he said. "All things considered."

"I suppose so, but I guarantee that that was rather more abrupt than he's used to."

"Hey, I didn't punch him, and I was damned tempted at the beginning."

"I'm sure you were. I know I don't need to ask because your playful tone and that lazy smile are answer enough, but I want to hear you say it."

"Say what?"

"That I get to keep my beautiful ring and that you still want to marry me after meeting my asshole ex and finding out exactly what dealing with him is like."

"Of course you get to keep your ring, gorgeous, and you bet your sweet heart I still want to marry you... even more than I did before, if that's possible." He kissed her. "I told you I wasn't going to change my mind because of Max. Do you believe me now?"

She angled her body closer to his, sliding her hands

between his arms and his ribs and splaying them possessively across his upper back. "With not one single doubt left. You've banished them all."

He took her hand and spun her like he might if they were dancing, then opened her door. "Since it appears Noah no longer has to spend New Years with his father, shall we head back to Northstar to finish out your vacation?"

"I'd love that. Noah, what do you say?"

"Heck yeah!"

"All right, then," Henry said after he slid in behind the wheel. "Let's go home so we can get to planning our future. Starting with whether we're going to live in Washington or Northstar."

"That's an easy one, isn't it, Noah?" Lindsay asked her son.

"It is, is it? Okay, which one?"

"You just answered that when you said 'let's go home,' Henry," Noah replied. "Northstar, of course."

"You're sure you don't need to think about it?"

"What's to think about?" Lindsay inquired. "You've said yourself that you were glad to be home on your ranch with your family. And it's where I'm happiest, and where my dream of opening my own catering business might actually become a reality thanks to you and your scheming and Marvin and Mary Struthers and June and Ben Conner for giving me the opportunity. How could I want to live anywhere else?"

"That's all well and good," Henry teased, "but what about Noah?"

"Henry," the boy said with a dramatic seriousness. "You live on a ranch. Life doesn't get much better for a kid than that."

"Twist my arm a little more, why don't you?"

"I don't think we need to," Lindsay laughed. "Is this really happening?"

"It really is," Henry replied, leaning across the cab to kiss her as he turned the key in the ignition.

"So," Noah said, sitting forward. "When do I get a little brother or a little sister?"

Henry joined Lindsay in laughter. "Let's give your mom a chance to get that degree she's always wanted to earn, all right, bud? Besides, I'm in no hurry because we already have you."

Epilogue

HENRY SPOTTED HIS WIFE making her way through the sea of students slowly flowing out the doors of the gym where commencement had recently ended. Dressed in a black robe and matching mortarboard with golden *summa cum laude* cords draped around her neck. She was possibly as beautiful as she'd been almost four years ago in her wedding gown. Maybe more so. Loose-fitting as her graduation robe was, it didn't obscure her growing belly, and memory of her joking this morning about being pregnant at her graduation for the second time in her life brought a brighter smile to his face. She'd followed the comment with an observation that this time she wasn't a scared teenager but a confident business owner and wife looking forward to the birth of their child with nothing but excitement. He couldn't be more proud of her.

Steve and Debbie Miller stood with him, along with his parents and brothers and their families. Beside him, Noah bounced, trying to see over the crowd of families waiting to congratulate their graduates.

"Do you see her yet?" he asked.

"Yep, she's almost here."

When she reached them, Henry wrapped his arms around her thighs and lifted her off the ground. Laughter spilled out of her, and she braced her forearms on his shoulders, then lowered her head to kiss him.

"So, gorgeous, how's it feel to be a college graduate?" he asked.

"Absolutely amazing," she replied. "I couldn't have done it without you."

"Sure you could have." He set her down and toyed with her honors cords. "These are all you, love. You worked your butt off these last four years, and I am so proud of you."

"Maybe I did the work, but your support made it possible for me to do it, so just hush up and accept your due praise."

"Yes, ma'am."

Debbie embraced her daughter. "I am so happy you've finally had a chance to go after your dreams and so proud that you've done it with such drive. *Summa cum laude!*"

Henry stepped to her side so the rest of their families could congratulate Lindsay. She might not have had the same wonder-filled experience he, her parents, or her friends had had in college, but she'd taken the knowledge and life experience and come out with higher honors than any of them.

Unable to help himself, he smoothed his hand over her belly. How incredible it was to feel that rounding and the persistent nudges of the baby's limbs. With sixteen weeks left to go, those movements were still small, but Henry was thrilled nonetheless. He couldn't wait to meet his son. "How's the munchkin?"

He liked the way her smile turned shy as she laid her hand over his. "Busy."

"Obviously." He turned to his mother. "Sorry the Hammond Curse struck again, Mom."

Tracie shrugged and pulled Jessie close. "I already have a granddaughter and three beautiful, wonderful daughters-in-law. Besides, with three boys of my own, I'm better equipped for grandsons."

"I know I'm definitely better equipped for boys," Lindsay remarked, pulling Noah close. "And I know my first will have a blast teaching his little brother why football is such a great game. Won't ya, bud?"

"Oh, yeah."

"All right, folks. We should probably get headed out to lunch if we want to beat the crowds," Henry announced. "Besides, I have a surprise for Lindsay, and I want to give it to her before Max and Giselle join us."

Debbie leaned close to him and remarked for his ears only, "You mean, you *don't* want to rub it in his face that you're a better man than he ever dreamed of being?"

"I have no need," Henry replied. "And anyhow, he's come around a lot in the last four years."

"So he has."

Henry didn't know if it was jealousy that Noah preferred him to Max, competitiveness, Henry's advice to appreciate what a treasure Noah was, or a realization that he might completely lose his son that had spurred Max to take a more active role in Noah's life, and it didn't matter. Henry was glad it had happened. They still weren't fond of each other, but he and Max were civil, and that was good for both Noah and Lindsay. Of course, he wasn't thrilled that Max had decided he needed a visit with his son this particular weekend, but he'd long ago promised he would encourage father and son to spend time together, even if that meant that his "encouragement" was sometimes nothing more than keeping his mouth shut.

They drove across town to Papa T's and managed to arrive before the restaurant filled up with other graduates. As soon as everyone had gathered around the long table, Henry pulled a plain white envelope with the logo of Lindsay's company—Blue Diamond Catering after her engagement ring—out of his back pocked and unfolded it before handing it to his wife.

"What is this?" she asked, frowning.

"Just open it."

She did and stared at the small receipt with a frown. "What is this?"

"It's a deposit receipt for twenty thousand dollars made to the account of Blue Diamond Catering."

"I know that, but what *is* it? Where did it come from?"

"It's the ten grand Mel paid me back plus interest and a little extra from—" He gestured around the table at the adults gathered, both the Millers and the Hammonds. "—your family. It should be more than enough to cover the rest of the equipment and signage you need for the new kitchen."

Lindsay pressed her fingertips to her mouth and met his gaze with watery eyes. "Thank you. Thank you all."

Henry leaned back in his chair with his ankles crossed and his hands knitted behind his head and listened as the others discussed Lindsay's plans for expanding her catering business now that she was finished with school and could focus her full attention on it. June's party planning business had taken off, and Lindsay had barely been able to keep up while she had classes and homework eating up so much of her time, but she'd already crafted a plan to not only meet the Ramshorn's need but expand into Devyn by hiring a few of her classmates to help her accomplish it. With her drive and talent and a new, fully equipped industrial kitchen, Henry had no doubt that she'd succeed spectacularly.

As for him... he had everything in life he wanted. His temporary move back to the Lazy H Ranch had become permanent, and like his brothers before him, his need for adventure was now fully satisfied by his wife and her charming son. He might not be making as much money as he had in Denver, but he enjoyed the work more than enough to compensate. And best of all, he had a wife he adored, a stepson he loved, and in a few short months, he'd be a father. For real this time.

Spontaneously, Henry jumped to his feet and offered his hand to Lindsay. When she took it, he settled his other hand on her waist and led her in a silly dance that soon had everyone at their table laughing.

"Looks like we salvaged more than just a night when you invited yourself to have a drink with me, Mrs. Hammond," he murmured.

"Indeed we did," she replied, pressing her lips to his. "We salvaged our hearts."

*****

Don't miss the next book in the
***Northstar* series:**

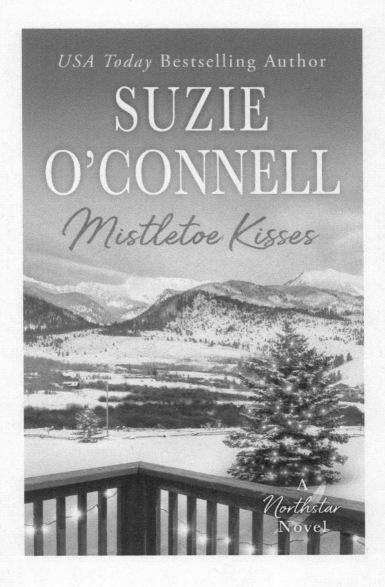

USA *Today* BESTSELLING AUTHOR

SUZIE
O'CONNELL

Mistletoe Kisses

A Northstar
Novel

Mistletoe Kisses

When Ty Evans stole a kiss under the mistletoe from his best friend Shannon O'Neil, he had no idea of the captivating desire it would awaken.

With Shannon's acting and singing career poised to take off and Ty's horse training business gaining acclaim, that reckless kiss might be the only one Ty ever gets... until a brush with the darker side of fame forces Shannon to question if she can handle the spotlight. Now she's back in Northstar to clear her head.

This might be the chance Ty has been waiting for—an opportunity to convince Shannon that their kiss under the mistletoe was just the beginning of something even more wonderful. Just one problem. He can't let her give up on her dreams, but if she pursues them, he'll have to choose between losing her again and abandoning his own dreams to follow her across the world.

AVAILABLE NOW
Visit www.suzieoconnell.com for more information.

ABOUT THE AUTHOR

Suzie O'Connell is the *USA Today* bestselling author of the Northstar romances. The series is the product of a love affair with Southwestern Montana that began with a two-week adventure at her stepsister's rustic cabin in her teens. That love affair shows no sign of abating.

She has been writing stories for as long as she can remember, and her love of writing and of Montana pushed her to earn a Bachelor of Arts in Literature and Writing from the University of Montana-Western. What else would you expect from a self-professed mountain-loving nerd?

When she isn't writing, you'll probably find Suzie in the mountains with a camera in hand and enjoying the beauty of Montana with her husband Mark, their daughter Maddie, and their golden retrievers Reilly and Angus.

Find Suzie online at www.suzieoconnell.com